No One Can Know

ALSO BY KATE ALICE MARSHALL

What Lies in the Woods

The Narrow

These Fleeting Shadows

Our Last Echoes

Rules for Vanishing

I Am Still Alive

Thirteens

Brackenbeast

Glassheart

Extra Normal

No One Can Know

KATE ALICE MARSHALL

FLATIRON
BOOKS
NEW YORK

NO ONE CAN KNOW. Copyright © 2023 by Kate Alice Marshall. All rights reserved. Printed in the United States of America. For information, address Flatiron Books, 120 Broadway, New York, NY 10271.

ISBN 9781250859914

This one is for my parents.
Which is kind of awkward, now that I think about it.
They're really lovely people, I promise.

No One Can Know

EMMA

Then

She looks at the body of her mother, sprawled in the hallway. If she turns her head, she will see her father, slumped in his chair by the fireplace in the next room, one fingertip still touching the side of a glass in which his whiskey, the ice long melted, still sits. She looks down at her hands to see if there is any spot or smear of blood, but they are clean.

She turns to her sisters. They stand apart from each other. She picks out details: the blood drying on the cuffs of the soft blue pajama bottoms, the wet hair hanging in stringy clumps, the hands rubbing together as if trying to get clean. She starts to speak, falters. She wets her lips and tries again.

"This is what we're going to do," she says, and when she tells them, they don't argue. They don't say anything. They simply obey.

Twenty-three minutes later, she picks up the phone from the kitchen counter and dials. When the emergency operator answers, she speaks in a level voice.

"My name is Emma Palmer. Our parents are dead. We need the police."

She looks at the clock on the stove. It is 5:13 A.M.

She hangs up. They walk together to the porch and wait. When the cruiser pulls up in front, they are still standing there. The lights flash over them. Red, blue, red, blue. Hair dry. Faces each a study of numb shock. Dressed in clean clothes—there will be no blood found on them, no bloodied clothes found anywhere on the property. None of them look at the others. None of them reach out for comfort, for reassurance, or offer it in turn. They are each a world of their own.

Emma holds a hundred questions between her teeth, biting down until her jaw aches. She doesn't ask. Will never ask.

It isn't that she's afraid of the answers.

She's afraid she already knows them.

"Our parents are dead," she says again, to no one in particular.

It's the last true thing she says for a long time.

1

EMMA

Now

The edge of the picture nipped Emma's finger as she reached into her purse for her keys. It was a flimsy thing, printed on glossy paper that felt plasticky under her fingertips. The image looked more like an off-brand gummy bear than a baby. She hadn't asked for it, hadn't really wanted it, but she hadn't seen a way to refuse when the doctor pressed it into her hands.

She realized she was standing in front of the door, not moving, her hand still in her purse. With a muttered curse she hooked her finger through her key ring. She turned the key in the lock, but it was already open—which it shouldn't have been, not in the middle of the day. The door swung open, and Emma stood frozen in the doorway. She breathed in. Testing, she knew and tried not to know, for the scent of blood, of sweet decay. Of everything happening again.

Then—"Emma?"

Nathan stepped out from the kitchen. He had a beer can in one hand. She stared at Nathan, at the beer, mind still on—*about nine weeks along*—the cheerfully sterile walls of the exam room. The slide of the ultrasound wand over her flat stomach.

"What are you doing home?" she managed at last.

An expression she couldn't read flashed over his face—guilt, defeat, something in between. "Why don't you come inside," he said.

She closed the door behind her. She set her purse on the little table in the hall, and now she saw Nathan's shoes discarded next to the shoe rack and his briefcase leaning against the couch in the living room. He was supposed to let her know if he was going to be home unexpectedly. She always had to know what she would find when she walked in the front door of her own home. She'd never told him why; he assumed it was just one of the quirks of her anxiety.

He was leaning against the kitchen doorway now, the beer can sweating in his hand. "We need to talk," he said.

That's my line, she thought.

Not a normal day off, then. She wiped her palms on her jeans. "Okay. What's up?" she asked, her voice too bright. He didn't seem to notice. He wasn't very good at reading people. That was one of the things she liked about him. She was keenly aware at all times how other people perceived her—too aware that it was impossible, really, to get things just right. You were too emotional, not emotional enough. Putting on an act, not acting the way they expected, or so on point with expectations that it had to have been rehearsed.

Nathan took things at face value. She didn't have to spend every conversation trying to ferret out what he really thought of her.

"Maybe you should have one of these first," Nathan said with a crooked smile, holding out the beer. Emma's stomach turned.

I shouldn't drink.

I need a drink.

She'd waited too long again. Frozen up. He lowered his arm and sighed. "I got laid off," he said, tossing a little shrug in at the end of the words.

She blinked at him, unsure what the proper facial expression to greet this news should be. How did one convey sympathy while also conveying *we are truly, deeply screwed?*

"Obviously it's terrible timing," he said.

"Nathan, we *just* had our offer accepted on the house," Emma said, voice shaking. "We paid the earnest money." More than ten thousand dollars. With multiple offers, their agent had told them it would help them compete.

"I'm aware of that," he said, voice a bit clipped now.

Emma pressed her palms to her face. Her cheeks were hot, her hands cold. She could still feel the remnants of the ultrasound gel, dried to tackiness under the waistband of her jeans.

She walked past him, shoulder bumping against his. She crossed the kitchen to the countertop and planted her hands on the Formica surface, staring at the grease stain that had been there when they moved in three years ago.

She straightened up. "Have you called Justin yet?" Justin was the man handling their mortgage, who had suggested that given Emma's spotty employment history and anemic income, Nathan should be the only one on the mortgage application. Emma had nodded along when he'd said to put the remaining medical bills, credit card bills, and car loan under her name to maximize Nathan's borrowing power, so now here she was in the negative—on paper, only on paper, they were a team—while Nathan smiled his way into half a million dollars' worth of house on credit. "The offer. There are—what are they—contingencies. We get our money back if the inspection doesn't go through, that kind of thing. Is there—"

"I got laid off before we made the offer," he said. She startled, her mouth dropping open. He made a dismissive gesture with one hand. "I had another job lined up. The house was perfect, and I was going to be able to start this week and it wouldn't even matter, they were paying *more*, it was golden, and then. . . ."

"No job," Emma said, voice strangled nearly to silence. "Nathan, why didn't you say anything?"

"Because it was handled!" he said. "If I'd said anything, the loan could have fallen through. Better to have the new job sorted first. Then the project funding got canceled at the last minute. The position was eliminated."

A hot fist of nausea lodged behind her breastbone. She'd been feeling a bit queasy lately. Nothing extreme. Not enough to notice, to wonder, not when there was the house hunt and then the mad scramble of putting together offers and getting the preapproval. Not when she'd had her period like clockwork (breakthrough bleeding, they'd called it, not uncommon) and had only gone in for an answer to her sudden, overwhelming fatigue.

The house had felt like a mistake from the start. The letter had arrived informing them that the duplex was going up for sale and they had sixty days to vacate, and she'd wanted to start looking for a new apartment. But Nathan had pointed out that with the rental market what it was, and with him finally having steady employment after a decade of patchwork contracts and canceled projects, it might be the perfect time to buy.

She'd blanched at the idea. Her work, which had once kept them afloat, had cratered after the accident, during the long weeks of her recovery. The rest had dried up after her biggest client went under and others tightened their belts. New websites weren't the priority when they were trying to keep the lights on. But Nathan had finally landed a permanent position. One that paid well—well enough to (mostly, nearly, almost) pay off their small mountain of credit card debt, Nathan's student loans, the medical bills from the accident.

"Because I technically lied about my employment, we can't get the earnest money back," Nathan was saying. "And we were already on the bubble with the loan approval. Justin doesn't think there's any way he can push it through, even if I miraculously get a new job offer tomorrow." He collapsed into a chair at the kitchen table.

Her mind churned quickly over the possibilities. The closing date would have been a tight turnaround as it was. Finding another rental wasn't an option until Nathan got a job, not without the cash that had now vanished into the hole of the offer that was too high but worth it, *completely worth it, when you think about our life there, our future.*

He was looking at her like he was waiting for her to tell him what to do. Because she always knew what to do. She was always the one with the plan.

"I'm pregnant," Emma said. Fingers curled over the edge of the counter. Gaze on the cheap vinyl tile. Were those meant to be roses in the corners? They looked like splotches of mildew.

"What?"

Her eyes flicked up. He stared at her, mouth slack, hair falling boyishly over one eye. Dark hair, blue eyes, a small scar on his chin she liked to set her thumb against right before she kissed him. They'd met at a coffee shop, back when she couldn't even afford internet, so she'd hidden herself in the corner away from the baristas' annoyed glances and ordered plain black coffee and nothing else for hours at a time as she worked. He'd been sitting at the table next to hers. When he bought her a chocolate croissant, she tried to wave him off, but he said it was for his sake, since her growling stomach was distracting him.

She took the croissant. And the latte that followed. It was a week before he actually asked her out, to a mediocre movie and good Italian food, and kissed her a gentlemanly kiss good night at her doorstep before she slid her hand into his hair and pulled him to her hungrily, drew him inside the tiny studio, undressed him in the dark.

He told people he'd fallen in love with her over pastries and coffee, but when they were alone he confessed it had been that night with her teeth against his neck, the certainty of her, the hard edges that she had hidden so well.

She told him she'd fallen in love with him with the taste of butter on her lips that first morning, but it was just a story. She had no idea when she'd fallen in love with him. But people needed stories to make sense of things, and she had learned to give them what they needed.

Now his face was pale. His lips shut. That face that couldn't hide anything failing to hide his unhappiness. "You're on the pill," he said.

"It happens," Emma replied helplessly. She'd missed a pill here or there when she was sick, distracted, traveling. Far from perfect use. "You want children." That was the point of the house, with its extra bedrooms.

"I do. Of course I do. It's just—now—" His throat convulsed. "If I can't find a job . . . We won't even have a place to *live* in a few weeks. We can't."

"What are you saying?" she asked.

Nathan wanted children, and she had said *yes, okay, someday,* because she wanted to be the person who could want that. Now, though, it was his face that had taken on a gray pallor. His eyes that dropped to the table. "It's not the right time. Maybe things work out. But what if they don't? And I wouldn't want to wait, and then—when it's further along—"

Emma put her hand against her abdomen. Still flat, no outward sign at all, and she realized she had already made a decision.

"I'm keeping it," she said.

His brow creased slightly, as if puzzled. Sometimes, she thought, she underestimated how well he knew her. He said *we want kids,* but maybe he knew that he wanted kids, and she said okay. "We're out ten thousand dollars, and that was *all* we had. The down payment was supposed to be another loan. I'm unemployed. We're getting kicked out at the end of the month. How are we supposed to raise a kid right now?" he asked.

"I don't know." Her hand became a fist against her belly.

He sat back in his chair, a look of consideration on his face. "What about your parents' house?" he asked, and there was something odd in his tone—like he'd been waiting to bring it up all along.

"What about it?" Emma asked, instantly wary. Her stomach tightened with a feeling like dread.

"Well, we own it, don't we?" he asked, eyebrow raised.

"Technically, *we* don't own anything. The trust does. You know I can't do anything with the house unless Daphne and Juliette both agree." They were the names of strangers in her mouth. "We can't take out a mortgage on it or sell it or anything like that by ourselves."

The way the trust had been set up, they hadn't been able to do anything with the house until Daphne turned twenty-one. By then, none of them had spoken to one another in years. It was easier to go on ignoring one another's existences. Ignoring the house, and the horrors it held.

"I'm not saying sell it—not yet, anyway. But there's nothing to stop us from living there," Nathan said. He looked excited. Here it was: the perfect solution to all of their problems. Emma's heart was rabbit-quick. He stood. He crossed the floor, put his hands on her arms.

"We can't," she said. It felt like she was forcing the words out against something solid. She never thought of it as the house where she'd grown up. Only the house where her parents died.

"This is the perfect solution. We move into your folks' old house. We fix it up, talk to your sisters about selling it, and then we can buy our own house. It's ridiculous that you've all just left it sitting there empty," he said.

"I can't go back there," Emma said, shaking her head. Not to the house. Not to Arden Hills.

He made a frustrated noise. "Why not? Come on, Emma. You're not being rational. We need a place to live. You own a house. It's not complicated." He gathered her to him, her face pressed against his chest. She closed her eyes and breathed in the familiar scent of him. "If you want to have this baby, we have to do this. We'll move into the house. We'll figure things out."

The button of his shirt dug into her cheek. She let him hold her, and said nothing.

Secrets shifted beneath her skin, ready to bloom.

––––––––––––––––

Emma had never lied to Nathan about her past.

Not exactly.

She'd told him she had two sisters, one older and one younger, that they hadn't spoken in years, that they had drifted apart after their parents died when she was sixteen. That they had inherited the house—four bedrooms, three bathrooms, two acres of land.

That Juliette, already eighteen when their parents died, had left for college and never came back. That Emma and Daphne had been shuffled off into foster care—split up and then spit out.

He'd asked how her parents died. Of course he had. Delicately, pressing a kiss against her shoulder, his hand against her hip, because that was the only time she ever talked to him about her past—stripped bare in the dark, looking anywhere but into his eyes.

She hadn't lied.

She'd let him lie for her.

"Was it an accident?" he'd asked.

"They never found the person," she had said, and let him think it was the answer to his question. Let him imagine screeching tires and winding roads.

Now, after the sun had set and they'd retreated to bed, she fixed her eyes on the slanted light from the street that stole through the blinds.

"My parents didn't die in an accident," she said. She felt him shift behind her, felt the weight of his attention. "They were murdered."

"Your parents were murdered?" Nathan asked, hurt and accusation and bewilderment braided together plainly in his voice. She could read every strand. She turned, finally, to face him, but the shadows stole the contours of his expression from her.

In the safety of the dark, she told him. How they had died in the house. Been shot. A bullet to the brain, a bullet to the heart. A missing gun.

"Why didn't you tell me?" he asked.

"I didn't want that to be what you knew about me," she said. "I didn't want to think about it."

He was silent. She could feel something between them, a rebalancing. His mistake weighed against her secret.

"You need to know," she said. She traced her fingertips down the side of his face and silently prayed as she had so many times—a prayer of a single word. *Stay, stay, stay.* "If we go back, you're going to hear some things."

"What kind of things?"

"You're going to hear that I did it," she whispered.

He was quiet for a long time. When he spoke again, his words were toneless. "Did you?"

"No. It wasn't me," Emma said. She wondered if he believed her. She wondered if anyone had ever believed her.

He rolled over, half on top of her, her legs trapped beneath his. "It will be okay," he told her. "We'll be okay."

His tongue slid between her teeth, and she wondered if he tasted the secrets lingering there.

The secrets still hidden within the walls of the house that was drawing them, inescapably, home.

2

EMMA

Now

Arden Hills was like a dead tree in a forest. Even as it rotted, new life had sprung up, feeding off the decay. Real estate agents and New York transplants took the place of beetles and fungi, that was all, and in a few years all that would be left of the version of the town Emma had grown up in would be a heap of rich loam beneath the new growth.

Outside of town, hobby farms cluttered the landscape, their chicken roosts decorated with faux-distressed signs reading LADIES ONLY or THE HEN HOUSE, decorated with shutters and windowsill planters.

"We could get chickens," Nathan said, startling Emma. This whole trip, they'd ridden in silence, thin as the skin on a cup of milk left out on the counter and yet never broken.

"You want chickens?" she asked, trying to imagine Nathan scattering feed to a quartet of clucking hens.

He nodded thoughtfully, thumbs tapping the steering wheel. "You said the house is on a bit of land, right?"

"A little over two acres out back," she said absently.

"We could do chickens, a vegetable garden. Hell, maybe we could get goats," he said. She didn't point out that he didn't even own a pair of boots, or that his one nonnegotiable expense when they moved into the duplex was hiring a landscaping company to handle the postage stamp of a yard.

She didn't point out that this was supposed to be temporary.

"Fresh eggs would be nice," she said instead.

He grinned widely at her, and her heart thumped once behind her ribs, hard. This was going to work out. Wasn't it? He wasn't angry anymore. He was talking about chickens.

"Are you sure you know what you're getting into, going back there?" Christopher Best had asked her. She'd called him three days ago, in the middle of packing up. It had been years since they'd seen each other, but she still called every once in a while. Kind of pathetic, that her lawyer was the closest thing she had to family.

"People in Arden don't forget," he'd said. But maybe he was wrong.

A few miles from the house, Emma directed Nathan toward the gas station and grocery store by the roadside. They'd need food, and she didn't know if there would be basic supplies like toilet paper at the house.

They got out of the car, stretching limbs that had started to calcify on the long drive. Nathan laced his hands over his head and arched his back. His shirt rode up, baring a lightly furred belly, lean but without definition. Emma watched him from the other side of the car, falling without meaning to into a game she often played—imagining she was seeing her husband for the first time, as a stranger. What would she make of the scruff of beard on his jaw, his unusually long and elegant fingers? If they met again, would they ever have a second conversation?

She turned the game on herself, imagining what he would see. Thirty years old, with auburn brown hair she kept in a low ponytail. Skin that tanned easily and broke out in freckles every summer, a wardrobe of jeans and T-shirts and slouchy sweaters to throw over them in the colder months. She always thought of herself as nondescript, which was why it had puzzled her so much when Nathan showed such ardent and consistent interest in the beginning. She was soft-spoken, sometimes quiet to the point of paralysis. She had always been more comfortable talking to clients through the anonymity of the internet. She wasn't good face-to-face.

"You're a hard one to get to know," Nathan had told her once, two

months in. She wished that he had told her when he figured her out. So he could explain to her who she was, what she was like.

"Penny for your thoughts?" he said.

"Just looking at you," she said, and he smiled, pleased at the attention. She tipped her face up to his to kiss him, and they walked into the store together hand in hand, the touch tender, as if each was afraid the other would pull away.

Inside, Nathan drifted off to peruse the shelves of novelty mugs. She grabbed a basket from beside the door and headed toward the groceries. Her stomach roiling, she shopped like a picky toddler—graham crackers and peanut butter, a bag of cashews, a loaf of bread, raspberry jam, cereal. She spotted a tub of candied ginger and scooped some into a bag, remembering vaguely it was supposed to help with the nausea, which had arrived with calamitous intensity, as if making up for lost time. She hadn't been able to keep a proper meal down in days.

She added some frozen meals, disposable plates, and cutlery to the basket. At the last minute, she grabbed a bottle of white wine from a rack. It wasn't champagne, but this wasn't the housewarming they'd planned, either. Still, it felt wrong not to have something to toast with, even if she couldn't have more than a sip. Nathan was waiting at the register, a pack of toilet paper brandished like a prize.

As the woman at the counter rang up the groceries, Nathan chatted with her, his usual patter of friendliness. He liked to talk to people. Strangers in line, on the bus, sitting next to them at the movie theater. People opened up to him. Told him about sick grandparents and empty bank accounts and cancer scares before they even knew his name. It was nice, having him around. No one ever thought to talk to Emma when he was right there beside her.

"ID?" the cashier asked brightly, cheeks rounded in a smile, still looking at Nathan. Emma handed it over. The woman's eyes flicked down, up, down again, and the smile creased into a frown. "Emma Palmer?" she said, voice pitched too high.

"Can I have my ID back?" Emma asked. She tried to keep her

voice level, but it hitched. Not this. Not again. Surely it had been long enough.

The cashier jerked, then shoved the ID back in Emma's hand. She finished ringing up the rest of the food without making eye contact. As soon as the groceries were bagged, Emma snatched them and strode quickly for the exit, ignoring Nathan's hand reaching to help with the load. She didn't slow down until they'd reached the car and she'd shoved the food into the back seat. She stopped then, hand on top of the sunbaked roof, a breeze making the frizz at the edges of her vision dance.

She drew in a deep breath and only then realized that Nathan was asking if she was okay.

"Fine." Gravel crunched under her feet. The scent of gasoline from the nearby pumps made her gut churn.

"She knew who you were," he noted neutrally.

"Seemed like it," she said.

"Is that going to happen a lot?" he asked.

"I don't know," she snapped.

He held up his hands in mock surrender. "Whoa, okay. I'm just asking," he said. "I want to know what we're in for here."

"Let's just get to the house," she said.

He seemed for a moment like he was going to object. But then he nodded and got into the driver's seat. She slid bonelessly into the passenger side.

The house lay on the eastern edge of Arden Hills proper. Here the streets were narrower, with a tendency to loop and wind around blind curves. At the turn leading up to the river, Emma made a warning sound to get Nathan to slow, and he cast her an annoyed look—then slammed on the brakes as the road twisted sharply, leading up to a narrow wooden bridge with steep slopes to either side. A broken guardrail showed where someone else had made the same mistake. Rattled, Nathan crossed the bridge at a crawl.

"Thanks for the warning," he muttered. She pressed her lips together, let it go.

In contrast to the farmhouses and scrubby pastures they'd driven by earlier, there was a manicured uniformity to everything on this side of the river. The cars were new; the houses loomed behind gates and ruthlessly trimmed hedges. Nathan wore a small frown, and Emma realized she hadn't prepared him for this.

The turn to the drive was easy to miss, concealed among the trees. "Here," she said softly, and Nathan braked, pulled in. He stopped in front of the cast-iron gates with their gaudy calligraphic *P* emblazoned on each.

Beyond was a long drive leading up to a circular driveway, an empty fountain in the center, and rolling lawns to either side, with sparse woods beyond the house. Hedges lined the lawns and their walkways. On one side of the drive stood a carriage house, its white sides and open wooden shutters exactly matching the house that stood in front of them. The house itself was a towering Colonial, a solid block of white two stories high—three, if you included the attic—with columns standing straight and proud out front. The door was black, and from this distance it looked like an absence, a void. Except for the gleam of the brass knocker at its center.

Emma's breath caught in her throat. *Home*, she thought, and wished it didn't feel true.

"*That* is the house?" Nathan said, gaping.

"Not what you were expecting?" Emma asked, unfairly, because she hadn't told him, had she? She'd pretended she was surrendering the truth, but it wasn't even close, and this was only the beginning of it.

"I thought . . ."

He had thought that this house would be like the others they passed. The cute little farmhouses and past-their-prime Colonials that dotted the landscape between the heart of Arden and here, at its outer reaches.

"Your parents were wealthy," he said, neither statement nor question. There was a tiny gap between the last two words, like he wasn't entirely sure which was the more polite thing to say. Like *rich* could somehow be a bad thing, rude to mention. Which she supposed it was, once you actually qualified. It was weird how often people got offended when you pointed out they had money.

"We were, yes," she said. "I mean . . ." And she gestured at the house. All the proof that was necessary.

"Okay." He wiped his lower face with his palm. "Okay."

"I'll get the gate open," she said.

"Right." He nodded reflexively, calculations running behind his eyes. She didn't know what the house was worth these days. Not that it mattered, if Daphne and Juliette didn't agree to sell.

She'd sent them each a message, telling them that she and Nathan would be staying at the house for a while. She'd left it at that, for now. Daphne hadn't responded at all. Juliette had sent one word—*ok*. She had no idea what they'd think about selling the house. She had no idea what they thought about anything.

She walked up to the cast-iron gates. There was a thick chain wrapped around them, secured with a heavy padlock. She tugged the gate use-lessly anyway, making the chain rattle.

"Don't you have a key?" Nathan called. He'd gotten out of the car but stood behind the open door, like he needed it as a shield. She under-stood the impulse. She looked past him. The trees kept them mostly out of sight, but she could see the house across the street, and the curtain twitching aside in one window there.

"Nope," she said ruefully. "I've got the house key, but that's it."

"Seriously, Emma?" Nathan said. The spot between her shoulders tensed up. "Who does have one, then? Someone's getting in there to take care of it." He gestured behind her at the well-manicured lawns.

"We pay for a service. And there's someone who comes out to check around every few months. I'm sure we can get the key from him," she said quickly, soothingly. "We'll deal with the gate tomorrow. Just leave the car here and we can go around. It'll be fine."

"The whole thing isn't fenced off?"

"Just the front here, for cars," she assured him chirpily. She popped open the trunk, hauling out the bag that held her essentials.

"I've got that," he said, moving to intercept.

"I'm not an invalid," she protested, even though her limbs felt like rubber after the drive and all she wanted to do was curl up in a bed—any bed—and sleep for a week.

"Don't be so stubborn," he chided her, reaching to take the bag from her. This time she let him, standing back uselessly as he grabbed his own suitcase as well.

With Emma carrying some of the lighter groceries, they tromped off to the right of the gates. The imposing height of the cast iron gave way to a chest-high wall farther along, and then even that fell away, leaving only the rows of trees that provided privacy from the road. They trudged toward the house, Nathan dragging his rolling suitcase across the grass with limited success.

"Is that an actual carriage house?" Nathan asked, looking askance at the extra building.

"It is. Not that it's seen an actual carriage for a century," Emma said. "The hitching post is original, too." She nodded toward the feature in question, metal trending toward rust.

"What about the house?" Nathan asked.

Her breath was coming fast, her heart galloping. She told herself it was just the exertion. That sickly-sweet trickle at the back of her throat, the lurching in her stomach, was just the inaptly named morning sickness. The way her vision narrowed as those steps grew closer . . .

"Hey." Nathan's fingertips bumped her shoulder. She jumped, twisting away from him, and his lips parted in surprise.

Crazy, you look crazy, she thought, imagined her hair gone to frizz and wild from the drive, her eyes wide, pupils panic-blown. She shut her eyes, drew a steadying breath through her nose. "The house. The house is—it was built in the 1980s. The original house burned down."

"You okay?" Nathan asked quietly.

"Let's just get inside," she said.

Up the steps. Suitcases off to the side. Find the key. Get the key to the lock, hands shaking—"I've got it," Nathan said, taking it from her. He turned the key. Pushed open the door. He looked at her, asking wordlessly if she wanted to go in first. She shook her head. She couldn't. But then he started forward and she grabbed his arm, fingers dimpling the fabric of his sleeve, a breath hissing between her teeth. He couldn't go in there. No one should go in there.

"Emma?" he asked.

"No, no," she said, dimly aware that it didn't make sense as an answer, that he hadn't asked a question, really. "Sorry. Go ahead." She eased her grip on him.

Still looking at her more than ahead, he stepped across the threshold.

"Jesus," he said. She stiffened and strode in after him, a wild anger filling her she couldn't explain, but when she stepped past the threshold she stumbled to a stop.

The grand foyer, her mother had called it, though it wasn't particularly grand. A staircase led up to the bedrooms. The drawing room was to the right, the formal dining room to the left, and straight ahead the hall that branched off to the kitchen, the "great room" that hosted her mother's prize possession—her piano—and what had been her father's study. The gun case, which had been in the foyer for as long as Emma could remember, still sat in its place of honor. In its heyday it had displayed a little over half of her father's collection of rifles, handguns, and shotguns, an inartful combination of antiques and whatever new weapon caught his fancy, but now it was empty.

That wasn't what Nathan was staring at. His gaze was fixed on the wall to the right, and the bright red graffiti scrawled there.

HAIL SATAN, it said, and beneath it, MURDER HOUSE. She could see the tail end of another phrase scrawled in the dining room. Numb, she drifted toward it.

The dining room, with its blue striped wallpaper and wide-open space, had been an easier target. MURDERER and KILLER and PSYCHO and a sloppy pentacle, an attempt at what might have been a gallows that had been crossed out. It was all done in the same color, but a few different styles of writing, like they'd passed the can around.

"This is seriously fucked-up," Nathan said. "We should get out of here. If there's someone dangerous in here—"

She looked at him blankly, then laughed, surprising them both. "'Hail Satan'? They weren't even that creative," she said, voice devoid of amusement. "Gabriel said something about kids trying to break in," she remembered. When had that been? Last year, the year before?

She hadn't told him they were coming, she realized, anticipation and anxiety twisting through her gut at the thought of seeing him again. He'd never left Arden Hills. Not even after everything that had happened.

"Who's Gabriel?" Nathan asked. "Why would someone write this shit? You said—people think—" He looked lost. On the verge of panic. But she wasn't anymore. She reached out and took Nathan's hand, and didn't drop it when he flinched.

"Come with me," she said. She drew him away from the scrawled graffiti, the old oak dining table covered in plastic, the china still neatly stacked inside the antique hutch in the corner. She led him back into the foyer and then down the hall, past the great room and the dust-choked piano, toward her father's study.

It was still there, a few steps from the study door: a dark blotch on the oak hardwood flooring. By the time she had seen it, the blood was no longer a vivid splash of red. There was no chance to imagine, even for a moment, that there was anything she could do to help her mother.

"This is where I found her," Emma said.

"Who?" Nathan asked.

"My mother. This is where she was killed," Emma said, meeting his eyes, because she needed to see every moment of his reaction. She needed to know where she stood.

His face creased with discomfort. He swallowed, Adam's apple bobbing. "Right," he said. A syllable to fill the silence. "And your father . . ."

She nodded past him. Nathan twisted, as if there was something lurking behind him, but it was only the empty hall. The study door was closed. "He was in his study, in his chair. He was shot in the head." These were facts. They were cruel but clear, and she could speak them without breaking.

"They thought you did it," Nathan said.

"The theory was that I had an older boyfriend my parents didn't approve of, and we conspired to murder them. To get them out of the way, or for the money, or just because," Emma said. Facts.

"Obviously it wasn't true," Nathan said.

"Obviously." Endless rooms, alternately freezing and sweltering. Adults who tried to comfort her, frighten her, befriend her, threaten her. By the end they had given up on asking her any questions except, when they were done explaining to her what they were so sure had happened, to ask "Isn't that right?"

But she'd never confessed.

And she'd never told.

3

DAPHNE

Then

The day after her parents are killed, Daphne sits alone in a police station. There is a clock on the wall, but it's broken. The room is not an interrogation room, not like the gray brick boxes on TV, on the shows she's not supposed to watch (*they'll rot your brain*). There's a table against the wall with an old coffeepot, a crust of burnt brown at the bottom. A minifridge sits beside it, and a bulletin board on the wall advertises the weekend church potluck and a dog walking service.

She is not supposed to feel like she is in trouble, she thinks, but that doesn't mean that she isn't.

The door opens. Officer Hadley walks in, looking grim. Rick Hadley is tall and lean, with brown eyes and a face that looks hastily assembled, the contours of his cheekbones and jaw and brow rough and jutting. He's her father's best friend, and she's known him all her life, but today he looks at her like he's never seen her before.

"Daphne," he says by way of greeting. His voice is rough. She would say it sounds like he has been crying, but men like Rick Hadley and her father don't cry.

"Hi, Mr. Hadley," she says softly.

Chief Ellis comes in behind him. He's a solid man, muscular, with thick fingers and broad hands. He shaves his hair down to the scalp, and today it's pink with a fresh sunburn. He's carrying a white bag shimmery with grease, a paper cup that steams. He sets them both in front of her, the corners of his eyes crinkling, though his mouth hardly bends enough to call it a smile. He takes a seat across from her. Hadley takes the other chair, off to her left where she has to turn her head to see him.

"Thought you might be hungry, Daphne," Chief Ellis says. She nods. She twists her thumb against the hard plastic of her chair, as she has been doing for—how long? She doesn't know. She looks again at the broken clock. Long enough that the skin is raw. She reaches for the bag; he pulls it back an inch. She freezes. She is in trouble, after all.

"I'd like to talk to you about what happened, Daphne," Ellis says with all the gentleness in the world.

"You haven't said much since this morning," Hadley adds.

Daphne hasn't said anything. She's afraid she'll say the wrong thing. Forget what Emma told her to say.

Ellis leans forward, folding his hands. The smell of whatever is in the bag, greasy and rich, makes her mouth water. "Daphne?" Ellis prompts. "You've got to talk to us, honey. We need your help to figure this out."

He is not a kind man, but he can pretend at kindness adequately enough, and she's as hungry for that as the food right now. She'll let him lie to her. It's only fair. Lies are all she has to give him, too.

"Okay," she says. Her voice is a croak. He smiles like she has performed a miracle and pushes the cup toward her. She drags it the rest of the way across the table and hangs her head over it, inhaling the steam. Hot chocolate.

"Can you tell me what happened, Daphne? In your own words," Ellis says.

She stares at the tabletop as she answers. It's a fake wood veneer, the image of wood grain printed on cheap laminate. She bites her lip to focus. "Mom and Dad. They were—Mom was in the hall. There was blood on her shirt and on the floor, and—"

She's practiced this in her head a million times, and still it's coming out in sputters, like a hose with a kink in it. Ellis holds up a hand, stopping her.

"Start at the beginning. Where were you last night?"

"Right," she says. "Sorry. We were—I wanted to sleep out in the tree house. We do that sometimes. When it's warm. It was warm last night. We were out there."

"All three of you? Emma and Juliette were with you?" Hadley asks sharply. Ellis gives him a look, which he ignores.

Emma screaming. The front door slamming.

Juliette pressing a finger to her lips.

Someone running through the woods.

Juliette stumbling in, dirty water dripping from her hair.

"Yes," she says. "We were all together. We stayed up for a little while talking, and then we fell asleep."

"Did any of you get up in the night?" Hadley asks. Ellis's voice is exaggeratedly friendly; Hadley doesn't bother to make it sound like anything but a demand.

She shakes her head.

"Are you sure, Daphne?" Ellis presses. "Maybe Juliette or Emma got up and you didn't notice."

"I would have noticed. I was sleeping in front of the door. They would have had to climb over me to get out," she says, and then she thinks this is a mistake. Emma always sleeps by the door. Juliette is afraid of falling and Daphne used to roll around in her sleep, so it's always been Emma. She stills, panicked, but Ellis just nods.

"All right." He leans back in his chair. "When did you go back into the house?"

"I'm not sure," she says. She frowns like she's thinking. "What time did Emma call?"

"Five thirteen," Hadley says impatiently, but she already knows. The number is burned into her memory.

"So maybe just after five," she says. There is a split in the wood veneer; she can see the particleboard beneath. She digs her fingernail against the gap, pressing down, feeling the fake wood give.

"Why did you go inside?" Ellis asks.

"I had to pee," she says, and her cheeks heat up.

"And what happened when you went back into the house?" he asks.

"I used the bathroom. The one downstairs," she says.

"Your mother was in the hall. Not far away."

She nods convulsively. "I didn't turn on the light. I didn't want to wake anyone up," she says. "I didn't see her until—until—" A sudden wave of queasiness rolls through her, and she whines, high-pitched, bending forward on herself.

"Hey, easy there," Ellis says, reaching across the table to touch her shoulder. She whips away from him. She doesn't want to be touched. His eyes crinkle again, but there's no warmth in them. "You saw her when you came out of the bathroom?"

"Yes," she whispers. Hadley is watching her intently. She's certain she's made a mistake already.

"What did you do then, Daphne?" Ellis prompts.

"I screamed, I think," she says. "I ran over to her, and I called for my dad. And then I turned around and I saw him, too. Then Emma and Juliette were there. Juliette tried to help Mom but Emma stopped her, because she could tell—she didn't think we should touch anything."

"You could tell they were dead," Ellis says.

She nods. "You could see things. In Daddy's head." She doesn't mean to use the word, babyish, juvenile. She's twelve, not four. But Ellis's face softens.

"Look. You can see his brain." A finger reaching toward the hole, smacked away.

She lets the shudder that she has been holding back ripple over her shoulders and pulls her knees to her chest. She likes to imagine that she can fold herself in half and in half again, over and over until she is a tiny speck drifting. Until she is nothing at all.

"And that's when Emma called 911?" Ellis asks.

"Maybe not right away?" she ventures.

"Take your time," he reminds her.

Daphne swallows, nods. "Juliette was freaking out. Emma was trying to calm her down. So not right away."

"You weren't freaking out?" he asks, eyebrows raising.

"Of course I was," she says quickly. Too quickly. She sees the momentary softness hardening again. She doesn't know how to act. What to say. What does a normal person do, when they find their parents dead? When they see bits of their father's brain on the rug? She has no idea. She feels like an alien, every word and inflection skewed and wrong.

"So then you called 911," Ellis says.

"Emma did."

"That's right. Emma called 911." A nod. "And we pretty much know the story after that, don't we?"

She doesn't like that he calls it a story.

Ellis shifts a bit. His fingertips rest against the table. She looks over at the bag, inhaling the grease smell. He hasn't said she can't have it. He hasn't said she can. He notices her looking, and his hand flattens against the table.

"Daphne, let's go back a moment." He uses her name a lot, she thinks. Like he wants it to sound like he knows her. "Now, you and your sisters spent the night in the tree house. And you didn't hear anything from the house? Gunshots?"

"I don't think so?" she says. "I woke up a few times, but I don't remember it being because of a noise."

"And you were up there all night. All three of you," Hadley says intently, staring straight at her.

"Like I told you," Daphne says, and can't suppress the irritated snap to her words.

Ellis sighs. "That is what you told us," he concedes. "But, Daphne, we know that isn't true."

4

DAPHNE

Now

Emma was going back to the house.

Daphne sat on the porch, a crocheted blanket around her shoulders, and watched a barn cat stalk purposefully across the yard. She liked this time of day. That liminal space between the end of work and the start of sleep, the few minutes when obligation eased enough to steal a moment to herself. A moment to take a breath.

In a way, the last fourteen years had been an in-between time like this. A rest. But if Emma was going back to the house, surely that couldn't last.

"Daphne?"

The screen door creaked open, and Jenny leaned out, her dark hair slipping free of its messy bun to fall around her face. "He's asleep. If you want to take off now, I can handle things."

"Are you sure? He'll need his meds in an hour," Daphne said.

"I know the drill," Jenny assured her. If it had been one of Dale's other two children, she wouldn't have considered leaving. Lisa always got flustered and worried she'd misread the dosage or mixed up the medications, and Drew wouldn't have offered in the first place, was rarely here despite living only twenty minutes away.

"I wouldn't mind an evening to myself," Daphne admitted.

"You've certainly earned it. You've been such a godsend," Jenny said. "Dad just adores you."

"He's a wonderful man," Daphne replied warmly, though she didn't have much of an opinion about him. She knew it was terrible, but she never really cared to get to know her clients. She worked better thinking of them not as people but as a series of problems to solve. It wasn't to say that she was cold toward them—after all, emotional needs were another part of the puzzle. Being kind, listening, offering the gentle chiding voice or the joke to brighten their mood, it was all part of the work. She liked to be good at things.

And when, inevitably, her clients died—she refused, in her own mind, to soften that with phrases like *passed away* or *moved on*—she considered the project complete.

She gathered up her purse. Jenny walked her to the door, and there Daphne stopped, waiting an extra moment because she could see the strain in Jenny's eyes, the need to speak.

"It's not going to be long, is it?" Jenny asked, when the silence grew into enough of an invitation.

"No. Not long at all," Daphne said. "Days, maybe a week or two, in my experience. Though I'm not a doctor."

"You've done this a lot, though," Jenny said, almost a question. Daphne nodded, and Jenny looked away, scrubbing a tear from the corner of her eye with a kind of viciousness. "It's not like we haven't known it was coming."

"That can make it easier, but it doesn't make it easy," Daphne recited.

"I should make sure Lisa and Drew come by," Jenny said absently. She shook her head. "Sorry. I don't mean to keep you."

"I'll see you tomorrow," Daphne reassured her, and Jenny flashed her teeth reflexively.

"Right. Tomorrow," she said. She stood at the door, watching the whole time as Daphne made her way to her car and pulled away, gravel crunching under the wheels as she drove toward the distant lights of the city.

Later, alone in her apartment, Daphne turned on the television for some ambient noise and opened up her laptop. She clicked through a few bookmarked links, navigating to the fake profiles she had set up on various social media sites. Emma didn't have any kind of social media presence, but her husband did. Nathan. Daphne had met him once. At the wedding. Emma had looked so shocked to see her there, it was almost funny.

She hadn't even recognized Daphne at first—which Daphne supposed she couldn't entirely fault her for. The last time they'd seen each other, Daphne had been a skinny teenager, no longer starved for her mother's approval but still starving herself. It took a fainting spell in the middle of class and Mrs. Sawyer's refusal to accept her excuses to get the help she needed, but slowly she had learned to cherish the taste of food melting on her tongue, and to love the soft contours of her body as they grew, the way moving through the world no longer hurt and how her body was no longer her enemy. Her face was full and round now, her eyes bright, her arms thick and strong. She took up space, and she liked it.

Once Emma had gotten over her shock, she had introduced Daphne to the groom, and with a kind of awkward haste attempted to integrate Daphne into the proceedings. She'd been all smiles and I'm-so-glad-you-could-make-it, but Daphne could tell Emma resented her presence, that this was not a welcome surprise.

As for the groom, she'd had only a brief conversation with him, and then her observations over the course of the evening to judge him by. It was enough to know he was a weak man. He preened when he got attention and sulked when he didn't, took anything but adoration as a personal affront. Emma deserved better—but then, she had always played the part of caretaker and martyr in relationships. She had no faith in any relationship based in equality.

Now Daphne perused recent photos of Nathan—Nathan alone, Nathan with Emma, Nathan at happy hour with friends. There was no sign of what could have precipitated the message until she found the comment at the bottom of a photo from a few weeks ago, posted days after the photo had been taken. *Love you, bro! We'll miss you. Sucks not to see you every day.* One of Nathan's work friends. So Nathan was out of a job, then.

Still, moving back home seemed extreme. Daphne sat back in her chair, tugging on her lip. Could it be possible that Emma had found something out? Remembered something? Was she going back because—

No. There was no reason for Emma to go back now. To renege on the agreement they had all sworn to, sealed with the blood of their parents. There was no reason to open that long-closed door. Not intentionally.

But it would be wrenched open.

Which meant that Daphne needed to start making certain preparations. She needed to get control of the situation, before Emma stumbled into something she shouldn't.

She considered whether to contact the colleague—not a friend, despite his best efforts—who sometimes filled in for her with clients. But surely she had some time—more than Dale did, at least. She could see this project through to its natural conclusion.

She pulled up another tab on her browser, another fake profile. This time she was looking at a woman with rich dark hair springing in wild waves around her face, all but smirking at the camera. "Hello, Juliette," Daphne murmured to herself, and began to dig.

5

EMMA

Now

The house had not changed—it had stagnated. Locked up away from the world, its wallpaper had yellowed, peeled. Its floors were grimy, its windows unwashed. The furniture lay under shrouds of thick plastic, and the plastic itself was coated with something gritty and strangely sticky under Emma's fingertips.

She started with the ground floor, piling the plastic coverings in heaps in the corners. She moved through the sunroom, the wicker chairs faded to dingy gray, the damask pattern of the cushions nearly indistinguishable. She skirted around the piano in the great room, avoiding it for now, and drifted through the living room, where a massive and now worthless old TV dominated the space. Then there was the formal dining room, the kitchen and breakfast room, the library, the study.

She moved the rug from the foyer into the hall to cover up the stain. It looked incongruous, the wrong size and the wrong shape for the space, making it obvious that it was covering something up. After a minute of staring at it, she moved it again. At least there weren't any stains in the study—the rug that had once sat under her father's favorite armchair was gone, and so was the chair itself.

Nathan joined her as she went upstairs. The doors on the second floor were shut firmly, and she stood at the top landing, unmoving. Nathan's hand rested on the small of her back.

"Are you okay?" he asked.

"Not remotely," she said. But she squared her shoulders. Her room first. That seemed easiest.

The door stuck, and she had to shove at it before it sprang open. She blinked in the dim light. She flicked the light switch. The bulb was out. Nathan walked past her to pull open the curtains, sending out a cloud of dislodged dust. Sunlight slanted over the white bedspread, the pale pink wallpaper, the delicate white vanity in the corner next to a matching dresser.

"Huh," Nathan said, turning in a circle to take it in. He gave her a curious look. "I definitely thought I was going to learn something about your boy band preferences, but you don't have a single poster."

He was trying to keep things light, but she grimaced. "We weren't allowed to put up posters. My mom chose everything in here," she said. When she'd left, she hadn't taken much. A suitcase full of clothes, a few odds and ends. The books lined up on the dresser were the sweet teen romances her mother bought for her. Emma had always preferred horror and science fiction, but her mother disapproved of anything violent or contrary to reality.

"Should we check out the master?" Nathan asked, somewhat unsubtly. Emma gave a stiff nod. Her parents' sanctum. Opening the door felt like a transgression, but with Nathan at her back she didn't feel she could stop.

Her mother's taste suffused this room, like the rest of the house. Airy and light, sophisticated and classic. Only the bed broke the mood—huge, and carved out of dark oak that gave it a weight and intensity that so overpowered the rest of the decor that it was like a gravity well in the middle of the room.

She walked across to the bed and ran a palm over the bedspread. The fabric was cool to the touch. Her hand came away dusty.

"Should we . . . I mean, are we going to sleep in here?" Nathan asked doubtfully.

"It would be ridiculous not to, wouldn't it? The rest of the beds are twins," Emma pointed out.

"It won't be too weird?"

She'd expected it to feel that way, but now that she was standing here, it felt more like walking into an unfamiliar hotel room than wading into the past. With a sudden surge of energy, she grabbed hold of the bedspread and yanked, pulling it off the bed and letting it fall in a heap.

"Help me, will you?" she asked. Together they stripped the bed. She marched to the hall closet, where she found a set of linens, stale-smelling but serviceable, and made up the bed again, fresh. She stared at it. Nodded once. Looked at Nathan. "This is our house now. Until we leave, it's ours, not theirs. What happened here doesn't matter. It can't matter. That's the only way this works." The only way she could bear it.

"Okay," he said immediately, though his eyes were troubled.

She walked back out into the hall. The sacred, forbidden places of her sisters' rooms, she invaded, flinging open each one in turn. The soft yellow stripes of Juliette's room and the pale green of Daphne's. Chosen, of course, by their mother. Daphne's closet was open and cleared out, and with a jolt Emma realized she must have come back at some point for her things.

She opened Juliette's closet, but most of her clothes were still there—all pale pastels and whites, delicate filmy dresses and cashmere cardigans. They all had clothes like that, but Juliette was the only one who would have picked them out on her own. She patiently straightened her hair each morning, taming its wild waves, or braided it into an orderly plait. She dressed in skirts and white stockings and used only the soft shimmer of lip gloss their mother approved of, tiny silver studs in her ears that she had waited for her thirteenth birthday to get. She practiced piano dutifully for an hour every day, two hours on Sundays, and never made excuses to get out of going to church.

Juliette had been the perfect daughter. Everything that Emma couldn't be. It wasn't that she hadn't tried. For years she'd contorted herself to fit into the mold that her mother wanted, but she'd failed. No matter how hard she worked at it, she was scrappy and sloppy and sharp-tongued and devious and unladylike, and finally she'd broken. If she was going to be the bad daughter no matter what she did, then she'd do whatever she liked.

And all the while, Juliette had *yes, Mother*-ed and *no, Mother*-ed her way into the golden light of her parents' approval. Never strayed a step out of line.

Except . . .

Emma stared at the orderly line of Mary Janes and ballet flats in the closet, and she thought of that night. Juliette stumbling through the door, her feet bare, her hair soaked, her clothes dry. *Not* her clothes. Clothes that Emma had never once seen her wear—a black tank top, an oversize red flannel button-up, black jeans that clung to her like a second skin.

"Your sisters," Nathan said from the doorway. She looked up, her mind scrambling for purchase, reorienting to the here and now.

"My sisters?" she repeated.

"Is this why you're estranged?" he asked. He hesitated. "Do they think that you . . . ?"

He was an easy man to read, Nathan. It had always comforted her. But now, she wished she could believe his lie. Believe that he believed. But it was there in his eyes, that glistening doubt. The *maybe* of it all, the *what if*.

Maybe she *did* do it.

What could she say? *I don't know if they think that I did it.* She thought Daphne must. When Emma had come for her, riding in on her white horse—well, a twenty-year-old sedan that coughed and rattled—meaning to whisk her away from her foster home, Daphne had refused to even come to the door. Emma had sent the wedding invitation in a fit of vain hope—the same reason she sent birthday and Christmas cards every year, only giving up when she started getting Juliette's back with *No Longer at This Address* written in her sister's perfect handwriting.

But Daphne *had* shown up, she and Christopher Best—*"an old family friend,"* she'd told Nathan, which was technically true—joining an anemic trickle of friends to fill out Emma's side of the church. Daphne had spoken to no one, and at the end of the evening had fixed Emma with a look and said, "I'd hoped for more from you." And then she'd left.

Maybe they thought she'd done it, and that was why they had abandoned her.

Or maybe it was not because of blame, but guilt.

Blood drying on the hallway floor.

Juliette in a stranger's clothes.

Daphne, her sleeves soaked with blood, sleeping soundly in the tree house.

She hadn't known what happened. She hadn't wanted to know. She had taken care of it. She had accepted the suspicion, had even leaned into it at times, to pull the attention away from her sisters.

They had paid her back by abandoning her. And now Nathan was looking at her with that quavering light in his eyes. With all the questions that she had choked on all those years ago. He wouldn't ever say it. But he would think it, every day. And eventually, he would walk away, just like Juliette. Just like Daphne.

She would be alone again. It was only a matter of time, unless she could make him believe.

But how could she, when there was still so much she'd kept from him?

———

The morning after they arrived in Arden Hills, Emma sat across the kitchen table, in the seat that had once been her mother's. She'd sat there each morning with her reading glasses at the end of her nose, doing the crossword puzzle in pearls. It is important, she always said, to keep one's mind sharp.

She said it that way, too. *One's* mind. She always talked like that, with a stiff precision she believed elevated her. She did not believe that achieving a certain station in life meant you could relax her standards, and shook her head at the women she called her friends who wore sweatpants in public despite the diamonds on their wrists.

Nathan was opening drawers in the kitchen, determined to sort and catalog every item in this place. She was reluctant to get rid of anything, but he insisted that rusted can openers and ancient packs of sandwich bags, at least, could go. She had taken charge of a box of papers, sitting at the kitchen table and searching for any documents that might prove important.

The windows set in the back door were filthy. She could barely make out the trees in the back. She couldn't see the tree house at all. If it was still there. Go far enough past the tree house, and you got to the old house in the woods, its roof long rotted, its walls home to countless generations of small animals. Stark photographs of the graffiti-covered walls and the refuse-choked fireplace had been splashed all over the papers, after what the police found there. Some kid had drawn a pentacle on the wall at some point in the past, and suddenly Emma had a "known association with Satanism."

"Why did people suspect you?" Nathan asked, startling her. He was frowning at the paperwork. "There must have been a reason, right?"

"It's complicated." She wetted her lips, looking away. Her eyes fix on a discolored patch of crown molding. She wondered if it was water damage. She had no idea what shape the house was in. Gabriel hadn't said anything about there being major damage, but he hadn't mentioned the graffiti, either. Though the last time he'd sent any kind of update was at least a year ago. The emails were always short, impersonal. She never replied. She assumed he preferred it that way. "It's okay. You can wonder. Everyone does. If it matters, I didn't do it."

"If it matters? Of course it matters if you killed your parents," Nathan said, appalled.

"I mean if it matters that I say so. I've said it all along, and it hasn't stopped people from assuming that I'm lying. No, I didn't kill my parents. No, I wasn't in the house when they died. No, I don't know who killed them."

"Then why do people think you did?" he asked insistently. He shut the drawer he had been sorting through. The black trash bag beside him bulged already.

She spread her hands. "Lots of reasons. It makes a good story, for one. And people knew I'd been fighting with them. Juliette was the golden child. I couldn't compete. So I rebelled. I was the bad daughter, so it made sense I turned on them, right? People said I had an older boyfriend and the two of us plotted together to murder them. Or that I was friends with Satanists and it was a human sacrifice to the devil."

He snorted. "Seriously?"

She made a face. "The Satanic Panic was alive and well in Arden Hills."

"And were you friends with Satanists?" he asked, and it took her a beat to realize he was joking.

"No. That would require having friends at all." She chased it with a brittle laugh, but Nathan didn't look amused.

"They never arrested you, though," Nathan said.

"I had a good lawyer," she said. "He stepped in, did what he could to protect me. You met him, actually. Christopher Best. He was at the wedding."

"You said he was a family friend."

"He was. One of my dad's friends," she said. They'd been close in high school, and "Uncle Chris" had come by the house now and then, always with a kiss on the cheek for Irene and gifts for the girls. When he'd shown up after the murders, the first thing he told her was to stop talking. Then he'd gotten rid of the lawyer the state had given her, who seemed mostly interested in getting her to say the whole thing had been Gabriel's idea. If it hadn't been for Chris, she might still be in prison.

"They never found out who really did it?" Nathan asked.

"No." She set aside a phone bill, picked up an invoice for detailing on her father's car—it went on the stack with the telephone bill.

"I don't care what other people think. Or what they say," Nathan said, nobly enough. She knew it wasn't true, but she imagined he believed it. Few people cared as much about what other people thought as Nathan Gates. He wanted to be liked—or rather, he was desperate not to be disliked. So much that he whittled down every edge that he had, in case someone should find them distasteful.

She had never before thought she could be another piece of him that needed to be carved away.

"If you didn't do it, who did?" Nathan asked, musing out loud.

"I have no idea," she said, not looking at him. She picked up another bill. Doctor's visit for Daphne. Memories eddied through her mind.

Daphne with her wheezing breath, face pale, eyes panicked. Her mother, face like stone, holding the inhaler out of reach.

Daphne with her sleeves soaked in blood, blinking away sleep.

Daphne seizing Emma's hand, and whispering four words.

"No one can know."

6

DAPHNE

Then

Daphne is aware that she is a peculiar child. Her grandfather told her as much, when Daphne stood beside the bed that smelled of rubbing alcohol and musty blankets and the less-pleasant scents of a body that could no longer tend to itself. His skin sallow, his breath rattling, Grandpa looked at Daphne by letting his eyes fall to the side, not even turning his head because it took too much effort.

"You're a peculiar child, aren't you? Always watching," he said, with a kind of revulsion that made Daphne go still. She's never forgotten that tone in her grandfather's voice. She has listened for it ever since, and heard it a handful of times, sneaking around the edges of syllables from her teachers, her parents, even from Juliette.

Emma is different. "You're weird. It's cool," she tells Daphne, when she talks to her at all, and lets Daphne babble about fungi and poisonous plants and the ancient Roman practice of divining the future in the entrails of sheep. Daphne is twelve, and somehow both an "old soul" and "young for her age," which means she doesn't have many friends. She has her sisters instead. Sometimes she thinks about them leaving someday and she is filled with a formless, all-powerful fear, a scuttling thing like insects under her skin that makes her want to scream or to hit things. But today that fear is far away. Tomorrow she will sit in a cold room across from Chief Ellis and lie, but today she's with Emma at the park, and everything is perfect.

Emma sits alone under an oak tree, perched on a root. She wears black jeans and an off-the-shoulder black shirt with flowing sleeves and a half-dozen silver rings on her fingers. She's sketching, as she so often is; her walls are covered with her drawings and paintings. The best, she has labored over all year, to prepare for her art school applications in the fall. Daphne doesn't like to look at them. The rabbit with its leg twisted backward, caught in a snare. The church breaking open, people rushing out with expressions of frightening ecstasy.

Even the ones that should seem normal, like the portrait of Juliette at the piano, her head bent. The colors are wrong. Like rotting things. The tendons of her fingers stand out, and her hair is pulled back in a bun so tight, the skin at her hairline looks bruised. Her parents can't seem to see that there is something wrong with the painting. They smile and say that it's lovely, not like the rest. They don't see that it's the worst of all of them.

Emma hasn't spoken to Daphne since they arrived in the park, which is typical and doesn't bother Daphne—it's not like they have much to say to each other. Except that now Daphne, who has been walking along the riverbank, setting each foot precisely in front of the other to make a perfectly straight line with her footprints, has remembered what they're called. The ancient Romans with their sheep guts. Haruspex. She is about to go tell Emma this vital piece of information when Emma suddenly stands up and grins.

It's rare to see Emma smile. A grin is unheard of. Daphne stands still and watches as Emma raises a hand and waves, then picks up her canvas messenger bag and hurries her way over to a man leaning against a picnic bench. He has a long face and full cheeks, with short, unruly hair. Daphne can't read the look he gives Emma. Half-resigned and half-cheerful. He shakes his head and gives her a friendly fist bump.

Daphne creeps along the edge of the river, getting closer. The breeze carries the sound down toward her, and neither of them looks her way. She's used to this. She is happiest when invisible. Getting noticed is never good for girls like her, peculiar girls who say the wrong thing and walk the wrong way and don't want the things they're supposed to want.

"You probably shouldn't be hanging out with me where people can see," the man is saying. Daphne is bad at figuring out how old people are, but she thinks he's too old to still be in school. She doesn't recognize him from church, and she wonders where Emma met him. Mom is always complaining about Emma's friends, but it seems to Daphne to be a way of complaining about *Emma* without saying that directly. Though maybe Emma has friends Daphne doesn't know about.

"It's not like we're doing anything wrong. I don't care if people see us," Emma says. She crosses her arms. The sun turns her shoulders freckly in the summer and sends golden darts through her hair. Daphne has only two states—pale and burned. Her mother urges her to stay out of the sun, to keep her perfect porcelain skin protected.

"Yeah, I'm not sure that's true," the man says. Boy? She can't tell. He scratches his arm, looking off to the side. "People in this town gossip. Your dad would be pissed."

"I don't care."

"Maybe you should," he says.

"I don't. I don't care what he thinks. I hate him."

"Don't say that, Emmy," he says. Daphne narrows her eyes. Emma doesn't let anyone call her that. But Emma just huffs.

"It's true. I hate them. Both of them. I wish they were dead." Emma sounds like she's ready to cry.

"Everybody hates their parents sometimes," the man says. "You won't be a kid forever. Once you're eighteen, you can get out of the house. Go wherever the hell you want."

"Mom would never let me. She wants to control my life forever," Emma says bitterly. Her voice is ragged, and she bites her lip hard the way she always does when she's trying not to cry. "She won't let me go until one of us is dead."

Fear wiggles its way through Daphne's body. She doesn't like the way Emma is talking. She doesn't like that Emma is saying these things to a boy Daphne has never met or seen before, and she doesn't like the way he reaches out, touching Emma's shoulder gently.

The fear is formless and nameless. It's like she can feel something rushing up behind her, but she can't see it. Her chest seizes. Her breath wheezes in her throat. She can't draw in enough air.

"Emma," she tries to say, but it barely makes a noise. Panic scrabbles through her. She thrashes up the hill toward Emma, her breathing making a horrible whistle. Emma looks up, startled. Daphne says her name again, and Emma rushes toward her.

"Where's your inhaler?" Emma says, sharp and authoritative. For an instant she sounds like their mother. Daphne shakes her head. "You forgot it?" Emma says, frustrated and anxious.

"What's wrong?" the boy asks, worry drawing his brows together.

"She's having an asthma attack. I have to get her home," Emma says while Daphne struggles to breathe, the world closing in until all that is left is the sensation of *not enough*.

"I'll drive you. Come on," he says. Emma grabs Daphne's arm, dragging her away. Now people are looking. People are seeing them following this boy, seeing Daphne keel into the back of his car while Emma rubs her back and murmurs words that Daphne doesn't hear. Mom is going to hear about this. The thought makes the fear surge higher, and Daphne gasps and gasps.

He drives, looking at Daphne in the rearview mirror every minute or so. Emma keeps talking to her.

"I shouldn't go in," he says when he pulls up to the house, like he's apologizing.

"I know. This is fine. Thanks, Gabriel," Emma says. Daphne wants to thank him. She can tell that the worry in his eyes isn't just for her. This is a risk, somehow, though she doesn't entirely understand it.

Emma pulls Daphne along. Daphne's feet drag. Every breath is a question mark. But they burst in through the front door and Emma leaves her leaned up against the doorway. She races inside shouting for their mother.

"What on earth is going on?" Irene Palmer says, stepping out from the dining room. Daphne tries frantically to draw a normal breath. Irene's lips press together.

"Daphne needs her inhaler. Daph, is it upstairs?" Emma asks, afraid but focused. Daphne shrinks in on herself.

"She doesn't need that thing. She needs to pull herself together," their mother says, folding her arms so that her fingertips rest neatly on her elbows.

"She can't breathe," Emma says.

"It's not asthma, it's a panic attack. It's in her head," Mom says. She stands straight and still and tall, her hair in a perfect honey-colored bob. The light of the chandelier reflects off the shiny black of her shoes. Daphne slides slowly down the wall, trying and trying and trying to breathe.

"She needs her inhaler," Emma says desperately. "It helps."

"It's a placebo, and I am done coddling her," Mom says. Daphne squeezes her eyes shut. She needs air she needs air and there's none, none, none. She needs to breathe. She needs to be normal—*peculiar child*—and if she can't be normal, she needs to be unnoticed, and right now she is neither.

Heels click on hardwood. She senses her mother crouching before her, and opens her eyes.

"Control yourself," her mother hisses. Her hand raises, and for an instant Daphne thinks she is going to slap her, but she only grabs Daphne's chin, her fingernails digging in. "You're too old for this."

With that she drops Daphne's face, stands, and walks away. Emma looks between them, her expression a wreck of uncertainty.

Daphne puts her head down and tries, again, to breathe.

7

EMMA

Now

Emma and Nathan lurched from one task to another in the house. They found a broom and some old rags and started to attack the dust and grime. Nathan made a go at cleaning off the spray paint. It quickly became apparent that it was a losing battle, but he kept scrubbing away, trying one cleaning product after another. As if by erasing the words he could erase what they meant.

Or maybe he was just avoiding her.

She wiped the dust off the lid of the grand piano in the great room. She lifted the fallboard and ran her fingers lightly over the keys.

"Do you play?" Nathan asked. She startled at his approach, turning.

"Not well. And I'm sure it's horrifically out of tune," she said. She'd sat at this bench for so many hours, mangling one song after another. Sometimes because her fingers never seemed to move correctly, tangling and tripping over the simplest scales. Sometimes for the vicious pleasure of seeing her mother's face twist in anger. "Juliette was the prodigy."

She reached to shut the fallboard. It slipped free of her fingers and fell with a resounding crack, and she jumped back, hand against her throat and heart thudding wildly. Her fingers ached, a sudden pulse of pain that vanished just as quickly. She rubbed them against the thigh of her jeans. Nathan was watching her with an uncertain look. He was nothing *but* uncertain looks.

"I need to go into town," she said, speaking the words even before she'd consciously made the decision. "I'll go by the hardware store. I can pick up cleaning supplies that aren't over a decade old and something to deal with the graffiti." They needed to look into renting a dumpster, too. Nathan's black bag hoard was getting out of hand.

"I'll go with you," Nathan said immediately.

"Cool. Good," she said, though the point had been not just to get away from the house, but also from him and his nervous energy. *Like I'm the only one with secrets*, she thought.

They took a few minutes to unhitch the trailer from the car, leaving it in the drive in front of the still-locked gates. She checked her email again. Still no response from Gabriel about the key.

At the hardware store, Nathan split off immediately to go look for bolt cutters, to get through the chain on the gate. Emma wandered, staring at aisles of doorknobs and hinges, sinks and countertops, lamps and painting supplies. There was so much to do at the house, so much to repair, and neither of them had a handy bone in their bodies. They should just sell it. But she hadn't been able to bring herself to make the suggestion to her sisters yet. Not after the utter nonresponse she'd gotten when she'd told them about moving in.

All she had wanted back then was to have them with her. She didn't know what had happened and it hadn't mattered—the only thing she had cared about was keeping them safe. Keeping them together.

But Juliette had left the day after the funeral and hadn't ever come back. Emma and Daphne had been split up. Then Emma aged out of foster care.

She'd had money from her parents—lots of it. That was, after all, one of the reasons the cops—and later the DA—had thought she killed them. The money was in trust until she turned eighteen, and on her birthday she donated all of it, choosing a charity almost at random. She'd thought that maybe that would finally convince everyone, but it hadn't made a difference. It just became evidence of a guilty conscience.

She'd fallen apart. She hadn't been able to take care of herself, much less anyone else, for months. Chris stepped in again, giving her a place to crash, finding her a job and an apartment. She put herself together piece by piece, and when she was close enough to whole, she went to find Daphne.

Daphne didn't want to see her.

She hadn't even come to the door.

Emma had gone to see Juliette after that, but the look on her face when she found Emma at her doorstep was enough to send Emma running back to the train station.

Her sisters had made it clear that they didn't want or need her in their lives. Only the house still connected them. She thought with a pathetic, desperate kind of hope about calling them one last time, asking them to come, just to get the house ready to sell. To make peace.

To say goodbye.

But it was too late for that.

"Emma Palmer. I didn't realize you were in town," a voice said, low and alarmingly close to her ear. Emma spun. A man stood only a couple of feet away, a good six inches taller than her and broad in the shoulders. It took her a moment to place the crude angles of his face, now half-hidden beneath a thick gray beard.

"Officer Hadley," she said. Her voice sounded scratchy. Her hand at her throat, she could feel the pulse in her neck, galloping.

"Emma," he said, giving her an almost imperceptible nod. He wasn't in uniform, just wearing a faded gray T-shirt and jeans. The memory of a cold gray room sprang up in her mind. Hadley's hand smacking the table, making her jump. His voice raised to shout as she curled in on herself, tears running down her cheeks.

"What brings you back here?" he asked. She'd last heard that voice nine years ago. It had taken him that long to stop calling her on the anniversary and on her mother's birthday, telling her that she would never be safe. He'd sent her letters, too. Unsigned, just vague enough that she couldn't claim they were actually threatening.

She refused to quail in front of him as if she were sixteen again. She straightened up, lifted her chin. "We're staying at the house for a while. Me and my husband."

Hadley scratched the side of his neck. "That so? Well, it is your house. Though you ought to know—people around here still talk," he said, like he wasn't the reason for that.

"People can say what they want to. It doesn't bother me," Emma said, and realized that she was quoting her mother. It was something Irene Palmer had said many times, chin tipped up just like this, and it had been every bit as much a lie. "And if you have a problem with me being here, you should just say so."

"It's your house," Hadley repeated with a shrug. "A nice early inheritance. Must be worth a pretty penny."

"What's that supposed to mean?" she asked.

A grunt. "Just saying. If you wanted to sell, it wouldn't be a bad time for it."

"It needs a lot of work," Emma said darkly.

Hadley leaned in toward her, voice dropping. "You've really got no problem sleeping in the house where your parents were murdered?" he asked. "Where your mother bled out on the floor?"

Emma wrapped her hands around the handles of the basket she was carrying, heavy with paint remover and glass cleaner and other odds and ends. "Stop," she said. It was barely audible at all.

"Your dad was my best friend. I swore I would bring the person who killed him to justice. You should know I still intend to keep that promise."

He'd never let it go. All these years later, he was still sure it was her. She felt the frantic need rise up in her, the urge to speak. She'd said so much back then, so many ways. She had started out trying to protect her sisters, but at some point fear had taken over. All that had mattered was convincing him that she wasn't to blame, but she couldn't absolve herself—not without condemning someone else. And so in the end she'd only been able to repeat the same things again and again. *I didn't do it. I don't know. I wasn't there.*

"Hey there," Nathan said, coming up behind her. He put a hand on her shoulder, his standard affable smile affixed to his face.

"You're the husband, I take it?" Hadley asked.

"Nathan Gates," he said. He put out his hand to shake. Hadley reached out, his own smile sharp.

"Rick Hadley. Officer Hadley, when I'm working," he said. "Welcome to Arden Hills, Mr. Gates. Your wife and I were just chatting. I've known her since she was a baby, you know. Her father was a good friend of mine."

"Stop," Emma snapped, wound close to breaking. Nathan gave her a startled look. She glared at Hadley, jaw clenched. "It's our house and we've got a right to live in it. Just leave us alone."

"Emma," Nathan said, giving her a baffled and embarrassed look.

"That's all right, Mr. Gates. Emma and I have some history. No hard feelings, Emma—and I'm happy to leave you and yours alone, as long as you don't make your business my business. Oh, and Emma? Say hi to Gabriel for me." He gave Nathan a nod—nothing for Emma— and ambled away casually.

Emma's skin felt flushed. Her grip on the basket was so tight her fingers hurt and she wanted to shout after Hadley, but she had no idea what she would say—what words could possibly turn the fear and hurt inside her back on him as she wanted to.

"What the hell was that?" Nathan asked.

She looked up at him. "He . . . Back when my parents died, he . . ." Her throat tightened.

"I know you have history, but you were coming across a little Karen-y there," Nathan said with infuriating cautiousness and an edge of humor she wanted to cut him with.

"You didn't hear what he said," she ground out.

"Look, you're not exactly in a good frame of mind," he said. He reached for the basket. "Why don't I check out. You can wait in the car."

"I'm fine, Nathan," she said—and realized she sounded like she was about to cry. Which was ridiculous, since she hadn't cried once—not finding out about the layoff, the offer, the baby, confessing her deep dark secrets to him. Except as soon as she'd thought it, it was like all of it hit her at once.

"Fuck," she said loudly. A man at the other end of the aisle looked her way.

She pinched the bridge of her nose. That ever-present nausea was surging again, and the store felt unbearably hot. She wanted to get outside under the sky and take a breath that didn't stink of paint fumes.

Nathan rubbed a soothing hand along her upper arm. "Hey, it's okay. Go wait in the car, turn the air-conditioning on. I'll go pay, and we can get out of here."

She nodded mutely. She walked out into the sun, a hand over her stomach. Still flat enough she could forget she was pregnant at all—except for the sickness and the sore boobs and the fatigue that walloped her by seven every night.

She stalked over to the car and clambered in. They'd parked in the sun and the heat inside was like a solid thing. She got the AC going and leaned her head back.

If she were smart, she'd leave. It wasn't like Hadley actually had anything on her. Let Arden Hills talk; she didn't need to listen.

Except that she couldn't put the genie back in the jar, could she? Nathan knew. And he knew that she'd lied about it, by omission if nothing else, which meant he had good reason to wonder *why*. Good reason to wonder *what if*.

Nathan arrived. He put the bags in the trunk and came around to the front. He opened the driver's-side door, leaned down. "Want me to drive?" he asked.

They swapped places, and Nathan reached for the key to start up the engine, then paused. "That guy, Hadley. He said to say hello to Gabriel? You mentioned a Gabriel earlier," Nathan said. Not making it a question—quite.

Emma looked over at him steadily. "He's a friend. Or he was. He looks in on the house sometimes. Deals with the maintenance people, since he's local."

"What's Hadley's issue with him?" Nathan asked.

"Can we not do this right now?" she asked. Her voice cracked.

Nathan frowned. "Fine," he said.

As they pulled away, Emma let her head drop back against the seat once again. She'd thought that they were well matched, she and Nathan. Her flaws balanced against his. But that was when she'd thought she would never have to come back to Arden Hills, or tell him about her parents. Or about Gabriel, for that matter.

Now the scales would tip, and tip, and tip, with each doubt-filled glance he cast her way.

Whether they stayed or left, it was only a matter of time.

———

"Crap," Nathan said, just as they were turning onto Royal Avenue, toward the house. He smacked his palm against the steering wheel. "We forgot the bolt cutters."

"It's fine. We can leave the car on the road for another day," Emma murmured. She just wanted to get inside the house. A strange sanctuary, but at least it was hers.

"What the hell? Someone's parked in the driveway," Nathan said, and now Emma straightened up. There was an unassuming silver car parked behind the trailer, but no driver. Nathan rolled to a stop with plenty of room to spare. Emma unbuckled and reached for the door handle. "Let me check it out," Nathan said, motioning for her to stay.

"Hon," Emma said, giving him a look, and he chuckled.

"Let me be noble and protective of my pregnant wife?"

"I'll stand behind you," she offered with a quirk of a smile. They both got out of the car and made their way toward the gate and the parked vehicle. True to her word, Emma let Nathan take the lead, but there didn't seem to be anyone there. Then she looked past him. The gate was open—and walking toward them from the house was the

lanky form of Gabriel Mahoney. He raised a hand in greeting from
a distance, picking up his pace to a loping jog to reach them. A smile
broke across Emma's face, warm and unexpected, but Gabriel's expression was neutral as he approached.

"Got your email," he said, nodding to her, then looked immediately
at Nathan, sticking out his hand. "Gabriel Mahoney."

Nathan seemed to hitch for a moment before taking the offered
hand and giving his own name. He snuck Emma a glance that she was
pretty sure she knew the meaning of. Gabriel was, no way around it,
gorgeous, with tousled brown curls that fall to his jaw and deep brown
eyes. The cheeks that had been soft and boyish at twenty-one had given
way to a sharp jaw and sharper cheekbones, accentuated by a close-
trimmed beard. His eyes were hooded, somewhere between soulful
and mysterious; she'd teased him for it, once upon a time.

"Sorry I wasn't out here sooner. My grandmother's been in the hospital, so I was with her," he said, still talking more to Nathan than to
her. The smile that had curled her lips faded.

What had she expected? That he'd be happy to see her?

"No worries," Nathan said immediately, bobbing his head.

"Is your grandmother okay?" Emma asked. "It's not—"

"Nothing to worry about, just a routine procedure," Gabriel said,
looking at her at last. "Still cancer-free."

Emma let out a breath, nodding in relief. Lorelei Mahoney had been
at her sickest the weeks before Emma's parents died, but even weak
from chemo she'd been unfailingly kind to Emma.

"So you two are old friends?" Nathan asked, breaking the awkward
silence and looking between them. Emma adjusted her purse strap,
shifting her weight.

"Sure. Friends. You could say that," Gabriel said, staring straight
at her. Then he turned back to Nathan, slapping a ring of keys into his
hand. "Here. Keys to the front, back, garage, gate. Only thing missing
is the carriage house—I don't have a key to that. Daphne or Juliette
might. I've already let the landscape company know you're in residence,

so they'll get in touch next time they're scheduled to come out. Sorry about the graffiti. I was going to get around to cleaning it, but it's not like there's been a rush without anyone living there."

"Does that happen a lot? Kids breaking in?" Emma asked. Gabriel seemed to resent every time he was forced to acknowledge her presence. His jaw worked before he answered.

"Early on, just about every week. Nowadays it's pretty quiet. Old news. Though with you being back, who knows? Lock your doors at night."

"I always do," Emma said, a little sharper than she'd intended.

"Well. I'll leave you to it," he said. He started past Nathan. Emma turned, staring after him.

"Gabriel," she said. He stopped, looked slowly over his shoulder.

"Yes, Emma?" he asked, wearily neutral.

"I just . . ." she stammered. "It's good to see you again."

He was silent for another beat. Then he offered a single nod. "Sure," he said. He opened the car door and slid into the front seat. Emma and Nathan backed away to give him room to turn, rolling over the grass and dirt as he squeezed past their car. And then he was driving away, the car vanishing around the bend.

"A friend," Nathan said, voice choked with skepticism.

"Yes. A friend. Isn't that what I said?"

"You weren't looking at him like he was just a *friend*," Nathan said. "Didn't seem like he was being very friendly, either. What are you leaving out? Is he the boyfriend? The one who you were seeing that your parents didn't like? The one they thought—"

"You mean the evil older boyfriend who seduced me—or wait, maybe it was the other way around—and helped me murder my parents so we could run away together?" Emma asked, venom dripping from her voice.

"That's not what I said," Nathan objected.

"It's what you were thinking," Emma said.

He was silent a moment. "He's older than you."

"Five years older," Emma acknowledged. She rubbed the back of her neck. How could she have been so foolish as to hope that things would be sunshine and roses between her and Gabriel? After everything that had happened?

"So he's my age, then," Nathan said. She raised an eyebrow at him. He raised one back. "Just saying. Maybe you have a thing for older guys."

"Five years is not 'older guys' once you hit your midtwenties," she said, rolling her eyes.

"No, no, I like where this is going. I could be your silver fox," Nathan said. She knew he was trying to lighten the mood, but that old frustration and fear wouldn't ease. No matter how many times she said it, they never believed her.

"*We weren't together,*" she insisted, voice rising. Nathan's smile fell. His face clouded over. She stalked past him. Grabbed hold of the gate to pull it all the way open so they could drive through.

First Ellis and then Hadley had tried and tried to make her admit it. Hadley with threats and bluster, Ellis with understanding and sympathy. They'd tried to get her to say she was sleeping with Gabriel. That her parents had found out. That they had plotted the murders to get rid of the obstacle to their relationship.

She didn't know how they'd gotten the idea that she and Gabriel were involved. She had been, naively, convinced that the truth would be its own defense. Eventually, they would realize they were wrong, and look elsewhere.

She had been horribly mistaken.

And Gabriel had paid the price.

8

JULIETTE

Then

Juliette's hands shake. They haven't felt warm since last night. She pulls her white cardigan tighter around her, but it's no match for the air-conditioning overcompensating for the muggy air outside. On Chief Ellis's desk, a paper flutters in the breeze the AC kicks up.

The door opens; Rick Hadley comes in. She smiles at him politely, a well-trained reflex. He smiles back, but the expression seems forced. "Thanks for waiting, Juliette."

"Of course," she replies, all sugar. "Are my sisters all right?"

"As well as can be expected, I think," Hadley says. She nods gravely. Her fingers twitch. She folds them in her lap to hide it.

"Officer Hadley—"

"Juliette, I've known you since you were a baby. You can just call me Rick," he says. She doesn't want to. She hates calling adults by their first names. Her mother always says—*said*—it's disrespectful. More than that, it's disorienting, skewing the lines between adult and child, disrupting the clear and easy rules of what she ought to say and do.

But she needs Hadley to like her. She needs him to keep smiling at her and tell her what to do, because there are no rules for what's happened, and no Mom to tell her what's right. Only an infinite number of potential mistakes.

Instead of walking around the back of the desk, Hadley leans against the front. Juliette blinks up at him, trying to look attentive, but she's sure she looks the way she feels—exhausted. Broken. Her mind snags on the image of a sharp fragment of bone, a single hair stuck to it with a smear of drying blood.

"I know this has been a hard day," Hadley says. He's trying to sound gentle, but he's bad at it. Anger glints in his eyes. Not anger at her, she thinks. At least, not yet. His finger taps the front of the desk. "We're doing everything we can to figure out what happened to your parents, Juliette. But we need your help. We need you to tell us the truth."

"Of course," she says immediately, eyes wide. *What does he know?*

"I asked Chief Ellis to let me talk to you myself first. So you could talk to a friend."

A friend. She supposes she has always given Mr. Hadley the impression that she likes him. She's good at convincing people of that. It's instinctual. So it shouldn't be a surprise that he thinks she'll trust him.

She tries to arrange her face into an expression of sufficient gratitude. She's cried so much in the last few hours that her whole face feels puffy, her skin oddly stretched. She's sure she looks like a wreck. Her mother would be ashamed.

"Now, you and your sisters all claim that you spent the night in the tree house," Hadley says.

"That's right," she confirms. This is easy. This is what they agreed on. The story is simple, and they will all tell it the same way every time, and everything will be all right.

"Could one of your sisters have left at any point?"

"No," she says immediately, but he gives her a skeptical look.

"Are you sure? One of them couldn't have climbed down while you were asleep, without you noticing?"

"I . . . I don't think so," she says.

"Who was sleeping nearest the door?"

"Emma. She always sleeps by the door," Juliette says immediately, and something about the look of satisfaction in his eye makes her afraid.

"Could Emma have left after you fell asleep?"

"No. I would have noticed," Juliette insists. "Probably," she adds softly, and hates herself for it. He glances over at the desk, flipping up the top page of a legal pad to look at something written beneath, as if he's reminding himself of something.

"Right," he says. "Okay, Juliette, let's change subjects for a moment. What can you tell me about Emma's boyfriend?"

She stares at him blankly. "Emma doesn't have a boyfriend," she says. Emma with a boyfriend? The thought is almost funny. Emma with her black clothes and sulky attitude and the way she snaps at everyone constantly. Emma who taunted Juliette the first time she went out on a date, and rolls her eyes at every hint of romance, real or fictional? No, Emma doesn't have a boyfriend.

"So you weren't aware that she was seeing anyone."

She thinks of a name, of a knowing look exchanged between her parents. She wonders if this is the reason for the fight last night—the reason Emma took off.

"I didn't know Emma has a boyfriend," Juliette says. And then she does something that she will regret for the rest of her life. She bites her lip, looks up at Hadley, and says guilelessly, "I do know Emma was fighting with Mom and Dad. And I think it was about a boy. I think his name is Gabriel Mahoney."

9

JJ

Now

Nathan and I are going to be staying at the house for a while. Wanted to let you know.

Emma's number wasn't even in JJ's phone, and when the unknown sender's text had arrived, it had taken her a solid thirty seconds of reading and rereading to figure out it hadn't been sent to her by mistake. And another minute to remember who the fuck Nathan was. It was over an hour before she mustered the coherence to text back.

What did she care if Emma and her boyfriend (husband? They'd gotten married, hadn't they?) moved into the house? It wasn't like she ever wanted to. She'd be happy if it burned to the ground.

She sat on the balcony, on the deck chair wedged into the narrow space next to Vic's alarming number of plants.

She reached into her pocket, pulled out the silver lighter. There was a bumblebee etched in the metal, landing on a flower. She flipped it open, closed it. Flipped it open again. Lit the flame. Flicked it shut, the sound satisfying.

Emma knew something. She'd found something out.

There's nothing to find.

We covered our tracks.

She had taken comfort in those words for years, but now they seemed tissue-paper thin, no protection against possibility.

She had never been sure what Emma knew—or guessed, or suspected—about that night.

She might not know anything. She might know everything. It was all the territory in between that frightened JJ the most.

"Here's what we're going to do."

JJ was the oldest. She was supposed to be the one looking after her sisters. And instead, it had been Emma who leaped into action, told them what to do. And then, when Hadley had settled on Emma's guilt, she'd still never said a word about what she'd seen. Emma had let all that blame and suspicion fall on herself. Carried all the sin and shame of her family.

"You can't change the past. You can't take back what happened, to you or to Emma. The best you can do is protect yourself now," Vic had told her more than once. Easy enough when protecting herself had meant staying quiet, staying out of the way. But that was over.

"That's it, then," she said to no one. Flicked the lighter open. Flicked it shut.

She remembered closing her fingers around that cold metal, hands in her pockets, water dripping down her back.

She hadn't run from her past all these years so much as she'd ignored it. It was finally done ignoring her. And now it was time to choose—stay here, and risk Emma destroying the life JJ had built for herself. Or find a way to protect it.

Except it wasn't really a choice at all. She couldn't just hide and hope that the world spared her.

If she wanted her secrets safe, she was going to have to do something about it.

10

EMMA

Now

Emma knew she wouldn't be able to sleep. Long after Nathan went up to bed, she remained downstairs, stalking from room to room. She furiously dusted a bookshelf, threw open a closet to shove old coat hangers and ancient wrapping paper into a trash bag, abandoned it to scrub the grime from the powder room faucet. She lurched from room to room and task to task, completing nothing.

And every time she walked through the foyer and the dining room, the words on the wall taunted her.

MURDERER

KILLER

PSYCHO

She'd heard them all. Whispered behind her, spoken boldly to her face. She'd left Arden Hills, but the rumors had followed her to her new high school. The principal and teachers had made noise about making sure the school was a safe place for her, but in their eyes, she'd seen the same questions.

She'd dropped out. Christopher Best had tried to talk her out of it, and her next foster family had reenrolled her in school, but with less than a year until she aged out, it wasn't like anyone was really paying attention when she just didn't go. It wasn't until she was on her own that she got her GED, got herself into community college—far away from Arden Hills.

MURDERER. KILLER. PSYCHO.

She found the bags from the hardware store. She pulled on a mask and rubber gloves, and she got to work. The fumes made her eyes water as she scrubbed at the words, watching them surrender to the chemical assault. She started to feel woozy, realized she hadn't thought to open a window. She yanked it open. The air was as swampy outside as it was inside.

She had outrun this. For a little while. All it had taken was lying to everyone she met. Lying to her husband.

She stripped off the mask. The chemical tang was heavy in the air. She threw the gloves and mask onto the end table nearby. The words were almost gone, but the trace of them remained. You could still read them, if you knew what they said.

She shouldn't be doing this. It couldn't be good for the baby. She needed to think of more than just herself. She needed to eat well and sleep and *avoid stress*, as the doctor had so helpfully suggested, like that was possible.

Emma's phone rang, startling her. She pulled it out of her pocket. Gabriel's name glowed on the screen. She hurried to answer, adrenaline coursing through her.

"Hello? Gabriel?" she said, pressing the phone to her ear. What time was it?

"Emma." A sigh, a silence. "Look. I'm sorry to call so late, but I wanted to tell you . . . I wasn't expecting to see you. I thought I could leave the keys and go."

"It's okay," Emma said at once. "I understand. The way we left things . . ."

"The way you left things, you mean," Gabriel said. "You took off. You didn't say a goddamn word."

"I didn't think you'd want to hear from me."

"You were right. That doesn't mean you didn't owe me an explanation."

"I never wanted any of it to happen," Emma told him. "I'm sorry. Sorrier than you can know. I didn't realize that Ellis was going to try to put it on you. I didn't know he even knew who you *were*."

"You lied, Emma," Gabriel said. She shut her eyes. "You told him you were with your sisters that night. And I know you weren't, because you were with me. You gave yourself an alibi and left me without one."

"You would have been in trouble if Ellis thought I was with you, too," Emma said. "You know how many times I told him you weren't my boyfriend and he didn't believe me? If he knew I was at your house—in your *bed* that night—"

"You know, if I've got to be falsely accused of something I'd rather it be sleeping with you than double murder, actually," Gabriel said bitterly.

"Gabriel . . ."

"What?" he asked, voice rough.

Emma looked at the words written on the wall. It didn't matter how thoroughly she scrubbed, painted, covered them up. They'd always be there. "I was with you that night. But not the whole night. You left."

"Yeah. I did," Gabriel said. "But, Emma? So did you."

Her breath hitched. He knew. He'd figured it out.

The silence stretched. Then Gabriel's voice came again, steady and calm. "Listen, Emma. I've helped out with the house. I didn't mind doing that. And I can't stop you from coming back, obviously. But I don't need you in my life. You only ever fucked things up for me."

"I never meant for you to get hurt," she managed. "I only wanted . . ."

"You wanted to use me against your parents. And they're gone, so you've got no more reason to keep me around, right? Goodbye, Emma. Don't contact me again."

The line went dead. She set her phone on the table and staggered to where she had abandoned her gloves and mask. She pulled them back on. Turned back to the wall. And started again.

Emma dragged herself up the stairs. Her hands felt raw. So did her throat. Her joints and her feet ached. The words were all but gone— would never be gone. The things Gabriel had said, his scarred-over anger, echoed in her ears.

Nathan lay sleeping, sprawled across the top of the covers, stripped down to his briefs. The house didn't have air-conditioning, and the upstairs was stifling. Emma peeled off her T-shirt and pants and lay on the bed next to him. A finger trailing across his chest woke him; fingertips against his lips stifled his mumbled question.

"You have to believe me," she whispered, pleading.

"I do. Of course I do," he said, pulling her close. He kissed her brow; she kissed his throat. Then he was awake, rolling to half pin her against the bed, his hands and lips on her skin. They moved with more desperation than desire, as if this could be the proof they needed, the proof they wished they could give.

With Nathan's cheek pressed against her stomach, her fingers playing in his hair, Emma said, "How can you be sure?"

"Sure of what?" he asked, voice muddy with sleep and the slow fade of pleasure.

"How can you be sure I didn't do it?" Emma asked.

Nathan lifted his head. His hand rested on her thigh, possessive. "You say you didn't. I believe you."

She shook her head. It wasn't enough. "You don't *know*," she said. "Even if you think I didn't do it, you don't know who *did*. So you'll wonder. And that means you'll wonder about me."

"I won't," he promised. He was such a bad liar.

"She'll wonder," she said. Her hand slid over her lower abdomen. "Someone will tell her or she'll go looking, and then she'll wonder, and I can't—I can't—"

Nathan curled his hand around hers, ran a thumb over her knuckles. "We've got a long time to figure it out." He paused. "She?"

"Just trying it out," Emma said. *It* and *the baby* didn't feel real. She needed it to feel real. She needed there to be a reason.

"A girl would be nice. I'd like that," Nathan said, and pressed a tender kiss against her stomach. She shivered. "Then a boy. One of each."

"My dad wanted a boy," Emma said. She hadn't remembered that in years. "He was so happy with Juliette, but that was before he started to think he wouldn't get a son. I was a disappointment. Daphne was a disaster. They kept trying after that. Mom got pregnant again when I was seven. She lost it when she was five months along. It was a boy. Mom wanted to name him Randolph Junior, but Dad said he wanted his *living* son to have his name. She named him Anthony instead."

Her mother had called them into the hospital room to meet him. Emma had expected him to look like her baby dolls, but he was rubbery and shrunken, swaddled in blankets that didn't look soft enough for his delicate skin. Her mother wanted them to kiss his forehead, touch his hand, hold him. Emma wanted to run away. She loved her brother but she couldn't see how this could be him. She darted out the door. Outside, her father caught her by the arm and slapped her in the face. He'd forced her to go back in.

He never went into the room himself.

She found herself telling Nathan this, something she hadn't thought or spoken of in many years, but now it seemed like the most important thing, the only thing. The words dried up on her lips, and she looked at him and instantly thought she had made a mistake. A look of revulsion pinched his features. He already knew she was damaged. She shouldn't have put this on him, too.

"That's awful," Nathan said, after too long. "Grief . . . it does strange things to people."

"It wasn't out of character for him," Emma said flatly. "Nathan. There's a reason people thought I might have killed my parents. I hated them."

"Everyone hates their parents," Nathan said.

Where had she heard that before? "I wanted to kill them. I thought about it so many times."

Nathan was quiet, his thumb playing back and forth over her thigh. She could tell he wanted to be anywhere but here.

"But the thing is," Emma said. She fell silent. Then pressed on. "The thing is, I never once thought about how I would *get away with it*. I never thought about hiding it."

"Maybe that means you didn't really want to do it," Nathan said. "You were just angry."

She made a noise that was almost agreement, but she didn't think that was quite right. It wasn't that she hadn't wanted to kill her parents. It was that she knew if she did, there would be no point trying to save herself.

That was why she had hated shooting so much, every time her father made her go out. Because every time she pulled the trigger, she felt like she wasn't just destroying something else. She was destroying herself, too.

She remembered the kick of the gun. Yelping. Her father's laugh. *"That's just the recoil. It's not gonna kill you."*

She'd known that if she killed them, there was no point trying to get away with it. There was no getting away. Not then.

And not now.

Something thumped downstairs. Emma jolted upright.

"What was . . . ?" Nathan began, and then Emma's nose, so sensitive since her little houseguest moved in, caught an alarming scent.

"Smoke," she said, leaping from the bed. She bolted out of the door and down the stairs, the sweat cool on her bare skin. She saw at once the warm, wavering light splashed against the foyer wall—the fire was in the dining room. The dining room, where the wall was covered in paint thinner.

She darted left instead of right, toward the library. The armchair there had been covered in a heavy drop cloth instead of plastic, and it was still folded near the wall. She'd grabbed it and was running back by the time Nathan came down the stairs—he'd taken the time to pull on his briefs.

"What—" he started, but she just grunted.

The fire was contained to the floor in front of the window—the window she'd left open. There was something in the middle of it, a lump, she couldn't tell what. The rug had caught at the edges, the fire creeping toward the curtains, toward the far wall, and the air was still thick with fumes. She threw the drop cloth over the fire.

It was out in a moment. Suffocated beneath the thick fabric, the smell of smoke joining the rank burn of chemicals.

Movement outside caught Emma's eye, and she whipped her head toward the window in time to see a figure leaping over the wall at the front of the property. She stepped toward the window to get a better look, but Nathan caught her arm.

"You're not wearing any clothes," he said, and she gave him a disbelieving look. She yanked her arm away, stalked to the window. The figure was gone. Had there just been one of them?

Nathan pulled up the side of the canvas, made a face. "I think that's flaming dog shit. I didn't think people actually did that," he said.

The fading adrenaline sent a shiver through her, and suddenly Emma *was* very aware that she was standing in front of the window completely naked. She wrapped her arms around her middle, fighting off a feeling of vulnerability. Exposure.

Idiot kids, she thought. *That's all it was.*

"I'm going to put some clothes on," she said, voice shaky with anger and fear, and marched out of the room.

They couldn't stay here. This had been a mistake. They couldn't have a *baby* here. But they couldn't leave now. Not until—unless—Nathan found a new job. Or she did, something steady, but who was going to hire a woman who would be leaving in a few months for maternity leave? Maybe she could hide the pregnancy. And then what? She wouldn't have been anywhere long enough to get paid leave, so they'd be back to where they started.

She pulled on a T-shirt and shorts and raked her hair into something she hoped made her look less manic. She wanted to collapse into bed, but she wasn't going to leave that vile mess on the floor.

Halfway back down the stairs, she heard Nathan's voice.

"—Thank you. No, we're not going anywhere. Okay." She stepped around the doorway to see him hanging up the phone.

"What are you doing?" she asked him.

"Calling the police," Nathan said. He rubbed the side of his neck. "They said they'd send someone out soon."

"Are you kidding me?" Emma asked. She wanted to strangle him. "Why would you do that?"

"Because someone tried to burn our house down?" Nathan asked impatiently.

She groaned, covering her face with her hands.

"We need to make a report," he insisted. "I'll talk to them. You don't have to say anything. I'm going to go get some pants on, okay?"

She didn't answer as he walked past her and up the stairs.

Just some stupid kids. Stupid kids who knew who she was and knew she was back, because why else would they have come? The house had been broken into before. It wasn't safe.

It was never safe.

She let out a choked scream and slammed the side of her fist against the wall, hard enough to send pain shooting up the bones of her arm. Nathan's footsteps paused in the hall upstairs. Then resumed.

Emma went out to the porch to wait, as she had when she was sixteen years old, for the police to arrive.

11

EMMA

Now

A cop car pulled up to the gate. It wasn't locked—they hadn't bothered. Maybe she should have put on shoes and gone out to let him in, but she stayed on the porch and watched as Rick Hadley got out of the car, swung the gate open, got back in. He pulled up. No lights, no sirens, no hurry. He got out of the car again. To Emma's surprise, the passenger-side door opened, and a second figure stepped out—still bald, his jaw gone jowly, his scalp flecked with liver spots. Chief Ellis.

Nathan stepped out on the porch next to Emma, dressed in sweats and a T-shirt, his hair rumpled.

"Emma. Mr. Gates," Hadley said. "Heard you had some trouble."

"Yeah. Someone tried to burn our house down," Nathan said, in a *so what are you going to do about it* tone that made Emma wince.

"Doesn't look like they did a good job of it," Ellis said affably. Ellis had done his best to play good cop to Hadley's bad cop, back in the day. Patting her shoulder, offering her sympathy and understanding. Like she didn't know that Hadley worked for him, that he wouldn't be in that room at all if Ellis didn't want him to be. He looked to Nathan. "Craig Ellis. I'm the chief of police here in Arden Hills."

"Pleasure to meet you," Nathan said. Some of the hard edge in his voice had dissolved.

"Why don't you walk us through what happened, exactly," Ellis said, reasonably enough, while Hadley stood with his hands on his hips, looking deeply unhappy to be here.

"We were upstairs in bed," Nathan said. Her eyes flicked to him; for a moment she wondered just how much he'd tell Ellis, if the appearance of an authority figure would have him specifying what they'd been doing, for how long, and in what position. "We were, uh, talking. And we heard a thump downstairs."

"A thump?" Ellis echoed.

Nathan nodded. "Then Emma smelled smoke. We got downstairs and the carpet was on fire. Luckily, Emma smothered it before it spread."

"So how much damage are we talking about?" Ellis asked.

"Well. The rug's a goner," Emma said dryly. Nathan shot her an irritated look.

"And what makes you think the fire was intentional?" Ellis asked.

"Because it was a bag of flaming shit someone threw in the window," Nathan half shouted, gesturing behind him. "Someone broke into our house and—"

"Broke in?" Ellis said, interrupting him.

"They didn't break in. The window was open," Emma said. She could feel Hadley's eyes on her. She just wanted them gone.

"They were trespassing," Nathan said stubbornly.

Ellis gave a slow, considering nod. "Okay. Well, it seems like there wasn't too much damage done. You got cameras?" Emma shook her head. "Might look at getting some. We get called out here a lot. Kids."

"Cameras. Okay," Emma said. *Just leave.*

"They probably didn't know anyone was even here," Ellis said. "You've been gone a long time."

She raised an eyebrow, tilting her head toward the car and the moving trailer, parked nearby. "If there hadn't been anyone here, the house really could have burned down," she pointed out.

"What if we were asleep?" Nathan asked earnestly. "I don't even know if the smoke detectors work in this place. We could have been killed. I mean, someone tried to light my house on fire with my pregnant wife inside it." Ellis's eyes snapped to Emma.

"You're pregnant?" Hadley said with a hint of a sneer. Her hand went to her stomach protectively.

"Well. Congratulations," Ellis said, a peculiar tone in his voice. He looked intently at the two of them, like he was trying to work something out.

"So you can see why we're so concerned," Nathan said.

"Sure, I see," Ellis said with a nod.

Hadley's eyes hadn't left Emma. "Of course, there's not much to do," he said dryly. "Sometimes people just get away with things."

"You could do your job. Investigate," Emma said.

"They are doing their job, Emma. They're out here, right?" Nathan interjected, giving Ellis a look that said, *you and I, we're the reasonable ones here.*

Emma snorted softly. "They just decide what they think happened and stick to it," she said.

"We followed the evidence, Emma," Ellis said. If she didn't know better, she might think there was a note of apology in his voice.

She made a half-feral noise in the back of her throat. "You had us in those rooms for hours without a guardian or a lawyer—"

"Emma. Come on. This isn't the time to bring that up, is it?" Nathan said, putting a hand on her arm. She jerked away. Ellis just raised an eyebrow.

"Your legal guardians were dead, Emma," Hadley said, ignoring Nathan. "We were just trying to find out what you knew. Since the three of you were our only witnesses."

She groped for words—for the thing to say to make him flinch. To make him feel even a fraction of what she felt. But she only stood frozen, glaring at him. "We don't need your help. I want you to leave," she said.

"All right, then," Ellis said, holding up a placating hand. "You know, there's a couple of kids who still hang out at the old Saracen house. I'll have someone swing past, see about scaring some sense into them." He gave a nod, like he'd made up his mind and they ought to thank him for it. "You give us a call if you have any more trouble. And look into those cameras."

"We will," Nathan promised. She could feel his irritation—not with them, with her. She was the one causing trouble, being rude. "Thank you for coming out."

"It's no problem," Ellis said. He reached into his pocket and put one foot up on the bottom step of the porch, leaning out to hand Nathan his card. "You notice anything else, you go ahead and let me know."

Ellis walked back toward the car, but Hadley lingered. His hand rested on his belt. He looked at Nathan consideringly. "She lied about where she was that night, you know. Don't know if she bothered to tell you that."

"What?" Nathan said, puzzled at first.

"Don't—" Emma started, but what could she say?

"She was with Gabriel Mahoney. There were boot prints in the blood in the house. Men's, size ten and a half. Same size as Mr. Mahoney. She'd been fighting with her parents about him that day, said she wanted to kill them. In case you think it was so wildly unreasonable to be asking her a few questions about what exactly happened."

"Get out," Emma said. Nathan didn't say anything, just stared bug-eyed at Hadley. Hadley didn't move.

"Rick," Ellis called, a warning in his voice, and Hadley turned away at last.

Emma stayed perfectly still until the car had pulled through the gate. They left it yawning open behind him. Not that it mattered. It wasn't like it had ever done a thing to protect them.

"You lied about where you were?" Nathan said in the silence that remained.

She gave him a long, flat look, her mind empty. And she walked back inside the house.

12

JULIETTE

Then

On a Saturday afternoon less than twelve hours before their parents will be shot to death twenty feet from where she sits, Juliette plays the piano.

The notes spill out, liquid and elegant. Juliette's hands dance along the keys. Her eyes flick across the sheet music. She feels like she is racing along ahead of some great galloping beast, always one stumble from being trampled into the ground. She hears people talk about being lost in music. She is not lost in the music but she is lost *to* it. It is dragging her hands across the keys in that runaway sprint of sound that is always, always, on the precipice of utter disaster, until she crashes to the ending and lets the last note linger.

Perfect. Every note perfect. She would gasp for breath, except of course her breathing is as controlled as everything else, because her mother watches for that. She watches for everything.

Her mother beams at her, eyes dark and sharp as a hawk's. "Wonderful," she says. Her hands come together, almost as if she is about to clap, but they only stay that way, palms touching lightly.

Juliette smiles demurely. "I thought I was a bit rushed in the middle," she says softly. She doesn't think anything of the sort, but she must not appear boastful or overconfident.

"Yes, I think you're right. Let's start again from the . . ." Her mother trails off. Juliette looks over her shoulder, following her mother's gaze to see Emma in the foyer, taking her shoes off. "Run through your scales for now," her mother instructs and walks toward Emma.

Even walking through her own house she glides, every step choreographed. On days like this, when they aren't expecting to see someone, she still puts on her full face of makeup.

Juliette's maternal grandparents died when she was very young, but she visited them once. They had a nice house and a rowdy dog. The carpets needed vacuuming. They spoke loudly, and Grandpa swore at the TV when his football team was losing. They had this bizarre way of always touching each other—hands on shoulders, quick hugs, casually putting an arm around someone. The whole time her mother sat stiffly on the couch with a look of deep embarrassment on her face. Juliette didn't understand then, but she thinks she does now—how her mother is so controlled because she is afraid that if she relaxes, she will slip up, and the friends she plays tennis with will somehow sense the electrician's daughter under all that cashmere and silk.

Juliette's hands move along the scales by rote. Her mother and Emma are speaking quietly; she can't make out the words. Then Emma's voice lifts—"You're a complete fucking hypocrite!"—and footsteps stomp up the stairs.

"Emma Palmer, get back down here!" her mother shouts, but then she follows, her footsteps quieter but no less angry. A door slams. Juliette lets her fingers go still on the keys, frustration rising in her chest. Emma is always fighting with Mom. It would be one thing if she were the only one to bear the consequences, but it all comes crashing down on the rest of them—because if Emma isn't perfect, Juliette had better be twice as perfect.

She hears the murmured tones of another voice down the hall. Her father, in his study. Who is he talking to?

She ought to keep playing, but her hands ache, and so does her head. She's running on only a few hours of sleep. She knows she's stretching herself too thin, but what choice does she have? At least with the end of school, she has a few weeks before she has to worry about keeping her grades up again. Soon enough, though, college will start. She'll be commuting in—no way would Irene Palmer let her eldest daughter move away for college, out of reach. Which means nothing will change. She will be watched every moment.

She stands, stretching her fingers, shaking out her wrists. Dad is still talking. Curious, knowing she shouldn't, she pads over toward the study door.

"That's not what we agreed to. I can't just leave this stuff sitting on my trucks. I'm taking a big risk here," he says. A pause, as if the other person is talking. "Fine. One week. But it's going to cost you."

She hurries away before he hangs up. Her stomach feels pinched. She knows she's heard something she shouldn't have.

She starts the scales again. The study door opens. In his house slippers, her father walks down the hall without hurry. She forces her mind to remain fixed on the movements of her fingers. His hand falls to her shoulder.

"Beautiful," he says. She doesn't stop.

A scent twines around her, escaping from his clothes. Jasmine and amber. She knows the woman the scent belongs to. She's seen her, in the passenger seat of her father's car. At the office. At a restaurant in the next town over. Kissing his neck. Sliding her hands over his chest. Laughing like he's the most brilliant man in the world. She's young. Twenty-three? Twenty-four? Not much older than Juliette, Emma pointed out, when she whispered the secret to her, side by side in the tree house as Daphne slept soundly beside them.

Juliette keeps thinking of how beautiful the girl was, with her shining hair and her dark eyeliner and the laugh that bared her long throat. Juliette's mother isn't beautiful. She's the kind of person you call beautiful because she is thin and has good teeth and an expensive haircut.

Everyone always says Juliette looks just like her mother.

Her father tucks her hair behind her ear. "You look nice, with your hair down like that. You should wear it that way more often," he says.

"You should remember to take a shower after you go into the office on the weekend," she says softly.

He goes quiet. She freezes. She knows that quiet. His hand drops to her shoulder again, his fingers tightening. She breathes quietly, not moving, not making a sound, and curses herself. She knows better than to provoke her father.

"Keep your nose out of my business," he says. She relaxes a fraction, though not so he can see. When he gets truly angry, there aren't any words or warnings.

"Randolph." Her mother comes back into the room. Her hair looks mussed, like she's been raking her hand through it.

"I was just listening to Juliette play," her father says.

"She is a wonder, our Juliette," her mother replies. She clasps her hands together. "Why don't you take a break, dear? You've been working so hard. Go get yourself a lemonade, and then we'll get back to it."

Juliette murmurs her thanks. She slides out from under her father's hand and crosses quickly to the kitchen. She pauses at the refrigerator, her hand out to open the door.

"Everything all right with Emma?" her father asks.

"Someone needs to get that girl under control. And apparently I can't manage it," her mother says sourly. "She was in the park with some older boy. Marilyn says she's seen the two of them together *several* times."

"What boy?" Dad asks. Juliette forces herself to open the fridge, get out the lemonade, but her attention is trained on the conversation in the next room.

"Gabriel Mahoney," her mother says, like this means something important.

What is Emma doing hanging around with Gabriel? She knows Gabriel, sort of—she sees him talking to Logan sometimes. He's soft-spoken, good-looking in an unusual sort of way. Has he seen her? Does he know who she is? Has he told Emma about her and Logan?

She tells herself to calm down. Emma doesn't know anything, because if she did, she wouldn't have been able to go ten minutes without crowing about it to Juliette.

It's still quiet. Juliette's skin grows cold. It has been too quiet too long, and her father speaks at last, but the cold is still there. "I'll handle it."

"I told you it was a mistake letting her spend time at that house."

"I said that I'd handle it."

"The last thing we need—"

"Irene." Randolph Palmer never uses his wife's name unless he's unhappy with her. And Irene Palmer knows that life is better for all of them when Randolph is happy. She makes a dismissive sound, not quite ceding the argument, and her footsteps click toward the kitchen.

Juliette springs into motion, pouring a splash of lemonade so it looks like she's already had most of it. When her mother comes in, she is downing a dainty sip.

"Let's get back to it," her mother says.

Juliette smiles. "I'll just clean up first," she chirps. Her mother nods. Juliette picks up the pitcher of lemonade with its heavy glass base. She imagines smashing it into her mother's perfect teeth.

She puts it away. She walks back to the piano.

She begins, once more, to play.

13

EMMA

Now

Emma went to bed alone. Nathan never came back, but she woke to find a plate with plain toast beside the bed. The doctor had suggested she try to eat something the moment she woke up, before even sitting up, to combat the nausea. Its presence seemed like a good omen, at least. She nibbled on the edge, nose twitching at the scent of coffee downstairs. Nathan didn't want her drinking coffee. The morning after she'd told him about the baby, he'd taken her mug out of her hand and dumped it down the drain. He'd memorized the lists of forbidden substances and was meticulous in checking that she wasn't eating soft cheeses or glancing too intently at deli meats. The bottle of white wine she'd bought for toasting was in the kitchen trash, unopened.

She'd at least convinced him a cup or two of coffee a day was fine, but that didn't stop the dark looks. If he'd made her some, maybe he was trying to apologize for last night.

Her stomach settled for now, she showered and dressed. In the bathroom, she looked through drawers still filled with her mother's makeup—a dozen nearly identical shades of subdued lipstick, foundation, blush, nothing that might be construed as gaudy or showy or, God forbid, *fun.*

There must have been good things about Irene Palmer. People had loved her, after all. But when Emma thought back all she could remember was her anger, and the feeling of being trapped. Juliette had been everything their parents wanted; Daphne had survived by smothering the parts of her that weren't, growing small enough that she didn't stray outside the lines. Emma couldn't. Or wouldn't. She didn't know which it was, only that every time her mother told her to sit still she wanted to run, every time she said to sing, Emma clamped her mouth shut.

Now she was going to be a mother. Theoretically. The chance of miscarriage still loomed. She wasn't out of the first trimester yet, and her brief foray into reading online pregnancy forums had been a deluge of horror stories and tragedy. She'd been pregnant once before, after a broken condom incident with a guy she'd been seeing for a couple of months. She hadn't even had the chance to make the appointment when she started bleeding. A pregnancy wasn't a promise.

But she wanted this child. She wanted to be a mother—a better mother than hers had ever been.

Instead, her child was going to be born to a mother whose life was clouded in suspicion and lies.

She opened the bottom drawer. It was mostly filled with ancient cotton balls and Q-tips, but at the back was a small opaque plastic container, which she opened in idle curiosity. More lipstick—a single tube, this one a bright red. A birth control container, three of the pills gone. A small plastic bag with six round white pills in the bottom, which Emma vaguely recognized as the ones her mother had taken for her migraines. The last object in the container was a jewelry case, which Emma popped open to discover a thin silver bracelet, set with three petite diamonds. The inside of the bracelet was etched with a minute inscription. *Forever yours.*

The inscription was probably chosen by Dad's secretary, though the birth control pills at least suggested there was some level of intimacy left in the relationship when they'd died. Oddly unsettled by the glimpse into her mother's private life, Emma put everything back where she'd found it and shut the drawer.

She went downstairs, braced to see Nathan, but there was only a note on the counter. He'd gone into town for more groceries.

Or maybe just to get away from her.

Emma pulled her laptop out of her bag and set it up on the kitchen table. They didn't have Wi-Fi at the house yet, but she set her phone to be a mobile hotspot and opened up a browser.

She had studiously avoided searching for herself over the years. It was not a famous crime, mostly by sheer luck—there had been a school shooting the week before, and the week after had seen a celebrity suicide, a deadly flood, and the arrest of a serial killer, all of which kept a comparatively everyday double murder out of the national headlines.

There were two Emma Palmers much more famous than she was, one a D-list reality star turned influencer, and one the author of extremely popular and extremely explicit werewolf romances. It made it easier to skate under the radar. But the articles were there. Easy enough to find.

Sitting at the kitchen table, just out of sight from the patch of hallway where her mother had bled out from a hole in her heart, she read them.

She had been braced for what she might read, but it still hit her like a physical blow, seeing the words in print. *Shot to death in their house—daughters sleeping only yards away—no suspects at this time— second daughter's relationship with an unidentified man—rumors of occult activity among youth* . . .

The last was tucked in with almost a note of embarrassment.

> *Randolph and Irene Palmer were home at their house in Arden Hills when an unknown intruder entered the house. The intruder appears to have entered Mr. Palmer's study. He was shot in the back of the head, killing him instantly. Mrs. Palmer's body was found in the hallway, as if she had come toward the sound. She was shot in the chest at extremely close range. Blood was tracked between the bodies, leaving boot prints identified as a men's size 10.5 Dr. Martens boot. The tracks exited from the back door of the house.*
>
> *The gun was never recovered.*

Emma took in a shaky breath. They'd been dead when she got there. Had been dead for a while, judging by the consistency of the blood. She'd panicked, looking for her sisters, convinced she would find their bodies next. And when she saw the blood on Daphne's nightshirt, she'd thought for a moment her fear had manifested.

"No one can know," Daphne had said.

She'd hushed her sister. Told her to stop talking. She was afraid that she knew what had happened—exactly what had happened. But that was before Juliette came stumbling into the house, wearing someone else's clothes, her hair wet. And long before she learned that the gun hadn't been one of Dad's. Those had all been matched to their registration, confirming that they were all in the gun case where they belonged, securely locked away. He had always been meticulous about that. He kept the keys on him, wouldn't let any of them touch the guns unless he was there. Not even their mother was allowed to lay a finger on them.

It had struck her as absurd, back then. He'd been so damn proud of those guns. Twenty-three of them. She'd counted once. Twenty-three guns and he'd never had the chance to even pick one up to defend himself.

She wondered where they were now. Not that she wanted them around. She knew how to shoot—you couldn't have Randolph Palmer for a father and not be intimately familiar with how to handle a gun— but she'd never enjoyed it the way Juliette had. Though even with shooting there was a delicacy to the way Juliette operated—the careful way she picked out her target, plucked out a shot. No wasted movement or bravado, an almost ladylike lethality. Daphne didn't seem to enjoy the exercise, but she was competent—lining things up, tucking her tongue at the corner of her mouth, and squeezing off a shot without flinching.

She navigated back to the article. The boot prints. Gabriel wore size 10.5 shoes. But the article said they weren't just any shoes—Doc Martens. Did Gabriel own a pair of Docs? She tried to remember, but all she could picture him in were sneakers. Not that she'd known him that well. She'd met him only a few months before her parents died.

It had felt like a lifetime. The moment they met, there had been a connection between them that she couldn't explain. Like he understood her, in a way no one else did. Sometimes she thought he must be humoring her, pretending to care about what she had to say, but if that was the case, he never slipped up. He took her seriously. He *liked* her.

For Emma at sixteen, that had been a miracle. She would have done anything for Gabriel. She would never have hurt him. Not intentionally. By the time she realized the position she'd put him in, it was too late. She couldn't admit her lie. Not without looking guilty.

Or revealing the truth.

She chewed her lip. Part of her wanted to close the article, pretend that she'd never read it, and go back to living as if only the present mattered. But it was too late for that. She needed to know—know *more*, at least, than she did now.

She grabbed her phone from the counter where it had been charging and sent a quick text to Christopher Best.

Are you free to talk? I have some questions about back then.

She assumed she didn't have to tell him what she meant.

The sound of car tires on the gravel outside drew her attention. She closed her laptop quickly, not quite sure why she had the instinct to hide what she was looking at from her husband.

A moment later the doorbell rang. Frowning, Emma made her way to the door, wondering if Nathan had forgotten his keys—but when she opened it, she found a stranger standing on the front steps. The woman had masses of dark, wavy hair that fell to her shoulders and tattoos of flowered vines wrapping up her arms, a snake twining among them on the left. She wore a loose, sleeveless black top with gaping armholes that showed off the turquoise bra underneath and a glimpse of pale ribs decorated with more inked-on flowers.

"Hey, Emma," the woman said. Her voice was low and rough and entirely wrong, but suddenly the half-familiar features clicked into place.

"Juliette?" Emma asked, gaping at her older sister. "What are you doing here?"

Juliette raked her thick hair back from her face. It flopped forward again as soon as she released it. Her gaze was wary and almost arrogant. "Can I come in?"

"It's your house, too," Emma said flatly. She turned and walked back inside. There was a moment of silence, and then Juliette followed her, shoes squeaking on the hardwood. Their mother would have killed them for wearing shoes in the house, but Emma didn't say anything as Juliette followed her back down the hall and through the great room, pausing momentarily to look at the piano before traipsing back into the kitchen.

"Coffee?" Emma asked.

"Sure," Juliette said, hands in her back pockets.

Emma waved at the coffeepot. "Help yourself."

Juliette's mouth pursed, but she walked past Emma, getting a dust-rimed mug down from the cupboard where they'd always been. She poured herself the dregs of the morning coffee.

Juliette held the mug in both hands without drinking. Emma stood across the table from her, arms crossed. "So," Juliette said. She raised an eyebrow. "This is awkward."

"Really?" Emma said, scoffing. "It's been a decade and a half, and you haven't spoken a single word to me. Yeah, that's awkward."

"Do you want me to say I'm sorry?" Juliette asked, eyebrow still cocked.

Emma choked on a laugh. "Which sorry would that be, exactly? 'Sorry I haven't called you anytime in the last fourteen years, nothing personal'? 'Sorry I never said a word to help when you were the top suspect in our parents' murders'? 'Sorry I left you in foster care, skipped your wedding, never so much as wrote you a birthday card'?"

Juliette had the decency to look away. "I was just a kid."

"So was I. So was Daphne. We needed you," Emma said, her voice raw. Pain she'd thought she'd left behind her long ago raked nails down her spine.

"I know. But I was a complete mess," Juliette said. "I wouldn't have been any good to you. I couldn't look after myself, much less you."

"That didn't mean you had to disappear," Emma said.

"Jesus, Emma. What was I supposed to do? Mom and Dad were dead, and you—" Juliette faltered.

Emma's lip curled. "And I what?"

"You told us what to do. We hid things. We lied," Juliette said in a whisper, as if there were anyone alive in this house to hear. "Then Gabriel Mahoney gets arrested and everyone's saying you two killed them. What the fuck was I supposed to think?"

"I don't know. What was *I* supposed to think when you came in the door wearing someone else's clothes, when you were supposed to be asleep in bed?" Emma shot back. "I never told anyone. I didn't say a goddamn word, but you were happy to sell me out."

"All I told Hadley was that you were seeing Gabriel."

"And that I wasn't in the tree house. But you let him keep thinking *you* were," Emma said.

"He knew we were lying. I was doing damage control," Juliette protested. Emma stared at her. Juliette wasn't like Nathan. She'd always been hard to read. She would arrange her features into demure smiles and simpering adoration for their parents, shoot poisonous glares at her sisters. And if you caught her when she thought no one was looking, she always had a peculiarly blank expression. Like she was waiting to be informed of what performance was required of her. Now her expression was wounded, defensive. But there might have been anything underneath.

"Juliette," Emma began.

"JJ," her sister said, with the tone of a correction. She set the mug on the counter beside her, the coffee untouched. "I go by JJ now."

"Fine. JJ," Emma amended, the name sounding false to her ears. "Did you come all this way to rehash the past?"

"No," JJ said. "I came to find out what you're planning to do with the house."

She is lying, Emma thought. But what other reason could she have for coming? "There isn't a plan," Emma said. "We needed a place to stay for a while. I figured no one else was using it."

"I don't understand how you could live in this place," JJ said, unconvinced.

"It's just a house."

"We should have sold it a long time ago. Or burned it down," JJ said, looking along the ceiling, as if peering into the soul of the house itself.

Isn't that what she'd wanted, too? Out of their hands or out of the world completely. But now, with JJ standing in this kitchen, Emma couldn't help but look at her as an intruder—an intruder in Emma's home.

"Is that what you want to do? Sell it?" Emma asked.

"It seems like the sensible thing, right? Then we can all pretend this place never existed," JJ said.

"And we can do the same about each other," Emma replied icily.

"That's not what I said."

"We need all three of us to sign off on selling the house," Emma said, ignoring her. "If you can get Daphne on board, fine. We'll talk about it."

"What does she think about the whole thing?" JJ asked.

"How should I know?"

JJ's brow furrowed. "You haven't discussed it?"

Emma looked at her evenly. "I've spoken to Daphne once in the last fourteen years."

"What?" JJ looked dumbfounded.

"You do know that she was in foster care," Emma said.

"You both were," JJ said. "You were together. It wasn't like I could take care of you. I was a college student in the dorms—then getting kicked out of the dorms. I couldn't . . ." Her teeth clicked shut.

"After I aged out, I got my own place and tried to get custody, but she didn't want anything to do with me. Neither of you did," Emma said. Her voice was steady but her hands clenched, holding tight against the surge of old anger, old grief.

"I didn't realize."

"Clearly." It came out a snarl.

"Emma. When you came to my door that day I was a mess. I'd dropped out of school, I was drinking and taking a seriously dangerous amount of drugs and doing the kind of sleeping around that ends with being dismembered in a dumpster."

"And now?" Emma asked. She had no idea what her sister did with herself.

"I got my life together eventually," she said, hesitant.

"What do you do, then? Bartender? Musician?" Emma asked.

"I work at a bank, actually," JJ said with a wry smile. "What about you? Did you end up going to art school like you planned?"

Emma's mouth tightened in a flat line. "No. I didn't go to art school." JJ's smile faltered. "You didn't come here to catch up. Or to talk about selling the house. You could have done that over the phone. So why are you really here, Juliette?" Emma asked.

This time JJ didn't correct her. "You being back here is going to make people start thinking about what happened. They're going to start asking questions again," she said. And there it was.

"And? Let them talk," Emma said dismissively, though she tasted something sour in the back of her mouth.

"If the police ask you what happened, what are you going to tell them?" JJ asked, gaze fixed intently on Emma.

Behind the carefully constructed mask, behind the performance of sisterly concern, Emma saw it. A flicker of fear. "What are you worried I might say?" Emma asked.

The front door opened. JJ jumped, nearly knocking the coffee mug over as she straightened. Nathan's familiar long stride approached, accompanied by his voice.

"Whose car is that in the drive?" he asked, and then stepped into view. JJ tucked her hands into her pockets, shoulders slightly hunched as he caught sight of her. "Oh. Hi."

"Nathan, this is my sister Juliette," Emma said neutrally.

Nathan processed this for a moment, eyebrows rising in surprise, then stepped forward and stuck out his hand. "Nice to meet you, Juliette. I'm Nathan. Nathan Gates. I've heard all about you, of course."

JJ took his hand and shook it slowly. "Really. How wonderful. And it's JJ, actually. I haven't gone by Juliette since I was a kid."

"Right," Nathan said with a sharp nod and a look at Emma like she should have told him. "What brings you by?"

"I just came to talk to Emma about getting the place fixed up to sell," JJ said, her expression open and friendly.

"Excellent. That's just what we've been talking about," Nathan said. They hadn't talked much at all, but he said it as if it were a done deal. "It definitely needs some work. But I was thinking, if you three are all on board with it, we could get a Realtor out. Come up with a plan. Right now, I'm focusing on getting things cleaned out and sorted, so we can decide what to do with it all."

"Sounds great. You just let me know if you need help," JJ said easily.

"Are you staying in town? Need your old room for a few days?" Nathan asked. Emma cut him a look, but his eyes hadn't left JJ, and for the first time Emma realized just how attractive her older sister was, next to mousy Emma in her T-shirt and ponytail.

"You couldn't pay me a million dollars to spend a night in this fucking place," JJ said blithely. She looked past Nathan at Emma. "We'll talk again soon."

"That will be novel," Emma said. JJ flinched, and Emma felt a faint flash of satisfaction.

JJ walked out without another word. Emma went to the counter and dumped out the coffee, watching it swirl down the drain. She didn't know what she'd expected to feel if she ever saw her sisters again. Had she really hoped for an apology? She wasn't sure there was an apology Juliette could offer that would mean anything.

What *was* Juliette doing here? Not checking out the house. Checking out Emma, maybe. Something about Emma coming back to the house had worried her. Spooked her, even.

Like maybe she was afraid that Emma was going to spill their secrets, and that Juliette was the one who would pay the price.

"Ah, shit," Nathan said suddenly. Emma gave him an empty look, uncomprehending. He snapped his fingers. "We should have asked her about the carriage house keys. Think you could give her a call?"

"No," Emma snapped.

"Whoa. What did I do?" Nathan asked, hands immediately up in surrender. The cold remove that had carried Emma through the conversation with JJ shattered.

"I'm sorry. It's just—seeing her again . . ." Emma covered her face with her hands, fighting the edge of a sob.

"Hey." Nathan stepped over to her, gathered her against his chest. "I'm sorry. You know how bad I am at subtext."

"That's an understatement." Her words were edged with the tears that always seemed to be on the surface these days. She wasn't sure how much of it she could blame on the hormones. "I don't even know what I'm supposed to feel about her. She left us, Nathan."

"Is there any point bringing that up now, though?" Nathan asked. He sounded almost annoyed. "We're going to have to work with your sisters to deal with the house. You keeping grudges isn't going to help with that."

She pulled away from him, wiping her eyes. "You're probably right."

"I get that you're emotional," he said. "But you have to let go of the past to move into the future, right?"

"Did you see that in a TED Talk or something?" Emma asked, struggling to keep the bitterness out of her voice.

He made an irritated noise. "Look. With everything you've gone through, maybe it's not surprising that you're not acting rational. Which is—it's fine. I can handle things."

He had always been the steady one, the optimistic one. The sane one. She had always gone along with what Nathan deemed to be the best. He was the one with the healthy relationship with his parents, the one who had managed to finish high school, get a degree, keep friends for more than six months at a time. Now she felt like she was falling apart more than ever, and maybe he was right. Maybe she wasn't being rational.

"There's actually something I wanted to talk to you about that's kind of related," he went on. He put a hand against the counter, the other braced against his hip. His gaze was searching. "I don't think it's a good idea for you to go into town. I can run all the errands and things. You should stay at the house."

"Why?" Emma asked, instantly bristling. "There's tons to do. It doesn't make sense for one of us to be stuck here."

"I don't like the idea of people gossiping because they saw you out buying milk, or whatever. Getting home and calling their girlfriends to go 'Oh, remember that psycho teen Emma Palmer, I saw her in the Stop & Shop.'" He put on a mocking little falsetto.

"People aren't going to stop talking just because I don't leave the house," Emma countered. He sounded like her mother, always worried about what everyone else thought. "*You aren't going to leave the house looking like that, are you?*"

He threw a hand in the air. "Emma, I am living here. I am in this house, in this town, I am *here* even after you lied to me about all of this. Can you not do this one thing for me? For fuck's sake. After everything you've put me through the last few weeks—"

"Everything I've put *you* through?" Emma asked. "I'm not the only one who screwed up, Nathan. And I'm not going to be a prisoner in this house because you're worried about gossip." The heat in her voice surprised her.

He looked at her with a baffled expression. "I don't know what's gotten into you," he said. "You're not acting like yourself. Last night, and now this."

No, she wasn't acting like herself—not the Emma that he knew, at least. Not the Emma she had created painstakingly, a rebuke to the girl she had been. But now she was home, and that old Emma had been waiting for her here the whole time. A ghost in this house.

Nathan didn't know that Emma. The one who always chose to fight instead of surrender, the one who was contrary and clever and sometimes cruel. He knew the soft Emma, the quiet Emma, the version who would bend and bend and bend and never break.

"Emma. I love you. I only want to do what's best for you. For us." He reached out, a sudden movement that made her flinch, and pulled her in toward him again. She surrendered and murmured a wordless agreement.

He said he wanted what was best for them. But this time, he was wrong. She couldn't keep hiding from what had happened. She had to know. For herself. For her child. For any hope of a future.

"I'll stay in. I won't leave," she said, lying as she had so many times before.

14

DAPHNE

Now

Dale had slipped away peacefully and on schedule. Daphne left her apartment in Colorado for Arden Hills the next day, arriving around the time that an embalmer was slitting open Dale's veins and shoving in a tube, swapping blood for formalin.

Daphne kept a tiny one-bedroom cottage in town, a few miles away from her childhood home. She'd unpacked her suitcase immediately, putting her clothes away tidily in the drawers. Whenever she traveled, she liked to do that right away. It was a way of having standards. One of her mother's favorite words, though she meant something different by it.

For Daphne, it wasn't about appearances, it was about reminding herself that she had value; that wherever she was, she belonged. She'd bought this house when she was twenty-one, newly married, her new last name on all the paperwork. The marriage hadn't lasted; it hadn't been meant to last. Jonathan had walked away with a sizable chunk of her money, but she'd kept the cottage. It was hers in a way few things were.

Before she'd left Colorado, she'd gotten a new haircut—sharp, straight bangs and a bob—and a new oak-brown color. It wasn't the most flattering, but it changed her face, making her look even less like little Daphne Palmer than the years and weight already had. When she'd walked past the house yesterday, in fact, Nathan had been collecting the mail out front. She'd almost turned around, but instead she'd walked right past him and nodded and said good morning, and he'd offered only a bland greeting in return before heading back inside.

It had encouraged her enough that she'd gone back this morning. This time, she had a dog with her—Winston, a small gray terrier, getting on in years. Not hers, of course. She'd been a dog walker in Arden Hills under her married name for years. She was good at it, the way she was good at all of her work, and her clients were always thrilled when she was back in town.

Dogs were easy. You just had to work out what they wanted—love, treats, praise—and make them understand what you wanted. A simple matter of communication. She'd messaged her regular clients and had her week booked before she even got into town. It was relaxing work in between her human clients, a way to spend a few weeks or a month or two resetting before she entered into the world of another family's grief again.

Besides, people didn't look twice at a fat woman walking a small dog, she'd found, sometimes not even once, and it gave her a plausible excuse to be strolling through the neighborhood.

With Winston in tow early in the morning, she had spotted Nathan's car pulling out of the driveway. He'd left the gate open behind him, and she knew she shouldn't, but curiosity got the better of her. She went in through the gate, turning off to the side quickly so no one would see her from the street. She left Winston behind the carriage house, dropping him a few treats to keep him content—he wouldn't wander off, she'd trained him well over the years—and stole around to the back door of the house. A glance through the windows didn't turn up any sign of Emma.

The back door proved unlocked. She remembered it creaked when fully opened, so she sidled herself through instead and stood in her parents' kitchen, waiting for memory to overwhelm her. It didn't. She felt almost disappointed at the discovery. She'd built this place up so much in her mind.

There was a phone on the counter, plugged in to charge. Daphne turned on the screen. The photo was of Nathan, grinning; the background was a beach. A vacation, maybe. It looked a few years old. Next to it was a bottle of prenatal vitamins. Daphne let out a little *ah*—all this urgency suddenly made more sense.

She looked through the cupboards briefly, noting the saltines and ginger candies. She listened for any sign of movement, but there was none, so she risked slipping her shoes off and stealing deeper into the house. Everything smelled of dust and cleaning products. The drawers of the credenza in the great room were all opened, the contents heaped or dumped in a trash bag beside it; someone was clearing things out. A little shiver of anxiety went through her. Was there anything left in the house to find?

No. Surely not.

She looked toward the stairs. She had been expecting since she stepped through the gates to be confronted. For Emma to stand in front of her, arms crossed, steel in her eyes—but that was the old Emma, wasn't it? This Emma didn't stand firm, she vanished. She receded.

Daphne walked slowly up the stairs, old habit guiding her feet past the places that creaked and sighed. At the top she paused, looking toward the smaller rooms where she and her sisters had slept. Nearly identical, except for the color of the stripes on the walls. And that had been the goal—three girls, identically perfect, distinguished by the color of their hair. Juliette's dark, Emma's auburn, Daphne's wheat-colored, wearing matching white dresses with ribbons at their waists. They had photos from every year just like that. Emma squirmed and made faces through every session, but their mother always managed to find the one in which it seemed as if they were all cooperating, a fraction of a second's shutter-click securing the illusion of success.

Emma had rebelled; Juliette had conformed and performed her part. Daphne had tried to be invisible, until one day she couldn't be. Even now, she felt small again, standing in this place. She pressed a hand against her chest, feeling the steady thump of her heart and the strength of her own flesh. She was not that sprig of a girl anymore.

But there was still utility in being invisible, she thought, and padded toward the master bedroom. The door was open a crack. She pushed it open farther and there was Emma, sleeping on her side on top of the covers wearing a T-shirt and shorts. She looked gaunt, Daphne thought, her skin sallow. She wasn't eating enough.

"Poor thing," Daphne said under her breath. She stood over her sister, watching her chest rise and fall, waiting for Emma's eyes to flutter open. She'd be caught. She would have to explain. There would be a joyous reunion—an angry confrontation—a confession, at last, overdue. The possibilities presented themselves one by one, and one by one they faded. Emma slept on.

Daphne drew away, half-reluctant and half-relieved. It wasn't time yet, she told herself. There were still things she needed to take care of before Emma could know that she was here.

She should leave, she knew. But before she did, she got down a loaf of bread and popped a slice in the toaster, started a pot of coffee to brew. Eating first thing, before even getting out of bed, helped with nausea, and there was nothing like the scent of coffee to make going downstairs less of a chore. While the bread was toasting she picked up Emma's phone, considered a moment, and entered four numbers to unlock it. It worked right away. Nathan's birthday.

Daphne wondered if Emma understood that using her husband's birthday wasn't a sign of how much she loved him but its opposite. For someone else it might have been a gesture of affection, but for Emma, Daphne thought, it was a way of reassuring herself that Nathan was the center of her world. And she wouldn't need reassurance if it were true.

Emma certainly wasn't the center of *his* world. That much had become clear, however well he thought he had covered his tracks. Anger burbled inside her. Emma deserved better. Daphne would never understand how her sister had let herself settle for a man like Nathan.

Daphne found the location tracking app easily. She checked the usage statistics—it hadn't been opened in the last three months. Perfect. She entered her own information, confirmed the link on her phone, and granted herself permission to track Emma's location. Then she closed the app, turned off the phone, and positioned it exactly where Emma had left it. Another quick trip to put the toast on Emma's nightstand—and then Daphne took a risk, and leaned over, pressing the softest kiss against Emma's brow before retreating. Emma, deep in sleep, did not stir.

She looked peaceful, Daphne thought as she exited the house. But you could see the signs of sickness in her. That was what all of this was; a restfulness that concealed infirmity. It couldn't last.

She walked back to where Winston was waiting, tongue lolling out. She gave the carriage house one long look. The door was locked, with no other good way to get in. She'd have to leave it for now. At least she felt better now, with Emma's location easily accessed. Hopefully it would prove an unnecessary precaution. But Emma had always been curious. Her artist's eye quick to pick up on things out of place. And if she started to see the things that had been hidden all this time . . .

Daphne shook her head, making her way quickly back to the street with Winston trotting alongside her. It wouldn't happen that way. Daphne would be there, to shape what happened next.

And she would do whatever she had to.

15

EMMA

Then

Two months, more or less, before she burns her sister's bloody clothes in the fireplace grate of an abandoned house, Emma stands examining a painting.

It has taken half a year of pleading to convince Emma's parents to let her buy oil paints. She has made do with acrylics and watercolor, but she glories in the romance of the oils. She researches their origins and ingredients, imagining herself the painter of older eras, grinding pigments from minerals and roots, mixing them into the oil herself. Her paints come, of course, from tubes, purchased with her carefully hoarded money one color at a time, so that the bloom of new hues across her canvases become a way to mark the march of time.

Lorelei teaches her. The hardest part is the patience, waiting for each layer to dry, unfinished, the promise of possibility shimmering in her mind's eye. Her mother hates the stink of it—the oil, the turpentine. The way it stains her fingers and her clothes, splatters and lines of paint crawling up her forearms, decorating her face. There is nothing ladylike and pristine about painting. She emerges streaked in umber and sienna, cadmium and vermilion.

Her work is always sloppier, clumsier than she would like. She rushes; she waits too long; the paint cracks, it smears. Lorelei tells her patience, patience. Worry when it looks perfect, because that means you've caught up with your own ambition and judgment. Dissatisfaction is the engine of creativity.

Lorelei is the one who encouraged Emma to consider schools farther from home. She has a talent, but that's not what Lorelei prizes. The girl has *drive*, the kind of hunger that won't be sated until she has the chance to give herself over to it completely, and that means instruction, proper instruction, more than Lorelei can give her. She needs to be surrounded by other people as hungry and obsessed as she is. The schools she tells Emma about are in Georgia, California, even Europe. Emma says again and again that she has to stay close to home, but the hunger says otherwise.

Emma has filled out the applications. It's absurdly early, she knows, but she wants the essays and forms out of the way so that she can focus on her portfolio. She needs eight—wants ten. She has, over the last year, managed seven she deems adequate. Three watercolors, two in acrylics, one in charcoal, and one, the painting of Juliette at her piano, in oil.

Today she stands in her room, scrutinizing what may be the eighth piece. It sits on her bed, propped against the wall, as she paces back and forth, examining it from every angle. With this, she will have enough to make her applications, and a few more months to manage a final two—or to replace some of those she is less certain about, like the watercolor that shows the bridge over the river near the house, with its curls of water folding in on itself and the light slanting low. It is competent, but it says nothing, and she worries that the judges will think her point of view is shallow.

This piece, though—she thinks she likes it. It is nothing special, in a way. Only a portrait. Gabriel, a three-quarter view, strong shadows over his face. He leans against a doorway, neither inside nor outside the room. He looks like he is about to ask a question. The question was *"How long do I have to stand like this,"* but she has left out the glint in his eyes, made him wearier. In his eye is the shadowed reflection of a woman. A girl. She calls it *Intruder: A Self-Portrait*. She worries it is too obvious, not obvious enough, pretentious, common.

She likes it.

She is not *satisfied* with it, the way Lorelei cautions her against; her colors are muddy in places, the anatomy just off enough to bother her, the reflection of the girl not as distinct as she'd hoped.

Gabriel likes it, too. But he doesn't like the title. "You're not intruding on anything," he'd said.

"Except your life," she told him.

"Consider yourself an invited guest," he said with his slantwise smile.

Their families hate each other. The details of it are murky to Emma. His father worked for hers until very recently. There were accusations of theft on one side, mismanagement on the other. But Kenneth Mahoney is a drunk and a deadbeat, and no one was surprised he'd gotten himself fired from another job.

"What is that?" a sharp voice asks.

She turns. Her mother stands in the doorway. She is dressed, as she nearly always is, as if she is about to walk out the door to a charity brunch at any second. Pearls at her neck and her nails shiny, perfect ovals, buffed and polished.

"It's a portrait of Mrs. Mahoney's grandson," Emma says simply, as if this is completely neutral information.

"We're painting portraits of boys now?" her mother asks in that same sharp tone.

Emma rolls her eyes. "It's just a portrait, Mom. It's not like I drew him in the nude."

Her mother stiffens. "I hear you've been hanging around together."

Tension locks into place down Emma's spine. There is danger in this conversation. The truth is no defense against her mother's suspicions. It would only make things worse. "He lives with Mrs. Mahoney. He's around the house a lot, if that's what you mean," Emma says.

"So you're not sleeping with him?"

"Mom!" She stares at her. She's never even kissed anyone. There isn't time for it, even if there were a boy in town who didn't think she was weird and unapproachable.

Her mother makes a noise in the back of her throat. "You should have been downstairs ten minutes ago. It's time to practice," she snaps.

"I'll practice later," Emma says. When her mother is in a good mood, sometimes she can get away with half an hour after dinner, instead of the full hour she's supposed to plink away at the piano. Her fingers are dexterous enough, but she can't hear the music the way Juliette can. It's all a jumble of disconnected notes to her, and it comes out sounding like it. Daphne is better than she is—competent, and uncomplaining during her hour. For Emma, it's torture.

"Now, Emma," her mother says. She waits; Emma complies. She thuds her way down the steps sullenly. In the great room, Juliette sits with her diary. Daphne is in the sunroom, nose in a book. Probably about something horribly gruesome like the black plague or witch trials, or a detailed explanation of *pressing* as an execution method, which Emma will enjoy hearing about later, out of their mother's earshot.

Emma takes her seat. "Posture," her mother tells her. She straightens her shoulders, stacks each vertebra in painful overcompliance. Fingers on the keys. "Hands," her mother tells her; she straightens her wrists, relaxes her fingers. She runs through simple scales mechanically as her mother stands ramrod straight and perfectly still at her shoulder.

Her mother selects the first piece. Emma knows what the notes mean; she can read music fluently enough. But the sequence never resolves in her mind to anything other than fragments of information, refusing to cohere. She can't *hear* it the way she can *see* a painting. She can't sense the whole, and so even when she manages to follow the notes precisely, it somehow never sounds like the same song that Juliette plays.

"Faster here," her mother tells her, and "Posture," and "Watch your breathing," but none of it changes the fact that she is a dull, plodding player, not a musician, not a *talent* like Juliette. Her fingers ache. She's held a paintbrush half the day already, and her back has a lick of acidic heat running up beside her spine.

"Pay attention," her mother snaps. "If you practiced more, you wouldn't struggle so much."

"Maybe the piano just hates me," Emma grouses.

Her mother glares down at her. "You are perfectly capable if you apply yourself. Keep going."

Emma grits her teeth. She plays on. She speeds up, speeds up more, until her fingers are stumbling drunkenly. Dropping a note, smashing down two keys instead of one, notes tumbling together in a muddle of noise. Her mother says her name. She keeps going. Brutishly forcing her way through the music, shouldering each bar aside to get to its end. Her mother says her name again—a third time—

Irene Palmer reaches out, grabs the fallboard, and slams it shut. Emma whips her hands back. Not quite fast enough. Emma shrieks. Pulls her left hand free, cradles it against her chest, two fingers in sudden agony. Her mother looks down at her with her mouth in a faint O.

Emma laughs. The sound is stretched obscenely, the pain making her shake. She looks down at her hand. The index finger is fine, probably, bruised. The middle finger is swelling quickly, and she knows at a glance that it's broken. "Guess I can't play now," she rasps out.

"Go to your room," her mother manages, pointing with arm outstretched, like she is claiming control of the situation in the only way she can.

Emma stands, hand still cupped against her chest. She looks at Juliette, who is staring at the floor. She looks at Daphne, staring openly from the sunroom, her book abandoned beside her. She laughs again, a sound that turns to brambles in her throat. Her mother sees that she isn't moving, isn't obeying, but her eyes flick away. To argue is to cede more control.

"Juliette, you could use another pass at the Brahms," she says briskly.

Juliette stands, setting her diary beside her. She walks across the room, eyes on the floor, and takes her seat, forcing Emma to edge away.

Emma shakes her head. She turns away at last and walks swiftly out of the room, her vision blurring with tears as the pain overtakes the outrage.

Behind her, Juliette begins to play.

16

EMMA

Now

Nathan had gone out to the hardware store again. After the third visit they'd caved and opened a credit card there, since it was becoming clear they were going to need a lot more than a bit of paint remover and a mop. The stairs on the back of the house had rotted through. The screen door sagged. The paint was peeling, the toilets flushed at their own whim and not yours, and there was a proud dynasty of squirrels in the attic, their ancestors entombed in the insulation. Nathan had finally gotten the Wi-Fi going and was now spending hours on YouTube, doggedly determined not to pay anyone a cent for what "any real man could figure out on his own."

Emma had just finished heaving up what little lunch she'd managed to get down and returned to spackling holes in the dining room. Her first batch had dried. She sanded them as smooth as she could, but there was still a slight bump where some vandal had put something through the wall. It wasn't the only one. Here and there were patches where the texture of the wall changed or a slight dimple marked a patched hole. She set her fingers over one, then made a fist and pushed her knuckles against the spot. But her hands were smaller than her father's had been.

Her phone rang. "Chris," she said, answering it.

"Emma. Sorry I didn't call earlier, things have been a bit hectic around here," Chris said in his resonant baritone. In the background she could hear several small dogs barking.

"What's going on over there?" Emma asked.

"I made the mistake of taking a little mutt in off the street. She gobbled down enough dinner to sate a pack of wolves and then gave birth on a five-thousand-dollar rug," Chris said.

"That's what you get for taking in strays," Emma replied, laughing a little.

"At least you never whelped a litter in my living room," Best said, with exaggerated gravitas. "You're back at the house."

Emma's smile dropped. "Yes. Juliette was here, too, actually. She dropped by."

"Ah," Chris said. "That must have been difficult."

"That's one word for it." Emma let out a breath, bracing a hand against her lower back. "I'm not sure why I even texted you, really. It's just—being back here, and trying to explain things to Nathan, I've been wondering a lot about what happened. What really happened."

"You never asked for answers about your parents' deaths. I assumed there was a reason for that," Chris said, voice free of judgment. For all that he'd done for her, she'd never told him the whole truth about that night. He had accepted that, and done his job.

"Chris, did my dad have enemies? I know he had affairs. Maybe there was an angry husband, or something," she said, speaking too quickly.

"I promise you the police investigated those angles," Chris said. "Emma. The investigation was never closed. Please don't give the police or the DA a reason to start thinking about you again. You are safer forgotten."

"It might be too late for that," Emma said, thinking of Hadley's hard stare. "Is there anything you can give me? A bad breakup, a business deal . . ."

Chris paused. The silence was a beat too long to mean nothing.

"Chris. What aren't you telling me?" Emma said, pulse thrumming.

He sighed. "It's probably not connected. I told the police all of it back then, and nothing came of it. But your mother approached me, a couple of months before her death. She told me that she had information about something illegal. She wanted to turn it over, but she was worried she might get in trouble as well. I got the impression it had something to do with your father, and so I told her I couldn't be involved personally, but I gave her the contact information for someone else at my firm. She never contacted him."

A memory shivered to the surface. Emma gripped the edge of the windowsill to steady herself. "Chris, did you write that number on a green Post-it note?"

"I have no idea. It was fourteen years ago, Emma."

"But did she show you—was there a flash drive?" Emma asked.

"She didn't show me anything. We just talked. Why? What flash drive is this?" Chris asked, concerned.

"It's nothing," Emma said. And it probably *was* nothing. A flash drive and a green Post-it note with a phone number scribbled on it, hidden away where no one would look for it. No one except a nosy teenager.

Something smacked hard against the back window. Emma startled, letting out a cut-off yell.

"Emma? What's wrong?" Chris asked.

"I have to go," Emma said. She hung up and dashed into the hall in time to see two figures sprinting into the woods behind the house, one of them giving a whoop. She caught an impression of a red shirt and a mop of blond hair.

She growled a curse under her breath and, before she thought better of it, shoved her feet into her shoes. She stalked out the back door, still in her pajama shorts and T-shirt, and ran across the back lawn toward the trees, her phone still in her hand.

She angled toward the familiar path on instinct. She couldn't see the kids anymore—if they were kids—but she didn't slow. She passed under the tree house, which sagged, probably rotten through. Footsteps crashed up ahead. Still she ran after them, not sure what she was doing, not sure why, her pulse thudding through her and her breath coming hissed between her teeth.

Then she slowed. She looked around. The path had petered out. There wasn't much undergrowth here, and it was easy to navigate, but she couldn't tell where they might have gone.

A voice broke through the low chatter of forest sounds. It was high and excited, and followed by a lower voice that burbled with laughter. Off between the trees, Emma could make out the graying side of a building. The old Saracen house. Hadley had said kids still hung out there.

She crept forward slowly. As she drew closer, the house became visible. It was low and narrow, the roof gaping on one side and sagging on the other. Nothing about it looked structurally sound, but voices were coming from inside.

"Oh come on. You were scared. Admit it," the higher-pitched voice was saying.

"I wasn't scared! You're the one who took off running."

"Yeah, because I didn't want to get caught." Both voices were male and young. Through one grimed-over window, an upper pane knocked out entirely, she could see two boys sitting on the leaf-strewn floor, posed like they'd collapsed in exhaustion.

She kept moving, around to the front door, which was hanging off its hinges. She stepped right over the two rotten steps, not trusting them with her weight, and onto the spongy floor inside. The walls inside might have once been white but had faded to a grotesque yellow, covered liberally in scrawled graffiti. The frames around the doors were carved with more scratching, names and words and symbols—pentagrams and anarchy symbols and others she didn't recognize but that looked vaguely occult. A moldering couch slumped in one corner, pale blue with the cushions chewed through. Another door led out the back, past a narrow galley kitchen, but given the way it was swollen in its frame, she doubted it was functional.

She walked toward the sound of voices, still congratulating themselves on their own daring. When she stepped into the doorway, one of the boys, the one with the mop of blond hair, yelped and jumped up to his feet. The other one was a second behind but quicker to realize there was nowhere to go, unless they wanted to try busting through the window.

"Hey, lady, we, uh, we weren't," the second boy said nervously, his Adam's apple bobbing. He was Black, heavyset, wearing a red T-shirt with a dragon curled around a twenty-sided die. The other boy was white, and about the color of a sheet of printer paper at the moment, his hands opening and closing at his sides with nervous energy.

She imagined how she must look to him. Hair wild, shoes unlaced, wearing cotton shorts and a T-shirt that had clearly been slept in. The murderer, chasing them through the woods. "What were you doing at my house?" she asked. Her voice came out rough.

They glanced at each other. "We were just messing around," the first boy said. "We didn't mean anything by it."

"Was it you? Last night?" she asked.

They looked at each other again, eyes wide. "No?" the second boy said. "I was at home last night. Swear to God. Whatever happened, we didn't do it."

"He's telling the truth," the other boy said desperately, and she laughed. Both of them looked startled. She combed her hair back from her face.

"Criminal masterminds," she said. The Black boy smiled nervously. "So, what? You wanted to scare the evil murderess? Then what?"

"I dunno. It just seemed . . . fun?" the white kid suggested.

"What are your names?" she asked them.

"Travis," the blond boy said immediately, and his friend gave him a dirty look. Travis didn't notice. "And this is Abraham."

"Travis. Abraham. Don't throw any more rocks at my fucking house, okay?" she said calmly.

"No, ma'am," Abraham said immediately. "Look, we didn't really think . . ."

"Yeah, I gathered," she said. She crossed her arms, looked around. "This where the cool kids hang out?"

"Well, we're here. So . . . no?" Abraham said.

"We're cool," Travis said, a touch sulkily.

Emma raised an eyebrow. He scuffed the floor with his toe. What had she expected? Kids with mohawks and nose rings, bullies out of a high school movie? "You hang out here a lot?" she asked. They both wanted to bolt out of there, she could tell, but she was still blocking the door.

"Sometimes," Travis acknowledged with a bob of his head.

"There are parties here, that sort of thing?"

Abraham shook his head. "Used to be, I think? But with the roof caved in and everything, I don't think so. When we found it, it was pretty fucked-up." They were still nervous, but starting to settle down. Convinced Emma wouldn't unhinge her jaw and devour them whole, maybe. She turned back to look at the living room. Feet shuffled behind her. One of them cleared his throat, but neither spoke.

"Kids used to come here," she said. "When I was your age, they were out here all the time."

"Yeah, we heard about that," Travis said, almost eagerly. "We heard there were, like, Satanic rituals and shit."

"There are occult symbols on the wall. There're pentagrams and that's called a leviathan cross?" Abraham said, pointing. "I looked it up. But, like, that stuff's not real. Just people messing around, right?"

"Probably," she agreed.

"We heard you came out here a lot. That you were one of the ones that . . ." Travis gestured at the wall. Emma snorted.

"I was too antisocial to be part of a cult," she assured him. She walked back into the living room, sticking close to the wall to read the graffiti. There were names—people who had been there, people they wanted to cuss out. Questionable reports of lewd activity.

The fireplace was filled with trash. Crumpled cans, shattered glass bottles. That was where they'd found the bloody clothing. Just a few centimeters of cotton fabric that had escaped the flames, no more than a few drops of blood on them. Enough to match the DNA to Irene

Palmer. Not enough to identify who the clothes might have belonged to.

"We heard . . ." Travis started, then grunted. She looked over her shoulder. Abraham had elbowed him in the ribs, judging by how Travis was rubbing his side.

"You want to know if I'm a psycho? A killer?" she asked, idly quoting the words scrawled on the dining room wall.

"Yeah. I guess," Travis said. Abraham looked stricken. "I mean, obviously you didn't, like . . . sacrifice them to Satan. But there's the theory that you did it because they didn't approve of your boyfriend. Or, like, a thrill kill? Or you were doing a bunch of drugs and . . ." He seemed to realize at last what he was saying and swallowed. His eyes were shining with excitement.

This was . . . different. She blinked slowly. "Would you be disappointed if I told you I didn't do it?"

"No," Abraham said immediately. Travis's shoulders climbed toward his ears. Emma just shook her head, turned away.

There were more words, more names carved in the doorframe that led into the kitchen. Her fingers moved over the grooves. KC+TM. That weird S everyone inexplicably became obsessed with drawing in middle school. A flower.

She paused, fingers under the simple carving. She knew this flower. She'd seen it doodled in margins, in fogged-up windows. A daisy.

It had to be a coincidence. It wasn't that distinctive. And yet there it was. Juliette had left those little flowers like a signature everywhere she went. Scattered behind her, symmetrical and sweet. Juliette Palmer, with her perfect hair and perfect grades and perfect manners, would never have been in a place like this.

But Juliette hadn't been home that night, either, had she?

Emma's fingernail scratched across the lowest curve of the bottom petal. Emma had left first that night. But Juliette hadn't been home when she returned. Had walked in the front door with bare feet, wet hair, wearing clothes that weren't hers.

"Where did you go, Juliette?" Emma whispered.

"What did you say?" Travis asked.

Emma turned. Narrowed her eyes at him. "Don't come near my house again," she said. She stalked past them. Both boys jumped out of the way. As she walked she took her phone out of her shorts pocket and pulled up a rarely accessed phone number.

I need to talk to you about Juliette, she wrote, and sent the text to Gabriel.

17

EMMA

Now

Lorelei Mahoney's house was a petite three-bedroom, exquisitely maintained by her husband for decades before his death and by Gabriel since. Lorelei's prize roses were still blooming out front as Emma pulled up, but there was something changed about the quality of the garden, and Emma knew immediately that it wasn't Lorelei herself tending to the flowers.

The old woman sat on her porch, wearing thick glasses and shaking her head at her phone as she scrolled. She was a petite woman, with her grandson's long face, her skin sun-weathered and creased with dozens of fine wrinkles.

Emma got out of the car, suddenly sixteen again. Then, coming to this place had been entering a sanctuary. She would open the door without knocking and make her way to the studio at the back of the house. Sometimes Lorelei would be there; sometimes Emma would work alone for hours before she was interrupted. The first time she'd met Gabriel had been one of those days, the whole of her focus absorbed by the canvas in front of her so that when Gabriel made a sound behind her, she had no idea how long he had been there.

"You're good," he'd said. That was all. Then he'd wandered off into the depths of the house. By the time Lorelei introduced them officially, Emma was already in love.

There'd been far less reason then for Lorelei to dislike her, of course.

She looked up now, and her face pulled into a deep frown. Emma stuck her hands in her pockets as she made her way up the walk.

"Emma. I was wondering when I might be seeing you," Lorelei said.

"Hello, Mrs. Mahoney," Emma replied, formal, and Lorelei didn't correct her. Emma stayed on the walk, not wanting to give the impression she felt entitled to intrude on Lorelei's domain.

"Are you looking for Gabriel?" Lorelei asked.

"I am," Emma said. Lorelei *hmm*-ed. Emma cleared her throat. "I know you're not my biggest fan, after what happened."

"You're saying that like you want absolution," Lorelei said. "You're not going to get it from me. I'm not going to tell you you're a horrible person, either, if that's what you're looking for. You share some blame for what happened, but hardly all of it."

"I never intended anything to happen to Gabriel. I didn't think—"

"That much was clear," Lorelei said. She pursed her lips, then gestured over her shoulder. "He's inside, if you want to talk to him." Emma nodded gratefully and scaled the porch. Lorelei turned back to her phone.

Gabriel was in the kitchen, emptying the dishwasher. He looked up when Emma entered, but he didn't look surprised, exactly. More like resigned. "I told you I didn't want to talk to you again," he said.

"I know. I'm sorry," Emma said. Seeing him was like a fist around her heart. She had missed him, even while she'd convinced herself she didn't.

He shut the dishwasher and wiped his hands on a dish towel, leaning back against the counter. "What do you want?"

"I just have a couple of questions. Then I swear, I will leave you alone and never bother you again," she said.

"All right." He crossed his arms. "What do you want to know, Emma Palmer?"

"You used to go out to the Saracen house," she said.

"Now and then. Not really my scene, though," he said. "You said this was about Juliette."

She nodded. "Did you ever see her there?" He hesitated. "It's important," she pressed.

"I didn't know who she was at the time," he said. "But yeah. I saw her there once or twice. I got the impression . . ." He trailed off. Rubbed a hand along his jaw. "I got the impression she and Logan Ellis were hooking up."

"Hooking up?" Emma said, incredulous. It wasn't a phrase she could imagine applying to her prim and proper sister. The Juliette who had been in her kitchen two days ago, maybe, but the one who practiced her concertos two hours a day and never missed a day of Sunday school?

She tried to picture Logan Ellis in her mind. He'd had the good fortune to take after his mother; he had always been good-looking, if a bit generic. He had long blond hair and eyes that looked both lazy and interested, and he always held himself in a relaxed way, disengaged and cooler for it. He'd been out of high school by the time Juliette started. Twenty-four, twenty-five the year of the murders.

"Do you and Logan still talk?" Emma asked.

He made a dryly amused sound. "No, Emma. After his father tried to have me arrested for double murder, a certain distance arose between us." He shook his head. "We were never friends. He provided goods, I paid for them."

Emma glanced back toward the front porch. Lorelei was visible through the window, the cloud of her gray hair lit by the midday sun. "Is your grandmother still . . . ?"

He gave a sniff, shook his head. "Nah. The pain went away when she went into remission. We weaned her off. It was bullshit, though. One doctor decides she's drug-seeking, dependent—of course she was fucking dependent, it was keeping her from being in constant pain. And then the only way to get her the medicine she needs is to pay off some lowlife like Logan."

"I'm sorry."

"You say that a lot," he pointed out.

She lifted one shoulder in acknowledgment. "Is Logan still in town?"

"He's bartending at Wilson's."

"That hole-in-the-wall on Tenth?" she asked. He nodded, and she grunted in dull surprise. "Can't believe that place is still open."

"It has its devotees," Gabriel said. "Emma, why are you asking about this stuff now?"

"I'm just trying to put it all together."

"Put what together, exactly?" Gabriel asked, brow furrowed.

"Juliette. I don't know where she was that night, but she came back wearing someone else's clothes, and there are other things. . . . It's just, maybe if I can figure out what happened, I can clear my name," Emma said, gesturing helplessly. "But I don't know where to start. Apparently I didn't even know my own sister."

He stared at her. His thumb moved over his mouth slowly, and gradually she realized what that look meant. Her lips parted.

"Oh," she said softly, reality rearranging itself around her. How had she not realized?

"Emma."

"You thought I did it. All this time?" she asked, her voice strangely calm.

"You told me you wanted them dead," he said hoarsely. "You left the house in the middle of the night."

"So did you."

"I went for a walk to clear my head. Where did *you* go?" he asked.

He'd known she'd left. He'd thought she did it. And yet he'd never said anything, she realized—not even when it could have thrown the suspicion off him and onto her.

"I thought you lied to protect yourself. But it was your sister?" Gabriel asked.

"Maybe," Emma admitted reluctantly. "I don't know. I just know it wasn't me. And I never thought it was you."

"Am I supposed to say thank you for that?" Gabriel asked.

"No. Of course not," Emma replied.

He considered her. "Why now?" he asked. "After all this time, all these years. You never once said anything that might make people look at Juliette, even when everyone called you a murderer. So what's changed?"

"I won't let my child grow up thinking I killed my parents," Emma said.

"You're pregnant," Gabriel said. He ran both hands over his lower face. "Emma. Listen to me. Sell the house. Go live somewhere else. Have your baby, live a happy life with your husband."

"I'm done protecting my sister. I need to protect my family, and she made it clear years ago that doesn't mean her."

"Exactly. You need to protect your family," Gabriel said. "Maybe Juliette had something to do with your parents' death. Maybe she didn't. Either way, do you really think that whoever killed two people in cold blood is going to want you digging up the past? It could be dangerous."

"Why does it sound like you know something?" Emma asked. They'd never spoken after the murders; their lawyers wouldn't allow it.

"I know that two people died, and that if you'd been in that house, you'd probably be dead, too," Gabriel replied. "I know no one in this town lets go of a grudge."

"Ellis told me just about the same thing," Emma said musingly. "He thought that's why you helped me kill my dad. Because he fired yours, and called him a thief."

"I've barely got the energy for my own grudges. Besides, he probably did steal something."

"I never actually heard that whole story," Emma admitted. "Just the version my parents told."

Gabriel looked lost in thought. "Kenneth was always spending more money than he had, and it wouldn't be the dumbest thing he ever did for quick cash."

"Your father wasn't a thief," Lorelei said. Emma turned; she hadn't heard the older woman enter. Lorelei's hair was white, puffed out like a cloud around her face, but she stood as straight as ever.

"Nana," Gabriel said. He sounded tired. Lorelei ignored him, looking at Emma. Her hand gripped the back of a kitchen chair.

"Kenneth was always a bit up and down with life. Struggled with his drink. Gabriel's mother, God rest her soul, had about enough of him before she even started showing, and I don't blame her a bit for kicking him out. He'd get on the wagon and get a job for a while, and then he'd fall off the wagon and we wouldn't see him for a few months—"

"Or a few years," Gabriel added.

"But he'd been sober for almost a year."

"Seven months," Gabriel corrected.

"He found something off in the numbers. He thought it was a mistake, brought it to your father. The next day, Randolph accuses him of stealing and fires him."

"Something off in the numbers? Like embezzling, or something?" Emma asked.

"No, it was something about the weights. The weights on the trucks. I don't know the details," Lorelei said, shaking her head.

"Did he ever report it?" Emma asked.

"He certainly did," Lorelei said.

"After getting hammered. He burst into Ellis's office still drunk," Gabriel said. "It's not exactly a surprise Ellis didn't take him seriously."

"He could have at least looked into it," Lorelei huffed.

But, of course, he wouldn't have. Randolph Palmer was a pillar of the community, after all.

"Where is he now? Kenneth, I mean?" Emma asked.

"Probably dead," Gabriel said. "He took off not long after that. He did that a lot. This time he didn't come back."

"That's not true. He came back," Lorelei said.

Gabriel looked surprised. "What? When? Why didn't you tell me?"

She put a hand on his arm. "He didn't stay, honey. It was while I was in the hospital. By the time I got the chance to tell you—well, you had a lot going on, and I didn't want to trouble you with it."

"Right," Gabriel said, carefully not looking in Emma's direction. Because she was the reason for that. It was after Lorelei got out of the hospital that Gabriel had been arrested.

It all came back to her family. To her.

Whatever her father had been involved in, it had cost Kenneth his job. Had driven him away, and so cost Gabriel his father. She shouldn't be here, dredging up the past.

"I should go," Emma said. Part of her wished that one of them would say *No, stay*. She'd wanted so badly to belong here, once upon a time. But neither of them said anything, and she walked back to her car alone.

18

EMMA

Then

Nine hours before she tells the 911 operator that her parents are dead, Emma sits in the sunroom, sketchbook balanced on her knees. The evening sun slants through the glass. The page in front of her is empty. Lorelei says one doesn't wait for inspiration but hunts it down, lays a trap for it, lures it in, whatever is necessary. But Emma is mired, her mind's eye producing only a faint gray haze.

She needs one more piece. Not another oil painting, she thinks, not charcoal, something else, something new to show her range.

Her applications are going out across the country, but she has her eyes and her heart set on UCLA. She's never been to California. She doesn't really care about California, actually, except that it is all the way on the other side of the country, and she can look at a map and imagine all that space between her and her parents. Lorelei tells her that their program is impressive, and that she is impressive enough for it. The distance and Lorelei's words are all she needs.

Her parents can't know that she is looking at schools beyond the one-hour radius permitted to the Palmer girls. She wants her applications completed and sent early, to avoid any chance that her guidance counselor or one of her teachers might slip up and mention the recommendation letters she's asked for, her requests for help on writing essays.

Daphne steps into the room. Her expression is, as usual, focused

No One Can Know   115

and hard to read. She is twelve but looks younger, bird-boned. Emma has always enjoyed her company. She's good at listening and she never talks about normal, boring things. Last month she became interested in poisons. She learned about something called a poison garden, where all the plants could kill you, and asked for one of Emma's sketchbooks so that she could plan it out. Emma had listened to the descriptions of how each flower and root could kill, and imagined slipping them into her father's glass of bourbon, her mother's iced tea or evening wine.

Daphne says, "Mom and Dad want to talk to you. In the study," and all the blood drains from Emma's face. No girl is allowed inside the study unless invited, and this occurs in only two instances.

The first is when their father decides that it is time for them to be educated in some way. Then he will summon them in, sit them on a stool near his left hand as he sits back in his chair, and instruct them on some aspect of life. The last time it was about men. Boys. What they wanted from her. It somehow managed to simultaneously imply that she was a sheltered fool who had no idea what sex was and that she was selling herself to the whole school on the weekends.

But Mom is there, too, and that means it's the second thing.

"Do you know . . . ?" she whispers, but Daphne shakes her head. Delaying will only make things worse, so Emma walks quickly past her sister. She tries to think of what she has done that might merit this kind of punishment. Not the snap of Mom's temper or one of Dad's *corrections* but the both of them, together.

"Come in," her father's voice says. She pushes the door open and steps in, lingering just inside the door. Her father sits in his armchair, back to her. Her mother stands next to it, facing the door, one hand on the back of the chair. Without turning, her father crooks two fingers in a beckoning gesture.

Obediently, sick anticipation curdling in her gut, Emma makes her way around the chair to stand in front of him. He leans back in his chair, regarding her steadily. He is a plain man, with pale hair that was nearly colorless even before it turned gray. His eyes are deep-set, his nose hawkish. Emma inherited that nose from him, and he likes to point it out, laughing about how he's spoiled her having any chance at being a beauty, but at least he knows she's his.

"Do you know why you're here?" her father asks.

Emma swallows. This is the first question, always. If you don't answer, your punishment will be more severe. But if you guess wrong, you're only inviting worse.

"I don't know," Emma says.

Her father's hand moves slowly, almost absentmindedly, to the small table beside his chair. Only then does she notice the thick fold of printed pages there. She can only see a sliver of what is on the top page, but she recognizes it, and her stomach twists. It's the UCLA application, which she printed out at school. Which she buried in her backpack in the back of her closet, where her parents wouldn't check.

"You didn't tell us that you were looking at out-of-state schools," her father says. He says it lightly, like it's a tidbit she has forgotten to share, like it doesn't matter.

"My guidance counselor said I should apply widely," Emma says with a shrug. "It doesn't mean I'm actually going. I know you want me to stick with an in-state school."

"It's not a matter of what we want. It's what's right for you," her mother says.

"Why do you even care?" Emma blurts out. She looks between them. "Why does it matter where I go to school?"

"You belong at home with your family," her mother says sharply.

"But why?" Emma asks. "It's not like you need me to work at the business or help around the house or anything. You don't even like me."

"That's enough," her father says. "Your mother and I decided—"

"Mom decided," she says, interrupting him, and his eyes flare. She knows that she's crossed a line. But it's too late now; she presses on. "Mom decided that we all have to live here and go to school here so we turn out just the way she wants, except I'm already not what you want, so what's the point?"

"You need guidance," her mother says, but her father holds up his hand.

"Irene, that's enough," he says. "We are under no obligation to explain ourselves to you, Emma. Your parents have made a decision regarding your education; your job is simply to accept it."

"That's ridiculous," Emma says. She knows she should shut up. She knows she's making it worse for herself, but she can't stop. "Why can't I just go to school where I want and come home on the holidays like everyone else?"

"You need to speak to your elders with respect," her father says.

"Respect? Why should I respect you?" she asks.

"Because I am your father," he says, and his voice is dangerous, but for once she doesn't heed the warning.

"Why should I respect a father who cheats on my mother?" she demands.

The slap is hard enough it sets her staggering, lights popping in front of her eyes. It isn't her father who moved but her mother, hand still out in front of her, fury in her eyes. "Don't you dare speak to your father that way," she says.

Emma clutches her face, letting out a disbelieving laugh. "You're mad at *me*? What about him? I'm telling the truth. He cheated on you. He cheats on you all the time. He—"

"My business is none of your concern," her father says, rising from his chair.

She looks between them and realizes her mistake. "You already knew?" she asks.

Her mother's face is still; there's the smallest of tremors, starting at the edge of her pinky finger, stealing up the side of her hand. She notices, covers that hand with its opposite, as if to hide it. She takes in a small breath. A flutter of her eyelids, a tremble of her lip—and her voice steady as she says, "We're done here."

Emma laughs, because that's the only thing left to do. The only sane thing in the face of the absurdity of it all. "You're pathetic," she says.

"This is all so fucking pathetic. I can't believe you'd just stand there knowing what he did."

"Irene," her father says, "Emma and I need to have a conversation in private."

Irene stalks out of the room without a word, and Emma is alone with her father. Her father, who has been quiet and calm for too long.

"We have let you get away with too much," her father says. "You think that you can live under our roof and disrespect us. It's time you learned that actions have consequences."

Emma stands, righteousness crumbling into dread. Her father remains in his chair. She looks beyond him to the door, a quick flick of the eyes, a brief fantasy of running. She knows it wouldn't do any good.

He rises out of his chair. She steels herself because she knows what is coming, but it doesn't hurt less for it. One quick strike to her stomach, doubling her over, and then he wraps her hair around his fist, yanking her up, bending her back. He spins her around as he does so, so her back is to him. Her scalp hurts, hairs at the edges tearing free. He stares straight ahead and holds her against him.

"You need to learn respect. Clearly, your mother hasn't done enough to instill that in you. I've let it slide for far too long, but that's over."

She wants to shut her eyes, but she knows better. It will be over quickly, she tells herself. He does not leave marks where they can be seen, he does not lose control. He does not strike them out of anger, he tells them. It is not punishment but a lesson.

Two more blows, at her side below her ribs, carefully calibrated. Pain, not damage. A horrid wheeze in her throat as she tries to take a breath.

He releases her. He leaves her there, still wheezing slightly, and walks out of the room. She collapses onto the ground, hand on her side where the pain throbs, trying to breathe, hating the tears that leak from her eyes. She isn't crying because she feels sorry for herself, though that's what he'll say if he sees it. She isn't crying out of sadness or fear—it's a purely physical response. Because she isn't sad or afraid. She's angry.

She sits seething on the ground as his footsteps move up the stairs. She doesn't move until she hears the sound of canvas tearing.

She runs for the stairs.

The utility knife in her mother's hands has a dull gray handle, wrapped in weathered tape. Emma keeps it in the top drawer of her desk for trimming paper and slicing away dried gobs of paint. Her mother wields it with brusque efficiency, opening a gash across the canvas in front of her, a yawning crescent of nothing splitting Gabriel's face.

Her mother whirls, face pale, lips clamped together. Her rage is genteel. It is contained. The marks on the canvas, three of them, are made with surgical precision to obliterate the image with the least amount of violence.

Emma screams. She throws herself forward. She's not sure what she's saying as she slams her open hands against her mother's chest, shoving at her. Strong arms wrap around her waist and pull her back. She claws at her father's arms, twisting in his grip, and manages to turn.

"Emma, calm down," her mother says, but she won't, she can't, she rakes a hand at her father's face—

The punch comes without warning, a quick pop to her eye. She thuds backward on her ass, stars sparking in her vision. The impact makes her teeth click together and pain jolt through her skull. There is suddenly silence.

Her father shakes his hand. "That's quite enough of that," he says. He flexes his fingers. Emma touches a disbelieving hand to her eye and finds her cheekbone exquisitely tender. She looks at her fingertips, as if expecting to find blood, but of course there's none. "Get up."

Her mother is breathing heavily, her eyes bright and a look on her face that might be regret or fear. Emma pushes herself to her feet. Her father looks down at her desk. One of the other portfolio pieces is there, a charcoal piece depicting a girl in the park, crouching down with a stick in one hand, which she is using to prod a dead bird. Casually, he picks it up and tears it in half.

This time, Emma doesn't move. She stands, shaking and silent, as he bends down to pick up the portfolio that holds the rest of her work. Each one, he neatly tears into four pieces. Then he hands her the pile. Only the painting of Juliette at her piano remains, propped up in the corner. Emma doesn't cry. Crying always makes things worse.

"Throw these out," he instructs.

She takes the scraps from him. Her hands are trembling. There's a lump in her throat that makes swallowing painful, and her vision blurs, but she doesn't cry. She looks down at the scraps of paper in her hands. Useless now. She'll have to start again.

She can't start again.

"Fuck you," she says.

"Emma," her mother hisses, and something in her tone makes Emma actually think for a moment she might be concerned for Emma's well-being—but this only lends a kind of comedy to the situation, and Emma bares her teeth.

"Fuck. You," she says again, the worst insult she can muster, fangless and ineffectual. She throws the stack of ruined work at her father, paper fluttering to the ground as he stands impassively, and she runs.

Her mother calls after her, but her father says "Let her go," and then Emma is at the door, shoving her feet into shoes, running out. He's letting her go because he knows and she knows that she will have to come back, and when she does, the punishment will be far worse than if she'd stayed.

She stops in the drive. If she turns back now, it might not be so bad. But the worst that can happen already has. Her work, her way out, is ruined. There's no way she can rebuild the portfolio in time, not one good enough for UCLA, for anywhere. And they won't let her go.

She can't be here, in this house, with these people. She starts moving again, walking swiftly with her arms wrapped around her and her eye throbbing in time with the beating of her heart.

As she makes her way down the road, she allows herself, at last, to cry.

19

EMMA

Now

When Emma arrived home, the neighbor across the street was mowing his lawn. He made no attempt to hide the fact that he was watching her as she got out to open the gate. She wished she were the kind of person to stare right back or flip him off. She kept her head down instead. She grabbed the bag that rested in the passenger seat—cameras from the electronics store, which she'd figured she'd pick up and spare Nathan the trip—and hurried inside without making eye contact.

Nathan was in the kitchen, taking a Brillo pad to the stove. She dropped the bag of cameras on the table, but he didn't turn.

"I got some cameras. They're the brand you wanted. They were pretty expensive—I only ended up getting two, but that's front and back, at least," she said.

"I thought we agreed you weren't going to go into town," he said, not turning. The bottle of white wine sat on the counter, half-empty. He must have retrieved it from the trash.

"I know. But I had a bit of cabin fever and I thought since you were so tired—" she began. He turned, eyes flashing with anger.

"If you were doing me a favor, why did you wait until I was asleep? Sneak out when I was taking a nap?" he demanded. She flinched, shying away from him. He made a disgusted sound. He hated it when she flinched. He'd never once raised a hand to her. Acting like she was afraid of him was insulting.

"I'm sorry," she said. "I didn't want to argue about it."

"Which means you knew it would piss me off and you did it anyway," he said.

"I can't be a prisoner in this house, Nathan," Emma protested.

"A prisoner? You're being way overdramatic," Nathan said.

"I just mean—"

"You're trying to turn it around and make me the bad guy. But you're the one lying and sneaking around," Nathan said, jabbing a finger at her.

"I'm not—"

"You didn't just go to the store," Nathan said. He crossed his arms. "Did you?"

"You tracked my phone," she said evenly.

"Can you blame me? I woke up and you weren't here."

"I sent you a text. I left a note," Emma said. She glanced over; the note was in the trash. He had found it, then.

"We're being harassed. I didn't know where you were. Whether you were safe. And apparently I was right to be worried, because you weren't where you said you were going to be."

"I made another stop," Emma said.

"Whose house was that?" he asked, voice dark with suspicion. "Is it Gabriel's house?"

She turned back to the bag, started taking things out in jerky, angry motions. She had her anxieties. Nathan had his. They'd argued about the tracking apps a lot, over the years. He claimed he wanted them in case of an emergency—what if one of them ended up crashed into a ditch? But he only ever brought them up at times like these. *I thought you were staying in today,* he'd say casually, or inquire about how Susan was doing when she hadn't told him she was visiting Susan that day at all.

She hated it. Hated the feeling of being watched, her every movement monitored, and feeling like she couldn't make a spontaneous trip to the new bakery in town without it being treated as suspicious.

"I take it that's a yes," Nathan said sardonically. Grime streaked his knuckles. There was a smudge on his cheek.

"I went to talk to Gabriel," she confirmed. That elicited another grunt, this one curled with satisfaction.

"What is it with this guy? It's like you're obsessed with him," he said.

"I don't think I've mentioned him more than three times since we got here," she said, temper beginning to simmer. What did he think, that she'd managed to fit a torrid affair into the five minutes she'd spent at the house?

"All that not-mentioning is pretty loud," he said.

She gritted her teeth. Talk about a thing too much, you're obsessed. Talk about it too little, you're hiding something. And no such thing as a middle ground. She could never get it right. That perfect balancing act of the *right* way to speak, to be, to look, to feel, so your innocence could be confirmed. Once you were tainted you could never get clean.

"Is it a first-love thing?" he asked. "The guy who got away?"

"It's not that," she said. She busied herself sorting out the cameras and mounting equipment. With only two, they wouldn't be able to cover the carriage house. They hadn't even been in there yet. There could be a whole family of serial killers nesting inside.

"Then what is it? Why are you hung up on this guy?" Nathan demanded.

"I'm not hung up on him. I was never . . ." She ran both her hands through her hair, looking up at the ceiling.

"Who is he to you?" Nathan asked, and she couldn't escape the feeling that he wanted her to tell him she was still in love with Gabriel. That he *wanted* there to be something between them. He couldn't be angry about her parents because that would imply he thought she might have something to do with it, so give him some other sin to hang around her neck, a reason for her to grovel and plead.

"Gabriel wasn't my boyfriend. His grandmother was my mentor—my art teacher, and she gave me private painting lessons. His dad took off and his grandma was sick, so Gabriel was living with her that year, and we hit it off. I had a schoolgirl crush on him."

"But he and you never . . . ?" Nathan prompted.

She sighed. "No. I was too young for him, and he wasn't that kind of guy." She didn't want to have to explain how that had been part of the point. Gabriel wasn't just kind and handsome and funny—he was *safe*.

"You're not too young for him now."

She rubbed her eyes. "I'm not cheating on you, Nathan."

"I didn't say you were. You know I trust you."

She looked away before she said something she regretted.

"Why didn't your parents want you spending time with him?" Nathan asked. "That was what the police said, right? They didn't like him."

"They wouldn't have wanted me to date him, no," Emma said. "But it's not relevant, since we weren't dating."

"He was cleared. Gabriel."

"Yeah," Emma said.

"How?"

"I don't know."

"How do you not know?" Nathan asked. "They thought you did it together, so don't you know how they cleared you?"

"It doesn't work like that," Emma said. "It wasn't like they gave me a certified letter saying *Congrats, you're innocent*. They were just investigating me until at some point they weren't. Chris stopped hearing from them and eventually the case wasn't being actively pursued anymore, and that was it." It had been a long, agonizing period of ambiguity. Every time Chris called, she'd assumed he was telling her she was going to be arrested. But the call never came.

"Why would he stick around after all of that?" Nathan asked. "You got out, why didn't he?"

"Lorelei won't go," Emma said. "That's the house she lived in with her husband for decades. She told me once that leaving here would be leaving him."

"Lorelei, that's his grandmother?"

Emma nodded. "She was an amazing teacher. An amazing artist, too."

"Right. You said she was your painting teacher," Nathan said. There was an odd tone to his voice, one that set the hairs on her arms on end, though it was perfectly civil.

"That's right."

He gave her an unreadable look. "You never told me you used to paint."

"Yeah. I did. Is that so strange?" Emma asked, shrugging one shoulder.

"It's just that I've never seen you even doodle a stick figure," Nathan said.

Emma neatly folded up the plastic bag the cameras had been in and took it over to the trash. "It was all I wanted to do back then. I was going to go to art school."

"Why didn't you?" he asked.

"I didn't even graduate high school, remember?" He'd made such a big deal about it when they were getting to know each other. How interesting her "alternate life path" was. How he respected different ways of finding success. "I needed something that would get me a job right away, and I got a scholarship for a web dev course. And then I guess . . . I don't know. You lose a dream and it starts to hurt to even remember you ever had it."

She was out of things to busy her hands with and folded her arms awkwardly.

"You keep coming up with new surprises," he said. "I can't help wondering what's going to be next."

"I've never hid anything from you about us. About the present. My past—I left it behind. I didn't want it to touch us."

"How can I believe that? What other secrets are you keeping?"

She didn't answer, looking away instead.

"I'm not the police. I'm not our nosy neighbors. I'm your goddamn husband. You know something about what happened, don't you? You wouldn't have to keep all these secrets if you didn't know *something*."

"We promised. All of us," Emma said.

His gaze sharpened. "Promised? Emma, did your sisters do something?"

"I don't know."

"Emma."

"I don't know," she insisted. "The things I saw could have meant a lot of things."

Her phone chimed. Eager for a reprieve from the conversation, she pulled it out of her pocket. It was a text from Gabriel, with a photo attached. *Found this. Thought it might be relevant*, it said.

It was a dark photo, taken in the Saracen house. The couch was filthy and stained, but not chewed through; the writing on the walls looked fresh. Logan Ellis, son of Arden's beloved police chief, had his arm around the shoulders of a girl with big brown eyes and dark hair, spilling loose over her shoulders. She looked nervous, but excited. She wore a plaid skirt and a low-cut blouse under a faux-leather jacket.

Juliette.

There were three other kids in the photo, two crammed on the couch and one sitting on the arm. Emma only recognized one—Elaine Chen, the chain-smoking lead singer of their high school's resident rock band. Next to her on the couch was a Black guy with a silver stud earring and a goatee who looked like he might have been college age. The other girl, the one perched on the arm of the couch, was white, slim, not exactly pretty but impossible not to notice, with sharp features and intense eyes.

She was wearing a red flannel shirt like a jacket, unbuttoned down the front. Emma had seen a shirt exactly like that before. On Juliette, when she stumbled into the house in the early hours of the morning, the day their parents died. It could have been a coincidence. Except for the other thing.

Juliette's shoes. She had her knees together, her body pinched inward in discomfort. On her feet were a pair of masculine black boots. Doc Martens, their laces cinched unusually tight.

As if to make up for the fact that they were too large for her feet. "What is it?" Nathan asked.

She hesitated a moment. And then she turned off the phone and put it back in her pocket. "It's nothing," she said.

He didn't know her sisters. He didn't love them. She couldn't explain why it mattered, but it did. She had to start from love. She could believe that Juliette had harmed her parents, but she couldn't stand the thought of someone else believing it—or believing it without also loving her.

Without understanding what it had been like in this house.

Without understanding that the first thing she had felt when she saw her mother's empty eyes, the blood speckling her throat, was relief.

20

JULIETTE

Then

Emma is fighting with Mom and Dad again. Juliette can't hear the details, and doesn't care to. There's always something. She hears a name—Gabriel—and remembers her parents' earlier discussion, but it still makes no sense. Emma doesn't hang out with boys. Ever. Dad makes comments here and there, jokes that aren't jokes about how she'd better be careful or people are going to start thinking she's a lesbian.

Of course, one can't be *too* interested in boys, either. Juliette has learned to walk that careful line. Learned it well, after she came home at fifteen with what her mother deemed a whorish amount of makeup and her father asked her if she'd done anything with that boy she ought to be ashamed of. She promised she hadn't—they hadn't even held hands—and he held her chin and stared into her eyes, and with his thumb smeared the peach-colored gloss from her lips. "Keep it that way," he said, and she did.

For a while.

Juliette puts her headphones on, turning up her music. The screaming is upstairs now. There comes a yell and a thump and then fleeing footsteps, and the front door slams. Juliette closes her eyes and hums, her body tense.

If Emma keeps provoking them like this, she thinks, *someone is going to wind up dead.*

At just past nine o'clock, less than six hours before she is going to die, Irene Palmer knocks on the door and pushes it open. Juliette takes off her headphones. Her mother's cheeks are flushed, her hair messy around her face, and she covers her forearm with the opposite hand in an odd way. "We're off to bed. I wanted to check in on you."

"I'm fine. Tired. Probably just going to sleep," Juliette says. It isn't yet ten o'clock. She isn't the least bit tired.

"Good, good," her mother says. She sighs. "At least there's one of my children I don't have to worry about."

"I love you, Mom," Juliette says. Her mother gives a tight smile and shuts the door. Juliette listens for the master bedroom door closing. Once Mom has checked on her, she's good for the night. Dad never pokes his head in, and Mom knows—believes—she doesn't need to check in again, like she does with Emma and Daphne. This is the advantage of playing along that Emma has never understood.

Just past eleven, Juliette throws back the covers and swings her legs out of bed. She goes to her closet and opens the box labeled WINTER SWEATERS. She removes the two sweaters on top and takes out her boots—Doc Martens, her prize possession—and a change of clothes. Jeans, a blue sleeveless top with a V-neck that slashes right down past her bra. She pulls on the boots, tying them tight. They're way too big, but if she laces them up and wears thick socks, she can walk in them all right. She found them at a thrift shop. Nina has a pair just like them.

Juliette's cheeks get a bit hot. She wonders if Nina will be there tonight. Nina with her smoky laugh and the short, messy curls she is constantly fiddling with, piling them on top of her head, sweeping them all to one side, stretching one coil out to its full length in front of her face and letting it spring back. She was a year ahead of Juliette in school. She left for college but often comes back over breaks. She'll be gone again at the end of the summer, but Juliette tries not to think about that.

She finishes changing and listens again for the sound of movement in the house, but there's nothing. Dad will be in his study, drinking.

Mom will be in bed with her glass of wine. Juliette eases up the window and swings a leg over the sill, then wriggles the rest of her body out. She closes it softly behind her, making sure it doesn't latch, and then it's easy to climb over to the corner of the house and scramble down the trellis there. She keeps to the edge of the lawn, out of sight of the kitchen in case someone is grabbing another drink, until she gets to the trees.

Her path takes her under the tree house. A light glows inside, and as she walks underneath, Daphne peers out. They look at each other, Juliette on the ground, Daphne up top, and Juliette presses a finger to her lips. Daphne does the same, retreating inside again.

Daphne won't tell. Daphne keeps everyone's secrets.

Juliette sets out through the woods, toward where she knows Logan is waiting for her.

She's seen Logan around plenty, but she doesn't think they actually had a conversation until last fall. She'd just had a fight that wasn't a fight with her parents. A rare slipup. She asked to skip a recital so that she could do a college visit trip with Stacy, and when Mom reminded her that she could look at colleges only in commuting distance, she pushed back.

"*Disrespecting your mother,*" her father had called it, and applied what he terms a swift correction. Just one quick strike to her stomach, so she'll remember.

She doesn't think she can complain, not really. It doesn't happen often, and it rarely even leaves a mark, and she lives a comfortable life. More than comfortable. They're rich, basically, and she has everything she could ask for, wants for nothing; it isn't like her parents are violent drunks who lock them in the basement.

But she was still smarting and still angry when Logan pulled his car up alongside her. He called over to her. "*Hey, Princess, want to have some actual fun?*" She isn't certain which one of them was more surprised when she said, "*Sure.*"

His car smelled of cigarette smoke and the glass cleaner he used obsessively. The seat was split, the foam padding bulging out, pock-marked like acned skin. The AC was broken, and she remembers the sweat trickling down her spine as Logan asked her where he could take her.

"Anywhere but here."

He took her to the Saracen house.

Each night she leaves, there is a moment of pleasurable adrenaline, a moment when she thinks, *You have no idea who I am.* A moment when that statement is a triumph, instead of a fearful whisper.

Who am I? I am a secret, she thinks, *every part of me concealed.*

Someday she will show them who she truly is.

Someday she will show them that she doesn't belong to them at all.

Logan is waiting for her at the edge of the clearing where the Saracen house stands. He grins when he spots her, flicking his cigarette onto the ground and stomping it out. He's striking, with strong cheekbones and pale eyes. He's twenty-five, but Juliette has trouble thinking of him as any older than she is; he acts like an overgrown kid.

He drags her in close and presses a hard kiss to her lips. He tastes of cigarettes. The kiss is all teeth. He gropes up under her shirt with one eager hand and she shoves him away with an exasperated sound.

"Cut it out, Logan," she says. His smile is crooked and unbothered.

"Just happy to see you," he tells her. She snakes an arm around his waist, her lips tingling. Walking next to him like this is awkward, making her steps uneven. His bony hip digs into her side. His fingers manage to dangle just over her cleavage. "Here. Take this," he says. He tucks a single pill into her palm.

"What is it?" she asks.

He shrugs. "Nothing too intense. You need to relax."

She sets it on her tongue; he follows the gift with a flask and she washes it down with what tastes like turpentine but is probably cheap bourbon. She needs something to take the edge off. This—the house, the crowd, and especially Logan—stopped being new months ago, stopped being fun shortly after. Without chemical assistance, it's turned deadly boring, in fact, but she isn't ready to admit it yet, because she's got nothing else.

Inside, a few of the usual faces are already there. A couple of them lounge on the couch, others sit splay-legged on the floor. It looks like a D.A.R.E. video, she thinks, and smothers a giggle that draws an odd look from Logan.

There is tinny music playing from someone's phone, a slow-rolling conversation that Juliette can't catch the thread of. Logan keeps his arm around her shoulder and kicks someone off the couch so they can sit there, the closest thing to royalty their little gathering has.

It's both exactly what everyone says about the Saracen house and far less interesting. At first the mere presence of alcohol and drugs— mostly prescription pills lifted from parents' medicine cabinets, plus Logan's premium supply—felt shocking, electrifying. The novelty has worn off.

Whatever Logan's given her, though, it's giving her that pleasant, floaty feeling. She burrows against Logan, and his hand finds its way inside her shirt again, stroking her hip. Kaitlyn is telling a story she's told a half-dozen times before, gesturing broadly and putting on voices. Elaine examines her fingernails, leaning against the wall with an expression that suggests she's just as over all of this as Juliette.

Then Nina walks in. Is it everyone who turns to stare at her, or is it only that she becomes all Juliette can see? She wears her standard uniform, a simple top under an unbuttoned flannel shirt, rolled up to the elbows. It's unpretentious, dressed up only with a few silver bangles. A tattoo of a sword decorates her forearm. She spots Juliette and walks toward her, stepping over a couple of people to get there.

"Scoot," she orders. Juliette wedges herself more firmly against Logan to make room; he grunts in annoyance as Nina drops into the gap she's created. The older girl taps a cigarette out of a pack and then holds up the pack to Juliette. "Want one?"

"She doesn't smoke," Logan says, but Juliette nods. Nina winks. Hands Juliette the cigarette and then, as Juliette lifts it to her lips, takes out her lighter. It's silver, with a bee and a flower etched in the metal. Juliette's eyes fix on her fingers as they flick it open, light it.

"Anything interesting happen while I was gone?" Nina asks. Then she laughs, tosses her head. "Never mind. Nothing interesting has ever happened here."

"Hey, remember when Seth sliced his arm open and had to go to the ER?" Kaitlyn asks.

Nina lets out a plume of smoke. "Oh yeah. That was kinda cool. Come on, we're sitting around like a bunch of losers. At least play some decent music."

Decent music is procured. Juliette manages a few puffs of the cigarette. When the ash gets too long Logan confiscates it with a laugh and puts something new into her palm; this time she doesn't ask what it is. It doesn't matter. It's something to make this anything other than depressing. It makes the colors bend, blur. It makes time braid into new shapes, so that she isn't sure at what point she stands up—Nina pulls her up—and starts to dance with her.

Juliette can never tell if Nina likes her. She's friendly, physical, quick to loop an arm through Juliette's or sling a leg over hers on the couch. But she teases Juliette, too, calls her Logan's pet, calls her prissy, taunts her for being a lightweight and having a curfew.

But here, now, the music is pounding and Nina is holding both of her hands and they're spinning around, and both of them are laughing, Nina's hands are around her neck, her hands are on Nina's waist, Nina is throwing her head back with a wild grin. She doesn't know if it is the alcohol or the pills or the simple intoxication of Nina's beauty, but it is like she isn't touching the ground at all. The whole rest of the world is gone, but that's fine, because the whole world is contained in the places where her skin touches Nina's, and this is the only thing that matters, the only thing that has ever mattered.

Nothing here counts. That's why she keeps coming back. It isn't real. None of these people are real, none of the things they write on the walls mean anything at all, nothing Juliette does is real or matters at all, and so it doesn't matter that she wants, more than anything, to kiss Nina. It isn't real, so she can have it. Just here. Just for a little while.

But then someone says "Kiss her!" and someone else whoops, and Nina, laughing, leans forward, and Juliette doesn't pull away, and they *are* kissing, to hoots and cheers, and Nina's hands are in her hair and her tongue is in Juliette's mouth. It is a few seconds, no more, and then Nina pulls away and she looks at Juliette with a grin, and Juliette stares back at her, feeling cracked in two, feeling real again, and broken, and Nina's mouth suddenly rounds in an O.

"Shit, I didn't—" she says softly, and then Juliette turns and runs.

21

EMMA

Now

Emma jolted awake that night to the sound of gunshots, impacts against the house. Nathan had his phone in his hand and called 911 before the fifth and final shot faded, and they sat huddled in bed until the police knocked on the door. Not Hadley or Ellis this time; a younger, female officer, blond. She was sympathetic as she showed them the bursts of soot against the siding and windows, the discarded scraps of cardboard and plastic. Fireworks, not bullets.

The next morning, Nathan installed the cameras.

Emma knelt in the garden bed midmorning, pulling up weeds and tossing them into the bucket at her side. Sweat trickled down her neck, slipping beneath the collar of her shirt. Above the front door, the blank black eye of the camera stared down at her. She kept glancing at it. Ever since Nathan had pulled his little trick with the phone tracker, she'd felt like she was being watched at all times. It should have been easy to feel swallowed up in that big house, but she imagined him monitoring the sound of her footsteps and felt his attention on her, inescapable.

The sound of a car turning into the drive brought her twisting around. It was a blue hybrid, nearly new. JJ was behind the wheel. She parked ten feet from Emma and got out, shading her eyes. Emma stayed where she was, kneeling in the dirt.

"I come in peace," she said. She pulled something from her pocket and held it up pinched between her thumb and forefinger. A key. "Nathan asked if I had keys to the carriage house. Asked me to bring them by."

"He's not here," Emma said. It seemed like he never was anymore. She stood, brushing dirt from her knees. As she rose, spots appeared in her vision. She wobbled.

"Whoa," JJ said, striding quickly over to her and reaching to take her arm. Emma yanked it away, which only made her almost topple over again, dizziness sweeping over her. JJ reached for her arm again and this time snagged it, keeping her steady. "Are you okay?"

"I'm fine," Emma snapped, except that her vision wasn't clearing.

"Come here. Put your head between your legs," JJ said, guiding her firmly over to the steps. Emma sank down in the shade, not out of obedience but because if she didn't, she was going to fall over anyway. JJ left her there, reappearing moments later with a glass of water. JJ hovered awkwardly as Emma took a sip, then handed it back.

"Thanks."

"You should be careful. Sunstroke's no joke," JJ said with the fleeting edge of a smile. Emma grunted. She levered herself up to her feet, but it was a mistake—her knees went rubbery immediately.

"Help me inside, will you?" she asked.

JJ looped an arm around Emma's waist, silently helping her up the steps and through the door. With the window AC they'd bought on credit, the house was slightly more tolerable than the outside, and JJ helped her into the living room and onto the couch.

A headache pounded behind Emma's eyes. She tried to sip the water, but it only turned her stomach again. She hated that JJ was here, seeing her like this.

"This is your fault," she muttered, splaying her hand against her abdomen.

"How is this my fault?" JJ asked, affronted.

Emma waved a hand. "Not you. The spawn."

It still felt more like a flu than a future. A collection of symptoms that would fade. Nathan didn't talk about the baby or the future, either. He used to—lying awake at night, fantasizing about the children they would have and the lives they would live. But as soon as it became real, he'd gone quiet.

"Nathan mentioned," JJ said. "Congratulations."

"Yeah. Well. I can't possibly be a worse parent than ours were, right?" Emma asked. JJ snorted, and their eyes met in a brief moment of understanding. Then JJ's expression shuttered again.

"When's the last time you ate anything?" JJ asked.

"Toast when I woke up. Nibbled on some crackers," Emma said. "Haven't managed anything else." It wasn't even that she felt sick, exactly, just that her body seemed physically incapable of allowing her to bring food to her mouth. Like it could tell that she was somewhere unfamiliar. Somewhere unsafe.

She eased herself upright. JJ stiffened, but the wooziness had passed. Emma moved gingerly deeper into the house. "Did you need anything else?" she asked.

"Just dropping off the keys," JJ said, trailing behind. In the great room she halted, looking around. "I didn't really stop to see anything the other day. It's weird, being in here again."

"Did you ever come back?" Emma asked.

"Hell no," JJ said. "Did you?"

Emma shook her head. "No reason to."

JJ drifted toward the right-hand hallway, which led to the living room and their father's study. The hall where they'd found their mother. "It was here," she said, looking down at the stain.

Emma joined her, setting her glass on the closed lid of the piano as she passed. "We tried to get the stain out, but it looks like we're going to have to patch the whole section of floor," she said.

Juliette rubbed a toe idly against the edge of the dark blotch. "And Dad was . . ." She moved forward with an unhurried kind of purpose. She pushed open the office door but stayed back. Emma joined her.

The room was arranged around that spot, now bare, from which he ruled his kingdom. They hadn't been allowed in here without explicit invitation. Now JJ stepped cautiously over the threshold.

"He was facing away from the door," she said. She lifted her hand, almost as if she were holding a gun. Barrel to the back of the head, boom. She seemed to realize what she was doing and dropped her hand, then walked quickly over to the wall and set her fingers against a gouge in the wainscotting. "This must be where the bullet lodged."

"I—I don't know," Emma stammered. She'd never thought about where the bullet had gone, when its work was done.

JJ looked back at her, expression unreadable. "It entered the back left side of his head and exited at the front right near the temple, then lodged in the wall."

"I never wanted to know the details," Emma said. The more she knew, the more she worried she would find out. And she hadn't *wanted* the truth. As soon as she was sure, it would stop being a matter of protecting her sisters. It would start to be a question of protecting just one. The equation stopped balancing.

"He didn't see it coming," JJ said. There was a strange mix of challenge and compassion in her voice. Her eyes were locked on Emma. "It would have been instantaneous, for him."

"But not Mom?"

"She was shot in the chest," JJ said. "Close range. The bullet only nicked the heart, so it took a minute or two for her to bleed out. A minute or two isn't that long, though." She sounded like she'd thought about it a lot. She sounded like she didn't quite believe that part.

"She must have heard the gunshot and come downstairs," Emma said.

"Must have," JJ said, not breaking eye contact. Must have, as if she didn't know. Maybe she didn't.

"You sneaked out to meet Logan that night, didn't you?" Emma asked. JJ startled.

"Who told you that?"

"So it's true."

Car tires crunched on gravel. JJ didn't answer, looking at her steadily. "Sounds like your husband's home," JJ said.

"Were you at the Saracen house that night? Where did you go?" Emma asked.

Juliette let out a breath between her teeth. "It's ancient history. It doesn't matter."

The front door opened. "Why are you so worried about people asking questions, Juliette?" Emma asked.

Nathan stepped into the doorway. He was carrying a duffel bag over his shoulder that Emma hadn't seen before. He looked between the two of them, clearly taken aback. "Oh. Hey, JJ," he said.

"She brought the carriage house keys. Like you asked," Emma said, words clipped.

Nathan smiled. "Great! Thanks for that. It's been driving me crazy, not being able to see what's out there."

"Probably just Dad's tools and a good way to get tetanus," JJ said with a shrug. She glanced at Emma. "There wouldn't be anything interesting out there."

"No, I don't think so," Emma said. Not in the carriage house.

"Still. Could be buried treasure," Nathan said cheerfully.

"Have at it." JJ tossed Nathan the keys.

He caught them deftly in the air and stepped aside to let her pass. As her footsteps moved off down the hall, he brandished the key at Emma. "Now we don't have to break down the door."

"You called JJ about the key?" Emma said quietly.

His affable expression darkened. "Yes. Gabriel—your good friend Gabriel, remember him?—did say she might have one, so yes, I called her."

"You didn't tell me you were going to, that's all," Emma said.

"I didn't think it was important."

"You didn't think it was worth mentioning that you were in touch with my estranged sister? My estranged sister who I *just* told you I was having trouble with," Emma said calmly, teeth clenched.

"It's not like we were conspiring against you," Nathan said. "I just want to get into the fucking carriage house."

"It's not a big deal, except that you didn't tell me you were doing it."

"Because I thought you'd be pissed," Nathan said.

"Yeah. I would. I am," Emma said. "Jesus, Nathan, come on. I pour out my heart to you about how horrible things have been since she took off and you, what, go onto my phone to find her number?"

"You're acting like I was sneaking around on you," Nathan said, rolling his eyes, "when you're making secret visits to your ex."

"Gabriel is not my ex, and it wasn't a *secret*, I just—"

"Just didn't happen to mention it," Nathan said.

"I'm not the only one with secrets," Emma said quietly.

"You can't hold the mortgage thing over me forever," he said. "I screwed up. I haven't kept lying to you about it."

"I wasn't talking about the mortgage," she replied, voice barely audible. He went quiet. His hand tightened at his side, knuckles flexing.

Only then did she hear the front door shut and realize that JJ hadn't left yet.

Nathan looked over his shoulder, realizing the same thing, and looked back at her with anger in his eyes. "You couldn't have waited two minutes to lay into me?" he asked.

"I didn't think I was laying into you," Emma said. His anger was like a pressure in the air, making it hard to breathe.

"I'm trying to do what's best for us. Trying to deal with this shitty hand you've left us with," Nathan said. "This fucking house, this fucking town." He took the satchel off his shoulder and slammed it down on the kitchen table.

"What is that?" Emma asked.

"Protection. Since a couple of dinky little cameras aren't going to do shit," Nathan said. He opened the satchel and pulled out a small zippered pouch. He unzipped it to reveal a handgun, black and angular—a Glock, her memory supplied.

"Where did you get that?" Emma asked, not moving or taking her eyes off the gun, feeling like an eel was sliding around in her guts.

"I found the bill for a storage place the trust has been paying for. It turns out that's where they stored your dad's guns. Plus some other stuff that could be valuable," Nathan said. "I've got the rest out in the car."

"You—" She took a breath. Tried to stay calm. "What exactly are you planning to do? Shoot at the next couple of kids to throw rocks at the windows?" Emma asked, thinking of Abraham and Travis, of shadowy forms in the dark and a trigger pulled in haste and panic.

"What if it isn't just kids and fireworks next time?" Nathan asked.

Bullet to the back of the head. She tasted something unpleasant in the back of her mouth. "You don't have a permit."

"I'll get one," Nathan said with a shrug.

"No," Emma said.

"They're our property," Nathan said, as if that was her objection.

"Nathan, I do not want those things in this house."

"I'm not going to sit here defenseless," Nathan said.

"Get rid of them," she said, voice flat and angry. And before Nathan could argue, she turned and marched out of the room.

22

EMMA

Now

Emma slept alone and came down the next morning to find a blanket on the couch and no sign of Nathan. A look out the front window showed the carriage house door was open. He'd gotten in at last.

They hadn't spoken after the argument about the guns, but she'd heard him the night before while she was in bed, loading them into the gun case. They were there this morning. Six rifles, two shotguns, more than a dozen handguns. Seeing them all in the wrong order, on the wrong shelves, made her weirdly twitchy. *He'll know you moved them*, she wanted to warn Nathan, and knew it was ridiculous.

They didn't fight, as a rule, she and Nathan. Emma had listened to her parents fight behind closed doors throughout her childhood; Nathan's favored screaming at each other in the open. Emma sidestepped the issue by not bringing up a problem until she'd worked out the solution that Nathan would find agreeable. If she couldn't, she'd let it go.

And she was careful—had been careful—never to be the source of the fight. Nathan was so easy to read, it was a simple enough matter to tell when he was irritated or angry long before the pressure built up enough for him to bring it up to her. She adjusted, bent, experimented until she could tell by the lightening of his mood that she'd found the source of his displeasure.

When had she decided that it was better to be miserable than to be alone, she wondered. Or had that always been the price she was paying?

Her parents had tried so hard to make her small, and she'd fought every moment of it. But for Nathan Gates she'd simply surrendered.

She couldn't do it anymore. She couldn't bend one more inch. Not for him.

The kitchen table was covered by a cheap tablecloth, folded in half. The Glock lay disassembled on top, with a cleaning kit half-unpacked next to it. It looked like Nathan had started in on the project and then given up.

Emma sighed. Her father at least had never cleaned guns at the kitchen table or any place where people ate. She gathered up the pieces and carted them to the living room instead, opening a window to let the inevitable fumes out. She set to work—dry brushing the chamber and barrel, wiping it out with solvent and a cloth, brushing again.

It was another several passes before the barrel was clean enough to have passed her father's inspection, back in the day. There was a meditative quality to the process, and she found herself falling easily back into the rhythm.

With the parts cleaned and lubricated, she assembled the gun, the movements coming back to her fingers before her brain.

"I was going to do that," Nathan said. She startled. He was standing in the doorway, clothes covered in the dust and grime of the carriage house. "I was going to look up a video later."

"Well, there are plenty more to clean, if you want to," she said. She tucked a strand of hair behind her ear, taking a breath to stay calm. "Nathan, I'd like to take these back to the storage unit until we can arrange to have them assessed and sold. I do not feel comfortable with them in the house."

"Right. You're a good little liberal who hates guns," Nathan said, rolling his eyes, and her carefully constructed calm cracked in half.

"Yes, that's why. It couldn't be because my parents were murdered with a gun. That I grew up with a dad who thought it was funny to point them at us as a joke," Emma said, cheeks hot. "Get rid of them. Sell them, have them melted down, I don't care."

"If you just want me to get rid of them all, why bother with cleaning it?" he asked.

"Because it was obvious you didn't know how," Emma said.

"I told you I was going to watch a video." He turned and strode out of the room, sparing her from making things any worse. She looked down at her hands, streaked with black and stinking of solvent. It was on her clothes, too, in her hair. She swiped her palm across her already soiled T-shirt, but it wouldn't scrub clean.

She took the gun to the foyer. She turned the key and swung open the glass door. She set the Glock in carefully, exactly as her father would have, and shut the door again, locked it.

An overactive imagination, her father had called it. The way her mind could so easily concoct the image of a gun in her hand, trained on a human being. The feel of the trigger under her finger. The kick against her palm, the calamitous sound. The heat of blood. All of it so vivid it could have been real. As vivid as a memory.

She pulled the key from the door and put it in her pocket.

She couldn't stop it. The pressure built too fast for her to bleed it off in the thousand small ways she had developed over the years to keep things steady and agreeable. The fight was coming—not an argument, a real fight, the kind she had avoided in all the time they'd been married. And she found that she no longer wanted to stop it. Enough silence. She wanted things in the open.

It was dinner when it finally boiled over. It started with a look, Nathan watching her, his fork in his hand.

"With everything that's happening, maybe . . ." He paused. "I mean, it's not too late. To change our minds."

"About what?" she asked, but the implication hit her before the words had fully left her mouth. She set her fork down. She hadn't touched her dinner. She knew she should be eating more. She'd started getting faint in the middle of the day, but she could still only manage to nibble at plain bread. Now the alfredo that she'd hoped would be enticing enough that she could get down a few bites was congealing on her plate. "No."

"You're not being rational about this. You can't tell me you have a good argument for keeping it. Why are you so set on having a baby right now?"

"That's not it," Emma said. It wasn't something she could break into a list of pros and cons, because there was only one *pro* that mattered— she wanted this child, wanted this little life to kindle inside of her. She didn't know why. She didn't need to. "It's not up for discussion, Nathan."

"There's a time limit on these things," he said, but she didn't answer. She thought of after the accident, after the doctor had told her that she might not be able to safely carry a pregnancy to term. The way Nathan's face had crumpled, and for the next week he slept with his back to her, could hardly meet her eyes. But she'd healed. Better than anyone had expected. He'd been the one to cry when they got the news, pressing his face to the crook of her neck.

He let out a frustrated sigh. "I just hate having to wonder how many more secrets you're keeping. It's like you've been putting on an act the whole time we've been married," he said.

"What do you want me to say?" she asked. For once, she couldn't tell. Should she cry? Should she plead? Should she shout at him in turn? Did he want her anger, or her confession?

"I don't know, Emma. The truth, maybe?" Nathan asked.

"I don't even know what the truth is. If I did, I would tell you, and we could be done with this."

"Come on. That's bullshit," Nathan said, slamming his palm on the table so hard she jumped. "You know plenty. You still haven't told me what happened. Why? Are you hiding something that would make you look guilty?"

She remembered, suddenly, standing in front of her father in the study while he sat in that huge chair with its oak arms and dark upholstery, a glass of amber liquid sweating in his hand. Remembered her silence, and all her meaningless noise as she tried to explain and justify and apologize, to find the secret code, the combination of contrition and logic that would spare her the punishment she had never once managed to evade.

Nathan's face was red, his jaw clenched. He wouldn't hit her. He'd never hit her. He was not like her father.

But there was nothing she could say to apologize, she knew that. He would push and push and push and she would have no answer, and this precarious balance of theirs would topple at last, and it would be her fault.

She couldn't stop it. But she could make it so that it wasn't her fault. Not only her fault.

She looked up at him, and her lips parted to speak. His face was ruddy with anger, lines deep at the corners of his mouth. *I know*, she could have told him.

She stood instead. She walked to the hall, plucking her purse from its place on the credenza.

"Where are you going?" Nathan asked.

"Out," she said. Because if she stayed, they would break. She would lose him.

"Emma." He put himself in her path.

"I just need some air," she said. She started to step around him. He grabbed her arm, jerking her to a stop. She looked down at his hand, fingers dimpling the skin of her upper arm. Tight enough to balance on the edge of pain.

He let her go.

She was afraid of so many things; he had never been one of them, and he wasn't now. But she couldn't be here.

"When are you going to tell me what happened?" he asked.

Never, she thought. "Soon," she said.

This time, he let her leave.

23

EMMA

Now

Wilson's was a bar utterly without personality; it didn't slouch into dive bar territory or manage the gloss necessary to be trendy. It was a bar you only ever ended up at because it was the only one open or the only one close by.

As soon as she opened the door she spotted the man she was looking for down at the end of the bar, pulling a pint. At forty, Logan Ellis had a few flecks of gray in his hair and more definition to his jaw, but little else about him had changed. Still good-looking in that slightly off-putting way, still with those pale eyes. His attention flicked up to her, and he raised a few fingers in a perfunctory greeting, not showing a glimmer of recognition. She made her way down to the other end of the bar and sat, watching as he delivered the beer to the only other patron in the bar before coming back her way.

Logan approached. A puzzled smile crossed his features, and he rested his hands on the bar. "Emma Palmer. My dad mentioned you were back in town."

"I'm sure he's thrilled," Emma said.

He laughed, not unpleasantly. "Yeah, he's not exactly your biggest fan. What can I get you? Club soda and lime?"

"Sure." His father must have told him that, too. He set the drink in front of her. There were tattoos climbing up his arms, smudged with age. Clumsy images of demons and dice, an anchor with an unreadable banner. She caught the edge of the smell of him, musk and soap.

She took a sip, remembering that she hated club soda. Studied him while he studied her. Her ice clinked in her glass as she tipped it back and forth in her hand idly.

"Why are you here, Emma Palmer?" he asked. "It's not for the drink and it's not for the ambience, so what is it?"

"You and my sister," she said.

"Me and your sister," he replied with a half grin. "So you heard about that."

"I was kind of hoping it wasn't true," she said.

"Can't imagine someone like me with the perfect princess of Arden Hills?" he asked, and laughed. It was an unkind sound, like a crow's warning call.

"Is that why you slept with her? You wanted to ruin the pretty princess?" Emma asked.

His face darkened. "No. Look. I liked her. I did. A lot more than she liked me, I think."

Emma considered him. She'd met Logan a handful of times as a kid. Her dad wasn't close to Ellis like he was with Hadley, but they were friendly. When Logan was a teenager, he'd been around the house a few times when they had dinner with the Ellises. She remembered a boy who couldn't seem to hold still, constant motion and a tension in the air that made her nervous. He seemed more settled now, but there was still a taut feeling to the air. Something getting ready to snap.

"Were you at the Saracen house the night my parents died?" she asked.

He set his weight back a bit, surprised. "Jesus, you don't beat around the bush."

"Were you?"

"Playing detective?"

"Just asking questions," she told him. "Please. Help me out?" she asked, and she didn't have to fake the desperate plea in her voice.

Something shifted in his face—a look of sympathy or maybe pity appearing briefly in his eyes before he nodded reluctantly. He glanced over at the guy with the beer at the end of the bar. Dropped his voice. "Sure, I was there at some point."

"And Juliette?"

He didn't answer right away. She just waited, eyes locked with his. "She was with me for a while. She took off," he said at last.

"Where?"

"I don't know," he said slowly, irritation roughening his voice. "She wasn't in a talking mood. We had an argument, sort of. She ran off on me."

"And you didn't see her again? You don't know where she went?" Emma asked.

"No," he insisted, but his eyes dodged away from her. He was lying, Emma thought—or hiding something.

"Did you give my sister anything?" Emma asked.

"Oh, that's low-hanging fruit," he said with a lewd chuckle she thought was a bit performative.

She rolled her eyes. "You know what I mean."

"She partook on occasion," he acknowledged.

"That night?"

"Probably."

"What?"

"I don't remember," he said. "Would've been oxy. Benzos, maybe. Look. Juliette was a good kid who wanted to be bad for a while. She would've gotten bored with me pretty soon, if things hadn't happened the way they did."

"But she took something, and she ran off. That's why you were looking for her," Emma said. She was still struggling to imagine Juliette out in the woods. Juliette high. Juliette having sex. In her memory, Juliette was a white cardigan and fingers resting lightly on ivory keys.

If Juliette had been on something and came back to the house, could she have lost it? Done something?

Logan folded his arms. "I wanted her to have a good time, that's all. I wouldn't have given her much. And she was a lightweight. Didn't take after her mother in that respect."

Emma jerked in surprise, her mouth dropping open. The flash of satisfaction on his face told her the effect was intentional. "You're saying my mother was a client?" she asked. She ought to have been offended, incredulous, but it made a certain amount of sense. The "migraine pills" Emma didn't remember her ever going to the pharmacy for, the way she would just seem to vanish from herself from time to time.

"Yeah. Now and then," Logan said with an easy shrug.

"What did she use?" Emma asked, and Logan gave her a strange look. She supposed she should have acted more shocked and less genuinely curious.

"Why do you want to know?" Logan asked.

"I'm not here to get you in trouble," Emma said, spreading her hands. "I want answers about my family. Help me out."

Logan grunted. "It's been a long time," he hedged. "She probably bought what all the rich not-that-kind-of-junkie junkies bought. Valium, Vicodin, oxy, whatever their preferred flavor. A few at first and then more and then too much, and either they got clean, got in trouble, or got above my pay grade."

"Above your pay grade meaning . . ." she prompted.

"Heroin," he said simply. Emma gave him a skeptical look. "Never heard of the opioid epidemic? Eventually the semilegal stuff stops doing the job. But like I said, above my pay grade. If it wasn't something you could at least theoretically get with a doctor's note, I didn't stock it."

"Right. So how long?" she asked.

"How long did I sell to her, you mean? I think about five years," Logan said, scratching his chin as he did the math in his head.

"Right under your dad's nose."

He smirked a little. "No risk, no reward, right? Besides, he's not the white knight he likes to let people think he is."

She thought of Ellis across the table, playing the concerned father figure while urging her to incriminate herself. How frustration had crept in quickly, his face turning red as his voice got louder.

"And what about now?" she asked. "Still selling?"

"Clean as a whistle," he said. Leaned an elbow on the bar. Leaned in *too* close. "Cross my heart and hope to die."

His eyes fixed on hers. He did have pretty eyes, she thought. Maybe that was what Juliette saw in him. Or maybe it was only that he was so unlike what she was supposed to want. That, Emma could understand.

"Did my mother always pay on time, Logan?" Emma asked lightly.

He chuckled. "Nice try. I wasn't even selling to her at that point."

"So she got clean, got in trouble, or went above your pay grade?" she asked. She would have known if her mother was using *heroin*, wouldn't she?

"Or she was getting it from somewhere else," Logan said.

"Where?"

He worked his jaw, like he was considering not telling her. "I can't say for sure."

"But you have a theory," Emma said, raising an eyebrow. He wanted to talk. He wanted her leaning in close, listening to what he had to say; he wanted to be important, and there were precious few opportunities to be important when you worked at a place like Wilson's, lived in a place like Arden.

"It's nothing." Logan shook his head.

"Does it have to do with my father?" Emma guessed, and Logan froze. Something illegal, involving her father. Drugs wouldn't have been her guess. Her law-and-order father thought they should bring the firing squad back, thought "druggies" should be rounded up and put in camps—preferably along with liberals, IRS agents, and anyone who called their pets "fur babies."

But she was realizing more and more how little she'd known him—or any of them. Her parents, her sisters. She'd been so wrapped up in her own anger and misery, she'd never looked twice at the people closest to her.

Logan wetted his lips. "Emma. I was a cuddly teddy bear compared to some of the people out there. I was a dumbass with a lucrative hobby, and I don't mind talking about it. Other people, they're not going to be so nice, if you ask questions."

"My father is dead. He's not going to hurt anyone," Emma said.

"Yeah, he's dead. And someone killed him."

"General wisdom says that was me," Emma reminded him.

"Nah," he said. "I never bought that."

"You might be the only one."

"I'm good at reading people," he said. "You might act tough, Emma Palmer, but you're a gooey chocolate chip cookie on the inside."

"You have a way with words," she said dryly.

He waggled his eyebrows. "It's not the only thing I have a way with."

"I'm married," she told him.

"And does he make you happy, Emma Palmer?" Logan asked, jokingly.

"He makes me feel less alone," she said. Logan fell silent, both of them startled by the answer. He shifted his weight, uncomfortable.

"Emma, all I know is that one of your dad's guys paid me a hundred bucks to spend a night shifting cargo between trucks after hours. I don't know what it was and I don't know where it came from, but it can't have been legal. But maybe go ask Gabriel Mahoney why his dad got fired. Or don't. Like I said, there's a lot of bad people out there. I wouldn't want a nice girl like you getting involved with them."

"I can look after myself."

"You sure about that?" Logan asked. All that sleepiness was gone. His gaze was intent. Intrusive. He put a glass in front of her and poured a trickle of amber liquid in it, barely a swallow.

"I can't," she said.

"One sip won't hurt anything, and you need it."

She picked up the glass, staring at it for a moment. Whiskey. Her father's favored drink, faithfully transferred to a crystal decanter each week. He didn't often drink to excess, but he drank steadily, from the time he got home to the time he went to bed. This stuff was cheaper than that; she could smell it from here. She knocked it back. Hardly a swallow, but it scorched all the way down.

"That's better," he said.

Emma made an unamused noise in the back of her throat. "I should go."

"But you don't want to," he replied, unsmiling.

He was wrong. She did want to go home. Because Nathan was at home, and she loved Nathan. Maybe she'd never fallen in love with him, but she loved him. She had to. Because he was the man who had never left her. Even when he had the option. She knew him. She knew his flaws and she knew the worst thing he was capable of.

That had been enough before. It would have to be enough now.

She rose, reaching for her wallet. "Thank you for the drink."

"On the house," he said. "And tell you what. Give me your number. Could be I think of a few things from back then. I can let you know."

She didn't trust Logan's affability, that easy way he let things roll off him. There was a hard glint hiding behind those eyes. He let things go in the moment, she thought, but she doubted he forgot them.

Still.

She scribbled her number on a napkin and put a bill down on the bar. "Thanks again, Logan," she said, and made her way to the door.

24

JULIETTE

Then

She's aiming for the door. She almost misses, banging her shoulder against the frame and stumbling down the front steps.

"Juliette!" Logan is behind her. She stops, closes her eyes.

Not like that. She wanted it but not like that, and she shouldn't have wanted it at all. She knows what she is. She knows it should be fine, but it isn't, not for her, not for her father.

Logan, laughing, catches her arm and pulls her around. "Hey. Babe. What's wrong?"

"I'm not—" she begins. She gestures. "I don't like girls."

"Aren't all girls just a little bisexual?" he asks. He sticks a finger through one of her belt loops and tugs her against him. "Come on. It's just for fun. It's hot." His breath is loud against her ear; he kisses her neck. He's leaning forward, enough that she can't hold up his weight, has to step back and back again, until her shoulders hit the rough bark of a tree. "Don't worry. I know what you do like."

He unbuttons her jeans. With her weight braced against the tree, his mouth against her throat, he works his fingers between her legs until she is stifling her cries, her eyes shut, her head tipped back. As soon as he's done, a familiar feeling of shame floods through her, the need to not be touched or seen. She turns her face away.

She remembers coming back from homecoming. Her date kissed her goodbye. Did more than kiss her, leaning in, opening his mouth to slip his tongue between her lips. She kissed him back, delighted by the novelty of it, even if she had no interest in the boy himself, who had all the substance of damp cardboard. Her father saw.

He didn't say anything. But the next day he asked her to bring him one of his guns, saying he needed to clean it, and then he spun the cylinder and sighted casually down the barrel at her and mentioned, as if out of nowhere, that he'd rather his daughters be dead than be whores.

Three weeks later she went out again with the same boy and she leaned his car seat back and fucked him in the parking lot behind the gas station, all of their clothes still on. She'd always assumed it would hurt, but it didn't. She didn't even bleed.

"My turn," Logan whispers in her ear. His hand goes to her shoulder, pressing down.

She shakes her head. "Not right now," she says.

"Come on. I made you feel good. And I know you can tell how much I want you," he says, pressed against her.

She doesn't mind them—blow jobs. The name is ridiculous and so is the act, but it's fine. Faster than sex, at least, and she doesn't spend the whole time trying to think of something to make herself excited, make herself come, because he's always so sulky when he knows she didn't. But everything is turning sour in her mind and her stomach, and his touch feels filthy with grit, feels unbearable.

"Not right now," she says, and shoves him away. Not hard. Not weakly, either. He steps back, spreading his hands.

"Whoa. No worries," he says, and she reminds herself that Logan has never pushed, only ever asked. He takes out his flask, offers it to her. She accepts, drinks deeply. It's warm in her hand, like the grip of the revolver when her father handed it back to her.

"Turns out it's still clean. Don't need to do anything about it yet."

"Maybe you'd rather go down on Nina after all," Logan says with a smirk.

"Fuck off," she says.

"I'm just saying. I wouldn't mind having a front-row seat, if you wanted. I bet she'd be up to it."

"Shut your fucking mouth already," Juliette snaps, panic rising in her throat like bile. Does he know? Can he tell? He can't know. No one can. Not until she gets away, and she can't get away until Daphne is out of the house, because Emma doesn't understand how the rules work, that someone needs to keep Mom and Dad happy so that they don't realize that Daphne is strange in a way that they haven't quite noticed and will never understand.

He gives her a look. "What's up with you tonight?" he asks. He reaches out to touch her cheek; she slaps him away.

"Don't touch me." *He knows he knows he's going to find out—*

"I'm just—"

"Don't touch me! Leave me alone! Fuck *off*!" she yells, shoving him hard in the chest, and then to her horror she bursts into tears.

Logan, baffled, stares at her.

"The fuck did you do, Ellis?" Nina asks, storming out of the house.

No, no, no, not her, Juliette thinks. Nina and Logan are shouting at each other. He throws up his hands. Nina stalks past, yells something at him that Juliette can't hear over the sound of her own sobs.

Then Nina has her arms around her, shushing her. "What did he do? Are you okay?"

Juliette shakes her head. He didn't do anything. He didn't do anything, but she can't seem to stop crying.

"Come on," Nina says. Holding Juliette close, she walks her away from the house. Nina guides her to a toppled log. Juliette realizes they're next to the road. "I parked a little farther along. I'll go get the car, you stay here. I'll take you home. Don't move."

Juliette nods miserably. Embarrassment is beginning to overtake the roil of emotions. She can't think. What is she doing?

She still has Logan's flask. She takes another drink. Her eyes feel gummy. Logan is never going to talk to her again, she thinks, and finds she doesn't care. She wishes she knew what he gave her, what they're supposed to do to you, because she can't tell which parts of what she's feeling are her and which are chemicals and whether it matters. She's alone. Nina isn't there.

She can't be alone with Nina. She can't. Because Nina knows, doesn't she? She knew when she pulled away from that kiss.

Juliette stands. Nina is going to be back soon. She can see headlights in the distance. She wipes her mouth on the back of her arm.

Alone, less than two hours before a shot is fired into the back of her father's head, less than five until her sister will instruct her in how to lie, she staggers into the trees, heading toward home, and dark waters close over her mind.

25

JJ

Now

Y*ellow wallpaper, white grip, red hand.*

The memories had been submerged for years, but here in Arden Hills JJ couldn't seem to keep them from looping through her mind.

Vic hadn't wanted her to come. They'd fought about it. Loudly, as usual, but that was always a relief. She always knew when it came to Vic that nothing went unsaid, no secret feelings smothered in the name of propriety and appearances.

"It's a trap," Vic had told her, chopping onions with a speed and precision that was both impressive and a bit intimidating.

"You think Emma is setting a trap for me?" JJ asked, hip propped against the counter, arms crossed. Vic had her hair in locs piled artfully on her head and a smudge of turmeric on her cheek; her palms were stained with it, too, and the kitchen already smelled divine from toasting spices for the curry.

"No, I think she's walking into the same trap that you are. It's not literal, it's spiritual," Vic said, gesturing with the knife alarmingly. She was wearing a white undershirt and bright pink boy briefs, since the kitchen in their tiny apartment was too goddamn hot for pants this time of year, by her own official assessment. It made it harder to argue with her. "You're going back there for, what, closure? There's no such thing."

"What if she finds something?" JJ asked.

"If there was anything to find, the cops would've found it back then."

"Hadley kept them focused on Emma."

"And that's what this is really about, isn't it? You feel bad that Emma took the blame. But that wasn't your fault."

JJ hadn't answered. She'd told Vic so much—more than she'd ever told anyone. But there were things she hadn't admitted even to her.

"If I'd told them everything, they wouldn't have been looking at Emma. They would have been looking at me," JJ said.

Vic chopped the end off a carrot with more force than was strictly necessary. "And that's a good thing?" She set down the knife and stepped over to JJ, putting her hands on either side of JJ's face. "Babe. Going back there is just inviting the worst kind of energy into your life. You want to fix things with Emma, call her. Don't go back there and stir up things that might hurt you. Hurt us."

JJ leaned her forehead against Vic's, breathing in the scent of her, of cloves and coriander. "All right. I won't go," she said.

Yet in the end, she had. She still couldn't tell if it was for the reason Vic assumed—a search for closure—or out of fear of what Emma might discover. She wasn't sure what she was going to do when she got there, only that she had to go.

Yellow wallpaper, white grip, red hand.

She hadn't had a plan, or even the notion of one.

She had always thought of herself as the one in control. The one who knew what to do, who understood the world and how to survive it. Emma was too angry and foolish, Daphne too strange and disconnected, but Juliette was practical, savvy, worldly in a way no one guessed. She'd believed it up until she'd stood there panicking, with her mother's body three feet away, and Emma was the one who spoke with perfect, frightening calm, laying out what they had to do.

Now she was turning that methodical bent to asking the questions JJ had been terrified of for fourteen years. JJ had gotten a Facebook message from Logan Ellis of all people, warning her that Emma was nosing around. The only reason no one had looked at Emma was they had no idea what Juliette had been up to, sneaking out with Logan. Now Emma knew.

And JJ still didn't have a plan.

She was sitting in a dingy motel room, flipping her lighter open and shut, when her phone rang. The number was unfamiliar and so was the voice, when she answered, but the woman said her name like she knew her.

"JJ. It's been a while," the woman said.

"Daphne?" she said incredulously.

"You and I need to talk. It's important."

"This is Daphne, isn't it?" JJ asked, brows drawing together.

There was a huff, impatient. "Yes. It's Daphne."

"Why are you calling?" JJ asked. "I thought you said I wasn't ever supposed to contact you."

"That was a long time ago. Things are different now," Daphne said.

"Different how?" JJ asked. What was Daphne doing calling her?

"Emma's back at the house, that's how," Daphne said, sounding a touch impatient. "They're going to be cleaning the place out. Rooting around."

"There's nothing to find," JJ said. They'd covered their tracks. "Emma made sure of it." She stood, pacing in a tight circuit back and forth on the cheap motel carpet.

"Emma didn't know about everything. She didn't know about the gun," Daphne said.

JJ's heart dropped. "What gun?" she whispered.

"You know exactly what gun I'm talking about," Daphne said deliberately.

JJ shut her eyes. *Yellow wallpaper. White grip. Red hand.* "It wasn't there. The police never found it."

"Because I hid it, JJ," Daphne told her. "I hid it in the carriage house that night, before Emma got home."

JJ couldn't breathe. She squeezed her eyes shut. "I gave Nathan the keys to the carriage house."

"I know," Daphne said with a sigh. "And that means that we need to decide what to do."

JJ sank down onto the bed.

Vic had been right. She shouldn't have come.

Everything was falling apart, and this time, Emma wasn't going to be willing to shoulder the blame.

26

EMMA

Now

Emma didn't go back right away. She sat in the park instead, letting time spool out in the hopes that it would give Nathan's temper time to cool. She drove home slowly, not eager to find out if her return would mean picking up the fight where they left off. When she pulled into the drive, the carriage house door was open a crack, and there was a light on inside. Rattling and banging echoed from the interior, the unmistakable soundtrack of Nathan's "organizing" spree that had spanned half the house so far.

Feeling cowardly, she went inside the house instead of checking on him.

It turned out she hadn't known Juliette at all. Hadn't realized her mother was on drugs. Hadn't known that her father was involved in some kind of criminal enterprise. What else hadn't she seen back then?

She'd missed something.

She was still missing something.

She walked through the rooms. They were gutted, their contents strewn over surfaces and the floor, stuffed into bulging garbage bags, collected in untidy heaps. They bristled with labels. KEEP, SELL, DONATE, TOSS in Nathan's careless blocky script. As if he had a right to any of it.

None of this held the answers she was looking for. She stood in front of the gun cabinet. On a whim she grabbed a pad of Post-it notes, scrawled TOSS on one, and slapped it onto the glass.

She walked to the study. Nathan had wanted to take it over, but she'd insisted he use the kitchen as his office instead. She couldn't stand him in here, steeping in the scent of this room, her father's sanctuary. The old whiskey decanter was still there, cap in place, two inches of liquid in the bottom. She turned up a glass—SELL—and poured. She held it up, the cold edge against her lip, inhaling the caramel and smoke smell without drinking. It was a different beast altogether than what Logan had served her. She remembered the taste of it, the way it had burned.

She'd been fifteen and rebellious; she'd sneaked a sip, and her father had caught her. Of course he had; she wasn't the one that got away with things. He told her it was fine, that she could have some. Have some more. He made her drink until she got sick, to cure her, he said, of the desire.

She set the glass down, walked to the desk. There were papers here, sorted into thick stacks. The silver letter opener—SELL. The crystal paperweight—SELL. The fountain pen propped up on a wooden stand—SELL.

She flipped through pages of papers. More bills, forms, letters, the kind of endless paperwork of a time before much of anything was digital. There was nothing that looked at all suspicious. If there had been, the police would have found it fourteen years ago. Dad didn't bring business home.

But her mother had known something. She'd told Chris as much. And then there was the flash drive. Emma closed her eyes, trying to picture it. The first time she'd seen it, her mother was kneeling in Daphne's room, rooting through the closet. Emma stood in the hall, watching her through the sliver of open space between the door and the frame. Irene Palmer had looked, for once in her life, disheveled. Out of breath, with a red mark on her jaw the width of a thumb. She had dragged something out of the back of the closet—a metal lockbox, the fireproof kind for important documents.

Her mother had taken a key from her pocket and opened the box. From the box she took a fat wad of bills and added more to it, securing a rubber band around the whole thing and throwing it back in. Then she'd reached into the pocket of her cardigan and taken out the flash drive, tossed it in after.

The front door shut. Irene had jumped and quickly closed the box, locked it, shoved it back into the closet. Emma had crept backward, slipping inside Juliette's room, since it was the closest, not quite shutting the door so it wouldn't make a sound. Juliette, sitting on her bed with a magazine, stared at her. She pressed a finger to her lips, and Juliette nodded.

For all that they'd fought, that rule was never broken. You didn't tell. You kept each other's secrets.

No matter what.

Emma set another page aside. The next paper was a phone bill. There was a handwritten note at the bottom, slantwise and sloppy, as if it had been written idly on the nearest piece of paper without regard for what it was. *Have to do something about Emma*, it said, a half-finished thought.

She walked with precise steps to the spot just behind where the chair would have sat. Like JJ had done before, she raised her hand, fingers extended like a gun barrel. Brought her thumb down. *Bang*.

The idea of him being murdered because of money or drugs was so bloodless against the raw hatred that still burned in her gut when she thought of him. But she couldn't discount the possibility. Whatever was on that flash drive, it was something her mother wanted hidden. The evidence she claimed to have, Emma could only assume. But the flash drive was long gone. She'd lost it that night.

The night they died.

27

EMMA

Then

She shows up on Gabriel's doorstep after dark with her eye already swelling and red, her nose snotty from crying.

"What happened?" he asks, and she tries to tell him, but fresh tears well up and she finds herself sobbing and trying to force words out as he draws her inside and pushes her firmly and gently down onto the couch. "Wait here."

He returns moments later with a bag of frozen peas wrapped in a kitchen towel. He sets it to her eye and guides her hand up to it, because she can't seem to remember what to do by herself. His jaw is tense and his eyes sorrowful as he sits on the coffee table, his knees knocking against hers. They have never been this close, she thinks, and of course it's now when she's the furthest thing from lovely, with the peas against her swelling eye and her face red and puffy.

"Are you hurt anywhere else?" he asks. She shakes her head; it's all she can manage. "Who did this? Your father?"

"They ruined it all. They took everything," she says.

"Who?" he asks, confusion written on his features. "What happened, Emma?"

"I can't go back," she manages. "I can't go back. They'll kill me. Please, Gabriel, I can't—you have to—"

He hushes her. He shifts to the couch and gathers her in his arms and she sobs against his chest as he murmurs meaningless things and strokes her back. She can hear his heartbeat, steady and strong within the cage of his ribs.

"Nana's still in the hospital, but you can stay here as long as you need to," he says. "I won't let anything happen to you."

When she is done crying, he takes her to his bed. It's a bed in Lorelei Mahoney's house, and so it is firm and has fresh sheets and smells of fabric softener, and he draws a blanket up over her. He sits on the end of the bed, leaning forward with his elbows on his knees. She shuts her eyes. Eventually, she drifts into a sleep unencumbered by dreams.

She doesn't know how much later his weight shifting on the bed wakes her. She keeps her eyes closed and her breathing even, letting him think she is asleep as he draws near.

"It's going to be okay," he tells her. She wonders if he knows he's lying. "You're safe here." He bends over her and brushes a kiss lightly at her temple.

He leaves. She holds still, fearing he'll know she's awake, that it will somehow ruin this moment. The front door opens, closes. Outside, a car starts. She pulls the blanket aside and pads out to the front room in time to watch his headlights disappearing. She stands alone in the house, shivering despite the warm night.

Gabriel is wrong. He is kind, but he is wrong—nothing will be okay. Nowhere is safe. Not unless she does something.

She slips on her shoes and heads out.

She leaves Lorelei's house with half a plan wrapped in fierce conviction. She can't go back home. She has to get away. And so she *has* to go back home, because she ran out of the door with nothing and she has nowhere to go. She needs clothes, needs supplies. Most of all, she needs money.

And she knows where she can find it.

It's after eleven o'clock as Emma walks up Grant Lane, then cuts through the woods past the Saracen house. There are flashlights and lanterns on inside and a couple of kids out front trying to stoke a sad-looking fire. One of them looks her way as she walks, but at this distance she's sure she's nothing but a dim silhouette. There is a light in the tree house as well, at the edge of the lawn. She skirts around it, giving it plenty of room so she won't be spotted.

Emma creeps her way through the house without turning on any lights and takes the stairs silently, well practiced. She looks behind her once at the sliver of light at the bottom of the study door, barely visible at the end of the hall. There's no sign of movement. At the top of the stairs she hooks a right to go to her parents' door. Here she hesitates. If she's wrong, and her mother is awake, the whole plan will fall apart.

But when she opens the door her mother is, as usual, sleeping soundly. The glass on her bedside table still has half an inch of white wine in it, and beside it is one of her migraine pills. Irene is sleeping half-twisted, the side of her face pressed against the pillow and one hand up next to it, the other flung behind her. It does not look restful, her face contorted as if she is having a bad dream. Emma stands watching her for a moment as her mother's eyes roll under her lids. She has thought many times about killing her parents. Finding a way to get a gun from the case or a knife from the kitchen, pressing a pillow to her mother's sleeping face. Irene Palmer is a slim woman who has stayed that way through deprivation; there is no substance or strength to her. If Emma wrapped her hands around that thin neck—

But every time, that's where it ends. There is no *after* to that fantasy.

Using only the tips of her fingers she opens the drawer in the nightstand and reaches all the way to the back, snagging the loop of a single small key. She draws it out and retreats. She doesn't glance back; she doesn't realize this is the last time she will see her mother alive, that their last words to each other have already been spoken.

The lockbox is where she remembers, nestled beneath layers and layers of pink and yellow sweaters and caps. Their mother keeps all of their baby clothes in spotless condition, though it became clear long ago that their father was never going to agree to have another child. Irene Palmer loved having babies. Loved their cooing and laughter and smiles, loved how she alone could soothe their cries.

She wanted more than anything to have that version of motherhood back. The one where she was the world, and she understood every need.

Emma claws aside the clothes and pulls out the lockbox. It opens readily to the key. Inside is a small envelope, a thick roll of bills, and the flash drive.

Emma peers inside the envelope. It contains her mother's passport, Social Security card, and birth certificate. There is also a green Post-it note with a phone number scrawled on it in an unfamiliar hand. Emma doesn't recognize the number.

None of this is particularly interesting, except that her mother is hiding it. Emma picks up the USB drive, frowning. If these were just important documents, her mother would keep them in the safe in the study. But she's taken them out, hidden them here. Why?

Downstairs, the study door opens. Emma swears under her breath. She shoves her mother's documents back in the box and puts the money into her pocket. On instinct, she grabs the flash drive, too, then piles clothes back on top of the lockbox, not bothering to leave them neat, and pushes the whole thing back into the closet.

In her own room, she throws clothes and everything she can think of into her backpack, zips it shut. The toilet downstairs flushes. Footsteps make their way back to the study, and Emma lets herself relax. She steals back down the stairs, heart hammering, and out through the kitchen.

She shoves her feet into her shoes hastily. She doesn't realize that one of them has come untied until she takes off running, until the lace gets caught under her foot and she sprawls at the edge of the yard with a grunt she's certain will be heard from the house. She scrambles back up and runs flat out, her backpack slapping against her back, the thick bulk of the roll of bills comforting in her jacket pocket. She knows the money is still there, and so she does not think to check for a small, undistinctive flash drive. She does not notice the face in the tree house window, watching her run. Watching her fall.

She does not see the small form climbing down the ladder and walking to where she stumbled to examine the glint of metal in the dirt.

28

EMMA

Now

She slept lightly, expecting Nathan's weight on the mattress to wake her at any moment, but it didn't. When she did wake, she didn't remember what had stirred her from her sleep; she had only the sense that she'd heard something. She made her way to the window. The courtyard was quiet. Still. There was a light on in the carriage house.

She looked at the alarm clock beside her bed, blaring out its glowing blue numbers. It was past midnight. Nathan had always been a night owl. She glimpsed him briefly, walking past the lit window on the ground level of the carriage house, and then drew the curtains closed.

If he was avoiding her, she wouldn't push. He would stay. Surely he would stay.

Yet dawn greeted her with unsympathetic light slashing through the blinds, and Nathan had never returned to bed. No toast this morning either. She threw up, brushed her teeth—which made her retch all over again—and stumbled downstairs, cursing her unborn and clearly ungrateful child.

Nathan's laptop was out on the kitchen table, taking up half the space on the table with its external keyboard and mouse and second monitor and a USB adaptor flopping aimlessly from one port. He even had a can of compressed air out—he was so meticulous about keeping crumbs and dust out of his keyboard. She'd always thought the point of a laptop was portability, but Nathan never used his without all his peripherals. She closed the lid and went over to her phone, which was charging on the counter where she'd left it.

She'd missed a call from a former client. She checked the voice mail and made a mental note to follow up, then idly scrolled through her emails, distracting herself as she pinched tiny bits of bread off and tried to fool her gut into thinking they were something other than food. A client had finally paid a tardy invoice—good, that would help.

No sign of Nathan still. Frowning, she wandered through the house. There was a blanket on the couch in the living room, like he'd slept there, but no sign of Nathan himself.

A momentary panic stabbed through her gut. He was gone. He'd left—but he hadn't *left*, she told herself. His things were still upstairs in the bedroom, his laptop on the kitchen table. And where would he have gone?

There was one place. The thought was traitorous. She looked down at the phone in her hand. She closed her email and swiped over to where the phone tracker app waited, her thumb hovering over it.

He'd gone out on an errand, or for coffee, or to get some air, she told herself. She wasn't going to be the one who didn't trust him. She turned off the display and jammed the phone in her pocket.

She got to work, as she had every day, without a particular plan. Today she went through the labeled items, actually throwing away the trash, surreptitiously removing some of the TOSS and DONATE labels for things she thought they'd need to check with her sisters.

She took an old vacuum cleaner—definitely on its last legs, but they didn't have the budget for a replacement—and went to tackle the rug in the front living room. Through the window she glimpsed the car, and stopped, frowning. Nathan hadn't left, then. So where was he? Not still out in the carriage house, surely. She bit her lip. If he was truly avoiding her that thoroughly, she didn't want to intrude. She grabbed a stray glass from a sideboard and marched determinedly back to the kitchen. She opened the dishwasher to put it in and paused.

There were two wineglasses snuggled inside the dishwasher, the purplish stains of red wine caked to the bottom. She lifted one, turning it in her hand. There was a lip print on one side, bright red. And there was the bottle, in the recycling. Empty. Someone had been here last night, while she was out. Someone who wore red lipstick.

Someone Nathan might have left with.

Reluctantly, she took her phone from her pocket and this time she opened the app before she could talk herself out of it.

The dot that showed Nathan's phone was indeed in the carriage house, practically dead center, and for a moment she scolded herself for letting her imagination run wild. But the dot was grayed out. A last known location, not his current location. She waited, thinking it might need a moment to load, but nothing happened. His phone was off.

And that was, in itself, bizarre. He was addicted to that thing. She had ground rules about putting photos of her on the internet, but every other part of his life was recorded, uploaded, and captioned. He followed celebrities on Twitter and replied like they actually wanted to hear his witty rejoinders and compliments. He kept up long text threads throughout the day—though that had been quieter lately.

He hadn't even turned off his phone when—

She cut off the thought. Anxious possibilities spilled from her mind, impossible to claw back once they were free. Nathan at the bottom of a ladder with his neck twisted around. Nathan in the passenger seat of a car, so eager to leave he didn't bother to pack. *Nathan slumped in a chair with a hole in his skull, in the hall in a pool of blood, shirt stained dark—*

She pressed the heels of her palms to her eyes. She should leave him alone. Give him space. She knew this. Except now those images were in her mind, and she could only spin through the same loop over and over again. *He's fine. Almost certainly fine. Except what if he isn't?*

She knew how this would go. She would sit on the couch, steeling herself unsuccessfully against panic, picking up one horrifying possibility after another and playing it through to its end. As if by working out the logistics of each fate, she could make it hurt less. The same thing seized her sometimes when he was even a few minutes late getting home from work. By the time he walked in through the door, she had worked out getting to the hospital or calling his parents to break the news, thought about where the life insurance documents were, imagined a rotating cast of doctors or police offers saying, *"Ma'am, we're sorry to have to tell you . . ."*

Nathan always found it amusing. He laughed at her for the grand tragic scripts she wrote out in her head. But it wasn't at all amusing to be inside of that relentless what-if. The only way she could bear it without panicking was to make those detailed plans.

"You could have just checked the app," he would always tell her, and she would try to explain how *that* would mean she really was being overly anxious and spying on him to make herself feel better. So instead she fretted and pretended not to, and stopped asking him to text her if he was going to be late, because he always forgot anyway.

He wasn't on the road and out of reach, though, he was thirty steps away, and she was being ridiculous. She would poke her head in. Say good morning. Say she was sorry, yet again, and hope that this time it was enough.

She put her phone away and arranged her face in an expression of what she hoped was only casual interest. She made herself walk unhurriedly out the door.

The lock on the carriage house door was undone, sitting on the step. She pulled the latch, swinging the heavy door open, and stood at the threshold. Dust swirled inside, lit by the slant of sunlight coming in; the interior was dim, and her eyes struggled to adjust. It had been decades since a horse or carriage had been inside this building, but two stalls remained to the far right. The rest of the space had been left open to store the actual carriages, but her father had converted it into a workshop, for those times when he decided that being a man meant cutting up pieces of wood and screwing them together in a different configuration. There were workbenches and a variety of tools set against the walls, including a table saw and a miter saw and other things that might have been worth a bit of money, if they were anything close to new or functional.

"Nathan?" she said. No answer. She could feel her pulse at her throat. "Nathan, are you in here?" she asked, though it was obvious that he wasn't.

Then where was he? Where would he go without the car?

Unless someone picked him up, she thought, and chased that idea off into the shadows again.

There were footsteps in the dust, crisscrossing the floor. She followed them inside, lacking anything else useful to do. She stepped around the side of the big worktable in the center of the room, and she froze.

Nathan lay on the ground beside the worktable. His eyes were half-opened. One leg was twisted awkwardly under him where he had fallen. His T-shirt was stained dark, a single neat hole in the fabric at his chest. His face had a look of vague surprise.

Emma stared. All her time imagining the grim possibilities of fate, preparing herself for them to become reality, suddenly made it impossible to comprehend that this was, at last, real.

Nathan wasn't dead. She was sitting on the couch, and in a moment he would walk in and tease her about it and ask how long she'd decided to wait after the funeral before starting to date again, and she would pretend to chuckle and the knot in her stomach would ease. Because it wouldn't happen. Couldn't. How utterly unlikely was it that one of those awful things she had imagined so many times would *actually* come true?

But she had always known they could.

She turned around, a ringing sound in her ears. She stumbled back into the open air, gulping down one breath after another that didn't seem to be sufficient, and suddenly the world tipped and her vision filled with brightly colored lights that swarmed and swelled, and she felt her knees impact the drive, gravel digging into her palms that splayed against the ground.

Then suddenly she wasn't alone—there was someone there, a blur of teal, the sharp bark of a dog.

"Here you go. I've got you," someone was saying. Emma was dimly aware of being helped to her feet, guided—or more like carried—toward the house. As she stepped inside, her vision went dark again, and she felt her legs giving way, heard the quick, alarmed exclamation of her rescuer—and then, mercifully, nothing.

29

DAPHNE

Then

The night her parents die, Daphne sits in the tree house, her arms around her knees. She's too old for the tree house. It's a child's refuge, the ceiling so low that even she has to stoop to fit inside. When they sleep together out here, it's so crowded they jam knees and elbows into each other all night long. Not that they ever sleep together out here anymore. Sometimes one or the other of her sisters will join her, but Emma hasn't in weeks, and Juliette always slips away after night falls, whispering to Daphne not to tell.

Everyone keeps secrets. Daphne keeps everyone's secrets.

If you are quiet enough, small enough, people begin to forget that you still have eyes and ears, that you can hear their murmured conversations and see their furtive errands. Daphne listens at the door to her father's phone calls, and she knows about the drawer of secret things that her mother only brings out on special occasions, when their father is out of town. She knows the two cars that come to the house on those days, the black Taurus and the blue Impala. They're both animals, the bull and the antelope, and she feels like this should mean something.

When the blue Impala comes, her mother puts on makeup. She slides into the passenger seat and rides away, and comes back breathless and giddy.

On those days Daphne worries about the smallest of her secrets. The things that she has gathered up, the things she can't prove but thinks about often. The color of her eyes, the skin that doesn't freckle in the sun, her cleft chin.

What her mother is doing is dangerous.

When the black Taurus comes, it's different. That man comes into the house. Her mother doesn't dress up for him. She hands him money. He leaves. But he hasn't been back since the last time, almost two months ago. "*I don't want to be involved*," he told her mother. "*This isn't what I signed up for. You can have them, but if anyone asks, I'll tell them I've never heard of you.*"

The secrets gather inside her. She's rarely told a secret, but she can't keep them all inside, so on days like this when the pressure grows too intense, she walks out to the bridge over the river. She takes her secrets, whispers them into a stone, and drops them off the side of the bridge to the rushing waters below. The stones carry her secrets to the river and the river swallows them up. But she has no stones now, no river, and so many secrets.

I told Dad about Emma's applications. I pretended I didn't know she wasn't supposed to be applying, but I knew.

She is furious with herself. She wanted Emma to stay, because if Emma leaves, it will just be Juliette. With only Juliette as a point of comparison, Daphne won't have any chance of pleasing their mother. Without Emma, Daphne won't have anyone to turn to when she *does* earn her anger. Juliette doesn't understand her like Emma does. She had to do *something*.

She scrubs her hands over her tear-stained cheeks. And then she hears it—the footsteps in the grass, stumbling and staggering. She looks out the window. In the darkness, it is hard to make out the figure below, to tell light brown hair from dark. Her sister—whichever of them it is—suddenly sprawls, stifling a cry of pain. Daphne almost calls out to her, but then the figure is back on her feet and running through the woods. She's dropped something: a bit of light from the house is enough to see the faint trace of metal in the dirt.

Daphne shimmies down the ladder, curiosity banishing her tears.

She scuttles forward, fingers already snatching at the air, the dirt. Her grasping hands find the small, cold bit of metal and curl around it. She knows what it is by feel. She considers tucking it away in one of her many hidey-holes, but her curiosity is not a patient creature. It turns immediately to kneading claws at the back of her mind.

Dad is in his study. Mom is safely asleep. Easy enough to go in the back door and to the computer in the corner of the great room. They're not allowed to have phones or computers in their rooms. The internet is, after all, a wilderness full of pedophiles and socialists.

The icon pops up on the desktop and she double-clicks it with a delightful churning of anticipation in her gut, hoping she's not about to read Juliette's English homework or something equally boring.

It isn't homework. She isn't sure what it is. Files and files. Images, mostly. Photos of pages in a notebook, columns of numbers. Other papers, typed up neatly, with more numbers. Dates and amounts. The paperwork is for Palmer Transportation. It is not the least bit exciting, and Daphne is disappointed. Then she opens another image file and she's looking at a photograph. It's taken through the window of a car at night. Three men are standing amid a landscape of gray rock, beside a car. One of the men is her father.

One of the men has a gun.

She is about to open another image file when a hand falls on her shoulder. She doesn't jump or make a noise—she goes instinctively still, frozen as a rabbit as a wolf stalks by.

"What do you have, Daphne?" her father asks. Steady and quiet.

"I found it," she whispers. "I think it's from your work. I was going to give it back to you." She unplugs the drive. Hands it to him. He's standing behind her with a blank expression, the most dangerous kind. She holds out the drive, her expression guileless. "Is it for taxes?"

"Yes. That sort of thing," her father says. He takes the drive from her but doesn't take his eyes off her face.

She smiles a little. "It looked boring enough to be taxes," she says.

Another long moment of silence as her insides quiver like Jell-O and her expression stays cheery. Then he gives her a pat on the shoulder. "You should get back to bed."

"I'm sleeping outside today," she says.

"Back to the tree house, then," he says, and nods his chin toward the door. "Go along."

She is rarely on the receiving end of her father's punishments. She's better than even Juliette at understanding what he wants. Juliette thinks it's only obedience, but really it's devotion. So she wraps her arms around his waist, and he puts a hand on the back of her head fondly before she skips away. Before she turns the corner to the kitchen she sees him walking back down the hall to his study, his fist tight around the drive.

She creeps along the side of the house, those needle claws still tickling at the back of her mind. She fits her small body against the house below the study window.

He's on the phone. "I don't know. One of the girls had it. No—I don't know how much she saw," he's saying. Then, "There's no need for that. I'll handle it." Another pause, and now his voice is angry. "Stay home. I told you I would handle it, and I will. You don't need to be here."

He hangs up. She peers over the sill, watches through the crack in the curtains as he opens a drawer in his desk and tosses the flash drive inside before pacing over to the liquor cabinet. He pours himself a hefty measure of whiskey. He stands, staring at nothing, for a long time.

His stillness frightens her. She falls away from the window.

Juliette is Mom's favorite. Daphne has always been puzzled by the knowledge that *she* is Dad's. Maybe it's because she was so small and quiet—he calls her *dainty*. Their mother is frequently horrified by Daphne's macabre interests, but they amuse Dad.

She suspects, though, that what amused him in a preteen will become less and less amusing as she gets older. That one day, it won't be any protection at all.

"I hate knowing you've got to grow up," Dad told her once, and something about it made her very afraid. Afraid like she is now.

She doesn't know what to do. Emma is the one who makes plans.

Something has to be done, she thinks. In the house, the light in the study stays on, and Daphne doesn't dare sleep.

30

EMMA

Now

When Emma was next aware, she was sitting on the couch in the living room, holding a glass of water. Her mouth tasted of vomit. Her hands were red and pockmarked with the impressions of gravel, grit clinging to her skin. She was alone, though she felt like she hadn't been a moment ago, had the vague memory of a woman's voice and gentle hands steering her inside.

Because she'd fainted. Because . . .

Because Nathan was dead. She drew in a long, steadying breath. Her stomach heaved again, but this time she gritted her teeth and kept it down, and took a slug of water as soon as it settled.

Nathan was dead. He had been shot, and she needed to do something. But for all of her what-ifs, she had no plan now, only the yawning impossibility of what she was facing.

She needed to call the police. Except that here, Hadley and Ellis were the police. And this was all too familiar. But what was the alternative? Pretend she hadn't seen? Hide the body? That was ridiculous. A notion born entirely of panic, of her sixteen-year-old self in the interrogation room.

Where was the woman who had helped her? Emma looked around, but the room was empty.

The room was empty, and Nathan was dead.

It still didn't feel true. She took her phone out. Nathan was dead and she needed to call the police. *They'll think you did it.*

The doorbell rang. The sound was so incongruous, the cheerful three-tone chime ringing out through the house, that for a moment she didn't process it at all. She stared through the doorway to the foyer, mouth slightly open. After a long pause, the bell rang again.

Now Emma forced herself to move. She stood, walking jerkily to the front door.

JJ was standing on her front steps. Her mouth was pulled into a frown when Emma opened the door, and her hands were jammed in her back pockets. When she saw Emma, she shifted her weight from foot to foot. "Emma. Hey," she said, not quite meeting Emma's eyes.

"JJ," Emma said, and then wobbled alarmingly. JJ made as if to reach out and then snatched her hand back, rethinking it. Emma grabbed the doorframe. She needed to sit down. "What are you doing here?"

"I came to talk to you. To tell you—shit," JJ said, and tucked her hair behind her ear. "I don't know how to—"

"Nathan is dead," Emma said, cutting her off, because it was suddenly unbearable that JJ could be talking and not know. That anyone could be talking about anything other than that fact.

"What?" It wasn't a question but a statement of shock. Emma gestured behind her.

"He's in the carriage house. He's been shot. My husband's been shot and I haven't called the police yet because they're going to think that I did it, because why shouldn't they? I'm the girl who killed her parents in this house, and now my husband is dead."

JJ looked back at the carriage house. Then at Emma, eyes wide with shock. "But you didn't," she said slowly.

Emma stared past her at nothing in particular. "It doesn't matter. Maybe I'll just tell them I did it. That way it'll be over with faster."

Her vision strobed at the edges. Her shirt was stuck to her chest, soaked through with sweat. JJ reached for her arm again. Emma wrenched it away.

"My husband is dead. I need to—I need to—" Her voice cut off in a sob, and this time when she swayed, she let her sister catch her.

JJ was the one who called the police in the end. They arrived with lights and sirens, filling the courtyard, along with paramedics who came purely to confirm they weren't needed. They'd have to wait for the coroner now. Emma sat in the kitchen, feeling so disconnected she could barely feel the weight of her own body.

"Emma. Emma," Rick Hadley was saying. He snapped his fingers, and she jolted. "You need to tell us what happened, Emma."

When he'd come to the house fourteen years ago, his face had been full of sympathy. There was none of that, now. His expression was hard, with an edge of something like vindication, maybe even a touch of excitement.

"Emma. Who shot your husband?" Hadley asked.

"Hey," JJ snapped. She was standing over at the side of the room, talking to the uniformed officer who'd come about the fireworks. "She's in shock. Leave her alone."

"Get her out of the room," Hadley said, jerking his head, and the woman put her hand out to usher JJ away. Then Emma was alone with Hadley, who pulled a chair around and sat so close his knees nearly knocked into hers. He braced his elbows on his legs as he leaned in to look at her. "Okay, Emma. Let's try this again."

She tried to keep track of what he was saying. She tried to answer, as best she could, but her words kept getting tangled up, and it was like his voice was dipping in and out. She'd seen Nathan in the carriage house last night around eleven. No, she wasn't sure it was him, but she'd assumed it was. She went out this morning and found him there. No, she hadn't gone in more than a few feet. No, she hadn't touched him. Yes, she had the key to the gun case. In the pocket of her other pants, probably.

Her words felt slushy in her mouth, like their edges had gone soft, and she kept losing the ends and beginnings of sentences.

She tried to tell him about the woman, the dog, but she couldn't make him understand. He kept asking her where the gun was; she kept shaking her head. Which gun? There were so many of them, and none of them had ever saved anyone.

"Rick," Ellis said. He was standing in the doorway, hand on his belt. "Look at her. She's barely conscious. Have the paramedics looked at her?"

I'm fine, she tried to say, but no sound came out. Her vision was bright with spots. She bent forward, covering her face with her hands. Then there was a new voice speaking to her, and when she opened her eyes it was not a cop but an EMT crouching in front of her and telling her very kindly that they were taking her to the hospital, which seemed all of a sudden like a very good idea.

A couple of hours later, she'd gotten treatment for shock, dehydration, and mild malnutrition. She lay in a hospital bed in the ER, listening to a child crying two rooms down. Her hand hurt faintly where the IV went in.

JJ was outside on the phone. Emma could just hear the conversation filtering through the door. "I know. But I need to be here. I need to find out what she knows. I have to—Vic, I'm being careful. I promise. Okay. I love you."

She stepped back inside, hanging up the phone. There were dark circles under her eyes, lines at the corners of her mouth where she'd been frowning.

"Boyfriend?" Emma asked.

"Girlfriend. Fiancée, actually," JJ said.

Emma's brow furrowed. "You're gay?"

"Yup. Huge lesbian, turns out," JJ said with a little awkward chuckle. She rubbed the back of her neck.

"Huh," Emma managed. Maybe she should have been more surprised, but it wasn't like she'd known anything about her sister's life to contradict it. Whatever image Dad projected outside the house, Emma had known he was a raging bigot when it came to his family. Juliette had always been so perfect, so eager to please. *JJ*, with her tattoos and wild hair, was a stranger. But maybe this helped explain how she'd gotten from one to the other.

JJ sat in the chair beside the bed. "She didn't want me to come down here. She thought it would just cause more trouble."

"Smart lady," Emma said, and JJ grunted agreement. "You don't have to stay, you know."

"I can't leave you here on your own," JJ said.

"Since when?" Emma asked.

JJ looked away. "Is there *anyone* I can call? Someone to take care of you?"

Nathan, she thought. She remembered when she'd been in the accident last year. A drunk kid in a borrowed pickup slamming into her in an intersection. Her head clipping the window, glass raining around her, a world suddenly defined by pain. She'd been on the phone with Nathan when it happened, and she could hear him shouting her name. He had gotten there while they were loading her into the ambulance, and followed behind. He'd never left her side. Concussion, broken pelvis. It had taken her several months to recover. She'd had to lean on him for help the whole time.

It had been draining, but he hadn't complained.

But Nathan was gone. She needed to call his parents, she realized. They were in Virginia. Retired, Mom on disability. He was their only child, and she was going to have to tell them he was dead.

Her husband was dead and she didn't have time for grief, because she was going to be a suspect. Maybe *the* suspect. She couldn't be lost in sorrow, but she would have to perform it, because thinking clearly was both essential and would be seen as a sign of guilt.

Innocent until proven guilty was for judges and juries. Right now she was dealing with reality, and she didn't have the luxury of sitting around hoping the truth prevailed. She needed to protect herself.

"I need to call my lawyer," she said.

"Uncle Chris?" JJ asked, voice dripping with distaste that Emma didn't understand. "Hadley's best buddy? That lawyer?"

"What are you talking about?" Emma asked, giving her a bewildered look. "They were friends in high school, so everything he did for me doesn't matter?"

"It's nothing," JJ said, shaking her head.

Emma sighed, leaning her head back against the pillow. "That woman. I can't remember what she looked like." She was a witness. She might have seen Emma coming out of the house, which could at least confirm her story for the police. She'd tried to remember details, but they just weren't there. Brown hair. Teal shirt. A dog barking. And nothing. "Everything's hazy. Or just missing."

"It's not unusual. Extreme emotional distress can cause blackouts," JJ said. "And you're already pretty physically trashed."

"Like amnesia?" Emma asked skeptically.

JJ shook her head. "Not amnesia. That would be when you lose a memory. When you black out, you're not forming memories in the first place. There's nothing to get back, because it was never there."

"Then I won't ever remember."

"Maybe some of it. But if it's not there, trying won't do anything."

Emma considered her. "It sounds like you have experience."

"Remember that thing about doing stupid amounts of drugs?" JJ asked. She sat on the bed across from Emma, raking her hair back from her face.

"*Oxy. Benzos, maybe,*" Logan had said.

"What do you remember about that night?" Emma asked softly. "We never talked about it."

JJ looked at her steadily, but there was the flicker in her eye, the fear. "I remember plenty. I remember you telling us what to do. How to lie."

"You were at the Saracen house with Logan Ellis," Emma said. "But you took off. Where did you go?"

"We're not doing this."

"Why not?"

"Because I don't feel like being interrogated by my sister," JJ said.

"I've learned more about you from ten minutes talking to Logan than I ever did living with you," Emma said, a little sadly.

"Logan doesn't know anything about me," JJ shot back.

"But he was with you that night. He said he never saw you after the Saracen house, but he was lying, I could tell," Emma said. It wasn't a question. She wasn't sure if she wanted an answer. "You know, I could never figure out if you turned your back on me because you thought I did it, or because you had."

JJ sucked in a breath, her eyelids flaring briefly before her face settled back into a calm expression.

"You're the one who said you wanted to kill them. You're the one who fought with them constantly," JJ said.

"You had a whole secret life."

"And I never got caught, did I? Things were working, and I knew all I had to do was wait," JJ said.

"Unless they found out," Emma pointed out. "What happened to the clothes you were wearing?"

"You're the one that hid them," JJ said.

"Those weren't yours," Emma said. "You were wearing someone else's clothes."

"If you're going to accuse me of something—"

"Why did you tell Vic you needed to find out what I knew?" Emma asked sharply.

JJ shoved to her feet.

"What were you doing at the house this morning?" Emma pressed, and JJ blanched.

"—going in there, so if you'll excuse me," came a voice from the hall.

Emma pushed herself up, brow furrowing. JJ's head twisted around toward the noise as Gabriel pushed his way into the room. A nurse appeared behind him, not at all happy.

"Sir, I told you, you cannot come in here."

"It's okay," Emma said, puzzled. "He's a friend." The nurse looked between them. Sighed. Walked away.

"I heard what happened. Are you okay?" Gabriel asked.

"You shouldn't be here," Emma said.

"I was worried about you. I've been thinking ever since you came over. Thinking about how I fucked up, not talking to you, blaming you for what happened. I was on my way to talk to you and I saw all the cops and one of them told me you were here," Gabriel said.

Her heart thumped in her chest. Gabriel was here. All these years later and she still felt safe when he was around, even if it had never been true. "I'm fine. Just dehydration, mostly. They're about to discharge me."

"Where will you go?" Gabriel asked. She hadn't thought about that yet.

"I don't know," she admitted.

"Then I'll take you to the house," Gabriel said.

JJ snorted. "Yeah, that'll look great. Going straight from your husband's murder scene to your boyfriend's house."

"He's not—"

"I know," JJ said sharply. "But that's what it's going to look like. Come on, Emma. You're the smart one. Be smart."

Emma's jaw clenched so tightly her back teeth hurt. Like she was going to take advice from JJ right now? "Just get me out of here, will you?" she said to Gabriel pleadingly. He nodded.

"Fine," JJ said. "Just—don't say anything. To anyone."

"I never did," Emma said quietly.

JJ hesitated a moment, and then strode out the door.

31

EMMA

Now

Lorelei said nothing when Emma appeared on her doorstep, only held the door open and gave Gabriel a look that could have been a whole conversation. Emma could only guess that Lorelei wasn't thrilled to have her here, to have Gabriel involved in her drama, but she'd made up the guest room already, and while Emma sat in the back garden, the wind catching at her hair, she brought out a cup of coffee.

Emma sat with her hands wrapped around the mug, staring at the tumble of green and bright flowers.

Emma didn't believe in luck or fate. But she understood, deep within her heart, that there were people who could be a curse on those around them. Their rot infected others and it spread and spread, it got into the blood, the marrow, the lungs.

Nathan was a good man, she told herself. His flaws were modest ones, suited to a modest life. He had grown up loved by two middle-class parents and gone to school and gotten good grades and a decent job, and if the last few years had been hard, had given those small flaws the chance to gain purchase, surely it was because of the dark seam at the center of her she had worked so hard to cover over. But it was like foul water seeping through layer after layer of wallpaper, revealing the shape of the damage.

If it weren't for her, she was certain he would still be alive.

"Emma." She didn't startle at Gabriel's voice as he stepped out onto the back porch. "Your coffee's getting cold."

She hadn't had a single sip. She lifted it to her lips. It was lukewarm and bitter. "JJ is right, you know. Me being here—it's going to cause you trouble."

"I'm not worried," Gabriel says. "I was at a jobsite most of the night. Cameras everywhere."

"Jobsite?" Emma echoed. "You know, I don't even know what it is you do."

"Carpentry," he told her, leaning against the doorframe. "I'm leading a renovation for this historic B and B. We had some delays with the supply chain issues, so I was up there with one of my guys trying to finish in time for their grand opening. The owner's paranoid about theft, so she records everything."

Gabriel was a carpenter. That felt right, somehow. She couldn't imagine him cooped up in an office doing IT work.

"Emma. Why didn't you want to go with Juliette? What's going on between you?" Gabriel asked.

Emma took another sip. "I don't know that woman. I don't know if I even knew Juliette, but this is someone else entirely," Emma said. Her words sounded pockmarked, pitted by the acid that seemed to always be burning away at her throat. "After my parents died, everyone I knew disappeared. They wouldn't talk to me. Didn't want anything to do with me, really. I figured if everyone hated me that much, they couldn't all be wrong. I decided I had to start over. Take myself apart and build someone new. Someone who had nothing in common with the old Emma Palmer. I made myself into a stranger and I found someone who could love her, but I couldn't ever let him find out who I was. And then he did, and he died."

"I'm sorry. Emma. I should have talked to you," Gabriel said.

"You had every reason to hate me," she replied. The sun, angled low among the trees, burned her eyes, half blinding her. She didn't look away. There was nothing she wanted to see.

"It wasn't entirely your fault," he said, and his voice cracked. "That night, when I left? I drove to your house." Now she did startle, looking at him with wide eyes. He rocked his weight back on his heels.

"Why?" she asked, her voice a whisper.

"You showed up on my porch with a black eye. Didn't take much to figure out who'd given it to you," Gabriel said. "And I knew it wasn't the first time. I was angry. I went there to—I don't know. I parked across the street. Tried to talk myself into going up to the door, tried to talk myself out of it. In the end I guess I came to my senses. I left. Came out here to clear my head."

"But you didn't do anything," she said.

He shook his head. "The thing is, someone saw me. They gave a description. A shitty one, but close enough. It wasn't just the alibi that made them fixate on me. It wasn't just your fault. It was my own terrible judgment."

"Why would you do that?" Emma demanded.

"Because I cared about you. I was angry," he said. "And I was young and hotheaded and I wanted to be a hero."

"You cared about me," she repeated.

"Of course I did," he said.

She set her coffee cup down on the small metal table beside her, the movement slow to give her time to think. "You put up with me," Emma said. "I followed you around like an annoying little sister and you were nice enough not to tell me to get lost."

"It wasn't like that," Gabriel replied. "You know it wasn't. I liked having you around. I liked talking to you, hearing about your art. You were never imposing. And I never spent time with you because I felt sorry for you."

She made a noise in the back of her throat. "I had such a crush on you."

He laughed a little, softly, kindly. "I know."

"It wasn't exactly subtle. I hope it wasn't too awkward," she said.

"No. I mean, you were too young for me, obviously," he said, and a half smile hooked the corner of his mouth. "But if you'd stuck around another few years? I don't know. But I definitely never thought of you as a sister. I'm sorry I didn't get in touch after, Emma. I'm sorry you were alone. But it wasn't because no one cared about you."

She'd wanted to hear those words for so long, but hearing them now, she struggled to feel anything at all.

A bird, small and brown, lit on the lawn in front of them, and both of them watched it, so they wouldn't have to look at each other. Its head twitched, examining them with one eye and then the other. Apparently unimpressed, it flitted away again.

"I'm sorry. It's a shitty time to be bringing this up," Gabriel said. "I don't mean anything by it. Your husband just died. I'm not trying to suggest anything, I'm just—"

"I know," she said. "Please, God, don't go away just because we liked each other over a decade ago. You're the only friend I have out here. Or at all."

"I'm not going anywhere," Gabriel said.

She wiped tears from her eyes with her thumb. "We weren't happy, you know. I don't think we had been for a long time. I tried to stay the person he married, but she was always a lie. And I think he could tell."

Gabriel didn't respond; she supposed there wasn't a way to respond to that.

"Gabriel, I need to ask you something," she said. She sat forward, elbows braced on her knees. She didn't know what to do with the weight of loss inside her. But she could get answers. She could do *something*. "Maybe it's nothing—maybe it's irrelevant. But your dad, when he got fired. Can you remember anything else about what he thought was going on there?"

"I wouldn't put much stock in anything he said," Gabriel replied. He put his hands in his pockets, squinting off into the distance. "Dad was a useless drunk before he got fired. He'd been through a half-dozen jobs in half as many years. He'd always claim he was getting his act together and then fall apart again. When your dad fired him, he kept insisting he hadn't stolen anything. That your dad was the one stealing. Nana believed him."

"You don't?"

"Addicts have been known to lie," Gabriel said. His weight shifted like he wanted to pace. "He was borderline functional before that. After, he went off the deep end. Kept saying he was going to find a way to make your dad pay for humiliating him, but the only people he ever made suffer were his family."

"And you don't have any idea where he is now," Emma said.

He was silent a moment. "Emma, Nana says that he came back right before . . . right when your parents died. Then he took off for good."

"What are you saying?" Emma asked.

He rubbed his shoulder with his opposite hand. "He was never violent. But I'd never seen him as angry as he was at your dad. What if . . ." He didn't finish the thought.

"What if he killed them," Emma said. The thought hadn't crossed her mind, but she couldn't deny it fit. A grudge. A disappearance. If Kenneth Mahoney had come to the house demanding some kind of justice, and things got out of hand . . . But her father had been shot in the back of the head. No demands. Just an ambush.

"It would explain why he never came back," Gabriel said, and she made a noise of consideration, noncommittal.

Her phone was ringing in her bag, and she pulled it out to check the ID. Chris. "It's my lawyer," she said. "I have to—"

"Yeah," Gabriel said, bobbing his head. "I'll be inside if you need anything."

Gabriel ducked inside, and Emma caught the call right before it got kicked to voice mail.

"Chris," she said.

"Emma. I'm in town," Chris said. "Where are you?"

"Lorelei Mahoney's place," Emma said.

"You mean you're with Gabriel," Chris replied, and heaved a sigh.

"I can be there in fifteen minutes. Try not to get into any more trouble before I get there, will you?"

"I'll do my best," Emma promised, but her voice sounded weak. "Chris, I'm really worried." *Tell me everything's going to be okay*, she thought.

"You should be," he said instead, and hung up the phone.

———————

He arrived exactly fifteen minutes later. Christopher Best was Black, nearly six foot four, and broad in the shoulders, the hair at his temples graying and a pair of glasses giving him a professorial air. He had a pre-dilection for fine suits and good brandy, and was the sort of man who read *Ulysses* for fun. What he called his "intellectual blossoming" had occurred after high school, which explained how he, Randolph Palmer, and Rick Hadley had ended up friends. Back then he'd been primarily concerned with football, beer, and girls—shared interests among the three. He'd left Arden Hills while the other two stayed, changed when they'd stagnated, but he'd maintained a friendly relationship with his high school buddies as an adult. Up until he became Emma's lawyer.

Chris wasn't a hugger. Or at least, not with her. She gave him a close-lipped smile as she opened the door, then stepped aside to let him pass. It might have come across as cold, given all that they had been through together, but Emma had come to appreciate the emo-tional distance. She had been so desperate for anyone to show her love back then that if he had offered her tenderness, she would have dissolved into it. She would have clung to him and never let go. But he was not her parent. Whatever warmth existed between them, there was also a careful remove.

They sat together in the kitchen, Lorelei and Gabriel having vacated to give them some privacy. Emma picked nervously at a loose thread on her jeans as Chris settled into his chair.

"What have you gotten yourself into?" he asked her.

"You tell me," Emma replied. "You've talked to the police?"

"I've talked to a number of people," Chris said. "First order of business, the Arden Hills Police are not investigating this case. The State Police will be stepping in."

"How did you manage that?" Emma asked.

"I pointed out to them the personal history between you and the two senior officers, not to mention the ongoing harassment the department's second-in-command has engaged in for years. The misconduct investigation a few years ago helped my case."

"An investigation? Of Hadley?" Emma guessed.

"Ellis," he corrected. "Abuse of civil asset forfeiture to fund the department. Mismanagement of city funds. Things missing from lockup that he claimed were a result of bad recordkeeping. The last decade hasn't been kind to Ellis. Word is he's holding on to his job here by a thread. Smart money would be on him retiring soon."

"And then Hadley's in charge? Not exactly an improvement," Emma said.

Chris's expression was regretful. She forgot sometimes that they'd been friends once. All the way up until Best became her lawyer. With that, he'd made himself Rick Hadley's enemy.

He was your friend, too, she remembered Hadley shouting at him.

That's why I'm here. Looking after his family, Best had answered.

"She's a bad seed. He knew it. She's the reason he's dead."

Of all the people who had asked her questions about that night, Best was the only one she had ever thought believed that she was innocent. And the strange thing was, he was the only one it didn't matter to. He would have done everything the same either way. He would have done his job.

"The detectives are eager to get a statement from you," Chris said in a tone that suggested this was entirely the detectives' problem, not his.

"I was pretty out of it when I talked to Hadley before," Emma acknowledged with a convulsive nod.

Chris raised an eyebrow. "You shouldn't have talked to them at all. You know better."

"I wasn't thinking clearly." She dropped her eyes to the floor.

"Good thing I'm here to do your thinking for you now," Chris said, only a little bit joking. He reached into the briefcase on the floor beside him and took out a pen and a legal pad. "Now. You are going to tell me every goddamn thing that led up to your husband's death. Not just the relevant things or the things you want me to hear, all of them. Understand?"

She nodded mutely. "Where do I start?"

"I think you have a better handle on that than I do," he said. He clicked the end of the pen. She wetted her lips.

She began with the house, the lost job, the move. She told him about the flaming shit bag and the fireworks, the kids throwing rocks, the arguments and the almost-arguments. She found herself skipping forward and back, filling things in, but he never interrupted, just took quick little notes as she went along. Every once in a while he asked a clarifying question, and it always set her stammering. When she got to the carriage house—*the body*—she faltered.

"You pretty much know the rest," she said.

He nodded slowly. "I believe so. Now, Emma—do you or Nathan own a gun?"

"Just Dad's," she said. "He got them out of storage. They were in the gun case."

"All of them?" he asked, glancing at her over his glasses as he scribbled notes.

"I think so." She chewed her lip. "Do you . . . do you think that what happened back then is relevant?" she asked.

"Why would it be?" Chris asked.

"It just seems like a massive coincidence otherwise, doesn't it? I come back here and start asking questions, and suddenly my husband is dead," Emma said.

"I think that the more distant from your past this current murder is, the better for you," Chris said.

"In other words, I shouldn't talk to the cops about that idea," Emma said.

"I wouldn't advise it."

Emma fidgeted, rubbing her thumb over the opposite palm in a repetitive gesture. "The thing is, I've been talking to some people. People that think Dad was involved in some dangerous things. Illegal things."

"Your mother's suspicions aside, I never saw any proof of wrong-doing," Chris said. She was silent. For all that he'd helped her back then, she'd never felt like she could tell him how she'd really felt about her father. As far as he was concerned, the narrative the police painted about a girl who hated her parents was a total fiction. Randolph Palmer had been his friend. "Who have you been talking to, exactly?"

"Logan Ellis," Emma said. "He told me that he used to sell prescription pills to Mom. And that Dad was using the company as a front for smuggling."

"Logan Ellis is a waste of oxygen who sold pills to middle schoolers," Chris said, his expression dark. "I wouldn't believe a word he says."

"But is there any chance it's true?" Emma asked. "If it was, couldn't that have something to do with why they died?"

Chris clicked the pen to retract the point and set it on the legal pad, then folded his hands. "We aren't trying to solve your parents' murders. We're not trying to solve any murder. We are trying to insulate you from this investigation." He let out a sigh. Rubbed the spot between his brows. "I'm sorry. After everything you've been through, you shouldn't have to endure this. And it's going to be hard. Very hard."

"Does that mean you believe me, at least?" Emma asked, hating the tremor in her voice, the way she couldn't quite look at him.

"I've always believed you," he told her.

"I haven't always told you the truth," she said.

"You told me the important thing. That you didn't do it," Chris said. The chair creaked as he adjusted his weight. "And this time?"

"It wasn't me," Emma told him. There was no real inflection to her voice, no strength. Just the words offered plainly, without performance.

"I'm going to do everything I can," he promised. She could see in his eyes that he didn't think it would be enough. "But, Emma, to protect you, I need to know what I'm protecting you from. Are you sure that you've told me everything?"

"I loved my husband," Emma said quietly. Her hands were limp on her lap.

"I don't recall questioning that," Chris replied.

"But people will. They're going to look at me and try to judge my grief. Whether I'm acting like a widow should. But it doesn't matter what you do. If you cry, they call them crocodile tears. If you ever laugh, you're a psychopath; if you never laugh, you're, wait for it, probably a psychopath. If you smile, you're remorseless, and if you don't, you're cold and unlikable."

"I wish I could tell you that you're wrong. But then, you've been through this before."

"Maybe I'm cursed," she suggested.

"Entirely possible," he told her, surprising her into a small, mirthless laugh. He settled back in his chair. "The police want to bring you in to ask you some questions. You do not have to go; you aren't being arrested. At least, not yet."

"I should seem like I'm cooperating, shouldn't I?" Emma asked. This time, she didn't need to lie or spin a story. She hadn't done anything. She wasn't trying to hide anything.

"It's your choice, but I'd advise against it, at least until we know more about what we're looking at here, and whether they're looking at *you*," Chris said.

"I'll go. Then we'll know what it is they want to ask, right?" Maybe they'd found some evidence, something they would share. Right now, there was nothing for her to hold on to, just endless whirling questions in her mind.

"It's your choice," he said again. "But I need to know that there isn't anything they're going to surprise me with in there. You're sure you've told me everything?"

He could see it on her face, she thought. Yes, there was one last thing. Something that shouldn't have ever mattered. That should have been allowed to fade, unremarked.

"There is one thing you should know."

32

DAPHNE

Then

Daphne has seen things die before. Last year she was in the garden on the old stone bench, not reading but rather holding a book and staring off into the distance, constructing a scenario in her mind in which her parents died in a car crash and she was badly injured. In the daydream she lost a leg and had a prosthetic. She ran a race and people wrote articles about her. Her sisters cheered.

The rat crawled out of the bushes. It pulled itself along the ground on its belly and stopped several feet from her. Its head rested on the ground, its black eye fixed on her. Its breathing was slow and labored. She knew immediately it was dying. It had probably been poisoned. Her father had the boxes set up around the house. He'd told her not to mess with them, and she hadn't, but she looked up the poison and exactly what it would do. The blood in its body wouldn't clot and it was dying from the slow accumulation of injuries created simply by moving, muscles flexing and tearing in microscopic ways that were meant to heal. Being alive just meant that your body could put itself back together faster than it tore itself apart. The poison adjusted the equation.

It could take days.

Several hours later her father found her there, still waiting for the rat to die. He made a face and got a shovel and brought it down three times, hard, stopping each time to check if the creature's sides still rose and fell, and then it was done, and she didn't find out how long the poison would have taken after all. Her stomach was twisted and pinched and her hands shook as she went to get the trash bag for her father.

"I put it out of its misery," he said, and she felt guilty that she hadn't thought of how horrible those hours had been. She teared up. "It was just a rat," he said, and shook his head in disgust.

Her mother's breathing is weaker than the rat's. It has a wet, gurgling quality to it, and it comes unevenly, but it persists. A faint pulse flutters at her throat, and her eyes are open to slits, unfocused but looking at Daphne, who kneels beside her. Daphne puts a hand against the wound on her mother's chest. She pushes down. Her mother lets out a noise, a whining moan of pain, and Daphne snatches her hand away.

"Shh, shh," she says, trembling hands brushing the hair back from her mother's face. She thinks of the rat and of the swift downward swing of the shovel, and thinks wildly that she shouldn't let her mother suffer like this. *Misery*, she thinks, and the word repeats in her mind. She pulls her sleeve up over her hand and lays it over her mother's mouth, pinching her nostrils shut, and holds it there. Her mother doesn't struggle.

A floorboard creaks. Daphne's head whips up.

She is not alone.

33

DAPHNE

Now

Daphne was worried about Emma. That wasn't anything new, of course. She'd spent most of the last fourteen years worried about her in one way or another. She hadn't wanted to leave Emma on the couch after finding her collapsed outside the carriage house, but she also hadn't wanted to explain her presence either to her sister or to the police.

She'd thought she was in control of the situation. She'd been wrong. At least Emma was safe for now.

She clucked her tongue to Tigger, the rambunctious goldendoodle she was walking. She had three daily clients now, along with a handful of others she'd done one-off walks for on referral; her credentials were flawless, her testimonials glowing, and it had never been hard to get business. She drove close to Emma's neighborhood with the dogs each day so she could walk past several times without raising too much suspicion.

She'd thought herself so very *clever*. But if she'd just knocked on the door that first day in town, told Emma everything, would any of this have even happened?

She steadied herself with a deep breath. Things had not played out the way she had hoped. But there was no reason to think Emma was in imminent danger. And she could get things under control again. She put the phone away as she walked past the house, keeping to the other side of the street. There were two police cruisers parked in the courtyard, and she could see the edge of a flapping piece of yellow crime scene tape over the carriage house door. Earlier, walking Domino the lab, she had seen officers carrying boxes out of both buildings.

The police had never searched the carriage house thoroughly after their parents died. There had been no reason. The carriage house had been locked, left undisturbed. Nothing but tools out there. A cursory check, that was all. But of course, now that would change. They would search.

Daphne had thought that she could take her time. Make the arrangements she needed to. She would tell Emma everything, but only once the pieces were in place.

She hadn't anticipated Nathan dying. In the grand plan, the one that was more fantasy than intention, he was removed from the picture, of course. He was no good for Emma, and Daphne had thought about ways to ensure that she was free of him. Not like this, though.

Tigger bounced at the end of his lead. She walked him back to his home, handed him off to his very blond and very distracted owner, and walked to her car. She pulled up her older sister's number. Her last four calls had gone to voice mail, but this time, JJ answered.

"Daphne," JJ said in a strangled voice.

"Is Emma with you?" Daphne asked.

"Daphne, Nathan's dead," JJ said. She sounded like she was barely holding things together. Daphne pinched the bridge of her nose.

"I know. Where's Emma?"

"She just left the hospital with Gabriel Mahoney," JJ said.

Daphne blinked, unsure how to react to that. Optics aside, she supposed that wasn't the worst place for Emma to be right now. "What happened last night?" she asked.

Silence. Then, "I fucked up."

Daphne sighed. "I'm going to send you an address. Meet me there in an hour."

"What are we going to do?" JJ asked, sounding lost.

"Just be there," Daphne said, and hung up.

34

EMMA

Now

Emma walked into the police station with Christopher Best beside her and tried to calm the galloping pace of her heart.

Detective Mehta was a round-faced woman with a stocky frame and a button on her shirt that was on the verge of falling off, hanging loosely in its hole with a stray thread sticking out.

"I want to state for the record that my client is here of her own accord, and is free to go at any time, but has chosen to cooperate with this investigation," Chris said.

"And we appreciate that," Mehta said, without looking at Chris at all. "Emma—can I call you Emma?—we have the statement you and Mr. Best have provided, of course, but I'd like to go over things one more time to make sure that we have all the details."

Emma nodded. They weren't looking for additional details, they were looking for inconsistencies. She went over things again, from the time she got home the night before to when the police arrived. Mehta had a good poker face, but Emma didn't think that anything she said had made the detective relax or trust her more by the time she was done.

"You came home around nine o'clock," Mehta said. "Is that correct?"

"Around then. I don't know exactly," Emma said. "I didn't come straight back from the bar. I sat in the park for a while. There were a few other people around."

"Any particular reason you went to that bar?" Mehta asked.

Emma hesitated. She didn't want to lie, but going too far down this road wouldn't be good for anyone. Not her, not Logan, not JJ. "I knew Logan worked there. I wanted to talk to him. You know what happened to my parents the last time I was in town, obviously. And you know . . ." Mehta, mercifully, nodded without making her spell it out. Emma shifted in her seat. "I wanted to talk to Logan a bit, about being back and what happened all those years ago."

"You and Logan Ellis were friends?" Mehta asked.

"Our parents were friends, I suppose. We knew each other, that's all," Emma said. "I thought he'd probably talk to me. We chatted briefly, and then I left."

"And you saw your husband in the carriage house," Mehta said, and then they were going back and forth over the timeline again. Emma stumbled only once, stating the wrong time and then quickly correcting herself, and Mehta looked up but didn't seem bothered. Best looked unhappy, but not enough to put a stop to things.

"Ms. Palmer, there were a number of firearms found in your house. Are they yours?"

"They belonged to my father," Emma said. "They'd been in storage, but Nathan went and got them. I didn't want them in the house. I told him as much."

"Any particular reason he wanted them?"

"Protection," Emma said, all too aware of the irony.

"He felt he was in danger?"

"We'd been having some trouble with vandalism," Emma said, keeping her voice measured.

"Bad enough that he thought you needed a firearm."

"Like I said. I disagreed," Emma replied.

"You said that you asked him to get rid of them. Did you handle any of the guns at all?" Mehta asked.

"Once. The Glock, just to clean it. Nathan didn't know how."

"Why would you clean a gun you didn't want around?" Mehta asked, eyebrow raised.

"Keeping busy, I guess," Emma said. It sounded glib, and Mehta frowned. "Was it . . . do you know if it was one of those guns that killed him?"

"We're still conducting tests," Mehta said. She laced her fingers, hands resting on the tabletop, and Emma's mouth went dry. This was it, then. The part she'd been dreading.

"How was your relationship with your husband?" Mehta asked.

"Not great, recently," Emma said. Mehta looked interested at last, straightening up. "Things have been stressful. It's the reason we moved out here." She explained about the house. The baby.

"It sounds like he screwed up pretty bad," Mehta said. Emma thought she was trying to sound sympathetic. Like they were venting on a girls' night out. But Mehta wasn't built for it.

"It was difficult. And Nathan had a hard time with coming here, given my history with the place," Emma said. "We were working through it."

"I see," Mehta said. She angled her body in a way that seemed to exclude Chris, making this conversation just between her and Emma. "I get it. Marriage is hard. You fight. Things fester."

"We didn't fight. Not really," Emma corrected, shaking her head. "We talked, that's all."

"That's surprising. Nathan lied to you. Cost you a house, your savings—forced you to move back to a place that's got to have a lot of terrible memories. You must have resented him for that."

"I didn't care about the money. Or the house. And being here . . . It's not hard because of Nathan. It's hard because of me. My past. That isn't his fault."

Isn't. Wasn't. Tense got slippery at times like these. She remembered once hearing someone in the next room saying, *Did you notice she said* didn't? *My parents* didn't *have any enemies. Past tense, right away. She didn't have to correct herself.*

As if that meant anything.

Mehta sat back in her chair. Her finger tapped against the table,

and Emma's eyes fixed on it. Her father used to do that. *Tap, tap, tap.*
Like a metronome; like a timer, ticking down.

Mehta sat forward, squared up. Next would come the blunt statement made into a question, meant to take Emma off guard and provoke
a reaction.

"Were you aware that Nathan was having an affair?"

She had expected the question. But still, she almost laughed.

Did she know her husband was having an affair? Of course she did.
It was a miracle that it had taken her as long as it did to find out. She
had known he was feeling guilty about something—easy to read even
when he was trying not to be—but she hadn't pried. She couldn't see
what good there could possibly be in knowing the answer.

It was the stupid shared calendar that had done it. He was always
on her to put things on it, and she was always telling him that she didn't
really *have* things to put on the calendar. Her anemic social life had
cratered after her accident, and she hadn't attempted to resuscitate it.
Anytime she had appointments and things, she handled them during
the day when he was at work, so she didn't see why he needed to keep
track of them, but she'd dutifully logged in once a week to add things
in, sometimes putting in random work deadlines just so that she would
have *something* to add.

One Monday, there it was: a woman's name and the name of a hotel.
Her chronically organized husband had put his romantic rendezvous
on the wrong calendar.

And, of course, he'd never disabled his phone tracking. She'd
glanced at it once at the time listed on the calendar to confirm where he
was. She'd already met Addison—a somewhat severe-looking woman
with bright green eyes and aggressively bleached hair who had been
awkward the one time Emma had dropped by the office.

Nathan used to sit Emma down to do what he called a "trust audit."
Every corner of their lives an open book to each other. It had started
when they first got serious. He would have her log into all of her accounts, and he would hand over his computer for her to do the same—

check through private messages and emails, even pull up the call logs on the online portal for their phone plan. He insisted it was a demonstration of how much they trusted each other, how they had nothing to hide. She would page through his Facebook and click a few random emails to satisfy him, but she never understood his reasoning. If they trusted each other, they shouldn't have to look.

Inevitably, he would find something that made him, in his words, a little uncomfortable. A too-familiar sign-off, an after-hours chat with a work contact about something not work related. He would trot out phrases about professionalism and respect for your partner. She would apologize—and beg off girls' night with the friends who he felt were a bad influence, cancel the coffee date with the male colleague Nathan found too forward. Then the whole thing would repeat a few months later.

Of course, he *had* been hiding things. And that day she had done what she hated, snooping through Nathan's emails and accounts. He had been a little careful, at least. He used a dummy email account, but he'd saved the credentials on the browser.

The emails and phone calls went back months. She didn't look beyond that. She didn't want to know how long it had been going on.

She supposed she must have felt numb, but that seemed like too restrained a term for it. She had felt more like she had ceded control of her body completely, handing it over to an operator with no investment in the situation. She forwarded emails to herself, erased the evidence of having done so, and put Nathan's computer back, all without having what she could identify as a genuine emotion.

She went upstairs. She sat on the end of the bed. She felt like she was pressing her ear to a wall, listening to muffled sounds on the other side. Only it wasn't the murmur of a conversation but the hideous thrashing of her own emotions. If the wall crumbled even a little bit, there would be nothing to stop the agony.

And what good would it do?

He would leave, or he wouldn't. He would love this other woman, or he wouldn't. If she confronted him, it would be a fight. It would be recrimination and sorrow and tears and screaming.

Or she could wait. And when he left her—if he left her—she wouldn't be surprised. She would have her things in order.

Or he would stay, and wouldn't it be better then, too, that she hadn't said anything? Because they could go on as they were, and she could keep it quiet, this horrible thing she knew.

She had so much practice, after all.

So she had waited. She had never checked his secret email account again, or tracked his movements on the phone. She had convinced herself that she was doing what she had to do.

Beside Emma, Chris shifted. He hadn't said a word yet. They'd gone over this. They had decided on what to say. It didn't make it easier. "Yes, I was aware of that," she said.

"Really." Mehta raised an eyebrow. She might have been expecting shock or a false denial; she seemed taken aback not to get either.

Chris was talking. Taking over. Explaining that she'd been aware of the affair, and how long, everything that she'd told him. She let him drone on, staring at the tabletop.

"Ms. Palmer," Mehta said. She'd lost track of the conversation. Mehta had asked her something.

"I'm sorry. What was that?" Emma asked.

"I asked whether you had confronted your husband about the affair," Mehta said.

"No. We never discussed it," Emma said.

"You knew your husband was cheating on you, and you didn't say anything?" Mehta asked.

Emma stared at the wall behind Mehta. Her cheeks were flushed, the back of her neck clammy. Mehta must think she was pathetic. "I didn't want him to stop just because he got caught."

"And did he?" Mehta asked. "Stop, I mean."

"I think so," Emma said.

"You're not sure?"

"I couldn't exactly ask him, could I?" Emma pointed out. "Do you know . . . did he break it off?"

Again, a pause. Again, considering whether to offer this information.

"The affair ended two months ago," Mehta said. Emma's stomach twisted. Then it hadn't been long after she found out. Before they knew about the baby, though—so he hadn't ended it because they came here. "But it appears that the woman was the one who broke it off."

Emma let out a breath that was almost a laugh. "I see." Then he hadn't chosen her after all.

"I think we're done here," Chris said.

"I still have questions," Mehta replied.

Chris shook his head. "I think Ms. Palmer has been more than co-operative, and she has been through quite an ordeal. We can talk about setting up another time to continue this discussion, but for now we are done."

"One more thing," Mehta said. She took a piece of paper from a folder and slid it over to Chris. "We have a warrant for Ms. Palmer's phone and computer."

"My computer is at the house," Emma said. "My phone—I need my phone."

"We can get you a phone to use," Chris said, looking the paperwork over. "This is all in order."

"We need you to hand it over now," Mehta said.

"Can I get some numbers off it first?" Emma asked, and Mehta nodded. Chris offered a pen and a pad of paper, and Emma sat frantically scribbling things down. When she was done, Mehta took the phone from her without so much as a thank-you, and Chris touched her arm, indicating that it was time to get up.

Back at the car he gave her a look that was not entirely pleased. They were standing on the street, baking in the sun. A few people passed on the sidewalk on the opposite side of the street, well out of earshot. Some of them cast curious glances at Emma.

"I'd like to have someone go talk to this woman," Chris said. "I'd like to know why she broke things off with Nathan, and what was going on between them. And most of all, I want to know what she's going to tell the police."

"Do you think I'm a suspect?" Emma asked.

"Of course you're a suspect. Right now, you're pretty much the only one. We need to make sure there is nothing that could bolster that suspicion, and it wouldn't hurt to have some alternate avenues to investigate. I want you to keep thinking about who else might have wanted to harm Nathan."

"Wait. The cameras," Emma said. She pinched the bridge of her nose. "Nathan got them set up, so there should be footage, right? We didn't have a camera covering the carriage house, but there was one at the front door and the back door. It would show me getting home and not leaving again. If someone else came to the house, they might be on it. That's got to help."

"Do you have access to the footage?"

"I think so. I'll have to use a computer," Emma said. "I can probably borrow Gabriel's."

"Ms. Palmer, do I need to point out the obvious?" He only called her that when he was frustrated with her.

"You're just going to have to deal with it. I can't give up the one person who actually likes me in this town. Someone I have never had any romantic involvement with at all, by the way," Emma said.

"All these years and you haven't gotten less stubborn," he muttered.

"Would you rather I ask JJ?" Emma said, watching him openly. He shifted uncomfortably. "She doesn't like you very much. Why not?"

"Your sister and I had something of a disagreement during the investigation into your parents' deaths," Chris said. "She thought I was, in her words, 'out to get her.'"

"Meaning what?" Emma asked, alarmed.

"Meaning I tried to convince her to come forward with any information she had that might help you," Chris said quietly.

"You weren't supposed to—" Emma began, and clicked her teeth shut. "You were supposed to protect all of us," she amended.

"I was trying to find a way out of the mess you'd gotten yourself into, Emma. And your sister wasn't my client," Chris said.

"You were Uncle Chris to her, too," Emma reminded him.

"It wasn't like I was trying to throw her to the wolves, whatever she might have thought. But I suspected that she knew something that might have helped you. And judging by how fiercely you guarded her secrets, I'm guessing you thought the same," Chris said. "You took a bullet for your sisters, Emma. And that's your prerogative. But right now, you ought to remember that they're not your only family anymore. And you've got other obligations."

Emma's hand started instinctively toward her abdomen, but she forced herself to drop it. "Believe me, I know," she said.

He made a noise of surrender. "Get the footage if you can and send it to me. I can pass it along to the police if they don't already have it—and assuming it shows what we expect it to."

"You mean, as long as it doesn't show me waltzing out with a gun to murder my husband?" she asked. "I'll get it."

"And then you stay put," he said.

Stay put. Sit tight. Wait for things to blow over—or not. That was the smart thing to do.

And there was no way she was going to do it.

35

EMMA

Now

It took Emma three tries to remember the password, but then she was looking at camera feeds. Gabriel had brought a laptop into the guest room and sat beside her on the bed as she pulled up the footage from the night Nathan died. Emma watched with her heart in her throat, but if she had hoped for a smoking gun, a perfect image of a killer stalking toward the carriage house, she was disappointed.

There were two cameras. One above the front door, which captured the courtyard drive but didn't show the carriage house itself; and one at the back of the house, overlooking the woods. The back door camera hadn't caught anything more interesting than a deer picking its way across the lawn. The front was what Emma had been more interested in anyway. She plugged in 7:30 P.M., the night of the argument, and sped up the footage.

There she was, walking out to the car. Her shoulders were stiff, her gait tense. She got into the car and drove away.

About fifteen minutes later, another car pulled in. The memory of the wineglasses in the dishwasher flashed through her mind, and for a moment she thought of Addison—but the car was JJ's. JJ walked up to the front steps carrying a bottle of wine and knocked.

Emma caught her breath as Nathan emerged from the house. The camera only showed the back of his head—it didn't show his face at

all. But still her heart squeezed, and she only realized she had made a
sound when Gabriel put his hand on her shoulder.

"We don't have to watch this," Gabriel reminded her. "I could do it,
or you could give it to your lawyer."

Emma shook her head. "No. It's fine. It doesn't show the carriage
house. It won't show the murder." She made herself finish the sentence,
refusing to trail off into the mercy of silence.

On the screen, JJ and Nathan had disappeared inside. "Did JJ tell
you she was there last night?" Gabriel asked.

"No. She failed to mention that," Emma said, voice brittle.

"You don't think that she and Nathan . . ."

"No," Emma said immediately, but what did she know? She remembered the way Nathan had looked at her. JJ said she was gay, but that
didn't make it impossible.

It was only twenty-five minutes later that JJ emerged, striding out
to her car with her hands cupped around her elbows. She threw herself in and sat there a moment. Emma couldn't see her face from this
angle, but JJ suddenly slammed her palm against the wheel and then
peeled away, kicking up gravel as Nathan stepped out on the porch.
He watched her go with a frown. His head turned, as if he was looking
toward the carriage house. He stepped off the porch.

Nathan walked to the carriage house and left the view of the camera.
There was nothing for a long time, just the lengthening of shadows, the
dimming of the light. An occasional car driving past. Maybe the police
could at least track those people down and ask if they saw anything odd.

The car pulled back into the drive. Emma returning. She walked
back toward the house, stopping to look toward the carriage house.
Emma tried to remember what she'd been feeling, but her grief was
superimposed over it. When she tried to remember looking at the carriage house, what she felt was desperate agony, the need to go inside.
She willed the Emma in the video to turn. To walk over there and
knock on the door.

But instead, the Emma on the video walked into the house.

Stillness. Seconds streamed by, minutes ticking over. Then an hour. Emma would have been in bed by now, grateful for once for the fatigue that dragged her so inescapably into sleep each night.

Then, suddenly, Nathan veered into the frame again, moving at comical speed, and vanished inside. It happened so fast that he was gone before Emma could scramble to pause, rewind, slow the footage down.

When she played it back at regular speed, he came jogging toward the house with an intense expression on his face, and he was carrying something. Holding it up like he'd been examining it.

"Is that a flash drive?" Gabriel asked, squinting. Emma's stomach dropped. She rewound frame by frame and paused on the clearest image. The object was the length of a thumb, squared off at the end like a USB drive. The resolution wasn't good enough to see anything better than that.

"I think so," Emma replied. She tried to keep her voice neutral. There was no reason it would be *that* flash drive. And no reason that if it was, it meant anything, she told herself.

"That's interesting," Gabriel said.

Emma thought of Nathan's laptop, all his gear splayed out across the table. The compressed air. The USB adaptor. "I think he was trying to see what was on the drive."

"Sure. That makes sense. Find a weird flash drive, the first thing you want is to know what's on it," Gabriel said, nodding. "It just seems a little odd that he would act so urgent about it."

What *had* happened to the drive that night? It had been in her pocket, and then . . .

It hadn't been there later. She was sure of it. But how had it ended up in the carriage house?

Nathan was inside for almost an hour. When he emerged again, he had his phone out. He was calling someone. Putting it to his ear. He looked agitated. His hand rubbed the back of his head. Then he nodded.

He hung up and went back inside. The conversation had lasted less than two minutes. He was inside for another three, and then emerged, the flash drive in his hand again, his phone sticking out of his back pocket. He walked toward the carriage house and out of sight.

"It looks like he found something on the drive," Gabriel noted. "Who did he call?"

"I have no idea," Emma said.

Gabriel reached over to speed up the footage yet again, but the time flew by and Nathan never emerged. There was no more movement at all. Not until the sky lightened into morning and Emma walked out of the house. Emma went to stop the recording, but Gabriel restrained her with a gentle hand. "The woman who helped you," he reminded Emma.

The footage kept playing. Emma walked into the carriage house.

Now Emma shut her eyes. She tried not to play it in her mind again. Stepping inside. Walking forward, knowing what she was going to find, thinking that knowledge somehow made it impossible. That what she feared couldn't come true. She was anxious. She was paranoid. Her fears were not supposed to be real.

"Damn," Gabriel said. Emma's eyes popped open. She was looking at an empty courtyard.

"What is it?" Emma asked.

"Here, look." Gabriel rewound, and Emma watched as her mirror self appeared at the edge of the frame, supported by a woman in a baggy teal shirt and black leggings. They skittered backward, the woman lowering Emma to the ground before gliding back out of the frame. Gabriel played it forward, and Emma watched the scene unfold properly, with the woman helping her to her feet and up the stairs.

"You never see her face," Emma said. "Maybe when she comes out?"

But when the woman emerged from the house, her face was turned slightly away and down as she dug in her purse. Then she walked across the drive, out of the gate, and out of sight. Emma sat back with a sigh.

"Maybe someone in the neighborhood would recognize her," Gabriel suggested.

"Maybe."

"Hold on," Gabriel said, frowning. He reached over and pulled the laptop toward her. His fingers tapped on the keys and the touch pad. "There. Look." He spun the laptop around so Emma could see the screen again. It was paused on a view of the courtyard. Empty. The time stamp indicated that it was right after Emma left for the bar.

"What am I looking at?" Emma asked.

"There, on the street," Gabriel said. He pointed. There was a woman on the sidewalk, walking by with a terrier at her heels.

"That's the same woman," Emma said. "Okay, so we know she has a dog and she likes to go on walks."

"Totally normal. Except look at this." Gabriel skipped forward. It was night now, and dark. And the woman was there again. Or at least, it looked like the same woman—no dog this time, though, and it was hard to tell from this distance, with only the streetlights to illuminate her.

Emma scrubbed through the footage again, eyes fixed on the space beyond the gates. She watched police cars arrive.

Watched the woman walk past, leading a black lab on a red leash. "Different dog," she noted. This time, the woman was looking at the house. The camera caught her full-on, in daylight, and Emma's mouth dropped open.

"Emma?" Gabriel asked, looking concerned.

"I think that's Daphne," Emma said. "When I saw her at the wedding her hair was blond and much longer, but . . . yeah, I think that's her."

Daphne had been watching them. Daphne had been there, when she found Nathan's body. Daphne had been in the house.

Daphne had been in the tree house, covered in blood.

Emma stared at the frozen image. That night, after she'd found the money—she'd run. She'd tripped. The flash drive had been in her pocket, but it must have fallen out. She hadn't seen Daphne in the tree house—she'd assumed she was asleep. But what if her little sister had seen her? It was the only way she could think that the flash drive would have gotten back inside. Assuming it *was* the same flash drive.

She needed to know what was on that thing. "Gabriel, I think I know where that flash drive came from," she said. "If it's the same one I'm thinking of, my mother had it hidden away. I think . . . I think it might have had something to do with what your dad found out. About what my father was doing."

"You think he was actually right about something going on," Gabriel said, and Emma nodded. He rubbed his hand over his chin and mouth.

"You're sure you don't know anything more about what he thought he'd found?" Emma asked.

"No, but—hold on." Gabriel stood and walked out without explanation. Emma sat, feeling adrift. The still image of the driveway glowed at her. She shut the laptop with a shudder.

A few minutes later Gabriel returned carrying a cardboard box, which he set on the bed. "Dad's stuff," he said. "This is everything he left behind. Nana's held on to it, for when he comes back." Disdain and sadness mingled in his voice. "He said he'd figured it all out. He claimed he had proof. I remember he had . . . Here we go."

He pulled out a palm-size spiral notepad. The cover was battered, the pages bent up at the end. He flipped through it, and Emma's eyes swam at the dense sets of numbers, scribbled without apparent regard for readability or the orientation of the lines. It was like he'd been trying to get it all down as fast as possible. Some of them looked like they might have been dates or weights or maybe tracking numbers, but she couldn't say for sure.

"I thought maybe looking at it again would make it comprehensible," Gabriel said with a helpless shrug. "I never could make heads or tails of it. You?"

Emma took it from him. "I have no idea what I'm looking at," she admitted. Maybe an expert would be able to tease some meaning out of this, but it was so chaotic she doubted it. Damp had gotten inside the box at some point, and the ink had bled, rendering whole sections unintelligible.

She turned to the last page with any text on it. Instead of the wild bramble of numbers, there were six dates written out. The earliest date was in 2008; the last one, early 2009. "Do these mean anything to you?" Emma asked.

Gabriel shook his head. Emma grabbed the laptop again. She opened the lid and quickly minimized the open window, pulling up another. She plugged the first date in, but the results were too broad. A thousand things happened on any given day.

"Try to filter by local stuff?" Gabriel suggested.

She tried Arden Hills, then went statewide. She'd crawled through five of the dates without anything popping up that seemed significant and was ready to give up when the final date brought up a result that stopped her in her tracks.

ONE DEAD IN TRUCK ROBBERY

Emma clicked through with her heart beating wildly. Her eye caught on fragmented phrases—*string of robberies*—*state task force*—before she calmed down enough to read through the whole thing. The article described the latest in a string of cargo thefts—both of goods and of trucks. None of the previous robberies had been violent. This one was different. Cargo had been stolen off a truck in New Hampshire; its driver was found nearby with a head injury, and died several days later. It looked like some kind of scuffle had resulted in him falling and hitting his head. Unintentional, maybe.

Still murder.

"Try those other dates again," Gabriel said, but she was already nodding, typing them in. This time, she added *robbery* and *cargo*, and there they were. Each of the dates corresponded to a cargo theft somewhere within about a hundred miles of Arden Falls.

"Palmer Transportation almost shut down at the beginning of the recession," Emma said raggedly. "Dad wasn't as good at managing the business as his father. But things evened out. Good luck, he said."

"He was moving stolen goods."

"Or he was the one arranging the thefts in the first place," Emma said.

"But then someone died. So they stopped," Gabriel said, filling in the blanks.

"But then your dad noticed something weird with the weights," Emma continued. "So he confronts my father. Maybe that's how my mom found out about it. She started collecting her own evidence."

"And Dad took off," Gabriel said. He straightened up. "Jesus. I didn't believe him."

"My dad didn't like to be challenged," she said quietly. "Your dad disappeared. What if he didn't just leave?"

Gabriel shook his head. "He came back, though. You heard Nana. He was in town right . . . right when your folks were killed." He swallowed.

"You don't think—"

"He blamed your dad for ruining his life," Gabriel said.

"You think he'd be capable of it?"

"Honestly? I have no idea. One of the things I've realized as I've gotten older is that I really didn't know the man at all," Gabriel said, voice laced with old pain that she understood, bone-deep.

The older she got, the less she thought she knew anyone at all.

36

JJ

Now

JJ approached the small cottage with trepidation. The house was secluded, tucked behind a white picket fence strewn with flowering vines. The lawn was shaggy, but the flower beds relatively well tended. Little statues of frogs and turtles dotted the garden, and a half-dozen wind chimes decorated the porch. It was the kind of house she had always imagined her sister ending up in, maybe with a black cat sitting on the steps to complete the look.

The woman who opened the door looked little like the Daphne she remembered and yet exactly the same. She'd gotten taller and gained weight, of course, but those were small details—her eyes still had that intensity that JJ remembered so well, but whereas before that intensity had a flitting, hummingbird feeling to it, she seemed immediately grounded now. Steady in herself. Her hair was cropped pixie-cut short, lightened to platinum blond. She wore high-waisted caramel-colored trousers and a black sleeveless top, cat's-eye eyeliner giving the look a playful edge.

"You're late," Daphne said neutrally. On the phone, her voice had sounded thinner, and JJ had been more able to match it to the bird-boned girl she'd left behind. In person, it was rich, a little deep.

"Took me a few minutes to decide whether to come at all," JJ said. She glanced at her surroundings. When Daphne had texted her the address this morning, she hadn't known what to expect. "You live here?"

"This? It's more of a vacation house," Daphne said. "You'd better come in."

The interior of the house was spare. The furniture looked dusty but otherwise almost untouched. The shelves were bare except for a few simple white display vases, and there were none of the small touches from outside that made it look like a home. All the walls were painted a simple white that JJ suspected had been done before the house was sold—here and there were flecks on the trim of far more garish and interesting colors.

"Can I get you anything? Tea? I don't have coffee."

She was acting like this was a normal social visit. JJ swallowed. "Nothing. Thanks." She stood in the space between the small galley kitchen and the living room. There was a faint scent of bleach in the air.

"Sit down. I'll get you some water," Daphne said firmly, in a tone that had JJ moving to the couch before she even realized what she was doing. Daphne brought her the glass and sat down across from her in a gray armchair. Her nails were painted bright red; JJ's eyes fixed on them. "How's Emma?"

"Okay, I guess. Given the circumstances," JJ said. Her right hand gripped the opposite biceps tightly.

"What did you tell her?" Daphne asked. She sounded so calm, but that was nurses for you. Vic was the same way when something had to get done. It didn't matter if you were scared or squeamish or overwhelmed, you did what needed doing.

JJ had never been like that. "Listen. Emma didn't kill him. Christ, if you'd seen her—she was so broken."

"I know," Daphne said. "Emma's not capable of that kind of violence. She never has been."

"No. Not Emma," JJ agreed, splinters of memory digging under her skin. "Daphne. The gun—it—"

"It's gone."

JJ startled, then nodded slowly. "That was you—the woman with the dog."

"I've been checking up on Emma," Daphne said. Something in her tone made JJ give her a sharp look. Her sister shifted uncomfortably. "I haven't been able to talk to her directly, but I've kept tabs on her. On both of you. And when she came back to town I was worried, so I've been kind of . . . watching her. I was keeping an eye on things and I saw Emma outside the carriage house. I knew the police would search it, so before I left I went in. The gun wasn't there."

JJ's mind raced. "You're sure it was in the carriage house? And you're sure it was gone when you checked this morning?"

"I left it in a toolbox under the floorboards in the northeast corner," Daphne said. "When I went in this morning, the toolbox was open and empty."

"Are you absolutely certain of that?" JJ asked. "Could it have been inside?"

"I looked at the gun case. The one from back then was a revolver with a white grip. None of them matched," Daphne said.

"It was Logan's," JJ said. "Logan Ellis. I don't think it was registered or anything. He said he had it for security when he was . . ."

"Selling drugs?" Daphne said mildly. At JJ's look of surprise, she shrugged. "I overheard him talking to someone on the phone one time when we were over at the Ellis house."

"You always were a little eavesdrop," JJ said, without acrimony, and Daphne grimaced.

"I know. I'm sorry."

"You have nothing to apologize for," JJ said. "I treated you like shit back then. Both of you."

"Is that how you remember it?" Daphne asked. "Because I remember all three of us doing whatever we had to so we could come out the other side alive. You didn't do anything wrong."

"Then neither did you," JJ reminded her, and Daphne gave a strained chuckle.

"Funny how easy it is to forgive everyone else," she said.

JJ looked away. There was so much she didn't remember about that night, obliterated by a haze of alcohol and pills.

How she'd gotten from the woods to the house.

What had happened after she left.

There were only those splintered moments in between, memories she had tried for years to convince herself were nothing but a nightmare.

Yellow wallpaper.

She'd sat in her room, crumpled on the floor by her bed, her mind swirling with panic and anger. She understood at last that Emma had always been right. There was no waiting it out, biding her time. She couldn't keep doing this—hiding herself behind a mask, surviving by destroying herself. She had to get out. She would die if she didn't get out.

But she would be leaving Daphne behind. Six years where Daphne would have no Emma to draw their ire and no Juliette to placate them. Just Daphne alone, and she was so small and so strange and so unsuited for the games this house required of you.

There is no way out. There is only one way out. *You're trapped.* You have to escape.

White grip.

She remembered the weight of it in her hand. It was a revolver with a white grip. A good size for a woman's hand. She'd held it before. Logan telling her how to set her shoulders and point her hips.

"I know how to shoot a gun, Logan," she'd told him, and nailed every shot. Cans in the woods, nothing fancy. She was better than him. A lot better. It made him laugh like a hyena, and he'd given her a playful bow, admitting defeat. *"Rematch? Winner keeps the gun,"* she'd joked.

Red hand.

"They deserved it," Daphne said, and JJ's head jerked up. She realized she'd been drifting, silent for long seconds. "They deserved to die." Daphne's lower lip trembled faintly, as if she was waiting for JJ to contradict her. "You always thought you were protecting me. You and Emma. But you couldn't always be around. Dad was always soft with me, but Mom . . . She was happy with you and I think she was afraid of Emma. But I was always there, and she knew I wouldn't tell. I never told anyone's secrets."

"What did she do to you?" JJ asked hollowly.

When Daphne spoke it was with a frank, factual tone. "She wanted me to admit that I wasn't really sick. That my asthma was all in my head—panic attacks. She was right that I didn't have asthma. But a panic attack—it feels like you're dying. There's nothing fake about it. She was convinced that if she could *prove* to me that it was psychological, I would get over it. So she would try to trigger a panic attack and then try to get me to stop. With all the malicious creativity she was capable of, as I'm sure you remember."

"I had no idea."

"Like I said. I'm good at secrets," Daphne said, her lips bent in the faintest of smiles. Then she shifted, and JJ braced herself. "JJ. What happened after I called you?" Daphne asked, gentle but probing.

"You mean after you casually dropped that you'd hidden a murder weapon in the carriage house, and I'd just given the keys to our overly nosy brother-in-law?" JJ said with empty humor. "I panicked."

"That much I figured from the way you hung up on me," Daphne said.

"Can you blame me?" JJ asked. She raked a hand through her thick hair. Once upon a time she'd spent so much effort trying to tame these curls. "I went over there last night. I thought I'd make peace with Emma, talk to her about getting a few things from the carriage house. But she was gone. It was just Nathan. And I figured—this will still work. We opened the bottle of wine I brought. We talked."

"And then?" Daphne asked, eyes hard.

"I left," JJ said, as if nothing at all had happened in between. She thought of the splash of red wine, the rasp of insincere laughter in her throat.

"What happened with Nathan?" Daphne asked.

"Nothing."

"JJ—"

"Nothing happened with Nathan," JJ repeated, forcing herself to look Daphne in the eye.

"What time did you leave the house?" Daphne asked.

"I don't know. Eight thirty, maybe," JJ said.

"Well, hopefully he died well after that," Daphne noted, and JJ stared at her.

"How are you so calm?" she asked.

"Panicking wouldn't do us much good, would it?" Daphne asked. "So let's assume you didn't kill Nathan."

"Yeah. Let's assume that," JJ said, sounding strangled.

"Well, *someone* did."

"Why would anyone kill him, though? No one in this town even knows him," JJ said. He'd seemed like such a normal guy. Certainly not someone to inspire a murderous vendetta in only a few days.

Daphne took a deep breath. "The thing is, the gun wasn't the only thing in the carriage house."

37

EMMA

Now

Emma sent Chris everything she and Gabriel had put together, and got a tired response telling her not to jump to conclusions. Looking through all the articles, Emma had been running on adrenaline, gripped with the certainty that they had found something vitally important—but with Chris's message came the crashing realization that they didn't really have anything. Nothing solid, at least. Whatever had been going on with Kenneth Mahoney and her father, they were both long gone.

Emma paced. Gabriel was sitting in a chair next to a small desk in the corner, slouched so far he was practically horizontal. "You need to take a break," he told her. "Take a breath."

"I need to figure out what I'm missing," she said.

"Emma—"

"The phone call," she said, remembering. "Nathan. He called someone."

"Right after he found the flash drive and took a look at it. Is there any way to get your phone records, do you think? Call the company or something?"

She gave a wry chuckle. "Trust me, I know how to get them," she said. Gabriel's laptop was still at the desk. He stood up and shuffled out of the way to give her space, and she took his place in the chair. It was simple to pull up the account, and it was one of the passwords she knew by heart.

"Here it is," she said. The most recent phone call was to a number she recognized immediately.

"Addison," Emma said, stone-faced. She wished she hadn't memorized it. She hadn't meant to. She'd seen it on his phone one day, ringing on the bedside table, and the numbers had seared themselves into her memory. "The woman he was sleeping with."

"Shit. I'm sorry," Gabriel said, not saying what they were both thinking. That if he was still calling her, maybe things weren't as over as Detective Mehta had thought.

Addison, who had nothing to do with truck robberies and murders. Addison, who might stoop to sleeping with married men but probably wasn't a killer. Emma's shoulders dropped, her whole body feeling on the verge of collapse.

Gabriel put a hand on her shoulder. "Look. This is the part where you give that to your lawyer and the cops and let them do their work," he said.

"Right," Emma agreed. She felt drained. She wasn't a detective, wasn't a cop. She was a freelance web developer with a dead husband and no idea what to do next.

Gabriel glanced at his watch, looking troubled. "I've got to pick Nana up from her appointment. If I leave you here, are you going to be okay on your own for a while?"

"I'll be fine," Emma said. "Go."

"Promise me you're going to be all right?"

"Cross my heart."

His presence had been a comfort as she'd gone through the footage, but she knew she couldn't ask him to stay, and wasn't sure she wanted to. There were things she didn't want him to see. Grief was an ugly animal, and hers was a complicated grief. She needed time to tend it in solitude.

When he had gone, she sat for a while with nothing but that sorrow, that anger. She had loved her husband. Hadn't she? Maybe she hadn't *fallen* in love with him. But she had chosen him, and wasn't that the same thing?

She had to remember how he'd made her laugh, not the way she had crept around the house during his foul moods, afraid of setting him off. She'd been good at it, hadn't she? They hadn't fought.

He'd been so good to her after the accident. She'd been bed-bound at first, drugged to the gills to help relieve the pain, her pelvis fractured in multiple places. He'd been attentive, patient, kind. He'd brought her books, watched movies with her, helped her to the bathroom during those humiliating times when she couldn't manage it herself. He'd organized all her medical records, chased down prescriptions, sponged her down so she didn't have to sit in the stink of her own sour sweat.

Shouldn't she forget all the rest, if that was true?

A notification popped up—she was being automatically logged out due to inactivity. She started to close the window with the call log displayed, then stopped. She navigated back one month, two. The number popped up on Nathan's call logs, frequent calls and texts at odd hours. It culminated in a frantic series of calls over the course of three days that eventually petered out. There it was—the shape of an affair. During Nathan's "audits" she'd never noticed. Nathan was always on the phone with someone; the number hadn't meant more than any of the others.

That frantic burst of activity must have been when Addison broke things off. Had she gotten bored? Grown a conscience?

Emma had thought all this time that he had chosen her in the end. But it hadn't been his choice. And if she were honest—if she were *truly* honest—maybe part of her had been disappointed by that. Part of her had hoped that he would leave, and she could stop spending every day afraid that he would discover all the reasons he should have left long ago.

If he had left, he would still be alive.

She paged back and back and back through the call logs, and realized the number had disappeared. She moved forward again. There—a few calls, here and there. And then several every day. Her eye tracked to the dates and her throat closed up.

The accident. It started the week after the accident.

She pulled up the email account he'd used. She still remembered the account name, the password—they were burned into her mind, but she had never again logged in. Now she combed back through it. The earliest emails came three weeks after a drunk driver slammed into the side of her car and pinned her in her seat. When she was at home, bedridden.

I don't know how I would be managing this without you. It's so hard, an email read. *When can I see you again?*

She let out a sound like a wounded animal. She backed out, back to the main inbox, and sitting there was an unread email she hadn't bothered to glance at. Like all the others, it was from Addison. This one had been sent right around the time Emma was on her knees in the gravel outside the carriage house.

What we talked about last night, it said, and Emma couldn't stop herself from clicking it.

You need to make sure the proceeds from the sale go into a joint account. That way they're commingled and they become marital property, otherwise you might not have a claim to them in the proceedings. I'll have the guy I mentioned call you about it. But do whatever you need to get the sisters to sign off already. I'm not waiting around forever.

The proceeds from the sale—she was talking about the house. About how to make sure Nathan had a claim on it if—when—they divorced.

That was why he'd stayed. Not her. Not the baby. The fucking money.

She felt like she was going to throw up. Or pass out. But she couldn't. There was no time to collapse, to feel even a fraction of this betrayal. Nathan was dead, he was *dead* and it didn't matter what he'd done, except that every one of his sins would be heaped upon her. Every bad thing he'd done would be a motive for killing him. She knew how this worked. She'd been here before. Every moment she spent on grief and confusion was a moment for the walls to close in around her.

The affair didn't matter. It didn't matter that Nathan had chosen Addison instead of her, that he had been manipulating her, pretending to want to stay, just to get the money. Because Emma hadn't killed him, and Addison certainly hadn't. No, this had nothing to do with Addison, and everything to do with Arden Hills. With Emma and her family.

But it was like a corroded nail stuck straight through her, the thought that Addison had been the last person he talked to.

Her eyes flicked over to the time stamps, and she paused, frowning. The log showed that the call had been nearly fifteen minutes long. Far longer than the one they'd witnessed—and later, too, though only by a few minutes. Long enough that she hadn't noticed or looked beyond that first entry.

Idiot, she chided herself.

She looked at the next entry down. There—one minute, fifty-eight seconds, to a phone number with a local area code. This one, she didn't recognize. She plugged it into her phone and hit the call button.

The call picked up almost immediately. "Hadley speaking."

38

DAPHNE

Then

Daphne sits in the tree house with her sisters, knees knocking against knees, shoulders bumping shoulders. It's a warm May night, and the earliest bloom of fireflies blink and bob outside. It could be any night like this, except that it is the last night like this they will ever have. In two months their parents will be dead. None of them know it yet, of course, but Daphne feels something in the air where it touches her skin, like a hum.

"Let me see," Juliette says. Emma sticks out her hand, and Juliette cradles it in both of hers, examining the bruised fingers, the swollen knuckles. She sucks her teeth. "That's bad."

"It doesn't hurt that much," Emma says, and Daphne can read the lie in the way her lips press together and her other hand closes tight into a fist.

"You shouldn't provoke her," Juliette tells her, softly chiding.

Emma pulls her hand back. "What, you're saying it's my fault?"

"That's not what she said," Daphne objects. They're not supposed to fight here. "Is it, Jules?"

"I mean that you know what she's like," Juliette says. "That's all. Just try to keep her happy."

"Easy for the teacher's pet to say," Emma replies. "We all know you're her favorite."

"I hate her," Juliette says viciously. "I hate both of them." She reaches behind her. She pulls a cold can of Sprite out of her backpack and holds it out to Emma. "Here. Put that on it."

Emma accepts the peace offering. She presses her knuckles against the cold metal. "I'm getting out of here. As soon as I can," she says. Daphne's heart gives one big, slushy thump in her chest.

"Where will you go?" Juliette asks.

"UCLA, I hope. I've already got my application done, mostly," Emma says.

"They'll never pay for it."

"So I'll take out loans," Emma says.

"If you even get in."

"She'll get in," Daphne says. She stares at the floor, her knees up against her chest. Emma is good. Better than good—brilliant. Their parents can't see that, but Daphne can—she sees all the ways her sisters shine, and all their shadows. "You'll get in and you'll fly far, far away, and leave us all behind."

"I would take you with me if I could," Emma says, guilt heavy as a stone in her voice. Daphne only smiles a little, shakes her head. Emma and Juliette share a look, and Daphne pretends not to see. She's the youngest, the baby, but that doesn't mean she's ignorant. What it does mean is that while both of them can reach out and wrap their desperate hands around the possibility of freedom, she is trapped for long years yet. Six years before she can escape, and she looks less like her father every day.

Juliette combs Daphne's golden hair back behind her ears. "Everything will be all right," she says. "We'll figure something out."

There are so few nights like this now. Not so long ago they would be out here every chance they got, but things have changed. Emma runs a finger along the back of her knuckles, and Daphne watches the movement. She knows her sisters would do anything for her.

Anything except stay.

But tonight, they're here. They lie down on their sleeping bags and whisper late into the night. This is a sacred place. A place that is not out in the world, where they have to keep up appearances, or in the house, where they have to watch their every step. Here, in the dark, they can say all the dangerous true things they keep locked away from the light.

Juliette falls asleep first. She always seems so exhausted these days. Emma drifts off next, but Daphne looks up at the roof. There are gaps in the boards, and through them she can see a tiny sliver of starry sky. She has memorized the constellations, but she can't see enough to pick them out.

Pressure in her bladder forces her to move. She nudges Emma until her sister sleepily scoots out of the way of the ladder, and Daphne scurries down. She runs barefoot across the lawn and slips in the back door.

There's a set of boots in the mud room. Men's boots, covered in gray dust. A shirt is draped over the edge of the utility sink. Her curiosity is like silt at the bottom of a stream, stirred up by a probing stick. Her needs forgotten, she drifts deeper into the house. There's someone standing in the great room, hands on his hips, looking down at the piano.

A floorboard creaks under her and the man turns. Dim light falls over his face, illuminating the eyes as blue as hers.

"Hello, Daphne. You're up late," he tells her, as if she doesn't know. He doesn't look at her any differently from how he looks at her sisters, though he's smart enough to add up forty weeks and wonder. That's all right with Daphne. Having one father is bad enough.

"I needed to use the bathroom," Daphne says. He's wearing his boots, dusty like the ones by the door. Her mother would be angry. Past him, in the hall, the bathroom door is shut; light spills out beneath it. She can hear the water running beyond it.

"You might need to go upstairs," he says, but then the water shuts off and the door opens.

Her father steps out, drying his hands on a blue hand towel, working it over his knuckles again and again. The skin on his hands is red, chapped. He sees her and an expression she can't read falls over his face, unhappy in a way that makes her want to shrink down until she can't be seen at all.

"Go on, then," the man says, nodding toward the bathroom. She swallows and steps past them. Both men are silent, watching. She closes the door. Feeling like their eyes are still on her, she pushes down her pajamas and underwear and sits. Her cheeks are hot at the thought that they can hear her peeing, but she bites her lip and does it anyway, and then hurries to pull her pajama bottoms up again and wash her hands. When she steps out, they're still standing there. The hairs on the back of her neck prickle and rise.

"Back to bed, Daphne," her father says. There is a warning in his voice. She drops her eyes. More gray dust clings to the cuffs of his jeans. He rubs the towel against his palm absently, as if trying to scrape something off.

She walks back to the door. She can feel their eyes on her the whole way. She can feel that something has happened here she shouldn't know about.

She lies down between her sisters. Here, with Juliette and Emma beside her, she's safe, she tells herself.

As long as she has this, she will be okay.

39

EMMA

Now

Emma jammed her thumb against the button to end the call and practically flung the phone away from herself. She sat back in the chair, staring straight ahead.

What the hell had Nathan been doing calling Hadley in the middle of the night?

Why had he even had Hadley's number?

Emma's unfocused gaze went to the wall. She could imagine it perfectly. Hadley sidling up to Nathan. Hadley offering an apology for that scene in the hardware store, Nathan insisting that no, it was Hadley who was owed the apology. A business card slipped into Nathan's hand. *In case you need anything.*

In case you notice anything.

In case you wise up to the fact that your wife is a nutcase who probably murdered two people.

Nathan had found a flash drive—*the* flash drive?—in the carriage house. He'd checked what was on it and immediately called Hadley.

Now Nathan was dead. And Hadley hadn't mentioned getting a call from him.

There was one place she was certain she could find Hadley alone. His house.

She took an Uber. She sat at the bus stop down the street for almost three hours before Hadley's SUV pulled up in front of the meticulously maintained two-story Craftsman. Emma waited another few minutes before she stood and crossed the street.

The doorbell had a camera in it. She pretended not to see it as she rang and stared straight ahead at the door, schooling her face into neutrality. Inside, a dog barked wildly, and she heard Hadley's gruff voice telling it to shut up.

Chris would be incandescently angry if he knew she was here. Gabriel would call her an idiot, and she couldn't deny it. But she wasn't waiting around for the police to find the wrong answers to the wrong questions again. This was on her.

The frantic barking approached at high-speed, accompanied by the skitter of dog claws on hardwood. She heard the dog smack paws-first into the door and start scrabbling, followed by heavy footsteps and Hadley's voice again.

"Goddammit, get *off*," he said, and then he opened the door, using his body to block a caramel-colored, curly-haired dog that appeared to be constructed from springs by the way it was bouncing up and down. Despite herself, Emma had to suppress a smile.

Hadley was dressed in his off-duty uniform of a black T-shirt and jeans. He looked her up and down, then scowled at the dog. "I said off. Sit. For fuck's sake," he told it. The dog, which looked like something between a teddy bear and a muppet, finally sank down on its wiggling haunches. The strain of holding in its boundless enthusiasm made it quiver. Hadley took a steadying breath through his nose and turned his attention back to Emma. "What are you doing here?" he asked. He sounded genuinely baffled.

She steadied herself, planting her feet. "Nathan called you," she said. "Last night. Why?"

He looked at her, his hand on the door, then gave a slow nod. "Why don't you come inside, Emma?" he suggested with faux cordiality, stepping back to give her room.

She hesitated, suddenly wary. No one knew she was here.

"Come on, Emma. You came here to talk. So let's talk. Before the mutt makes a run for it," Hadley said, and the spike of annoyance at his tone gave her the spur to step over the threshold. He had left little enough room that she had to brush past his solid chest, catching the edge of his body heat and his scent, Old Spice and shoe polish. She didn't like putting her back to him but forced herself to walk inside.

The instant she was past the threshold the dog's obedience reached its limit, and it sprang in her direction with a delighted whimpering. Its paws caught her in the midsection, only to be immediately yanked back by Hadley's hand on its collar.

"Damn it, dog," he said.

"It's fine," Emma said quickly, flinching at the rough way he handled the dog. When he released it, this time it wriggled forward without jumping up, and she extended a hand to be bathed.

"He's my wife's," he said defensively. "She doesn't train him."

"I don't mind," Emma said. She'd always wanted a dog. Dogs didn't give a shit about your past, they just wanted your love. Nathan was allergic.

With the dog trotting happily at her heels, she followed Hadley deeper into the house.

The house had hardly changed at all since she'd last been in here. They'd had dinner with the Hadleys at least once a month. Marilyn would cook, which she'd hated, and they would pretend it was delicious. The girls would sit in silence as the adults talked, and then at the end of dinner, Hadley and their father would go out to the back porch to drink and talk while the girls did the dishes and the "ladies" slid poisoned barbs under each other's skin while smiling over their glasses of chardonnay. A choreographed dance that rarely changed.

"Is Marilyn home?" Emma asked. Everything in the house was white. White kitchen, white dining table, white couch in the living room in front of a white marble fireplace. There was a mug of coffee out on the kitchen counter and a stack of dishes next to the sink, which she couldn't imagine Marilyn tolerating.

"Marilyn moved to Portland eight years ago," Hadley said. "Married some accountant." He said this like she'd married a cannibal.

"Sorry," Emma said, without particular inflection.

"Alison," he said. She blinked a moment before realizing it must be his new wife's name. He nodded toward the mantel, where a series of artfully arranged photographs showed Hadley with a blond woman who had to be at least fifteen years his junior. They were outnumbered by pictures of the dog.

"I'd ask you if you want coffee, but somehow I doubt this is going to be that kind of visit," Hadley said.

She grunted in agreement. He jerked a hand toward the kitchen table, and she took a seat. The dog immediately settled at her feet with a contented sigh. Hadley leaned up against the kitchen counter nearby, forcing her to crane her neck up at him. The heat of the imminent confrontation flickered and faded in her chest, leaving her feeling tentative, vulnerable. He crossed his arms and looked down at her with a frown.

"Emma Palmer," he said, like her name was a revelation. "You've been through the ringer, haven't you?"

"What's that supposed to mean?"

His face remained calm. "I mean you've had a hell of a life. Losing your parents and your husband so violently," he said. "I'm saying you've been through a lot, and I'm sorry for your losses."

"You think I killed my parents," Emma pointed out.

He made a noise like he disagreed. "I think you lied about where you were, and there's good evidence that your boyfriend—your *friend*, sorry—was in that house," Hadley said. "I know you thought it was me causing all your problems, but I wasn't in charge then, and I'm not now."

"You made it very clear you thought I did it," Emma said.

"Sure. I did. I'm not completely convinced I was wrong. But Ellis was the one running the show. He was the one fixed on you. He played things nicer than me, that's all."

"Nathan called you," she said. That was why she was here. Nothing else.

"Did he." He looked at her steadily.

"He talked to someone right before he died. I called the number. You answered. It was you," she said, but the corner of his mouth curled and her certainty wavered.

"That was you, then," he said. "Do me a favor, Emma. Google that number."

Emma hesitated. Then, reluctantly, she pulled out her phone and did as she asked. The first result was a directory for the Arden Hills Police Department. *Chief Craig Ellis.*

"I answer the chief's phone when he's out. All of us do, from time to time," Hadley said, and Emma remembered now the card Ellis had handed to Nathan, that night with the fire. "Yes, your husband called the station the night he died, a fact that Detective Mehta is perfectly aware of, for the record."

"Why?"

He gave her a considering look. "I am not your enemy in this situation, Emma. I could be a help to you. And God knows you need all the help you can get. Your husband is dead. Shot. By someone who knew how to avoid the cameras on the house."

"Meaning me."

"Did you know that someone was sending threatening messages to Addison James?" Hadley asked, and Emma startled.

"Threatening messages? No. About what?" She couldn't help the edge of hysteria that crept into her voice. *What now?* she thought. What new thing was going to become her fault?

"About leaving Nathan alone," Hadley said, which she supposed should have been self-evident, given that he was asking her about it. He scratched his jaw with the side of his thumb. "Not you, then."

Emma gave him an appalled look. "No. Not me. I wouldn't have."

"No, from what I can tell, you have never once managed to stand up for yourself," Hadley said.

She rocked back in her chair as if physically struck. "Excuse me?"

He spread his hands. "You've been lying since the night your parents died, but if you didn't kill them, that means you were covering for someone else. Even when it destroyed your life, you kept lying. Then you know about your husband's affair for how long, and you don't say a word to him? That person doesn't go threatening the mistress. But then I have to ask, who would be sending Ms. James those notes? And I'm wondering, who is Emma Palmer going to lie for? And the only thing I can think is how close you three were. So why did you stop talking to each other? You know something about one of your sisters, don't you?"

He was almost right, she thought. Except that they hadn't been close, really. They'd been utter strangers to one another. All that loyalty had been an invention of her own mind, in the end. A wish for a sisterhood she didn't really have.

"So which of my sisters are you suggesting is a murderer, then?" she asked. She thought of Daphne. Daphne, so quiet and serious and strange. Daphne with blood on her clothes, Daphne who had been in town for God knows how long and hadn't said a thing.

"What do you know about what Juliette's been up to since she left?" he asked.

"A bit," she allowed. If he thought she would give him anything now just because he was treating her with a modicum of civility, he was wrong.

He dipped his head, all deep consideration, taking his time about speaking again. "Did you know she has an arrest record? Possession. Assault," he said. She twitched, chin tilting slightly with interest, and his gaze sharpened in answer as he confirmed he knew something she didn't. "Seems she had a fondness for getting into fights."

"Recently?" Emma asked, and she knew from the silence that it wasn't. Old news. "What happened messed me up for a while, too. I'm not here to talk about my sister. I'm here because—"

"Because you want to know why Nathan called Ellis," Hadley finished for her, and once again she had the sensation that she was standing on a beach with the waves stealing the sand out from under her feet. Nothing was solid. "But that's what we're talking about,

Emma. Nathan called the station because he found something. Something to do with your parents' murders."

Emma's fingers curled into tight fists in her lap. She could hear her own pulse thudding in her temples. The dog at her feet looked up and whined, as if he could sense the tension. "What was on the drive?" she asked.

Something flashed in Hadley's eyes. He sat back. "He only said he'd found something, not what it was," Hadley said. "He was going to bring it by the station the next morning. But we got your call instead."

Emma said nothing. The dog sat up, tucked its chin in her lap. She buried her fingers in its curly hair. It was small and wiry under all that fur, vibrating like a plucked string.

"Emma, I know you didn't want anything to happen to your sisters back then. But you have to consider your own well-being," Hadley said.

Emma was looking off to the side, her fingers loosely splayed over her mouth as she thought. "Juliette wouldn't have threatened Addison James," she said, letting her hand drop. "She doesn't know a fucking thing about my life. She wouldn't have cared enough to bother."

"Who would?" Hadley asked.

"No one," Emma said. Hadley gave her a pitying look, but she felt none for herself. She'd chosen her own life. "Juliette was the one who gave Nathan the keys to the carriage house. If there was something in there she didn't want him to find, she wouldn't have done that."

"If she even knew it was in there." He thumped the side of his thumb idly against the table. "The threats against Addison James might not be connected."

"Maybe none of it is," Emma said. "Did you ever think of that? Maybe we're just cursed. Maybe it's all just random and none of it means anything at all."

"Do you think you're cursed, Emma? Because I don't," Hadley said. "I think that you've been dealt a shit hand in life, sure. But I think that's someone's fault. And I think you know who it is. Even if you don't want to admit it to yourself."

"You know what's funny?" Emma asked. She tipped her chin up as she looked at him. "You aren't really admitting that you were wrong, are you? You're just saying your aim was a little off-center. You want one of my sisters because then you didn't *really* get it wrong."

"I just want the truth," Hadley said.

"It wasn't Juliette," Emma said, and tried to believe it. Doubt made her voice shake.

"Nathan found something, and he was dead within hours," Hadley said. "I saw the video footage. Juliette was there earlier that night. All three of you lied back then, Emma, but Juliette is the only other one in town."

Emma froze for a moment, not answering, and by the time she collected herself it was too late—Hadley's brow furrowed.

"Is Daphne in Arden Hills?" he asked.

"I haven't spoken to Daphne in years," Emma said, but the hitch in her voice betrayed her. She stood abruptly, startling the dog to its feet.

It had been a mistake coming here.

"I can help you, Emma," Hadley said.

"That's what you said back then, too," Emma reminded him. She turned to go, feeling sick. Juliette had swooped in to help. Daphne had been at the house. Were they checking up on her?

Or were they watching her?

40

EMMA

Then

Emma sits on the bed in Gabriel's room. Her bag is packed on the floor next to her, but she hasn't touched it. Eventually, the front door opens; his footsteps approach down the hall, and he looks in on her.

"Emma," he says.

"Don't," she says, stopping him, though she doesn't know what he might have said. She doesn't want to know.

He sits near her but not too near. He bows his head, and for a moment they sit like that, without saying anything, and Emma knows it's because the moment they do, something will fracture. So she doesn't ask where he went. He doesn't ask where she has been. He lets out a long breath, as if he is in pain.

Then he straightens up. The light from the street catches his eyes, makes them gleam.

"You can't stay here," he says softly.

"I know."

"If my grandmother were here, that would be different, but I can't—"

"I know," she says sharply, shutting him up. Because it can't just be that she needed somewhere to go and he was there for her, a friend. It's dangerous for both of them, her being here. People will talk. They already talk. If things get back to her parents, they'll both suffer for it.

"Is there anywhere you could go?" he asks.

"I was going to leave," she says.

"Leave?"

"I could take a bus somewhere." Where, she doesn't know.

"You're not eighteen. You can't just leave," he says.

"I have money."

"Do you have a way to rent an apartment? Get a job? Go to school? Do you know what happens to runaways?" he asks.

"I can figure it out," she says, but she's smart enough to know he's right. She blinks away tears, furiously staring at the carpet.

"Hey," he says. "You've got what, one year of high school left? Ten, eleven months. After that, you're eighteen, you've got a diploma, things get easier."

"They won't let me go," Emma says. "They'll never let me go."

"They can't stop you," Gabriel said. "Once you're eighteen, the only control they have is what you decide to give them."

"You don't know my parents."

"I'm more and more happy about that every day," Gabriel says, and she laughs ruefully. He touches her, carefully—a hand on her shoulder, as innocent a touch as he can engineer. "You don't have to do this alone. A few more months. You can make it."

She thinks again of the bus. Of a road leading out of Arden Hills, headlights cutting through the darkness. She can picture herself on it; she can picture it vanishing in the night, in the distant gloom. But there is nothing at the end of that road. She can imagine leaving, but she can't imagine arriving anywhere. She realizes with a slow seeping defeat that she never did want to go anywhere. She only wanted to be gone. In her fantasy, she disappeared into that night, and there was no other ending but that.

Gabriel is wrong. She cannot survive another few months. She doesn't see how she possibly could. But the only place she can go is home.

"I'm going to get some water," she says. Gabriel starts to offer to get it for her, but she waves him off and walks into the kitchen. She gets down a glass and fills it but doesn't drink. Instead she reaches up above the fridge, carefully taking down the old cookie tin in which Lorelei keeps her "emergency fund." In the last six months Emma has seen her get it down many times, and when she eases open the lid there are only a few bills loose inside. Emma takes the thick roll from her pocket and nestles it in quietly, replacing the tin back where it was.

Gabriel is still on the bed when she comes back out. "I'm going home," she says. She sees in his eyes that he wishes he could save her. She knows the cost of trying would be too great, but she still wishes he would.

"I can give you a ride," he says. She nods, because she knows it will let him feel like he did something, at least. "You don't have to leave yet. Stay a little while, at least. Rest."

"Okay," she whispers. She stays, and curls on top of the covers, and without meaning to drops into a dreamless sleep, deeper than any sleep she's had in a very long time.

41

EMMA

Now

Emma slunk back in the door feeling like a teenager sneaking in after curfew. The window air conditioner was doing its best to keep up with the heat, but the inside of the house was still sweltering. Gabriel was in the living room, and when she entered he stood abruptly, concern creasing his features. "Where have you been?" he asked. "Is everything okay?"

She couldn't help the diseased laugh that emerged from her lips. "Not remotely, but I don't *think* they've gotten much worse," she told him. "I talked to Hadley."

"Is that a good idea?" Gabriel asked.

"Probably not," she admitted. She scraped her hair back from her forehead. "Nathan called Ellis the night he died, right before he called Addison. He said he found something that had to do with my parents' death."

"The flash drive," Gabriel supplied.

"The only thing I can think, the only thing that makes sense, is that it had evidence on it," Emma said. "My mom had it, and I know she told Chris she had something on my dad. Which your dad knew about, too."

Gabriel's hands were in his pockets, his stance seemingly relaxed, but his eyes were hard. "Emma. We know my dad came back right around when your parents died. He hated your dad. Had some choice words for your mom, too," Gabriel said. "He had a temper. A violent one, sometimes, when he was drunk. Which he usually was. If he killed your parents . . ."

"We don't know that," Emma said. "We don't know anything for sure."

"We should talk to Lorelei."

Emma hesitated. "Are you sure?"

"He might have told her something, when he came back. She might not have realized it was important. Just don't tell her that he might have . . ." He trailed off, unable to finish the sentence.

She thought suddenly and vividly of the portrait she had painted of him all those years ago. The question on his lips; the weight of responsibility already in his gaze; the raw youth of him. She wished she could paint him again the way he was now. Those two paintings, side by side—

But of course, there was no painting of Gabriel at twenty-one any longer. And she hadn't put a brush to canvas in over a decade.

He gestured toward the back of the house, beckoning her to follow him.

The garden out front was orderly and formal, but out back Lorelei had always let things run a bit wild. Ivy snaked along the fence, sweet peas clambered up trellises, daylilies jostled with peonies for space. Lorelei sat on a cushioned bench out back with a sun hat on, squinting at a text on her phone.

"Your cousin is attempting to communicate with me through a strange runic language," she said as Gabriel stepped out.

"Those are emojis, Nana," Gabriel said.

"I'm aware of that. I'm not stupid, just old. It doesn't change the fact that it's gobbledygook," Lorelei said. Her eyes tracked to Emma. "Emma. Goodness, you look terrible."

Emma darted a look at Gabriel. His expression flickered with brief embarrassment, which she took to mean he'd thought the same thing, just hadn't said it out loud. "It's been kind of a terrible week," Emma said.

"Gabriel's been keeping me apprised," Lorelei said. Her lips pursed. "I've made it clear that I don't think it's a good idea for either one of you to be spending time together right now, but you're grown adults and I can't control you. Now, I assume you didn't come over to admire my garden, Emma Palmer." Emma thought she detected a hint of a warning in those words.

"She wants to talk about Dad," Gabriel said. Lorelei's brows rose.

"Seems like you've been very interested in my son lately," she said.

Emma shifted uncomfortably. "Kenneth was right. My dad was involved in some really bad stuff. And I've been wondering if it had something to do with why my parents were killed."

Lorelei sighed. "If I'm going to talk about this, I'm not doing it craning my neck. Get us a couple of chairs, Gabriel," she commanded. Gabriel ducked his head and emerged a few minutes later with two light kitchen chairs, which he positioned on the back deck so they could face each other. Emma sat at the edge of her seat, not wanting to look like she was settling in.

"Your grandfather, he was a stern man, but fair," Lorelei said, looking off into the distance. "Hard, but not cruel."

"I don't really have fond memories of my grandfather," Emma said. "I don't think he knew what to do with three granddaughters. He gave us presents. Pink, frilly things he thought girls must like." His wife had died young—when her father was a child. Her grandfather had raised her father on his own. Their relationship had always seemed more like that of an employer and employee, or maybe a senior officer and one of his men, than a father and son.

"I don't think that every child needs one father and one mother to come out right, but they do need love. And your grandfather, whatever his skills, had no idea how to show that," Lorelei said. "In any case, I don't have to tell you who your father was."

Emma nodded mutely, and Lorelei *hmm*-ed.

"Kenneth and your father were in school together. Them and Rick Hadley, and that other young man—your lawyer."

"Christopher Best," Emma supplied.

"Now, he couldn't draw a stick figure to save his life, but anyone could see he was the smartest out of the four of them. Kenneth was the clown of the group."

"Wait, the group?" Gabriel asked, surprise in his voice. "They were all friends?"

"Back then, sure," Lorelei said. "But then the other three left for college, and Kenneth didn't have the grades for it. When they came home, he expected things to go back to the way they were, but the others had moved on. He's always resented that. I think that's why Randolph offered him the job in the first place. He felt bad for the way things had fallen apart. And that's why it stung Kenneth so much. It wasn't just that his boss fired him, it was that his friends turned on him. Randolph fired him. Rick wouldn't listen to him. And, of course, Christopher caused all that trouble for him."

Emma's stomach twisted. "Chris?"

"Oh, he sent those letters, full of 'desist' this and 'severe penalties' that. Convinced Kenneth the best thing to do was to shut up and move on," Lorelei said. "Then the things he said about Gabriel."

"He was doing his job, Nana," Gabriel told her, looking uncomfortable. To Emma he said, "He and my lawyer had some sit-downs. He never suggested I did anything, but he was pretty skeptical about our relationship."

"He didn't tell me about that," Emma said, lacing her words with as much apology as she could muster.

"You say you're wondering if what Kenneth found got your parents killed," Lorelei said. She gave Emma a shrewd look. "But you know perfectly well I don't know anything that could tell you about your father's business. You want to know about Kenneth. Whether he might have done it."

Emma swallowed. "You said he came back while you were in the hospital. That means he was in town right around then, right?"

"Kenneth had a temper on him. I'm not saying he wouldn't have tried to hurt your father for what he did, but he wasn't a killer. He'd have decked him, but he wouldn't have shot him in the head. And he certainly wouldn't have shot a woman," Lorelei said. "I see why you'd wonder, but you're wrong."

"Then why was he in town? What did he say about it?" Gabriel asked.

"I don't know. I never saw him," Lorelei said.

Emma frowned. "Then how do you know he came back?"

"Because he left me money," Lorelei said. "He always left me money in my emergency stash, because he knew I wouldn't take it from him if he offered. When I got out of the hospital it was there, so I knew he must have come by. He was a good man. He was, Gabriel, even if his demons got the better of him more often than not."

Emma felt dizzy. Kenneth Mahoney had never been home at all. She'd been the one who left that money, and Lorelei had imagined her son coming home all these years when he never had.

"Look, honey. This is my Kenneth." Lorelei held out her phone, and Emma took it gingerly. She studied the photo Lorelei had pulled up: a man about her age, with Gabriel's hooded eyes and wide mouth, his chin up, mugging for the camera. She took in his smile, his short curls, the denim jacket he wore. There was a port-wine stain splashed across his jaw.

He didn't look violent or angry. He looked like his son. "I need to go," Emma said.

"What exactly is all of this about, Emma?" Lorelei asked.

Emma reached for the words to answer, but they slipped through her fingers like sand. Kenneth Mahoney had never come home. Lorelei had held on to the idea that he had returned, that he had wanted to take care of her, but it had been Emma all along giving her that false hope.

"I'm sorry. I shouldn't have bothered you about any of this," Emma said. She stood. As happened so often these days, she wobbled. Gabriel immediately rose and took hold of her hand, steadying her gently.

Lorelei made a *hm* sound, looking up at them with a discerning expression. "You both be careful, now," she said.

"Nana," Gabriel said, and nothing more. His hand touched the back of Emma's arm, ushering her into the house, and the contact made little zips of sheer awareness travel across her skin. Inside the house his hand dropped but the sense of touch remained. "Sorry about that."

"She didn't say anything," Emma said.

"She said plenty," Gabriel replied.

"I left that money for Lorelei," Emma said. She could feel the shift in the air when he worked out what that meant.

"I came to the conclusion a long time ago that he had to be dead," Gabriel said. "Figured he'd done it to himself, one way or another."

"I wanted it to be him," Emma said. "It's terrible, but I did."

"It's not terrible. If my father was responsible, your sisters weren't."

Her throat closed up. She turned away from him, stepping deeper into the house.

"Emma," he said, and there were fourteen years of things left unsaid hidden in those two syllables.

All the lights were off inside, and here in the narrow hallway between the back door and the living room, it was dark, all the doors closed. One step in front of her, sunlight slit open the shadows, a hard line of light she didn't cross.

"I wish . . ." Emma began, but she couldn't finish it. She thought of her parents, his father. Of Nathan, and how quickly he was vanishing into her past, along with all her other ghosts. How easy it was to let him.

Gabriel stood close enough that she could feel the warmth of him. Strange how strong the feeling was of him *not* touching her. If she didn't look at him, they could have this intimacy.

"I know. Me, too," Gabriel said.

"I should have left him a long time ago," Emma said softly. "None of this would have happened if I'd just left him when I should have."

"Why didn't you?" Gabriel asked, in a tone that said he knew it was intrusive to ask.

"He chose me. He stayed," Emma said. "And I chose him. So I had to stay."

"Did you even love him?" Gabriel asked.

"Of course. Yes," she said. It wasn't the kind of love in books and movies. But it was the kind of love that she could have, in her castaway life. It was all she was capable of. It was all she had earned.

Gabriel's hand touched her back. A soft touch, a whisper of pressure between her shoulder blades, as if he was ready to steady her if her balance faltered. "You deserve better," he said.

"You can't say that. Not when he's dead," Emma said, swallowing against something hard and painful in her throat. What was wrong with her, that she wanted to hear those words? What was wrong with her, that she wanted more than that ghost of a touch? But it was gone already, Gabriel's hand withdrawing.

She turned toward him, breaking the fragile moment of intimacy. The shadows across his face made his expression difficult to read.

She thought for a moment of stepping forward. Of putting her hand against his chest, of kissing him—here in the dark where no one could see, no one would ever know. Where for the space of a few seconds it wouldn't matter that her husband was dead, that she should be—was—grieving. If Nathan had been alive, she would have. But with Nathan dead, the betrayal was more stark, more unthinkable, than it ever could have been if he had lived.

"We can't," she said instead, and took a step backward, out of the shelter of the shadows and into the light.

42

JJ

Now

Vic was fond of reminding JJ that whatever she had done, she couldn't change the past. But she could be drawn back into it, and as she pushed through the door into a bar she'd never stepped foot in, she was somehow back there, dragged through the years by the simple knowledge of who she was about to see.

He ought to have been a footnote to her history. A distraction she used for a time to endure her last few years at home. Instead, what had happened meant their dysfunctional courtship was trapped in amber along with everything else from those final days.

There was something perverse about finding Logan here, in dingy unremarkable environs with no signs of success or suffering hovering obviously about him, proof that the world had lurched along without apparent regard for the importance of their tragedy. Logan looked like any other middle-aged man you might find in a bar like this, and whatever image she'd built up in her head of him crumbled immediately as he caught her eye.

There was another employee inside, a woman with slate-gray hair and a thick neck. She caught JJ's eye as she entered, but JJ walked deliberately toward Logan.

"Juliette," Logan said. "Of all the gin joints, et cetera." He smiled but it had no warmth to it. JJ made herself walk forward, take a seat at the bar. She was breathing too quick, prickles of sweat at the base of her neck.

"*He said he never saw you after the Saracen house, but he was lying, I could tell,*" Emma had said.

His eyes tracked the curl of a vine up her arm.

"Logan. It's been a while," she said.

"That's an understatement," he said. He cocked his head. "You're not here for a drink."

"No," she answered, though, God, she wanted one. She had a rule with Vic. No drinking alone, no drinking before five o'clock, never more than one drink. She'd broken them just about every night since she got back to this godforsaken town.

Logan took a survey of the bar. JJ had hardly noticed the other patrons when she entered—a couple having burgers and beers in the corner, a woman in a pink T-shirt and work boots. "If you're not going to drink, I'm going to take my smoke break," he said. "You can join me, if you like."

A dip of her chin in a nod, and she was following him toward the back door. Behind the bar was nothing but an empty lot. The air stank with indistinct sour smells from the dumpster nearby, but Logan didn't seem to notice. He pulled a pack of cigarettes from his pocket and lit one unhurriedly.

JJ reached out. She'd quit years ago, at Vic's insistence, but she still snuck one now and then. Logan offered a light, and she leaned in. His fingertips were calloused and stained. He met her eye as he held the trembling flame up to the tip of the cigarette, his own dangling from the corner of his mouth.

"Long time," he said again, like it was the only thing to say.

She leaned back, weight on her back foot. She took the cigarette from her lips and let the smoke spill from her mouth slowly, savoring the familiar flavor and sting of it. It wasn't a thing she'd ever liked, exactly. It was more like a ritual or a talisman, a way to mark in the moment who she was. Who she wasn't.

"Miss me?" she asked, the trace of a smirk in the corner of her mouth as she remembered who she meant to be.

"Now and then," Logan allowed with a half smile of his own, relaxing a fraction. He gave her a look that encompassed her scuffed-up boots, her skintight jeans, the loose blouse that did nothing to conceal the bright purple bra she had on underneath, the tattoos she'd accumulated over the years. "You look good. You look—I dunno. I would say you've changed, but I feel like this is what you were always supposed to look like," he said.

"Thanks, I guess," JJ replied. "You haven't. Changed."

"Never got around to it," Logan said. "I've stopped trying to be more of an asshole than I already am, at least."

"That's something," she offered, and it did feel like she was giving something to him, a gift as real as the cigarette she lifted to her lips again. It was strange looking at him and seeing in his aged face the face of the boy she had tried so desperately to want. By the time she'd gotten into his car that first day, she'd started to be worried about the fact that the boys in the back seats and teenage bedrooms held no attraction to her, to panic about the way her heart thudded when she caught a glimpse of Sara Williams applying a careful layer of lip gloss to her ample lower lip.

So she'd tried for a while to want Logan. She'd gotten as far as liking him, despite him being an asshole, despite him being, at best, a loser and a drug dealer and a sleaze. She thought she might still like him, maybe even like him more, without the pressure of anything more.

"What's that look?" he asked her.

"You don't want to know," she told him, with a shine of humor on it to keep the mood light. It did its job; he chuckled, ducked his head.

"Your sister came by. Asking questions about you," Logan told her, lifting his eyes to hers.

"So you mentioned," JJ replied, trying to sound casual, her pulse quick and loud. "What did you tell her?"

"Some of it. Not all of it," Logan said. "She wanted to know about that night."

She grunted. "You told her you didn't see me after the Saracen house. She thinks you're lying." The arch of an eyebrow, turning it into a question, a demand, but he only let out a long smoke-wreathed breath and didn't answer. "We never talked, you and I. After that night."

"Seemed like the smart call," Logan said. There was guilt there—or fear, maybe. "I figured you didn't want people knowing what you'd gotten up to."

"Very insightful of you," JJ said, throat tightening. "Not at all self-interested."

"So what if it was? No one wanted to touch that mess with a ten-foot pole," Logan said. "It was bad enough they found those bloody clothes at the house."

"The police talk to you?" JJ said.

"You mean my dad? Yeah," Logan replied. "That was a lot of fun, let me tell you. He didn't actually ask the questions, got Hadley to do it, but he was there."

"What did you tell them?"

"What do you think? Sure, I went there sometimes. Can't remember specifically when that night, can't recall ever seeing any drugs or underage drinking, can't recall, can't recall," Logan said. His eyes were on the pavement. He shuffled his feet.

"You said something else," JJ said.

"Look, it was a moment of weakness. I panicked a bit," Logan said. He looked up at her. "Hadley said it like they already knew. I thought if I lied, I'd be in deep shit."

"Said what?" JJ pressed.

"He's asking about the Saracen house, right? Who's there, when, what they did, all of that. And he said he knew the Palmer girl had been there, and had I seen her, so I said yeah, maybe, I thought I remembered seeing her but I could be wrong. I kept it ambiguous. Just trying not to get in trouble."

"Wait, he knew I was there?" JJ asked, brow furrowing, and then she played his words back in her mind. "The Palmer girl."

"He was all 'You're sure you saw Emma Palmer,' and at that point I guess I panicked. Said yes," Logan said. "I thought I was protecting you."

JJ stared at him. Her mouth was dry. "Why would I need protecting, Logan?" JJ asked quietly.

He fixed his gaze on her. Held the silence long enough that ash dropped from the tip of his cigarette, ghosting down to the ground to vanish against the gray concrete. "What do you remember?"

Yellow wallpaper. White grip. Red hand. Splinters of memory under her skin, no more. The rest a wide blank.

She wetted her lips. Swallowed. "Not enough," JJ admitted.

"Maybe that's for the best."

"You do know something."

"I know a lot of things, Juliette. You did a lot of things," Logan said. "I've thought about that night a lot. Trying to come up with a way none of it was my fault, right? But I think it was, at least a little. I knew I gave you too much. You were done with me. I could tell. I thought maybe if there was something else you wanted from me it might last a bit longer, or if you were more relaxed, you'd actually have some fun, and then . . ."

He trailed off. She let him stew in the silence.

"Just tell me what happened," she said, trying for a gentle tone. She didn't do gentle or sweet much these days. It sounded strange, and Logan gave her a look like he could tell she was out of practice.

"You really don't remember. I guess that's not surprising, given how fucked-up you were when we found you," he said.

"We?" she repeated.

"Me and Nina. When you took off, I figured you were just going to cut through the woods and go home, but she was freaked-out. Wanted to make sure you were safe. So we drove around a bit to see if we could spot you. We were out there for what—forty minutes, maybe? An hour? Nina was fucking pissed. I was just about to call it when we saw you. You don't remember any of this?"

No point in lying to him now, though she realized she should have let him think she remembered at least part of it. Leave him uncertain what he could lie about. "It's patchy," she said, and she could tell he didn't believe her.

"You were walking on the side of the road. Barefoot. Soaked through. You were fucked-up, like I said. Barely making sense."

"What did I say?" JJ asked, throat tight enough to hurt.

"I don't remember," he hedged, and she made a skeptical noise. "You weren't making sense. Nothing you said meant anything, as far as I'm concerned."

"What did I say?" JJ demanded.

"You said someone was dead. 'They're dead.' And you kept apologizing," he said. "We didn't know what had happened. We just thought you were high. Figured we should let you sleep it off. So I took you back to my place. We stayed there awhile, and then I drove you home."

"That part I remember," JJ said. Waking up in his bed, musty sheets tangled around her legs. Her hair still wet—it had always been so thick, so slow to dry. Logan telling her to get up. Get moving. Get in the car. Get out of the car. Brusque in a way she hadn't understood. She figured she'd done something. Said something. There was a weird taste in her mouth, metallic. Noises were too loud and strangely muffled, and she was gripped with the feeling that she was running from something, but she couldn't remember what.

She'd been so exhausted, her thoughts so muddied, that she hadn't even thought to sneak around the back of the house when Logan dropped her off. She just stumbled up the front drive and in through the door. She heard her sisters' voices and followed them.

Then the rest. Memory snapping back into her mind. *Yellow wallpaper. White grip. Red hand.*

"You were with Nina? The whole time, before you found me?" she asked.

"Yeah." It was almost a question.

"You weren't with me."

"No, Juliette, I wasn't with you," he said, angry now at having to repeat himself. "Whatever the fuck you did that night, you did it without me."

She wrapped an arm over her ribs, took a drag from the cigarette, and tried to decide if she was disappointed. She needed the answers. She didn't know if she wanted them. "Did you have your gun with you that night?"

"What? No," he said. Shot her a glance that bordered on alarm. She was losing him. The momentary camaraderie between them was guttering out as he realized—remembered—the depth of the trouble she carried with her.

"Where was it?" she asked.

"Why do you want to know?" he demanded. Not angry—scared. Confused.

"You're not stupid, Logan. You know enough of that answer to know you don't want to hear the rest," she said. "Tell me where the gun was and I'll walk away right now. I won't talk to you again and you won't have to know anything that makes you uncomfortable."

"Fuck," he said. "You have changed."

"Adapt or die, right?" JJ said. She gave him a minute. Let him look off into the distance and take a drag of his cigarette and tell himself he was in control—of this situation, of his life, of some corner of the universe. It was a lie everyone had to believe at least a little to get from one moment to the next.

"I've been waiting to get asked about that night for a long time. You and your sister weren't the ones I thought would be doing the asking," he said at last. His expression was shuttered when he looked at her again. "I've done fine without you around, Juliette. I like fine. Fine is all I could ever hope for out of life, and I don't want to fuck it up. You got questions, find someone else to answer them."

"Logan—"

"We're done here," he said. "I'm going to finish this and go back inside. I'd rather you weren't there when I do."

"Got it," she said in a rasp of sound. She let the cigarette fall from numb fingers and ground it out with her heel.

JJ stalked back inside and up to the bar. The other employee eyed her with something that didn't quite qualify as curiosity as she approached.

"Whiskey. Don't care which," JJ told her. The shot arrived; JJ downed it. Let it chase the taste of tobacco smoke. She pulled out her phone and stabbed in Nina's name. Social media images popped up. Nina on a beach in a wedding dress, leaning in to kiss her dapperly dressed bride. Nina and her wife with curly-haired, brown-eyed babies on their shoulders. Nina with a good life that didn't need JJ disrupting it.

She drank another shot, and then a third, and then slapped a bill down on the counter and strode out before Logan could come back in.

She'd hoped Logan could fill in the gaps. Could, maybe, absolve her. But the pieces she couldn't remember didn't matter, in the end. She knew what had happened.

And the time was coming soon when she couldn't keep hiding from it.

43

EMMA

Now

Three days after her husband's death, Emma walked through the door of her house once again.

Gabriel drove her. She had her phone back, too. Apparently it hadn't taken that long to scrape every crumb of her life off the device to sort through. Her car had been taken in, searched for evidence, and she had instructions on how to retrieve it. There was still crime scene tape fluttering here and there, and heavy shoes had tramped their way through the flower beds.

"You're sure you want to be here?" Gabriel asked her.

"I always end up back here," she answered. He looked puzzled, but she didn't explain as she walked in, leaving him to close the door. Thick drifts of dust floated through the light, and she lifted a hand, stirring eddies through them.

"You can go," she told Gabriel. He stood in the foyer, hands in his pockets, clearly reluctant to obey. She gave him a steady look. "I'm okay here. Really. You've been a huge help, but right now I just want to be alone."

"You're sure?"

"Please stop asking me that," she said.

"Call me if you need anything," he told her.

Gabriel closed the door behind him. Emma walked to the great room and stood there with her arms crossed, letting the scents and sensations of the house settle against her skin.

Hadley wanted her to believe that her mistake back then had been covering for her sisters when they didn't deserve it. He was wrong. Her mistake had been covering for them without understanding what had happened.

She took out her phone and made a call. JJ picked up on the second ring.

"Emma," she said, in a tone that suggested she had been dreading this call.

"I'm back at the house," Emma said. "We need to talk. All three of us."

"I know. We'll come over," JJ said.

"We?"

"I'm with Daphne. She called me. We had some things to talk about. I think you need to hear them, too. I think it's time."

Emma shut her eyes. She'd expected a fight. Without one, she wasn't sure exactly what to do. "I'll be here," she said. The line went dead.

———

Emma waited on the porch for her sisters to arrive. They pulled up in separate cars. JJ got out and tucked her hands in her back pockets, coming up to the house with her eyes scuttling left and right nervously. Daphne approached at a steady gait, seemingly unbothered by the strange circumstances of their reunion.

This Daphne was far closer to the version she'd met at the wedding than the one on the cameras. She wore a sharp blazer over a crisp white top and rust-colored skirt, lace-up boots clinging to her calves. Her sunglasses flattered her face, and so did the pixie cut—no more blunt bob or brown hair, no more shapeless tunic. The transformation made the hair on the backs of Emma's arms stand on end.

The three of them stood spaced a few feet apart, no one quite moving to greet the others. Only Daphne managed a smile. "Here we all are. I wasn't sure this would ever happen," she said, upbeat.

"Why don't you both come in," Emma suggested, to spare either her or JJ the need to formulate a response. She walked in, and the others trooped after her. She brought them into the living room. "If you want coffee or water or anything, you're going to have to get it yourself." She sat down, arms crossed, on one end of the couch.

"Oh, I'm fine," Daphne said, with a determined kind of pleasantness. She set her purse down next to her on the floor as she took a seat in one of the armchairs. JJ walked to the other but perched on the arm instead of sitting in it, shoulders stooped inward defensively.

"So," JJ said.

"So," Emma echoed. She had tried to plan this moment, but every time she imagined it, the pieces fell apart in her mind. Her imagined conversations were braided fragments of words and anger and blame and confusion that didn't add up to anything. "Where have you been?" she asked.

"You're the one who took off," JJ pointed out.

"I didn't trust you," Emma said.

JJ's chin dipped sharply. "Yeah. I got that."

"Let's not start out being angry at each other," Daphne said. She fidgeted with her sleeve.

"How long have you been in town?" Emma asked, looking to Daphne. "I know it's been at least a week."

"About that long," Daphne acknowledged.

"You were spying on me."

"Checking on you," Daphne corrected. "I didn't know if you'd want to see me. Or if I was ready to see you."

Emma grunted. JJ's rejection she'd always understood, in a way. Daphne's was the one that broke her. She'd thought that the two of them understood each other. They didn't like to get noticed, didn't know how to play along. She'd been able to bear it, knowing that Daphne and Juliette had been estranged from each other, too. That all three of them had cut themselves adrift—or been cut. She'd been able to convince herself this was just the way that things were always going to be.

But now they were here together. They'd been talking. Sharing secrets. She was in the dark, and maybe she always had been.

"And was that what you were doing here?" she said, looking at JJ. "When you brought a bottle of wine to the house, were you checking up on me?"

JJ's throat bobbed. "No," she said.

"Then what?" Emma demanded.

"I didn't know you wouldn't be home," JJ said. "I came to talk." But she couldn't look Emma in the eye.

"She went because we needed to get into the carriage house," Daphne said.

"You needed to get the flash drive," Emma guessed. Daphne looked almost pleased that Emma had figured it out.

"You dropped it that night—it was you, wasn't it? I picked it up," Daphne said. "Dad found me with it. I hadn't seen much—at least nothing I understood—but he was angry, in that quiet way of his. The dangerous way. I overheard him talking on the phone, afterward. He told someone that one of us had seen, and that he'd take care of it. I didn't know who he was talking to, but I knew it sounded dangerous, so after I found the bodies, I took it. And I hid it."

"In the carriage house," Emma said, and Daphne nodded.

"What was Dad up to?" JJ asked.

"I think I know. Some of it, at least," Emma said. They looked at her quizzically. "He was involved in some kind of cargo robbery scheme. Moving the stolen goods. Mom knew about it. She was going to turn him in, I think. Or use it as leverage to get away from him."

"I guess she finally got tired of him cheating on her," JJ said.

"She was cheating on him, too," Daphne said flatly.

"Are you sure?" JJ asked.

Daphne laughed a little. "Trust me. I'm sure."

Emma thought of the bracelet. The makeup hidden away in her private drawer. *Forever yours.*

"Wait—Dad said one of us had seen. Did you look at what was on the drive?" JJ asked.

"Yeah. It was mostly numbers—ledgers, I think. It looked like two sets, maybe one real one and one fake? I couldn't make heads or tails of it, but there were photos, too."

"What kind of photos?" Emma asked.

"I only saw one. It was taken from a distance, like through a car window. There were three men. One of them was facing away and it was dark, so you couldn't make him out at all. But Dad was there. He had a gun. I think it was at the old quarry," Daphne said.

"What about the other man? You said there were three," Emma asked.

Daphne shook her head. "I didn't recognize him. All I remember was that he was white. Dark hair, I think? And he had a birthmark. Like a port-wine stain," she said, pointing to her jaw.

Emma's stomach twisted.

"That sounds like Kenneth Mahoney," she said. She swallowed. "He disappeared. A couple of months before—before our parents died."

That flash drive was evidence of her father's misdeeds. Smuggling, yes. And a photo of Kenneth Mahoney. Of her father. Of a gun.

Kenneth had accused Randolph of smuggling, and then he'd disappeared. No one questioned it, because Kenneth Mahoney was a drunk. He'd disappeared before. And then there was his mother saying she knew for a fact he'd come back months later.

Daphne's mouth opened a little, surprise and realization. "There was this man who came by the house a few times. I think he was a private detective. Mom must have hired him to get photos of Dad cheating or something, but he got more than he bargained for. I think he took those photos. He gave them to her and told her never to contact him again."

"Okay," Emma said slowly. "Okay. But what I don't understand is why you needed the flash drive so badly. If what you're saying is true, there's nothing on there that would incriminate either of *you*." She waited. JJ spoke first.

"It wasn't just the flash drive."

"JJ," Daphne said, almost warningly.

"That night," Emma began. Her voice failed. She tried again. "That night, I didn't know what had happened, but I thought—I assumed—that one of you had killed them. Juliette was acting so strange, and she was wearing the wrong clothes. Daphne had blood on her. I thought the best way to protect you was to hide everything."

"You made me change," Daphne said. "You washed my hands. Under the fingernails, too. There was blood in my hair and you trimmed it off."

She'd taken the clothes and sneaked back to the Saracen house, which by then was empty. She burned them in the old fireplace. Not quite well enough to obliterate them, but enough that no one ever connected the clothes to Daphne. The ashes in the fireplace and the graffiti on the walls were enough to start the Satanic rumors—and link the crime to the teens who used the Saracen house as their crash pad. Including, occasionally, Gabriel.

The hair, just a half inch from the end and enough to even it up and make it look natural, she'd scattered here and there in the woods as she went, letting the wind catch it and carry it away.

She'd checked Juliette's clothes for any sign of blood, but she hadn't been able to find anything. She'd debated burning them, too, but in the end she simply folded the clothes and put them away in the bottom of Juliette's drawers. She supplied them each with fresh pajamas, changed her own clothes—leaving her discards in the hamper. And she'd told them what they should say.

They'd been sleeping in the tree house. Daphne had to go inside to use the bathroom. Emma figured Daphne was the least likely to be suspected. People always thought she was just a little girl, treated her like she was six instead of almost a teenager.

She kept it simple. The lie didn't need to be complicated, it just needed to be consistent. But it had still fallen apart. Tiny mistakes that added up. Then the police finding out about Gabriel, combined with Hadley's vendetta.

"I thought one of you must have done it," Emma repeated carefully. She couldn't quite look her sisters in the eye. "I didn't want to know who. I didn't want to know for sure."

JJ's teeth bit down on her lower lip until it blanched white. She looked like she was about to speak, but Emma cut her off.

"It doesn't matter who killed them." Her voice shook, but her words were clear. "We wouldn't have all survived. We wouldn't have all made it out of that house alive. This way we did. So it doesn't matter who did it. It had to be done."

"They didn't deserve to die," JJ said, but she didn't sound like she believed it.

"Plenty of people die who don't deserve it. They at least deserved it more than most," Daphne said with a shrug. "They were abusive. The things they did, maybe they weren't—maybe we never would have been taken away from them. We had everything we needed. Food and a good house and money and healthcare, and it's not actually illegal to hit your children, as fucked-up as that is. But I wanted to—not die, but—"

"Disappear," Emma said, hollow.

She'd never really had the chance to grieve her parents. The investigation had swallowed up any opportunity to pause and feel what was happening, and now it was like all that emotion had been stitched up inside of her and the seams were coming loose.

Did they deserve to die? She didn't know. She'd hated them in a way that was indistinguishable from love, loved them in a way that might have been hatred. She had feared her father and resented her mother and wanted to leave forever, but there were good memories, too, there must be, she would remember them soon. A good birthday, a day at the park, a kind word. She knew they existed, but they skittered away from her groping mind now. All she could remember of her parents was the sound of a blade tearing through canvas and the darkening shade of red against her mother's pale skin.

"I hated them," JJ said. Her fingernails dug into the meat of her arm. "I thought that I could keep pretending to be Perfect Juliette until Daphne got out of school. But eventually they were going to find out what I was up to."

"I never told anyone. Never," Emma said. "Not about the blood, Daphne. Or your clothes, JJ. I kept quiet because I'd never been able to protect you. Not from Mom and Dad. But from the police . . . I could do that. But then you left me. Both of you." She didn't mean to sound so pathetic. "Did you think that I did it? Did you think—"

"I was afraid," Daphne said, and Emma fell silent. "There were letters. Anonymous notes. They would say things like 'I know' and 'You'll never be safe.' So I thought I had to keep quiet, or my sisters would die. I thought I could keep you safe by staying away."

JJ looked startled. "I got the same kind of letters," she said.

Emma frowned. "I never . . ." she started, but then she realized she was wrong. "I thought they were from Hadley. He used to call me all the time, I assumed the letters were him, too, trying to get me to talk."

Daphne's head tilted. "So you thought it was Hadley trying to get you to confess, and I thought they were someone trying to get us to keep quiet?" she asked. "Seems like whoever it was had a messaging problem."

Emma barked out a laugh, startling all of them, and she clapped a hand over her mouth. She stood, pacing a bit, needing the movement.

She'd missed them. Her sisters.

They hadn't always liked one another. They hadn't always helped one another. But they'd been in this house together, and together, they'd stayed alive. They'd survived, and they'd needed one another to do it.

She didn't want to know. She just wanted to be with them again. To be *home*. And for all the rest of it not to matter—their parents and Nathan and all of it.

"Emma," Daphne said. She folded her hands in her lap, her expression apologetic.

She couldn't avoid it. She couldn't have her sisters and her ignorance, and let the rest of the world fade.

She had to know.

"Tell me," she said, and they did.

44

DAPHNE

Then

Daphne kneels beside her mother and stares at Juliette, standing in the doorway to the study.

Juliette has the gun.

She holds it at her side with a strange ease, so relaxed that it's almost as if she's forgotten she's holding it. There is a streak of blood on the side of her thumb and a speckling of it on her shirt and her face, fine glistening drops that smear when she raises her hand to wipe her cheek. "What are you doing, Daph?" she asks, her voice oddly toneless.

"I—I was—" Daphne says. She looks down and realizes her mother has stopped breathing. The pulse at her neck has gone still. *Out of her misery*, Daphne thinks.

"Come look," Juliette says. She gestures with the gun. Its barrel sweeps over Daphne and she cringes.

"Juliette, please don't—"

"Come on," Juliette says, impatient. Daphne lurches to her feet, balling her hands into fists and forcing herself to approach. Juliette doesn't quite have the gun pointed at her, but it isn't pointed very far away, either. None of it makes sense. Juliette shouldn't be here. Juliette shouldn't have the gun.

In the study, their father's body is slumped in his chair. There is no misery for him. No way he is still alive, or lived for more than a moment after the bullet smashed through his skull. Juliette approaches and Daphne follows.

"Look. You can see his brain," Juliette says, pointing, her finger so close to the wound that it almost touches.

Daphne slaps it away with a sound of horror.

Juliette stares at her. "Is this real?" she asks. Her face crumples. She looks like she's going to cry. What's wrong with her? "No, no, no, no," she's saying, and she puts her hands to her head, the gun still gripped in one of them.

"Juliette. Juliette, stop," Daphne says. She has her finger on the trigger. Daphne can see the bullets still in the gun, two chambers in the revolver empty. "Juliette, put down the gun, please."

Juliette looks in seeming surprise at the gun in her hand. Daphne reaches for it, and Juliette doesn't resist as she takes it. Her fingers wrap around the barrel. Her fingerprints are on it, she thinks. Juliette's, too. They have to get rid of it.

Juliette is stumbling away. She makes choked sounds that are almost like sobbing but more animal. Daphne starts after her but then she stops. Her eyes drift across the room, to the drawer where her father put the flash drive.

She still doesn't know what the files on the flash drive meant, but she knows they were dangerous. Could still be dangerous. She darts across the room. She snatches the drive from the drawer and turns. She is staring right into her father's face. His eyes are open, bulging. There is a ragged hole at his temple. Even so, she half expects him to straighten up. To fix her with those hard, angry eyes and demand to know what she thinks she is doing.

She runs past him into the hallway. Juliette stands in the great room, eyes unfocused.

"They're going to kill me," she says, looking at Daphne.

"Stay here," Daphne begs her. She grabs the key to the carriage house from its hook by the front door. Inside, she moves aside boxes until she finds a plastic toolbox abandoned at the back of the building.

She grabs a rag, wraps the flash drive in it, and shoves it inside. She takes the gun to the corner of the building, where the floorboards have rotted through—another thing their father is always about to get around to—and the dirt underneath is visible. She digs down with a spade fetched from a table. Six inches deep, she buries the gun, and then pulls a crate over the hole to hide it. She runs back into the house.

Juliette is gone. There are bloody boot prints leading to the back door but no Juliette. Daphne runs outside. She opens her mouth to call for Juliette, then shuts it. Juliette's gone. She's alone. Her parents are dead inside and no one is here to tell her what to do.

"Juliette?" she whispers into the dark. There's no answer.

She doesn't know what to do. And so she does what she always does when things get to be too much. She climbs into the tree house, and curls on her side. She squeezes her eyes shut and she doesn't cry, though she thinks probably she should.

She drifts off to sleep.

45

JJ

Now

Yellow wallpaper. White grip.
Red hand.

If she closed her eyes, she could remember the weight of the gun. The charcoal and sulfur smell. The deafening crack.

She remembered the bits of bone and hair and pink tissue in the hole through her father's skull. Heard, echoing in her mind, her mother's scream, and felt the heat of her blood as JJ knelt down and put a hand against the gushing wound on her chest. Her mother's hand had closed briefly around her wrist as her breath gurgled in her throat, and then it went slack.

She had tried so hard to think of any explanation but the obvious one.

"Something changed that night," she said. The others were silent, giving her time to find her words. "I realized I couldn't keep doing it—pretending. Eventually they were going to find out what I was up to. I kept thinking that they'd kill me. And I kept thinking about how much I hated them. I'd taken something and had too much to drink—I was out of it. I had Logan's gun, and . . ."

"How did you get the gun?" Emma asked.

"It was Logan's," JJ repeated.

"Right. But how did you get it? Did he give it to you? Why?" Emma asked.

"Does it matter?" Daphne asked.

"She's asking whether I planned to do it. Whether it was premeditated," JJ said, and Emma gave her a nod. It would matter if it came out. "I honestly don't know, which I assume means it wasn't—at least, it wasn't a plan I made while I was in my right mind. I didn't have the gun when I left the Saracen house. I must have gotten it after, but I can't remember much. Just Mom and Dad, and then—then the next thing I remember is you."

Emma's look was bewildered. "What about your clothes? Your hair?"

"According to Logan, he and another friend found me out of my mind and completely soaked through. I have no idea why," JJ said. "They gave me the clothes I was wearing and got me home."

Emma didn't say anything for a long time, sitting with her fist pressed against her stomach.

"You saved me," JJ said. Emma's eyes lifted to hers. "They never pushed me too hard. And when they tried to make you sound bad, I didn't fight them. I let them suspect you so that they wouldn't suspect me. I'm sorry."

"It's what I chose," Emma said, her voice a croak.

"I was the oldest. I was supposed to protect you," JJ said. And she never had. All those years in this house, she'd told herself she was being smart, that she was keeping her parents happy and that it mattered. But she'd never stepped in to take a punishment for Emma. She'd never told her parents off for the way they treated Daphne.

Emma looked away. Tears shone in her eyes, but she blinked them clear. "Did you kill Nathan?" she asked.

JJ's throat constricted. "No," she said, as clearly and fiercely as she could, and Emma turned to look at her. "No," she repeated. Emma's chin dipped once, almost imperceptibly, and she felt something knit itself together between them.

"What happened?" Emma asked.

She hesitated. "I brought over a bottle of wine. He invited me in.

We had a glass. We talked. I figured we'd chat and I'd find a way to mention the carriage house and ask if I could poke around. But I—it didn't work out."

She didn't mention the second glass. The way he'd leaned in toward her and the way she hadn't leaned away, because it was useful, and she'd laughed brightly and let her hair spill to the side the way guys always liked. She hadn't realized things were going too far until he put his hand on her knee, in that way perfectly calibrated to be excused as innocent if she reacted badly. And she had reacted badly. His expression shuttered. He all but kicked her out.

She couldn't pretend she hadn't known what she was doing. But she hadn't expected him to be so eager to cross that line.

"I left. Nothing happened," JJ said.

"Nathan called Ellis that night. Told him he'd found something," Emma said.

"That's good, isn't it? If Ellis knows what was on the drive—" JJ began, but Emma shook her head.

"He didn't say *what* he'd found, apparently. Which makes it seem just as likely that it was something that would implicate me. Or one of you two, and either way, they'll think I eliminated the threat. Or they could just ignore that and say I killed him over the affair. The woman he was sleeping with got threatening emails from someone trying to break them up. I'm sure they assume it was me."

"Nathan was cheating on you?" JJ said, eyebrows raising. "Fuck that guy."

Emma's hand cracked across JJ's cheek. JJ reeled, grabbing at her face. Emma reared back, mouth dropping open. "Shit," she said. "JJ—"

"It's fine," JJ said, clipped. She rubbed her jaw. "I shouldn't have said that. I'm sorry."

Emma cradled her hand in the opposite one, looking appalled at her own violence. "You're right, though," she said. "He was—he cheated on me. It started after I was in an accident. I couldn't—it was months before he and I . . ." Her cheeks colored. "There was a lot on his shoulders. It was hard on him," she finished.

"If I say anything, I'm going to get slapped again," JJ said, unable to keep the disgust from her voice.

Emma winced. "Hell of a family reunion," she said.

"We're out of practice," Daphne replied generously, and Emma laughed.

"It's not like we ever got along," Emma said.

But that wasn't true, was it? There had always been those few stolen moments, when they escaped their parents' world and found their own. Those nights in the tree house, shoulder to shoulder, whispering their secrets to the night.

Emma stood.

"Where are you going?" Daphne asked.

"I need to think," Emma said.

"Emma. No one can know about this," Daphne said.

Emma's eyes tracked from her to JJ. JJ's lips pressed together, but she said nothing. "We'll see," Emma said, and turned away.

JJ sat in the sunroom, watching fireflies appear and vanish again, lazy in their luminescence. She was breaking Vic's rules again, on her second drink, Dad's decanter on the side table next to her.

The house was so strange without them in it—her parents. She'd expected to find it haunted—not literally, of course, she didn't believe in ghosts. But for all that things were largely the way she'd left them, the most curious thing was how absent her parents really were. All these years she'd had the sense that they were still out here, just hidden away inside these walls, only for her to discover that the house had been nothing but an empty box all along.

The house wasn't haunted, she was forced to admit. She was.

"Mind if I sit?" Emma asked. JJ startled; she hadn't heard her come in. She waved to the other chairs in an *I won't stop you* gesture, and

Emma settled in. She glanced at JJ's drink on the side table and leaned forward, nudging a coaster across the coffee table in her direction.

JJ winced. "Sorry. Vic hates how much of a slob I am."

"It's fine," Emma replied. She regarded JJ, a knuckle set against her teeth. "You were such a neat freak when we were kids."

"I had to be," JJ reminded her. Irene Palmer had very much been of the "cleanliness is next to godliness" school of thought. Your hands weren't clean until you'd scrubbed under your fingernails and left your skin red. Owning anything you didn't actually need was an invitation for a lecture on clutter.

"You never knew how to pick your battles," Emma said.

JJ laughed. "Isn't it the other way around? You made everything a fight." It had frustrated her to no end, watching Emma turn every tiny thing into a war. The instant their mother suggested she do something, Emma had to do the opposite, even if she'd meant to in the first place.

"You broke yourself avoiding the smallest reprimand," Emma pointed out.

"Yeah. And then I overcorrected," JJ said, wincing. "One of the hardest things Vic and I did was figure out how to fight without hurting each other."

Emma made a noise in the back of her throat. She looked out the window, her hands limp in her lap. "Nathan and I never fought."

JJ bit back her immediate response. That maybe a fight was what they'd needed. Emma had mentioned the affair like it didn't even faze her. The Emma JJ had known would have been absolutely feral if someone treated her like that. The slap had been the first glimmer of the old Emma that JJ had seen from her so far.

And that was her fault, wasn't it? She was the reason that Emma had to learn silence. Learn how to hide. Emma had never bent a millimeter to protect herself from their parents, but to cover for JJ she'd broken herself completely. And JJ had done nothing to earn it.

"Guess we were both fucked-up in our own special ways. Turns out yours was healthier, though. It didn't turn you homicidal." She looked down at the glass in her hand. "I never said I was sorry. Or thanked you."

"Was it worth it?" Emma asked. It wasn't the question JJ had expected. Emma sat with her body pinched forward, elbows on knees and hands tightly pressed against each other. "I don't mean you lying. I mean what I did. Tell me it was worth it."

"I like my life," JJ said. "Did my best to fuck it up for a long time, but now—Vic, and the apartment, and even my job . . . I've been happy, Emma. More than I thought I ever could be. Yeah. It was worth it."

"Then I'm glad I did it," Emma said.

JJ looked at her in disbelief. "How can you say that, after everything you went through?"

They'd all hid. And so none of them had been able to help one another. Each wrapped up in their own tale of survival, their own dream of escape. It had taken disaster for them to offer anything to one another, and by then the only thing they had to give was silence. No wonder they had scattered.

"What if I'd told them the truth? We could have told people what they were like. Maybe . . ."

"They wouldn't have believed us," Emma said. "It wasn't the simple kind of evil that you can understand. They were mean to us. So what. Dad hit us every once in a while. There wasn't any sexual abuse—right?" She looked carefully at JJ.

"No. Not me. I don't think Daphne," JJ said, revulsion making her voice strained. At least they'd been spared that much.

"He was obsessed with us being virgins," Emma said. "Remember how he used to make us sit in front of him and he'd hold our chins and look us in the eye and make us swear we'd never done anything with a boy?"

"Yeah. That was when I realized I was way better at lying than I thought," JJ said. She'd been terrified the first time she'd had to go through that little ritual after her interlude in the car. But he'd looked at Emma with far more suspicion than at her.

"When did you . . . ?" Emma asked.

"Long before Logan," JJ allowed. She wasn't embarrassed by her past, but it was different talking to someone who had known her before—who had known the mask she wore.

"It never got back to Dad?"

"I was careful only to fuck guys who also had something to lose," JJ said. "Or guys who weren't from town."

"But you're gay," Emma said, and JJ gave a bray of laughter.

"Yeah, but I also wasn't that self-aware," JJ said. "It was never about the guys anyway. It was about doing something for myself—something forbidden. Less fucking, more a 'fuck you.' Did you . . . ?"

"No. I was actually—I didn't have a boyfriend until I was twenty-two. He was the first," Emma said, cheeks coloring. "Took six months to work up to it. It's not like I'm a prude, it's just—it always felt danger-ous, to be that vulnerable."

Sex had never made JJ feel vulnerable. Not even when it was stupid and risky. It had made her feel invincible.

"I slept with Nathan on the first date," Emma went on. "I knew that I would mess things up. Run away. Find a reason not to trust him, not to stay, not to care about him. So I decided that I would never be the one to leave. That I would choose him, starting then, and never waver."

"Even when he cheated on you."

"That was his choice. I made mine," Emma said, defiant.

"You don't think you deserved better than that?" JJ asked.

"No one has ever loved me more than Nathan did," Emma replied, and JJ couldn't say anything to that. Emma stood up. She walked around the coffee table and then perched on its edge, only a couple of feet separating her and JJ. She reached out and took the tumbler out of JJ's hands, and JJ offered no resistance. Emma swirled the whiskey in the bottom of the glass, inhaled.

"I won't let anything happen to you," JJ said fiercely. "I won't let you go through that again."

"We'll get through it," Emma said. "It's not going to be okay. It's already not okay. But we're going to survive it."

"That's not good enough," JJ said. She looked away, blinking back tears. "You've got a baby coming. You've suffered enough for what I did already. If it helps you at all, we have to tell the truth." She'd been given fourteen years; she couldn't ask for more, not at this cost.

"They're not after me for our parents. They think I killed Nathan, and you didn't do that."

"You have to—"

Emma stood, cutting her off. She gave the glass back to JJ and sighed. "Juliette—confess, or don't. But don't tell yourself you're doing it for me."

With that, she walked away.

JJ had thought that confession would bring—what? Peace? Some kind of release, at least. But it hadn't changed anything. She'd waited too long, and now her truth alone couldn't save Emma.

Maybe nothing could.

46

EMMA

Now

The dusty silence of the tree house wrapped around Emma like a blanket. She couldn't decide if it was comforting or smothering.

She had expected the space to seem smaller than it had felt back then, but it was almost more disorienting that it didn't. The planks were leached of color, and moss grew in the cracks, but it was the same room, the same scent, the same sensation of isolation. You couldn't see the house from up here. The window faced east and the door west, the house hidden behind a solid wall.

The sound of someone clambering up the ladder made Emma stiffen. Daphne appeared, levering herself carefully up over the lip of the platform. She looked around the small room with an expression of fondness.

"I'm surprised this thing is still standing," she said, scooting inward. The floor creaked but held.

"Careful. It might not last," Emma said.

"It would be kind of funny if we plummeted to our deaths at this particular moment," Daphne said, and Emma's lip twitched in what was very nearly a smile. "Are you okay?"

That was an impossible question to answer. "You knew the whole time. About Juliette."

Daphne bit her lip. "I saw her with the gun, but I didn't know exactly what had happened."

"You never asked."

"Neither did you."

Emma dug her fingernail against the soft wood of the wall, inhaling the half-rotten scent of it. "I missed you. So much."

"I missed you, too," Daphne said quietly. "I wondered all the time if it was a mistake, staying away."

"What do you think now?" Emma asked.

"That depends on what happens next," Daphne said, and Emma nodded, understanding. "I'm sorry about Nathan."

"Yeah," Emma said raggedly. "I don't like being spied on, you know. I wish you'd just told me you were in town."

Daphne's eyes dropped to the floor. "Emma, I should tell you. I dropped by once when you were asleep. I authorized myself to track your location."

"Jesus, Daphne," Emma said, eyes wide.

"I was worried. I wanted to make sure I could find you if anything happened," Daphne said. She didn't quite meet Emma's eyes, but she didn't sound apologetic, either. "I realize that you may be angry."

"Angry? You broke into the house, you took my phone, you—I don't like to be watched. Followed. Everything I do under a microscope."

"I know. I'm sorry," Daphne said. Her voice was steady. "Everything I've done was to protect us. Protect you. All I've ever wanted is for my sisters to be safe."

"Nathan tracked everything I did," Emma said. "He was always so fucking suspicious, and he was the one cheating."

"He was an asshole," Daphne said. "He didn't deserve you."

"You don't get to say that. I don't get to . . ." Emma said, but she couldn't finish.

"He's dead. He doesn't care what you say about him," Daphne said. "I knew at the wedding he wasn't good enough for you. You don't have to pretend he was better than he was just because he died."

"He was my husband, not some kind of villain," Emma objected.

Daphne sighed. "I see a lot of death. Sometimes my clients are lovely people. Sometimes they're terrible. Usually, they're a bit of both. But the thing with the terrible ones is that there's always some family member who wants to revise history. Make them a saint even if it means pretending all the hurt they caused doesn't exist and doesn't need space to heal. He was a bad husband, Emma."

"So he deserved to die?"

"I didn't say that."

Emma's head lolled back against the wooden wall. She felt sick, and for once she didn't think she could blame it on the baby. "You know the worst part? Every awful thing he did is just another reason they're going to think I killed him."

"But you didn't. We know that, and we'll prove it," Daphne said. "It all comes back to the flash drive, right?"

"But no one else even knew it was in there," Emma said.

"Nathan called Ellis, you said," Daphne replied.

"But he didn't say that he'd found the flash drive. Just that he'd found evidence," Emma said.

"According to who?" Daphne asked.

"Ellis, I guess," Emma said, and frowned. Daphne raised her brows. "You think he was lying?"

"It's the only thing I can think of that makes sense," Daphne said. "*Someone* had to know Nathan had it, right? And had to know what was on it."

"You think it was Ellis Dad was talking to that night, on the phone?" Emma asked.

"Maybe," Daphne said slowly, considering it.

"The third man in the photos. Could it have been Ellis?" Emma asked.

"I couldn't see anything more than a shadow," Daphne said. "Do you really think he could have been involved in a murder?"

"I don't know," Emma said.

"Emma?" JJ's voice came from a distance. Emma frowned.

"Shall we?" Daphne said. At Emma's nod she exited, and Emma followed at a somewhat ungainly scramble. She reached the base of the precarious ladder to find JJ walking across the lawn toward them, her phone in her hand.

"What's going on?" Emma asked, getting a look at JJ's face and knowing it was nothing good.

"Chris has been trying to reach you. He says he has bad news," JJ said. "He said he needs to talk to you in person."

Emma's heart sank.

There was only one thing she could think of that he might mean.

47

EMMA

Now

JJ gave her a ride. Emma wasn't fond of being carted around like an invalid, but she didn't have time to go prize her car out of the jaws of the justice system. JJ shoved random detritus off the passenger seat with muttered apologies. Emma sat scrunched against the corner between the door and the seat back, trying to get her galloping heartbeat to slow.

"I would have told them, you know," JJ said suddenly, startling Emma. "I wouldn't have let you actually go to prison. I just wanted you to know that." She sounded like she was trying to convince herself as much as Emma. It was true now, Emma thought—she believed her about that. But she thought it was more a wish about the past than a reality.

"I know," Emma said. They fell silent again. JJ stopped at a red light. A woman walked in front of the car, two daughters in tow. One of them had a book open, and her mother put a hand on the back of her head to make sure she didn't veer off into traffic. The other skipped by, turning her head to stare straight at Emma and JJ until she was forced to look forward again.

"Did you know that Daphne is tracking my phone?" Emma asked.

"Tracking your phone? You're sure?" she asked.

"I take it that's a no," Emma said.

"Why would she be tracking you?" JJ asked. She slowed as she approached the bridge over the river. It was a two-lane bridge with a walking path on one side. Here, the river was deeper and faster than out behind the house, and the sound of it filled the car.

"To protect me, I guess," Emma said wearily. Who knew why Daphne did the things she did?

The car bumped and jostled on the wooden planks. To either side of the water, the bank dropped down at a steep slope, and on the far side a couple of teenagers were picking their way down.

People used to jump off the bridge when they were kids, until a boy drowned the year Emma started high school. People said he was a daredevil, that he must have hit the water and gasped, or hit his head on a rock.

"Do you trust her?" Emma asked.

"Daphne? Why wouldn't I?" JJ asked, startled.

"I don't know. Maybe it's wishful thinking, but I keep wondering— you don't actually remember killing them. Right?" Emma asked.

"I don't remember pulling the trigger. But Daphne saw me there. Mom was still alive. It couldn't have been more than what, two minutes? So what's the alternative? Someone kills them and runs out the door, and I don't see them?"

"You don't remember seeing Daphne, either," Emma pointed out. "You don't know where you got the gun. You don't know how you ended up completely soaked."

"I wanted them dead," JJ said hoarsely.

"We all did," Emma replied. She shook her head. "I don't know. Something about it all doesn't make sense."

"Please, don't," JJ said. Emma cast her a curious look. "I've worked so hard to accept what I did, Emma. I can't afford to wonder."

Emma nodded, fell silent. She thought she understood what JJ meant. Yet it still bothered her. The gun, the gaps in JJ's memory, the fact that Daphne hadn't *seen* her shoot them.

What if they thought they'd been covering for one another, but it had been someone else all along?

Or maybe it was only a fantasy. Now that she had her sisters back with her, she wished she could wash the blood from under their fingernails, like she had so long ago. Brush their hair and tug their clothes into place and be blameless, be innocent. Go back to before she knew.

They didn't speak again until they reached their destination.

Chris was working out of a borrowed office. He still had enough friends to call in a favor, and Emma and JJ walked to the back of Quincy Real Estate to find him ensconced in a small room decorated with photos of a blond woman flanked by two massive Great Danes. The nameplate on the desk read KATIE GREER.

"You don't look much like a Katie," Emma said as she entered, her voice too loud to her own ears. Chris looked up from his laptop. His expression was grim.

"Emma. Juliette," he said, eyes tracking to JJ. "It would be best if you waited outside. Emma and I need to talk alone."

"I'd like her here," Emma said.

"I have to insist. This is a conversation that you want protected by privilege," Chris said, and Emma wavered. She looked over at JJ.

"I'll be right outside," JJ said. Emma nodded, grateful, and JJ stepped into the hall, closing the door behind her.

"So what's going on?" Emma asked.

"You should sit down," Chris said.

"I'm fine standing," Emma replied stiffly, both hands wrapped around her purse strap.

Chris adjusted his glasses, eyes on the tabletop. "Emma, I'm afraid you're going to be arrested," he said.

She'd expected it, and still she felt as if she'd been struck. Her balance faltered. She gripped the back of a chair for stability. She stepped around the side of the chair and sank into it. "Why? What—what do they have?"

"I don't know the extent of the evidence they've collected," Chris said. "I will, of course, find out as much as I can as quickly as I can so that we can resolve this, but I need you to stay calm. This isn't the end of the world, and it isn't a conviction. There's still a long way to go, and while this isn't going to be pleasant, you're safe, you're alive, and we're going to get through this."

"There must be something. Some reason they think . . ." Was it the affair? The emails to Addison?

"Emma. The forensics revealed that the gun that killed your husband was the same weapon used to kill your parents," Chris said.

And so they thought that because Emma had killed her parents, she must have killed Nathan, too. The truth burned like a coal in her chest, but she stayed silent. It wouldn't help, sacrificing JJ to save herself.

"Emma, remember, don't panic. We have time, we have resources, and we have the truth on our side. None of them are a guarantee, but right now the important thing is to stay positive and stay calm," Chris said. He'd given her that exact speech fourteen years ago, she reflected. Had it worked back then? Right now all she could feel was the terror coursing through her.

"Are they coming here?" she asked.

"No. I arranged to have you surrender voluntarily tomorrow morning," Chris said. "You're expected at six A.M.; I'll collect you and drive you. Hopefully, we can get you in front of a judge and get bail set so you don't have to spend the night in jail."

"How the hell am I going to get the money for bail? Will they even let me out on bail at all?" Emma asked, words coming fast and frantic.

"I don't want you to worry about that," Chris said. "It's my job to convince the judge, not yours. And don't sweat the money. If the judge sets bail, I'll make sure it gets paid."

"That's very generous," Emma said, a bit stiffly. Chris gave her a curious look. She wetted her lips. "Why have you always been so helpful?"

Chris's brow creased. "Emma, you know I've always been fond of your family. Of you. Do you have to ask, after all these years?"

"Yes. I do," Emma said hoarsely. "You sent threatening letters to Kenneth Mahoney."

He sat back in his chair. "Kenneth Mahoney? That was years ago."

"Did you know what my father was doing?" Emma demanded. He was silent. She looked away, blinking sudden tears from her eyes. "You knew. And you didn't say anything."

"I knew that your father was up to something. *Not* when I wrote the letters to Kenneth Mahoney," Chris said. "That was doing a favor for a friend who said that an angry employee was slandering him. In retrospect, I shouldn't have agreed to do it. I didn't know there was anything else going on until later."

"There were robberies. A series of truck robberies, and someone died," Emma said. She wasn't sure she was making sense. She wasn't sure anything would make sense ever again. "It was Dad. I don't know if he was part of the actual thefts, but he moved the goods."

"I remember those robberies," Chris said. He sat back in his chair, rubbing his chin. "Ellis was part of the task force. There was speculation at the time that there might have been someone feeding the thieves information from the investigation."

"Kenneth went to Ellis about it. Ellis blew him off." Emma's mind churned through the possibilities. If Ellis was the source, if Ellis was involved . . .

"No one took Kenneth seriously," Chris said. "And I don't see what any of this has to do with your husband's death."

"Kenneth Mahoney found out what they were doing, and then he disappeared. No one questioned it because it wasn't the first time he'd taken off, but he always came back."

"Okay," Chris said slowly, his tone cautious.

Emma plowed on. "When my mom came to you, she said she had evidence on a flash drive, right? Well, I found it fourteen years ago—but I lost it. I think Nathan found it. I think that's why he's dead. He called Ellis that night. He *told* him he'd found something. What if Ellis was involved? What if—"

Chris held up a hand. "Emma. Slow down. You don't have this flash drive now, do you?"

"No."

"And the last time you saw it was fourteen years ago."

She hesitated, then nodded stiffly. No need to bring Daphne into this—not yet. He folded his hands on the desk, looking down at them.

"This is all wild conjecture," Chris said. "I can talk to Mehta, and I can look into things on my end. Maybe there's something to all of this. But there is no benefit to rushing here. Nothing is going to happen in time to stop you from being arrested. Given that, it is far better to do things *carefully* and be sure of what we have."

"You're not the one who's about to be arrested for her husband's murder," Emma snapped. She stood, pulse thudding in her temple and skin flushed. She started to leave.

"Tomorrow morning," Chris said in a firm, warning tone.

"I'll be waiting," Emma pledged, venom in her voice.

"It's going to be okay, Emma," Chris said.

"You can't promise that," she told him, and left the room without saying goodbye. Outside, JJ sat in a chair in the hallway, chewing her thumbnail. She jerked as the door opened and surged to her feet, all pointless motion.

"What's going on?" JJ asked. "What did he say?"

"Let's get home," Emma said wearily. "I'll tell you on the way."

48

EMMA

Now

They left downtown, slithering onto the sun-dappled lanes that separated the busy heart of Arden Hills from its outskirts. Emma had never felt at home here when she was young, but now, driving these roads, it felt like this was where she belonged. It was not a comforting realization.

"We'll tell them it was me," JJ said.

Emma made a noncommittal noise. She was still thinking about the gun—about how it had ended up in JJ's hands. About what it was Daphne had seen, and what she hadn't, and all the things that looked like facts but were just assumptions. Juliette had the gun. It didn't mean she'd fired it.

Kenneth Mahoney went to Ellis, and then went missing.

Ellis was on the task force investigating the robberies, and no one ever got caught.

Red and blue light swept over the dashboard, followed by the short whoop of a police car.

"What the fuck?" JJ asked, looking into the rearview. Emma twisted to look behind them. Her heart sank at the sight of the Arden Hills PD SUV. JJ put on her blinker, started to slow down.

"Don't stop," Emma told her, suddenly frantic. She grabbed JJ's shoulder. "Keep going."

JJ gave her a surprised look. "What? I can't just keep going," she said. Quietly, she added, "Emma, come on. If I run away from a cop, what's that going to look like?"

JJ was slowing. Was stopping at the side of the road.

"It's okay," JJ said, giving Emma what was probably supposed to be a reassuring look. Emma sat back hard against her seat, pressing her body into the leather as if she could sink entirely within it. Emma wrapped both hands around the seat belt strap, focusing on the sensation of it biting into her palms.

The SUV pulled in behind them. The door popped open. Rick Hadley stepped out, moving with the unhurried gait of someone who wants you to know they don't mind keeping you waiting.

Emma's stomach clenched. JJ rolled down the window as Hadley approached. He leaned over, looking in at them one by one. His sunglasses turned his eyes to voids.

"Juliette. Emma," he said.

"Why did you pull us over?" JJ asked.

"There's a warrant out for your sister's arrest." He spoke to JJ but was looking at Emma. She stared straight back at him, at her own reflection in his sunglasses.

"Her lawyer arranged her surrender. Tomorrow," JJ said.

"I haven't heard anything about that."

"She's not supposed to be arrested until tomorrow. Go ask. Call it in, or whatever. They'll tell you," JJ said.

"Step out of the car, Emma," Hadley told her.

"You can't arrest her. You don't have the authority," JJ insisted.

"I'm sure we can sort that out with a quick chat, but in the meantime, Emma is going to step out of the vehicle." Hadley's tone was almost cheerful.

"You can't—" JJ started, but Emma put a hand on her arm. Her fear was still wrapped around her throat, but she knew there was nothing to do.

"Call Chris." She handed JJ her phone. She unbuckled and opened the side door.

Hadley beckoned her to approach the back of the car. She kept her hands loose at her sides, focusing everything she had on taking one breath and then another, and walked to join him. He waited for her to catch up and then put a hand on her arm. "Let's have a little chat," he said. He kept her walking all the way back to his car, and she didn't protest.

"What is this really about?" she asked him when he stopped. His hands on his hips, he looked at her inscrutably. "What do you want, *Uncle Rick?*"

"I want you to stop playing games," he said. He didn't sound cheerful anymore. His voice was low and dangerous.

"I don't know what you're talking about."

"You've been playing dumb for fourteen years," he said. Emma's hands shook. She balled them into fists to keep them still. "Pretending you didn't know what happened that night. Pretending you had nothing to do with it."

"I didn't," Emma said. She gave him a hard look. "Did you know what Dad was doing? About the robberies?"

"What the hell are you talking about?" he asked.

"I think Ellis knew. And I think Nathan told him *exactly* what he found, and what was on that flash drive," Emma said, aware that she wasn't explaining herself properly. She watched Hadley carefully. Her father's best friend. Ellis's second-in-command. Was it possible he didn't know? "He thought he was doing the right thing. He thought he could trust the police, and now he's dead, just like Kenneth Mahoney."

"Now, that's a name I haven't heard in a long time," Hadley said. He paused, as if considering long and hard. His thumbnail scraped along his jaw. "All right. Let's say you're right. Where is this flash drive?"

"I don't know," Emma said, frustrated, and then she noticed the intensity in his voice. The spark of paranoia in his eye. She backed away half a step. "I don't know," she repeated.

Hadley took a step toward her. She fell back on instinct, but he grabbed her arm, wrenching her toward him, and Emma realized she'd made a mistake. A terrible one.

"Tell me where the flash drive is, and we can clear this all up," he said. JJ's car door opened. She stepped out, but didn't approach. "Tell me, or I will shoot you in the fucking head and tell them you reached for my gun. You already killed your parents and your husband. You think they won't believe me?"

"I don't have it," Emma said. And neither did he.

"Emma—" he began.

Tires squealed, and JJ's car reversed—barreling toward them.

49

JJ

Now

JJ sat in the car, her knee bouncing with nervous, jangly energy. She watched Emma and Hadley walk toward the SUV. He couldn't just arrest her, could he?

Chris. She was supposed to call Chris.

She looked at Emma's phone and realized it was locked. Did she even have Chris's number on hers?

The screen lit up. She was about to ignore the call when she saw the local area code. Something made her stop. She answered. Held the phone to her ear.

"Hello?"

A pause. "Juliette?"

"Logan. What the hell are you doing calling my sister?" she asked.

"I was actually trying to reach you," he said. "I didn't have your number. Look, I felt bad about the way things went when we talked. It freaked me out, that's all. And I'm not repeating this to anyone who could vaguely be construed as an authority figure, okay?"

"What are you talking about, Logan?" JJ asked. What were Hadley and Emma doing? She popped open the door and stepped out, keeping the phone to her ear.

"The gun. My gun," Logan said. "I promise you, you didn't have it that night. Neither did I. I hadn't had it for a couple of months."

"Who had it?" JJ asked. She watched as Emma stepped back, and back again. As Hadley reached for her.

"I got caught with it. He took it off me, let me go with a warning."

"Logan. Who took it?" JJ asked, urgency in her voice.

"Rick Hadley."

Hadley had the gun.

Red hand.

She could almost remember pulling the trigger.

Almost.

But she couldn't have had the gun that night, could she? Not if Hadley had taken it. If the gun had been at the house that night, so had he.

JJ threw herself back into the seat, barely closing the door before she threw it into reverse.

Hadley spun as JJ accelerated. He stood frozen, staring as if he couldn't comprehend what was happening. Emma scrambled back away from him. At the last second he tried to throw himself out of the path of the car, but it clipped his hip. Not enough to do real damage at that speed, but it sent him sprawling, right against the hood of his own car. There was a crack as his head connected, and he fell to his hands and knees. He grabbed the side of his head, dazed.

"Juliette, what—" Emma started.

"Just get in!" JJ screamed at her, leaning over to throw open the door, and Emma leaped inside. JJ rammed the car into drive and floored the gas pedal, her blood roaring in her ears.

"What are you doing?" Emma demanded, finishing her thought. She turned in her seat. JJ looked in the rearview mirror to see Hadley getting up slowly, one hand braced on the hood of his car. Then the road bent, and he was out of sight.

"Hadley had the gun. Hadley had the fucking gun," JJ said. *Yellow wallpaper. White grip. Red hand.* But Rick Hadley had the gun, and she'd been wrong. She hadn't done it. It wasn't her, and relief and fear knotted together inside her.

She barely braked as she threw them around a hard turn, tires skidding along the dirt at the edge of the road. Emma was thrown against the door. She fumbled for her seat belt. JJ yanked the wheel, taking the final turn before the bridge.

"JJ, we're going too—" Emma said at the same moment that JJ realized where they were, how stupidly fast they were going. But it was too late.

They careened around the corner. The road kinked to the right. They kept going straight. JJ slammed on the brakes. The car jolted over the edge of the road, slammed into the already-broken guardrail with a sound of protesting metal, and then they were shooting over the edge of the drop-off, into the water below.

They were in the water. JJ must have blacked out for a moment when they hit because she woke with a mouthful of river water and Emma shouting her name.

The car had careened over the bank and jammed against a rock, with the passenger side sticking up out of the water. Emma was bracing herself in her seat, her seat belt wrapped around one arm, or she would have fallen. Water flowed over JJ's mouth and nose, choking her. She arched wildly, trying to get above it to take a breath—

"JJ! Your seat belt. Get your seat belt off," Emma said, sounding strangely calm. JJ scrabbled for the release. Then she was free, and shoving herself up above the water level, gasping. Emma crouched on her seat, eyes bright but steady.

"You okay?" JJ managed, coughing.

"For now. But the current's strong, and if it shifts us, we could go deeper," Emma said. "We're only a few feet from shore. I can't get my door open, the current's holding it shut. We're going to have to go out your window." The driver's-side window was still open. Through it, JJ could see the course of the river winding away from them, the water rushing past, the dark bulk of the bridge. JJ searched for headlights, sirens, any sign that someone had seen them. There was nothing.

"You still a good swimmer?" JJ asked. It wasn't far to shore. The current was swift, but it slowed past the bridge.

"We'll find out," Emma said. She shifted, and a look of pain flashed across her face, her hand going to the arm that had been wrapped in the seat belt.

"What's wrong?"

"Nothing. Let's get out of here," Emma said, but she said it through gritted teeth. "You first. I'll follow you out."

JJ hoisted herself up and out of the window, sitting on the sill a moment before swinging her legs over. There was no point trying to get her feet under her. She clung to the car to keep from being swept away and held on as Emma clambered across the seats, following her lead. Emma got her head and shoulders out, then one leg, the other foot braced against the sill.

Her weight shifted, and she let out a sharp cry. Her grip slipped, and in the next instant the current snatched her, tearing her away from the car. JJ cried out, flinging out a hand, and caught her wrist, her other hand holding tight to the car frame. JJ's hand was numb. Her grip on the car was slipping. She couldn't hold both of them.

JJ let go of the car in the same instant that Emma let go of her.

50

JULIETTE

Then

She is in the water. She is under it. It is rushing around her and she can't breathe—

She is on the bridge. The night is warm but she is cold. The blood makes her palms night-dark. It pools in the creases, cracks on her knuckles when she bends her fingers. She wipes her hands against her shirt, smearing the blood across it, but her hands won't come clean.

She remembers—*yellow wallpaper*—the sound of her footsteps, too loud. Dragging herself up the steps. Her parents' voices. They're angry. She leaves the door open behind her. She goes upstairs, to her room, knowing she shouldn't be here, not looking like this, not feeling like this. She still has Logan's flask, and she curls up on her floor and drinks and drinks and waits to be found. They're going to kill her, she thinks. He's going to kill her.

She remembers the gun—*white grip*—in her hand. She is a good shot. She likes to picture people when she fires off a shot, whoever she's angry with. She doesn't want them dead, but it keeps her aim toward center anyway. Emma. Logan, sometimes. Dad. Mom. She points the gun at the target and squeezes the trigger—bang.

She's holding the gun, but it isn't a paper target in front of her.

She's on the bridge and there's—*red hand*—so much blood and she doesn't remember how it got there.

She does remember.

She can't get it off. She has to get it off. To get away.

She's in the water, and it's over her head, and it's dragging her down. She kicks, but her feet are heavy, clumsy. Her shoes are too big. She was so happy when she found them, in that thrift store. Paid too much, didn't try them on, because Mom was going to be back at any minute and couldn't see her with them. She buried them under blouses and skirts in the bag and sweated the whole way home. They were too big after all, but she tied the laces tight and made do.

Now they pull at her, and she can't get a breath of air. They weigh her down, and the water takes her deeper.

Before the water, she's on the bridge. The moon is bright overhead. She sits on the rail. Kids used to jump off here until one of them drowned. A terrible accident, everyone said, he must have hit his head. But Juliette knows a girl who was there, who looked into his eyes the instant before he jumped and knew then that he wasn't going to come back up. That he didn't want to.

There's blood all over her and she can't get clean.

There's blood all over her and she can't go home.

She jumps. She falls. She goes under.

She's in the water and she kicks, twists, wraps her hand around the heel of one boot and yanks. The boot is too big and it slides free, and then she gets the other one loose. It's stuck. She yanks at the laces, her lungs burning, fighting the urge to gasp. Then at last the boot comes free and she's kicking up toward the surface, toward the light of a swollen moon.

Before the water, before the bridge and the woods and the blood, she is in her room, curled on the floor with an empty flask in her hand and a buzz in her head like a hornet trapped under a glass. She stares at the pale yellow wallpaper, orderly stripes surrounding her. Her mother and father have stopped shouting.

The gunshot makes her jump. She scrambles to her feet and stands for a moment, panting, at first not comprehending the sound and then waiting for a scream, a flurry of activity to mark what she has heard. There is nothing.

She creeps into the hall. Down the stairs. The front door is still open, the way she left it. Her thoughts a slurry, she stumbles into the great room. It's empty. Still. Then she looks to her right, toward the hall to the study.

She is in the water, and the gunshot is an echo in her ears, but the rush of the current bears it away from her at last; she forgets it was ever there.

But before the water she is in the hallway, and her mother is dead. The images in front of her are reduced to color: splashes of red, fragments of yellow white. The gun is on the ground. She picks it up; she forgets she picked it up. She looks down and sees it in her hand, and it's as if it's always been there.

She is in the water. She lets go of everything she can, every horrible memory, but shards of it lodge inside her. She will remember the yellow wallpaper, the white grip, the red hand. She will lose the pieces that could have saved her, but those will burrow into her flesh.

After the water, she is on the road when headlights spill across her. She's in the back seat of a car, struggling into someone else's clothes. Nina is telling her it's going to be all right, cupping her cold hands to warm them. Then Nina is gone, and Juliette slips her hand into the pocket of the oversize shirt that isn't hers, and finds something cool and metal there. Her thumb traces over the bee engraved on the lighter.

She is in the water, breaking the surface, taking in a breath that she wasn't sure she wanted until it filled her lungs, but now she knows. She wants to breathe. She wants to live. And so she lets her memories sink; lets the river take them. Everything else about this moment she will forget, except for that: She wants to live. She wants to endure.

The current is gentler this time of year, sullen and slow, not the galloping rush after the rains that will gladly slam you against the rocks or pin you to the bottom, but still it's carrying her along. She strikes out toward the shore. She is a good swimmer, and she has no fear of the water. It will not take her unless she wants it to.

After the water, when she is sitting in a cold room and answering questions, she will remember she wants to breathe; she will keep her secrets and stick to her lies and let her sister drown in her place.

But in the water she is, finally, alive. She breaks the surface. She takes a breath.

51

EMMA

Now

Emma was conscious of movement, of thunderous noise. She couldn't find the surface. She couldn't find air. And then there was an arm around her, hauling at her painfully. Of water surging over her face and the scrape of rocks under her. Then she was coughing, JJ's arms around her, holding her against JJ's chest as she murmured in her ear.

"I've got you. I've got you," she was saying, and Emma blinked awake under a blue sky, in the mud of the riverbank. The bridge was on her right, which seemed wrong. They'd gone into the water upriver of the bridge. Had they been swept that far?

Emma tried to speak and just coughed instead, the taste of river water filling her mouth. She managed to straighten up, pulling away from JJ, and braced herself against the ground with one hand, the other pressed to her abdomen. Her shoulder felt like it had been packed with ground glass.

"Emma?" JJ asked.

"I'm okay," she managed, more optimism than observed reality. JJ had a nasty gash on her forehead. Her thick hair was plastered in tendrils to her cheeks, hanging soddenly around her shoulders. Emma assumed she didn't look much better. "You?"

"I'll live," JJ said shakily. "Wasn't sure you would for a minute. You let go."

"I didn't want to drag you down with me," Emma said. "I might have overestimated my memory of high school swim lessons."

JJ's teeth chattered. "Emma—" she started.

The river almost hid the crunch of boots on the rocks. JJ twisted, Emma struggling up to her feet as Rick Hadley emerged from the trees. His gun was in his hand, and as JJ stood, he pointed it straight at her. Emma started to put her hands up, only for sudden pain to shoot through her shoulder, lancing down to her fingertips. She let out a strangled scream, and JJ lurched toward her in alarm.

"Stop," Hadley said, jerking the gun at her. "Tell me where the drive is."

"You were the one working with Dad," Emma said, cradling her arm against her body. "Did you kill Kenneth Mahoney when he tried to turn you in?"

Hadley laughed. "Ken didn't try to turn anyone in. Not at first, at least. First, he tried to blackmail your father. You can guess how far that got him."

"All the way to the old quarry," JJ said dryly, and Hadley flinched, just a bit.

"And then Dad called you and told you that one of us knew," Emma said. "What happened? Did you realize you needed to tidy up your loose ends?"

He gave her a strange look. "I didn't do anything to your parents. I loved Randolph like a brother. I loved—" He stopped. His throat bobbed, and Emma sucked in a breath.

"You were sleeping with Mom," Emma said. "You had Logan's gun."

"No, I didn't," Hadley said.

"You did. You took it from him," she insisted.

"And I gave it to your mother," he shot back. "She said she was afraid of Randolph. She needed a gun he didn't know about. That no one knew about. It was already in the house, Emma. And so was Juliette. Just like she was at the house the day Nathan died. All Nathan told Ellis was that he might have found something that cleared you. Not your sisters, *you*. You tell me where that drive is, and I'll back you up. Juliette's the one who attacked me. Juliette's the one with the criminal record. Just tell me where it is, and I'll make sure you don't have to give birth in a jail cell."

Their father had told him about the flash drive. Told him that one of *them* had seen it. And death had come to their house. Hadley had worked so hard to keep the suspicion fixed on Emma. No need to look anywhere else.

Until Nathan found the drive. And foolish, trusting Nathan had called Ellis right up. And, of course, Ellis would tell Hadley—Emma Palmer's husband found something. He's coming by in the morning.

Except, she thought.

"Hello? Helloo-oo!" called a voice. Hadley froze. Emma straightened up, staring at the tree line as Daphne strode out, clad in a bright pink top and striped leggings and waving frantically. "Is everyone all right? I saw a car in the river and the police car and I heard voices and I thought, *Oh my goodness, there is something going on here and I'd better check that they don't need help!*"

"Ma'am, please go back to your car," Hadley said. He turned, letting the gun drop to his side.

Emma saw the moment he recognized Daphne. His eyes went wide. His arm tensed. And Emma launched herself forward. Two staggering steps and she threw her arms around him, bear-hugging his arm against his body, ignoring the flash of pain. Between his surprise and her momentum he lost his footing and the two of them crashed to the ground together.

JJ was there an instant later, wrapping both hands around the gun and stomping on his elbow. He yelled, lost his grip. JJ flung the gun toward the water. Hadley rolled on the ground, pinning Emma beneath him. His hand was on her throat. His weight bore down on her windpipe, his face contorted in rage.

Above him, Daphne appeared. In both hands she held a rock the size of a football. With a look of utmost calm and concentration, she brought it down on the back of his head. Once. Twice. Three times.

Hadley toppled to the ground. Emma writhed out from under him, clutching at her throat, breath coming in sobs. Then JJ was there, hands under her armpits, hauling her back from Hadley—but Hadley wasn't moving.

Daphne dropped the rock. It landed with a thud next to her, one side slick with blood.

JJ sat with Emma, holding her semi-upright. She could feel the frantic beating of her sister's heart.

"Is he dead?" Emma asked hoarsely. Daphne knelt beside Hadley.

"He's breathing," she said. "But he doesn't look good. I hit him pretty hard."

"How did you—?" Emma began.

Daphne bared her teeth in something resembling a smile. "I guess it's a good thing I was tracking you. I saw your phone was in the river. Then I saw Hadley's car and I was sure something was wrong."

"Thank you for being so nosy, Daphne," Emma said with feeling. She reached out. Daphne caught her hand, their fingers lacing, and their eyes locked. Daphne let out a shaky breath, and Emma felt a shiver go through her. Not so icy calm after all. In the distance, sirens wailed, growing closer.

They were going to have a lot of questions to answer.

"It was him," JJ said. She sounded dazed. "I remember. I didn't kill them. I found the gun on the ground. It wasn't me. And he must have—when Nathan called Ellis, he must have told Hadley."

"He killed Nathan to stop him from turning over the drive and the gun," Daphne said. "He knew everyone would just assume it was Emma."

"Right," Emma said softly, not quite meeting her sisters' eyes. *Except.* Except that Hadley hadn't had the drive.

Her sisters were perfectly silent and perfectly still. JJ with her arm around Emma, Daphne's hand gripping hers.

They looked at one another, and the sirens grew closer. Daphne brought her other hand up, clasping Emma's hand between both of hers. She leaned in close, pressed a kiss against Emma's cheek, and whispered in her ear.

"No one can know."

Emma said nothing.

Just as she always had.

52

EMMA

Now

Emma missed out on the most intense questioning, thanks to being once again in the hospital. She had a torn ligament in her shoulder and a racking cough from breathing in the water, which made the doctors worry about pneumonia, but she was alive and the baby's heartbeat kept up its steady whooshing. She stayed overnight for monitoring just in case, aware that somewhere else in the building, Rick Hadley was clinging to life.

He did live. Or at least, he hadn't died yet.

Rick Hadley's house was searched. Hidden in his garage, they found a revolver with a white grip. Cleaned of prints, but its ballistics matching the weapon that killed Irene and Randolph Palmer. That killed Nathan Gates. And with the gun, a flash drive.

The flash drive was almost fifteen years old, but still functional. It contained records showing that Palmer Transportation had been falsifying its shipment records to hide extra loads—cargo that matched up with robberies in the area, around the same time. It also contained photos of two men forcing Kenneth Mahoney into a car. Driving him to the old quarry. You couldn't see Hadley's face in any of the photos; couldn't even really tell it was him. But it was his car they were driving, his old blue Impala, and the photographer made sure to get a clear shot of the plates.

They'd even tracked down the guy who took them. He thought he was going to get a shot of Randolph Palmer and some twenty-five-year-old mistress. He'd gotten the fright of his life instead.

So this is the theory the police suggested: Rick Hadley finds out about the flash drive. He knows that one of the Palmer girls has seen the evidence. He knows Randolph isn't going to let him do what needs to be done. Maybe they argue, maybe there's other bad blood already—maybe Hadley's taking the opportunity to eliminate his mistress's husband. Whatever the reason, he goes over to the Palmer house and puts a bullet in Randolph's head. But he can't find the drive. He can't find the girls. Irene finds him instead. He doesn't mean to kill her, probably, and when they struggle with the gun, when it goes off, he drops the gun in horror. He flees.

But Juliette picks up the gun. Daphne makes a logical conclusion. They all conspire to silence, thinking they are protecting themselves and one another.

Perhaps they could be forgiven.

For years, they all stay quiet. Hadley knows that one of them has seen the drive, but he doesn't know which. He sends his threatening letters, he hounds Emma so she knows she'll never be safe. Life goes on.

But then Nathan finds the drive. He calls Ellis. And the past isn't the past anymore, and Hadley has to do something. He drives to the house where his lover and his best friend died. Nathan has seen the photos, of course, but he wouldn't recognize Hadley, not steeped in shadow. He has no reason to be afraid. Let me see what you found, he says, and Nathan hands him the gun.

It explained why he came after Emma and JJ, afraid of what they knew. Or perhaps he was beyond all reason by then, and that was why he attacked them, threatened them, was certainly going to kill them if Daphne hadn't intervened. If she didn't bring that rock down as hard as she could, until she was sure he wouldn't get up.

It was a good story. People need stories to make sense of things, after all.

So they were safe. And they were free.

And it was time to go home.

53

JJ

Now

They went back to the house. They always ended up back at the house. It was like a gravity well, a black hole from which nothing could escape, not even light. JJ hadn't been back here since the river. The accident. Hadley. She'd stayed at the hotel or the hospital. With Christopher Best at her side, she'd sat again in a cold room and recounted what had happened the night her parents died.

Most of it, at least.

She'd told them about the pills and the drinking, Logan Ellis and the Saracen house, the strange state she'd been in when she wandered back into the house. She'd told them about the gunshots and picking up the gun from the ground. She hadn't killed her parents.

It should have been a relief.

Remembering that night was like seeing light bend through water. The angle kept changing when she moved her head. She remembered the water, the bridge, the blood, the gunshots, the gun. And if she held still, and tilted her head just the right way, she remembered the moment she turned toward the hallway.

Her mother is holding a gun. Juliette sees her, but despite the fact that she is standing only a few feet away, her mother doesn't seem to see Juliette. She doesn't seem to see anything at all.

Irene Palmer lifts the gun, turning her hand to rest the barrel against her sternum. Juliette steps forward. Reaches out for her, letting out a wordless cry. Her mother pulls the trigger. Hot flecks of blood burst across Juliette's cheeks.

Like a glimmer of light, it fractured as the water rippled. She couldn't be sure of it.

But she knew.

She sat in her childhood bedroom. The yellow wallpaper was the color of pus.

She had watched her mother shoot herself in the chest. Part of her had preferred her own guilt.

Irene had told Hadley she was afraid of Randolph. That she was getting ready to leave him. And then he'd found out she was preparing to turn him in. She must have thought she had no choice but to kill him.

Or maybe he had told her that one of the girls knew. Maybe she had realized she had to act, to protect her daughters.

JJ wished fervently that she could believe that was why.

Maybe she couldn't face what she'd done afterward. Maybe it had always been the plan—maybe she had always known that there was no true escape.

It was strange to realize that she hadn't known her parents enough to even guess why they'd done what they'd done. She'd spent so long trying to map her parents' moods, but in the end they were mysteries to her.

She knew one thing for sure. All these years, she had struggled to tease apart her guilt and her grief, unable to tell one from the other. Only now that her guilt had been lifted away did she realize that there was nothing else there.

She might have grieved once. But there were no more ghosts in this house.

JJ was done being haunted.

54

EMMA

Now

"We need to talk," Emma said.

"Do we?" Daphne asked, not quite pleading.

They were gathered together in the living room. Daphne sat; Juliette perched on the arm of a chair; Emma crossed her arms and stood near the doorway.

They hadn't had a moment properly alone since the river.

"We're not doing this again," Emma said. "Here, with the three of us, we tell the truth. All of it. We're not spending another fourteen years hiding from each other."

"The truth," Daphne echoed, and Emma saw something flicker behind her eyes. She was deciding how much to reveal—or how much she had to.

"Hadley didn't kill Mom," JJ said. Emma's eyes cut to her. JJ blew out a ragged breath. "She killed herself. I was standing right in front of her."

"You can't be certain of your own memories," Daphne pointed out.

"I know. But I think I'm right," JJ said. "But I don't understand why she would do it."

Emma's arms were crossed so tightly across her body that her ribs ached. "Dad knew that she'd collected that evidence, right? He had to guess it was her. Which meant she was in danger. She told Hadley she was afraid of him. If she was the one who shot him, and then she wasn't able to face what she'd done . . ."

"We said it was Hadley," JJ said.

"The police said it was Hadley. We just told them what we knew," Daphne replied.

"But we have to—"

"Tell them what, exactly? That you've recovered a new drug-addled memory, and unlike the previous two things you were absolutely sure of, this one is definitely correct?" Daphne asked sharply, and Emma held out a restraining hand.

"JJ, you're right. We should tell the police. But we can't," Emma said steadily. JJ gave her a wild look, uncomprehending.

"Why not?" JJ asked.

"It complicates things," Daphne said. "And right now, we don't need anyone asking questions they think they know the answers to. It's safer this way."

"He still came after us. He still murdered Nathan," JJ said.

Emma didn't answer. She looked at Daphne, and Daphne looked at her.

"Emma," Daphne said. Her voice was tender, soft. "Rick Hadley is a very bad man."

"Yes. He is," Emma said. Her heart was beating fast, but she could hardly feel it. She felt outside of her own body, like she was watching the whole scene from above. "But he didn't kill our parents. And he didn't kill Nathan."

JJ looked at her blankly. "Of course he did. He had the gun. He had the drive."

"No. He didn't," Emma said. "He tried to get us to tell him where it was. Which means he didn't have it." JJ's eyes widened. In all the chaos, she must not have remembered. Must not have put it together the way Emma had.

"Emma," Daphne said again, almost chiding, almost pleading.

"No more secrets. Not between us," Emma said. Not this time. "Tell me."

55

DAPHNE

Now

She didn't intend for Nathan to die. She wanted to make that clear. It was obvious that he didn't deserve Emma, of course. He was strangling her by degrees. She wouldn't survive staying and she wouldn't ever leave, but no, Daphne hadn't *planned* to kill him. She'd gone into the carriage house to find the drive, that was all. The drive and the gun; once she had those, he could tear the place apart for all she cared.

She hadn't *intended* for him to find her on her knees, pawing around in the now-empty toolbox that should have contained the flash drive. She certainly hadn't intended for him to grab the gun from the table and point it right at her. She'd even tried to talk to him, but she didn't like the way his finger was on that trigger, clamped right over it, and all of him shaking with adrenaline, and she'd started thinking about that phone call she'd just overheard, all the things he'd been saying about her sister to that woman he was sleeping with, about how he was going to try to get full custody from his crazy, probably murderous wife with her criminal family, about how he was going to take her money and run. And Daphne started thinking, was that the man she wanted raising her little niece or nephew? Was that a man who ought to be in a child's life at all?

So yes, she'd reached for the gun. And then he definitely *had* been intent on shooting her, and then it was less a matter of fault and more a matter of who was stronger, wasn't it?

No one expects a fat woman in a paisley tunic and Crocs to be strong, but she spent her days moving patients and she'd always stayed fit, lifting weights so she could tend to her clients' needs without strain. She liked lifting weights—getting strong, without all that obsession about looks and thinness.

Anyway, Nathan wasn't a strong man.

She hadn't planned for it to happen, but it wasn't like much good would come from getting caught, so she took the drive and the gun. She thought about placing an anonymous call—she hated the idea of Emma finding him, but she couldn't think of a way around it. She'd walked by several times that morning, anxious to see if there were police cars out front, if Emma would be okay. When she'd seen Emma in the driveway, she knew she should have walked on, but she couldn't bear to leave Emma alone like that.

It had been stupid, of course. Just like it had been stupid to assume that Nathan was done with the carriage house for the night. She'd known it at the time, and when she got home, shaking and crying and generally panicking, she had made herself sit and think. Think about what Emma would do.

Someone was going to have to take the blame for Nathan's death. Daphne. Emma. Maybe even Juliette.

Emma had protected them once. Now Daphne was going to have to do the same. It wasn't enough to not be discovered. She had learned that the hard way. For fourteen years, the lack of an answer had haunted all of them in different ways. It had driven them apart. There needed to be an answer. One that wouldn't harm anyone who didn't deserve to be harmed.

And wouldn't it be lovely if Nathan could do this last thing for Emma? Maybe the only really good thing he would ever do for her. Provide her the answer, the exorcism, that she needed. Yes, that was the thing. Let the new problem solve the old one. It's not like she hadn't prepared, though she hadn't been entirely sure what she was preparing *for*. She texted Rick Hadley's new wife to ask if Tigger needed a walk today.

He did. He always did, and she was always busy, and had no idea what to do with a rambunctious goldendoodle her husband despised and which she'd mostly bought for the Instagram boost of getting a new puppy. Daphne had made sure to walk by when she was struggling with the pup, her own three client dogs trotting obediently beside her—her only three, which she'd had to do some wrangling to schedule for the same time of day, but it was about the optics. A sympathetic noise and a quick chat later and Mrs. Hadley had a new dog walker. Daphne had given her a false name, of course. Mrs. Hadley, who should have been less trusting given her husband's profession, had given her a spare key. She was so busy, and so tired of coming home to puddles on the floor, you see.

They found the gun in Hadley's garage workshop. White grip. Three bullets missing. As a place to hide a gun, it wasn't bad. Not like anyone suspected the man investigating the murders, after all, and no one else went out there, not even his wife. Though if a neighbor had glanced outside a few days before Rick Hadley took a rock to the skull, they might have seen the new dog walker letting herself in.

The harder trick had been getting them to look in the first place. She'd known she couldn't come out and accuse him, but she'd thought she might be able to nudge her sisters into figuring out enough to point the finger, and Christopher Best was bold enough to follow through. It had almost taken too long, though. It had almost gotten Emma and JJ killed.

But it hadn't. They were all alive and safe and healthy—the baby was healthy. It wouldn't grow up with a mother in prison. It wouldn't grow up with Nathan Gates as a father, and thank God for that. Could you imagine if he had a daughter? Could you imagine if he had a son?

It was better this way. They were all together after so long. And the man who'd threatened them, kept them apart, was no longer a danger to them. It wasn't like he was innocent. He'd helped kill Kenneth Mahoney, hadn't he? He'd tried to pin the Palmers' deaths on Emma, to stop people looking where he didn't want them to. He'd destroyed the lives they should have had.

Maybe he didn't deserve to *die*. Hardly anyone did, really. But some deserved it more than others.

And something had to be done.

EMMA

Now

Gabriel met her by the river. It looked less peaceful, now that she'd been in it, she reflected. The rush of it was less a pleasant ambience and more a demand for her return. But she sat on the old picnic table, wearing a jacket despite the summer heat, and watched the water tumble by. Gabriel approached quietly and stood next to her, hands in his pockets. He scuffed a foot against the ground.

"I should have come to see you. In the hospital," he said.

"You had a lot to deal with," Emma said.

"I think there's a line about the pot and the kettle that might apply here," he told her, smiling slantwise in a way that didn't temper the sorrow in his eyes. She wanted to kiss him. She had wanted to kiss him since she was sixteen years old. The timing had never been worse.

"Have they found him yet?" she asked.

"A few hours ago," he said. "Just bones, but they think it's him."

"I'm sorry."

"Me, too. But it's been a long time. I might not have known exactly when or how he died, but I knew he was gone," Gabriel said. "Maybe I'd be angrier if your father wasn't already dead, and Hadley wasn't— well. I don't know if there's any of him left in there, but I doubt he's happy if there is."

"You think he got what he deserved?" Emma asked.

"He killed at least four people," Gabriel said.

"What if he didn't?"

"What if he didn't kill my father? Whether he pulled the trigger or not, I think the difference is pretty academic at this point," Gabriel said.

"No. I mean the rest," Emma said, forcing herself to look at him. She knew the lines of his face, the contours, every fleck of color in his eyes. She didn't need more than moonlight to read his expression. "What if he didn't kill my parents? What if he didn't kill Nathan?"

"Then who did?" Gabriel asked. She didn't answer. She couldn't. Not yet, at least—not until she was sure what that answer should be. Gabriel didn't let the silence last long. When he spoke, it was carefully, each word like a bead slipped onto a string. "I think the way things are right now, people have a story that finally makes sense. Three mysteries with one answer. You start picking that apart, and none of it is going to feel as solid."

It was what Daphne had given them—a way out. Rick Hadley was not an innocent man. He was not a good man. He had killed Kenneth Mahoney, slept with his best friend's wife, hounded Emma and her sisters relentlessly. He would have killed them by the river, Emma thought—he had no way out with them alive. Once he knew where the drive was, they would have died.

Rick Hadley got what he deserved.

And Nathan?

She wasn't sure how much she believed Daphne's version of what had happened. That she'd only grabbed the gun because he was pointing it at her; that shooting him had been more an accident than anything else.

But all the things Nathan had said about her, all the things he'd been planning? That, she believed.

"Can I tell you a secret?" Emma asked. She sounded young, she thought. She sounded sixteen again.

"You can tell me," he said.

"I don't think I loved my husband," Emma said. It was, finally, the reason she could never figure out when she'd fallen in love with him. The simplest answer possible, really, but she'd convinced herself otherwise—had stopped even asking the question. "I know that's awful. He's dead. He didn't deserve it."

"Love? Or dying?" Gabriel asked.

"Maybe neither," Emma said.

"I think . . ." Gabriel said slowly, "I think that you should consider what it is that you deserve, Emma. What you want."

What did she want?

The same things she always had, she thought. Her sisters. A home she wasn't afraid of. A life spent without looking over her shoulder.

The boy who had never treated her like an intruder, even when she felt like one.

She got down from the table. She approached Gabriel with steps as careful and intentional as his words, and took his hand. There, in the dark, she looked at him, meeting his gaze steadily. And then she rose on the tips of her toes and pressed her lips to his.

The kiss lasted only a moment. His hand on her waist, her thumb against his jaw. Then she sank back down. "I have to go," she said.

"Emma." She didn't understand how her name on his lips could have that kind of power, to mean a thousand things at once. It was a question, an invitation, a plea.

"We keep getting the timing wrong," she said, stepping away.

"Maybe next time," he told her.

"Next time," she echoed. She turned and slipped away into the dark. She drove home carefully, along the winding roads with their blind turns and dark stretches between the homes. You paid a premium for privacy on this side of Arden Hills, for the luxury of secrets.

She pulled through the gate. It was left open now, unlocked. It had never been protection for anyone here. The danger never came from the road. She walked inside and found her sisters waiting for her. The three of them stood in the foyer. JJ, her mascara making shadows under her eyes, her hair a dark cloud around her head. Daphne, with her calm intensity. And Emma.

"All right," Emma said. She took a breath. "Here's what we're going to do."

Now

The best thing Nathan ever did was contribute half his genetic material to the child currently giggling in Daphne's lap. Baby Wren had a full head of brown curls when she was born and exquisitely chubby limbs. JJ had at first been skeptical, but the day Wren learned to smile, JJ was a goner.

And Emma? Daphne knew to the instant when her sister had fallen in love—at the very first look. The first touch. Daphne had never seen Emma smile the way she had when she held her daughter in her arms.

Wren was six months old now, with dimpled cheeks and a single tooth starting to force its way rudely out of her gums. She had a tendency to drool on her auntie Daphne's shoulder, but Daphne reflected that her three most recent careers—nurse, dog walker, and now occasional nanny to her utterly delightful niece—required a high tolerance for bodily fluids.

Right now they were in the sunroom, recently refreshed with new furniture that was less likely to jab a spur of wicker into curious palms. Vic and JJ were visiting; Gabriel was coming by later for dinner. The house was more alive than it had been in years.

Gabriel was spending quite a lot of time at the house, in fact. And when he wasn't at the house, Emma was often with him. They hadn't gone out on a date quite yet. Eighteen months, Daphne was guessing—that's how long it would take for Emma to start feeling like she could live life post-Nathan properly. Personally, Daphne would have given the man six months tops, but she recognized that Emma had a certain attachment to him.

It really was for the best that he was gone. *Something* had to be done.

And people were so rarely willing to do it.

Like her mother. Daphne had known as soon as her father made that call that something terrible was going to happen. She'd gone to her mother, woken her up out of her deep sleep—her stupor, really. She'd told her that he had the drive, that he knew. Something had to be done. But her mother was in denial. She thought she could talk him down. Daphne knew she was wrong. And she knew where her mother kept the gun that Rick Hadley had given her—the gun he'd taken from Logan Ellis.

She'd stood on her tiptoes and lifted the gun high to shoot him. The kickback had hurt her wrists, but she'd been worried that they would be able to tell it was someone short who'd done it. She needn't have worried so much; *CSI* turned out not to be terribly representative of small-town police departments.

Part of her had expected her mother to thank her. Instead, Irene Palmer had stared at her with no expression at all, and then told her to hand over the gun and get out. So Daphne had done what she was told. Until she heard the second shot.

She had to protect them. All of them. Something had to be done, and she'd done it.

It was why she'd done everything. For her and for her sisters. To protect them. Nothing else mattered. No one else mattered. It was Emma and Juliette and Daphne—and Wren.

But they were safe now. All of them. There were no more questions to ask, only answers, neat and final. Maybe there would be some trouble if Hadley ever woke up, but the odds of that were vanishingly low.

Really, someone ought to put him out of his misery.

"Misery, misery, misery," Daphne crooned, bouncing Wren on her knee. The baby laughed, hands wrapped tightly around Daphne's index fingers.

Emma watched Daphne cooing at Wren, Wren laughing uproariously. It was hard to know which of them was more delighted.

The whole house was coming together, piece by piece. At first, they fully intended to put in the work and then sell it, but as the weeks turned into months, they had stopped talking about that possibility as much. Vic and JJ spent as much time here as they did at home. The wallpaper was gone; the hardwoods patched; the study converted into a second master bedroom. Gabriel was even helping to put in an en suite, stealing some square footage from the ostentatiously useless great room.

"She's good with kids," JJ noted, hands in her back pockets, a smile curling at the corner of her mouth. Emma turned toward her.

"I don't know what I would do without her to help," she confessed. And she didn't.

Daphne was a wonder, and there was nothing she wouldn't do for her family. Wren included. Emma knew that.

She knew other things, too.

She knew that her mother was entirely capable of murder.

She also knew that her mother was the kind of woman with an exit plan. She wasn't like Emma. If she had decided to kill her husband, she would have had a way out afterward.

She knew that Daphne was still keeping secrets.

But no one could ever really know another person, could they? Everyone had secrets.

JJ was in the sunroom now, pulling faces at Wren. Emma looked around the house. She'd tried to run from this place, but it had always been her home. *Their* home. It belonged to them, and they belonged to one another.

And that was all she needed to know.

Emma smiled, and went to join her sisters.

ACKNOWLEDGMENTS

No One Can Know is my thirteenth published book, and I think I may be running out of ways to say thank you—which is quite inconvenient when the list of people I am grateful to only keeps growing. This book was a particular challenge to write; untangling the three sisters' pasts and presents was a difficult and sometimes maddening task, which I absolutely could not have achieved without the help of the No Name Writing Group—Rhiannon Held, Corry L. Lee, Shanna Germain, Rashida Smith, Erin M. Evans, and Susan Morris. Special thanks to Erin and Susan, who are absolutely brilliant and went above and beyond the call of duty to answer my plaintive cries for help.

This book is dedicated to my parents, and I feel like as well as a thank-you I owe them an apology for the sheer number of terrible parents in my books. In my defense, if I just wrote about kind, supportive, loving parents like you, it would get pretty boring.

Thank you also to my wonderful spouse, Mike, who knew what he was getting into when he married me, and to my kids, who remain frustrated that I don't write proper books with pictures in them.

I owe an enormous debt of gratitude to my agent, Lauren Spieller, and my editor, Christine Kopprasch, for being this book's earliest and most dedicated advocates. And thank you to everyone at Flatiron who helped bring it to life—the Flatiron team has been an absolute dream to work with from the start, and I couldn't be happier.

About the Author

KATE ALICE MARSHALL is the author of *What Lies in the Woods* and multiple novels for younger readers. She lives in the Pacific Northwest with her family.